Praise for the novels of Sherryl Woods

"Readers who adore family dramas will again dote on Woods' newest romance."
—*Booklist* on *Wind Chime Point*

"Sweet and charming."
—*RT Book Reviews* on *Wind Chime Point*

"A reunion story punctuated by family drama, Woods's first novel in her new Ocean Breeze series is touching, tense and tantalizing."
—*RT Book Reviews* on *Sand Castle Bay*

"Sherryl Woods writes emotionally satisfying novels about family, friendship and home. Truly feel-great reads!"
—#1 *New York Times* bestselling author Debbie Macomber

"During the course of this gripping, emotionally wrenching but satisfying tale, Woods deftly and realistically handles such issues as survival guilt, drug abuse as adolescent rebellion, and family dynamics when a vital member is suddenly gone."
—*Booklist* on *Flamingo Diner*

"Woods is a master heartstring puller."
—*Publishers Weekly* on *Seaview Inn*

"Once again, Woods, with such authenticity, weaves a tale of true love and the challenges that can knock up against that love."
—*RT Book Reviews* on *Beach Lane*

"Woods…is noted for appealing character-driven stories that are often infused with the flavor and fragrance of the South."
—*Library Journal*

SHERRYL WOODS

WIND CHIME POINT

mira

mira™

Recycling programs
for this product may
not exist in your area.

ISBN-13: 978-0-7783-3383-8

Wind Chime Point

First published in 2013. This edition published in 2023.

Mira
22 Adelaide St. West, 41st Floor
Toronto, Ontario M5H 4E3, Canada
www.Harlequin.com

Printed in U.S.A.

Dear Reader,

Welcome back to Sand Castle Bay! I hope you're enjoying getting to know the whole Castle family and the men in their lives.

I'm sure many of you will be able to relate to Gabriella's story, not because you've discovered you're pregnant and have been fired and dumped all in the period of a few days, but because you've simply been through one of those times when life just seems to hit a downward spiral. Sometimes it's not even the major crises that slam us all at once, but the steady drip, drip, drip of petty annoyances that start adding up to overwhelm us.

For Gabi, of course, it's that huge trifecta of major life changes that sends her back to Sand Castle Bay and the loving arms of her family. And with so much on her plate, it's little wonder that sexy, attentive Wade Johnson seems almost too good to be true. But Wade truly is one of the good guys. Not perfect, by any means, but caring, generous and steady as a rock.

I hope you'll enjoy this latest installment in the Ocean Breeze series and will be anxious to read *Sea Glass Island* to see if the sisters' grandmother has found the perfect guy for Samantha. Come on! We're talking about Cora Jane. Of course she has.

All best,

Sherryl

WIND CHIME
POINT

One

Unemployed and pregnant! Those were two words Gabriella Castle had never envisioned applying to her, at least not in combination. Now, in a twist of fate she couldn't possibly have anticipated, she was out of work and, just as shocking, expecting a baby. So much for years of fast-track career dedication and workaholic tendencies!

Sitting in the middle of her comfortably furnished living room in Raleigh, North Carolina, Gabi stared at a painting that had cost more than some people made in a year. Her sister Emily had talked her into it when she'd stayed overnight a few weeks ago. She'd seen it in some fancy auction catalog—Sotheby's or someplace like it—and insisted it would be just the thing to pull all the colors in Gabi's haphazardly decorated living room together.

"Besides that, it's a great investment," Emily had said enthusiastically. "In a few years, it will probably triple in value."

Gabi wondered if she could simply get her money back now. She was probably going to need it.

In the meantime, she couldn't help wondering if her sister could come up with a painting—or a magical formula—that would pull her life together.

Even though it had been three days since she'd walked into her boss's office expecting to be commended on her latest public-relations campaign for their biomedical company, only to leave the room with a severance package, she still couldn't quite believe what had happened. She'd been working since she was eighteen, climbing the corporate ladder since she'd turned twenty-one.

Driven by ambition and the determination to prove something to her father, she'd worked out a career plan even as she'd scheduled her college classes, taking a succession of internships and summer jobs to gain the experience that would land her a top-notch job after graduation. She'd hoped that job would be with her dad, but Sam Castle had turned her down flat.

Once hired by a competing company and more driven than ever, she'd made a meteoric rise to become the company's top public-relations executive by the time she was twenty-eight. Everyone had assumed there would be a vice presidency in her future. She'd certainly earned it.

Unfortunately, it seemed that particular career path didn't blend with being an unmarried mother, not in certain circles, anyway.

Not that her boss had dared to fire her. No, Amanda Warren had just made it impossible for her to stay. She'd outlined a plan that would keep Gabi well hidden from the judgmental world for the duration of the pregnancy. Beyond that, well, the handwriting had been on the wall.

Her days of being a high-profile spokeswoman for the company were over.

She could have stayed and fought, but still reeling from the news that she was pregnant, she hadn't had the energy for a legal battle. She'd opted instead to negotiate a buyout that would give her a smidgen of dignity, a decent severance package and time to consider her options for the future.

A future that included a baby! That was, of course, the real kicker—the unexpected news that had first left her stunned and shaken and launched this downward spiral.

It wasn't that she hadn't understood that no method of protection was a hundred percent foolproof, but she'd thought birth control pills and condoms together were reasonably effective. Her boyfriend of five years, Paul Langley, had thought so, too. In fact, he'd been so certain of it, his first reaction had been to suggest that the baby couldn't possibly be his.

Then, once convinced of the truth, he'd said she was on her own, that a baby wasn't part of their deal. She hadn't even been aware that their relationship was a "deal" only as long as it was convenient for him.

As she was pondering just how wildly out of control her life suddenly was, her phone rang. According to the caller ID, it was her older sister, Samantha. Knowing Sam would just keep calling until Gabi picked up, she answered, trying to inject an upbeat note into her voice.

"When you didn't answer your cell phone, I called your office and was told you no longer work there," Samantha said, sounding suitably stunned. "What's going on?"

Gabi sighed. So much for any chance of keeping

her professional catastrophe a secret from her family, at least for a while longer. "I quit," she explained to her sister. "Or was forced out, depending on your point of view."

"But why?" Samantha inquired, her tone indignant. "Not because you took some time off to go help Grandmother after the hurricane, I hope."

"No, of course not. They understood about that, and I had a ton of vacation time coming to me. They owed me that time off. If that had been an issue, they'd have let me go months ago."

"Then why?" Sam asked, sounding gratifyingly bewildered. "You gave that company a national presence. What's wrong with those ungrateful wretches?"

Gabi smiled at the fierce defense. "Actually, it was the work that gave them a national reputation. I just spread the word."

"There you go, being all humble, but we both know the truth." Samantha hesitated, then asked, "What are you going to do now, Gabi? Have you decided? I know how important that job was to you. It was your life."

"And how pitiful is that?" Gabi said, seeing clearly for the first time what a mistake it had been to focus almost exclusively on work. Her relationship with Paul had definitely taken a backseat, something that had suited them both. Unfortunately, given his attitude over recent developments, she doubted that even full-time devotion would have changed anything.

"You'll do things differently next time," Samantha soothed. "Now you know that no corporation is worth expending all that time and energy on, not when they can treat you like this. Have you started looking yet?"

"I'm still trying to wrap my mind around what's

happened," Gabi admitted, which was putting it mildly. "With the severance package they gave me, I have some time."

"Well, you know some other company will scoop you right up. Call Dad. He has a million contacts in that whole biomedical research world down there. Maybe he'll even rethink his previous stance about not hiring family and hire you himself."

"Not now," Gabi said. Not only did she not want her father to know about the pregnancy just yet, she had a hunch it would pose a problem with other old-fashioned employers, as well. As for her dad, well, his reaction wasn't something she was ready to contemplate.

"Why not now?" Samantha pressed. "This is one of those rare instances when Dad really could help. He'd even want to."

"I'm not so sure," Gabi said. Her father was as conservative as anyone. He was very conscious of the need in their field to make the right impression, to demonstrate a seriousness of purpose, no mistakes allowed, personal or professional. He'd been equally rigid with his family. She had a feeling he'd side with her boss and, if that was the case, she didn't want to know it until she had her feet back under her and a plan in place.

"Is there something you're not telling me?" Samantha asked suspiciously. "I know you. It's not like you to let any grass grow under your feet. I'm surprised you didn't have another job lined up by the end of the day."

"Haven't you heard? These are tough times."

"And you're very good at what you do and have the perfect mentor in Dad. Of all of us, you're the closest to him. Why don't you want to ask for his help?"

Since it was clear Samantha wasn't going to let this

go, Gabi sucked in a deep breath, then blurted, "Because I'm going to have a baby, that's why." She nearly choked on the sob that came with the words.

Dead silence greeted the announcement, before Samantha finally said softly, "Holy saints in heaven! A baby, Gabi? Are you sure?"

"Do you think I'd have mentioned it to my boss if I hadn't been sure?" Gabi said dryly.

"And that's why they let you go?" Samantha asked, clearly shocked. "Isn't that illegal?"

"Technically they didn't let me go. They demoted me, so I negotiated a buyout. A win-win for everyone, according to Amanda. Who knew she was a better spin master than I ever dreamed of being?" Gabi said, unable to keep a bitter note out of her voice.

"Okay, let's forget the job for the moment. It doesn't matter," Samantha said. "The baby's Paul's."

Gabi was grateful that there'd been no question mark at the end of her sister's statement. "Of course."

"How'd he take it?"

"As if I'd committed a felony. Needless to say, he's no longer in the picture."

"The rat," Samantha said with feeling. "I never did like him."

Despite the tense atmosphere, Gabi smiled. "You never even met him."

"And that's precisely why I didn't like him. What kind of man doesn't want to meet his girlfriend's family? He never even showed his face when we were helping Grandmother after the hurricane."

"And what a blessing that probably was. Give him a hammer and he'd probably do more harm than good."

"Not what you need in a man," Samantha declared.

"Now Wade Johnson? He's the kind of man to have around in a crisis."

Gabi stiffened at the out-of-the-blue mention of the man who'd been underfoot nonstop while they were making repairs to the family restaurant, Castle's by the Sea, after the hurricane. "Why would you bring him up?"

"Because he *was* around after the storm, just like Boone. And I saw the way Wade looked at you, as if he'd never seen anyone so perfect in his entire life."

"You're crazy."

"Let me remind you that I said the same thing to our sister about Boone, and look at the two of them now. In a few months Emily and Boone will be married, assuming he can convince her to finally set a date. I'm good at this stuff, Gabi. I recognize heat between men and women, even when they're both in denial."

"Well, you're wrong this time. Besides, don't you think the timing is just a little off for me to be thinking about a relationship? I'm going to be having another man's baby in a few months."

Samantha sucked in a deep breath at the reminder. "Are you at least happy about that?" she asked hesitantly. "A baby, Gabi! That is so incredible."

Gabi rested a hand on her belly, felt the faint stirring there. The first time she'd felt that tiny life inside her, she'd fallen in love. Being pregnant might be inconvenient. It might not have been the result of a love match. It might have cost her a job, but she already loved this baby more than anything. She'd do whatever it took to protect it and make sure it had everything it deserved... including two parents who would treasure this priceless gift when the time came.

"I'm thinking about adoption," she admitted to Samantha, deciding to test the idea she'd mentioned to no one else.

Her words were greeted by stunned silence.

"Samantha? You still there?"

"You'd give up the baby?"

Gabi closed her eyes. "I think it's the only way to make sure it has a good life. And, to be honest, I don't want to be tied to Paul through this child. I don't want to take a cent of support money from him. I don't want anyone so selfish in this child's life."

"Oh, sweetie, forget Paul for the moment," Samantha protested. "*You* can give this baby a good life. You can surround him or her with a whole family who'll fall in love the instant he or she is born."

"Babies shouldn't start life with an out-of-work single mother," Gabi said wearily.

"It's not as if you're going to be destitute. And you'll find another job when the time comes," Samantha insisted. "Plus, we'll all help. Me, Emily, Grandmother, even Dad will be on board. His first grandchild? You know he's going to be thrilled about this."

"Is he really?" Gabi asked skeptically, sounding more like Emily than herself. Emily was the one who never gave their father credit for having deep feelings for any of them. Besides, Sam Castle had hardly noticed his own children unless they were in trouble. It seemed unlikely he'd be over the moon about a grandchild. The image of him sitting in a rocker cuddling a baby was so incongruous, it was laughable.

"Well, you don't have to decide right this second," Samantha said, backing off to give her breathing room. "We'll talk about it when I see you."

"When you see me?" Gabi asked suspiciously. "Since when are you planning a trip back down here?"

"I'm driving home tomorrow," Samantha said, as if the trip had been scheduled for days, rather than minutes. "Meet me in Sand Castle Bay. You don't have anything to keep you in Raleigh right now, so no arguments. You've already said you're not looking for work just yet, so you might as well enjoy this unexpected time off. You need sunshine and sea breezes to put this in perspective. You know you do. You'll see things much more clearly then."

"I'm not sure I'm ready to lay this on Grandmother just yet."

"Be there or Emily and I will come and drag you over there bodily, if we have to," Samantha insisted, refusing to cut her any slack.

"Emily's there now?" Gabi asked, surprised. "I thought she was working night and day at this new job in Los Angeles."

"She also has a wedding to plan. And she's still after Grandmother to do a little modernizing of the decor at Castle's. She and Boone flew in a couple of days ago. She claims she wants our opinion on the wedding plans. That's why I called in the first place, to let you know we've been called into action."

Gabi laughed. "Since when does Emily listen to anything you or I have to say when it comes to her life?"

"She says there are incredible weddings on those soaps I've been on, and I should know a thing or two. And we're both her sisters, and we're to be in the wedding party. I'd suggest if you don't want to wind up wearing a very unflattering shade of whatever color's in fashion in Hollywood these days, you need to be there to speak up. Listen to me. I'm the oldest. I know best."

Gabi laughed. "Since when? I've always been the sensible one. Everyone knows that."

"If that were true, how'd you land in this mess?" Samantha taunted. "See you tomorrow, sweetie. And don't worry. This is going to work out. I promise."

Gabi hung up and sighed. Sand Castle Bay was the very last place she wanted to go right now, but Samantha was right about one thing. It was exactly where she belonged.

Wade was sitting in the middle of his sister's living room floor with two kids under the age of three climbing all over him. Well, one was climbing. The other was cradled against his chest, drooling.

"Unca Wade?" Chelsea whispered, crawling into his lap and snuggling close.

"What's up, kiddo?" he said, shifting baby Jason to give her more room.

"Me wants a kitty for my birthday," the almost three-year-old announced.

He smiled, fully aware he was being manipulated. Once either of his nieces turned their big blue eyes on him, he pretty much gave them whatever they wanted. A kitty, though? Louise would have a fit. His sister had vowed there would be no pets in her household until every last one of her children were out of diapers—and preferably out of college, if he knew Lou.

"What does your mom say?" he asked the toddler, who'd rested her head against his chest with a deep sigh.

"No," she admitted sorrowfully.

"Then I'm afraid that's the way it has to be. Maybe

when you're older and can take care of a kitty all by yourself."

"But I'm going to be *three*," she reminded him.

"I think you need to be a little older than that," Wade said. "Having a kitten is a lot of responsibility."

He glanced up to see his sister towering over him, hands on hips.

"Good answer," she said, then frowned at her daughter. "And you. Did we not talk about you going to your dad or your uncle to try to get something I've already said you can't have?"

Chelsea gave her a winning smile that could normally charm anyone whose path she crossed. "But I want a kitty really, really bad."

"And I said no really, really firmly," Lou told her, though the corners of her mouth were twitching. "Now, go wash your hands before dinner. Daddy will be home any minute."

Chelsea heaved another resigned sigh, then dutifully scampered off.

"That child is going to grow up to be a sneaky politician making backroom deals," Lou predicted.

Wade chuckled. "Or a smart lawyer like her mama," he suggested. "A weaker man would have brought her a kitten first thing tomorrow, but I know how she operates. I've also heard the no-pet rule about a thousand times with the older kids."

Lou sank down on the edge of the sofa and for an instant he could see the exhaustion on her face. He frowned and scooted closer, then handed the baby over to his sister. He gave her a sideways glance as she instinctively rubbed her knuckles over Jason's soft-as-silk cheek and seemed to relax.

"You okay, sis?"

"Just trying to juggle too many balls in the air. What was I thinking having all these kids and trying to have a career, too?"

"You were thinking what an incredible mom you'd be, what fabulous children you and Zack would have and that you'd always have backup from me."

She managed a weary smile at that. "You are a godsend," she agreed. "Having you here for a couple of hours when I first get home from the office really helps me to hang on to my sanity. The kids adore you and I have some breathing room to get civilized before Zack walks in the door. Believe me, my husband appreciates that."

"Hanging out with your kids works for me, too," Wade said quietly. "Especially now."

Lou reached over and gave his shoulder a squeeze. "You're so blasted cheerful and easygoing ninety-nine percent of the time, sometimes I forget that your life hasn't exactly been a bed of roses the past couple of years."

"Don't go there," he pleaded. "Talking about Kayla and the baby... I'm just not up for it."

"It's been two years," Lou said quietly, ignoring his plea. "I know losing your wife and your baby tore you up, Wade, but you've *never* talked about it. Bottling up all that pain can't be good."

He gave her a wry look. "I come by it naturally. Johnsons don't talk about their feelings. Isn't that the lesson we learned from Dad? After Mom left, he never mentioned her again. We weren't supposed to, either."

"And we both know how that ate him alive," Lou

said. "I won't let you follow in his footsteps. If you don't want to talk to me, then talk to someone else."

"A professional? Not likely."

"Do you plan to hold on to the pain for the rest of your life, never go on another date, never marry and have children?" she demanded. "That would be a crying shame. You're meant to be a dad, Wade. Ask any of my kids. They'll give you testimonials. Well, except for Jason here, but I'm sure he'll be on board as soon as he can talk." She smiled at the baby, who'd wound his fist in a strand of her hair. "Won't you, buddy?"

Wade smiled at that. Seven-month-old Jason had come as an unexpected blessing, though with two older brothers and two older sisters, his arrival had been the last straw for Louise, who'd sent her husband off for a vasectomy and had her own tubes tied for good measure.

"Save the pep talk, sis. My life's okay these days. I'm not living like a monk."

Lou's expression immediately brightened. "Really? Do tell."

What could he say? That he'd finally met a woman who'd caught his attention? That she hadn't really given him the time of day? That she lived clear over in Raleigh and hadn't been to Sand Castle Bay in weeks? That his only contact was through her meddling grandmother's reports? Yeah, like that would reassure his sister.

"I'll fill you in when there's something to tell," he said eventually. He stood. "Now, I think I'll take off."

Lou regarded him with surprise. "You're not staying for dinner?"

"Not tonight. I've been working on a new carving. I'd like to get back to it."

"And you can't put that off for an hour to have some spaghetti with your family?" she inquired skeptically. "You're not fooling me, Wade Johnson. You're trying to get away from my prying."

He smiled. "Then let that be a lesson to you," he advised. "Stop prying."

She stood and wrapped her arms around him. "Never. You're my brother and I love you. It's my job to worry about you and pester you and make sure you're happy."

"I'm happy enough," he assured her. "Stop worrying."

As he drove away, he spotted his brother-in-law pulling into the parking spot he'd just vacated and gave Zack a wave. Lucky son of a gun, he thought. He wondered if Zack knew what a blessing that family of his was and how much Wade envied him.

But despite this attraction he'd felt toward Gabriella Castle, he wondered if he'd ever have the courage to risk the kind of pain he'd been through with his first marriage. Could a man even survive that kind of loss more than once in his life?

Since it was midday when Gabi arrived on the coast, she drove straight to Castle's by the Sea. She knew that's where she'd find her grandmother and, more than likely, Emily, who bit by bit was transforming the restaurant's decor. Her efforts were progressing at a snail's pace because their grandmother was resistant to change and because Emily was spending more and more time back in Los Angeles on a project near and dear to her heart.

It was close to two when Gabi arrived. Since Castle's served only breakfast and lunch, the crowd had already thinned out, and the door had been locked to keep new customers from entering after closing. Gabi walked around to the side deck, then slipped into the kitchen.

As she'd expected, her sister was tucked in the tiny office with fabric samples. Gabi poked her head in. "Any luck on selling the idea of new upholstery for the booths?" she asked.

A frustrated look spread across Emily's face for just an instant, but then she was on her feet, enveloping Gabi in a hug. "A baby? How exciting!"

Gabi blinked. "You know already?"

"Samantha filled us in when she called last night. She thought it might be easier if you didn't have to break the news yourself."

"Really?" Gabi said doubtfully. "Or was she trying to line up you and Cora Jane to be on her side?"

"I didn't know there were sides," Emily said, her expression a pitiful attempt at innocence. Samantha the actress could have pulled it off, but Emily failed miserably.

"I'm considering putting the baby up for adoption. Samantha disapproves. Does that ring any bells?"

"She might have mentioned it," Emily said. "But let's not get into that now. I'm just so glad you're here. Boone and I have news."

"You've finally set a wedding date," Gabi guessed, knowing that had been the hot topic since before Christmas.

Emily nodded happily. "June 2. Surprisingly, I suddenly realized that I want a traditional June wedding." She shrugged. "Or maybe that's what Grandmother really wants. Anyway, that's the date. I think you and Samantha will look stunning in pastel dresses. I took that into consideration, too."

"You do realize I'll be very, very pregnant by then. Are you sure the aisle will be wide enough for me?"

"We'll take out the pews on one side if it's not. I'll talk to Wade about it."

Gabi's gaze narrowed at the second deliberate mention of his name in two days. "Wade?"

"He is a master carpenter, after all," Emily said blithely. "He pops in from time to time, looking for you, I think. Grandmother thinks so, too."

Gabi shook her head as she rested a hand on her very visible baby bump. "It's an odd time to be matchmaking, don't you think?"

"Not matchmaking," Emily insisted. "I'm just saying he's around, eager to make himself useful. Actually, it could be he's courting Grandmother. He does seem to be excessively fond of her pies."

"Whatever," Gabi said. "I'd better go into the dining room and face the music. Just how upset is Grandmother about all this?"

"Her eyes lit up when she heard the news," Emily said. "If you were expecting shock and disapproval, I think you'll be disappointed. She's always been on our side no matter what mistakes we've made." She covered her mouth, her expression immediately filled with regret. "Not that the baby is a mistake, Gabi. I didn't mean that. You know I didn't."

Gabriella hugged her sister. "I know you didn't. And amazingly, all things considered, I never once thought of it that way, either. Even if I do decide to give the baby up for adoption, it will be a blessing for a family who desperately wants a child."

Even as she said the words, though, there was another of those little fluttery sensations in her stomach that made her heart catch in her throat. It had been one thing to make the whole adoption decision early on. She'd been furious with Paul, even more furious with herself. The baby hadn't been real to her. Now it was.

And that, she suspected, was going to seriously complicate her determination to do the right thing.

Two

Wade told himself he was stopping by Castle's almost every afternoon for a slice of whatever homemade pie Cora Jane had on the menu, but the truth was he was here because it was usually served with a mention or two of Gabriella. Hoping for tidbits of news about a woman he hardly knew, a woman who'd held herself aloof from him, was pitiful. No question about it. But given his lack of a social life of any kind since the deaths of his wife and baby, he considered this unrequited fascination to be progress on his long road to recovery.

He'd taken two bites of today's excellent peach pie with a scoop of vanilla ice cream on top when the kitchen door opened and Gabi herself walked through it, then came to a dead stop. Wade came close to swallowing his tongue at the sight of her. She was every bit as beautiful as he'd remembered. She was also very obviously pregnant, a situation not even her loose-fitting T-shirt could hide. If anything, on her petite frame, the shirt only emphasized the baby bump.

Now *that* was a turn of events he hadn't anticipated.

His heart thumped unsteadily as too many memories came crowding in, memories of Kayla at this stage of her pregnancy, the way she'd glowed, the excitement they'd shared. It had been such a blissfully happy time, only to be shattered by tragedy and inconceivable loss.

He dragged his thoughts away from the dark past and drank in the sight of Gabi, who despite her natural beauty couldn't hide her bone-deep weariness. A natural protectiveness kicked in. Before he could stop himself, Wade was already considering ways to take care of her. It was ironic, really, since of all the women he'd ever known other than his sister, Gabriella was the most independent and capable. That didn't seem to matter to this knight-in-shining-armor side of his nature.

Then he was struck by another, far more disturbing thought. Had Gabi gotten married? Surely that was something Cora Jane would have mentioned, rather than encouraging Wade's interest in her with a litany of less-than-subtle hints. Nor could he imagine why Cora Jane hadn't mentioned the pregnancy to him, since she knew perfectly well he'd been hanging around not for pie, but for scraps of information about her granddaughter. Was it possible this was going to be news to her, too?

He noted that Gabi still hadn't budged. Her eyes could be adjusting to the dim lighting, but it seemed to him she was actually reluctant to step into the dining room. He guessed she wasn't looking forward to seeing Cora Jane. After she'd hesitated for what seemed like an eternity, she finally drew in a deep breath, then walked briskly into the room, an expression of grim determination on her face.

"Looking for Cora Jane?" Wade inquired when Gabi would have walked right past him.

She gave a startled little gasp, then managed a half-hearted smile. "Wade! I didn't see you there."

"And I wasn't expecting to see you today, either," he said, then cast a pointed look at her tummy. "Guess we're both full of surprises. Who's the lucky daddy?"

She visibly flinched at the question. "Unfortunately, the daddy doesn't consider himself to be all that lucky. Haven't seen him since I broke the news."

She said it blithely, as if the man's irresponsible behavior was no big deal, but Wade detected the hint of hurt in her eyes.

"The man's a fool," he declared with feeling. "You know that, don't you?"

"There's a growing consensus about that," she admitted.

His gaze narrowed. He might as well ferret out the whole truth here and now. There'd been mention of a boyfriend back in August, but when the man had never shown his face, Wade had been as skeptical about the relationship as her sisters clearly were. They'd been pretty outspoken on the subject, though usually out of Gabi's hearing. While he'd worked on custom cabinetry, he'd kept one ear tuned to their conversations, especially whenever Gabi's name came up. Okay, sure, there were rules about eavesdropping, but come on, this was Gabi and he was just a little bit infatuated with her. Was he supposed to tell them to lower the volume a notch?

"Were you in love with him?" he asked, keeping his tone neutral and his gaze on her face.

He saw the surprise in her eyes before she slid into the booth opposite him.

"You know you're the first person to ask me that."

"Seems like an obvious question to me," he said. "Or did your family know better all along?"

She smiled at that. "I think they did. Samantha said she knew he was a jerk when he wasn't here helping out after the storm. I'm not sure why I was still making excuses for him then. I imagine on some level I knew he would never really fit in."

Wade nodded. "So, what's your plan? Before you try to deny having one, remember that the word around here is that you started making plans in grade school and never lost the habit."

She chuckled. "Actually, it was high school, but point taken. Amazingly, though, I'm still figuring things out. I got hit with too many unexpected changes all at once. A baby, the discovery that my significant other is a jerk, losing my job."

Wade whistled. "You lost your job, too? Talk about a trifecta, and not the winning kind."

"My boss wasn't impressed with my moral character."

Thus that weariness he'd noticed, he concluded. Wade was surprised she looked as good as she did with that many blows all landing at once. He suspected she'd come to Sand Castle Bay to spend time with the family and heal, but this might be his one and only opportunity to show her that not all men were idiots.

"You know what you need?" he declared, impulsively seizing a moment that might never come his way again.

"Aside from a plan?" she asked wryly.

"That'll come," he said with confidence. "You need dinner and a movie. It'll take your mind off everything. How about tomorrow night? I'll pick you up at six, unless you'd like to go for an early bird special. I remember when Kayla…" He tripped over the mention of his wife's name, shifted gears. "When Lou was pregnant," he corrected hurriedly, "all she wanted to do was sleep."

"Lou? Your wife?"

He laughed at the disapproving expression that accompanied her question. "Not all of us are jerks, sweetheart," he said, glad he'd not opened the whole sad tale about his wife. "Don't you remember Louise, my big sister? She has five kids now, all of them little hellions, which if you ask me is exactly what she deserves for all the grief she gave me when we were kids."

Her expression brightened. "Of course I remember Louise. Five kids? Wow! I thought she planned to be a lawyer."

"She did and she is. The two of you are a lot alike, both driven. Not much gets in the way of what you want. I'll have to get the two of you together. She can tell you what to expect when your baby turns your life upside down."

"This baby's already accomplished that," Gabi reminded him.

"So, about dinner? Will six o'clock work?" he pressed, determined not to let this opportunity slip away. In his opinion, Gabi not only needed family right now, she needed a friendly, impartial ear. He could provide that.

A frown settled on her face. "I don't think it's a good idea, Wade," she said. "My life's just too unsettled."

"And you think if you stay home tomorrow night and concentrate real hard, you'll figure everything out?" he asked skeptically.

"No, but—"

"Okay, then. I'll see you at six," he said, sliding out

of the booth and dropping a casual kiss on her forehead. "Don't even think about standing me up. I have allies."

He could tell by her resigned expression that she knew exactly who those allies were. Maybe if she hadn't taken so many hits recently, she'd have fought him harder. As it was, she merely sighed.

"See you at six," she said, then glowered at him. "I want my own bucket of popcorn."

He grinned. "Of course you do."

He couldn't seem to stop smiling as he paid Cora Jane, who'd remained suspiciously out of sight during his entire exchange with Gabi.

As she handed him his change, she threw in a piece of advice free of charge. "You hurt that girl and there will be no place around here for you to hide," she said. It was a pretty fierce warning from a woman who stood five foot two in her sneakers.

"Got it," he told her somberly, dropping a kiss on her cheek. "No worries."

"If I didn't believe that, you wouldn't have spent five seconds alone with her just now," she said, proving that her avoidance of his table had been deliberate. "Not when she's this vulnerable."

"You want to come along tomorrow night to chaperone?" he asked, only half in jest.

"Don't think I wouldn't do just that, Wade Johnson, if I didn't think you're going to be exactly what she needs. Don't prove me wrong."

"Understood."

Even more than Cora Jane probably realized. He'd seen for himself just how fragile Gabi was. Seeing her like that when he knew firsthand the sort of confident, successful woman she'd been just a few months ago had made him want to smash his fist into something. That idiotic ex's jaw came to mind as the perfect starting point.

Cora Jane found Gabriella exactly where Wade had left her. She looked as if the weight of the world rested on her shoulders. Cora Jane leaned down and pressed a kiss to her cheek before nudging her over to make room beside her in the booth. Cora Jane settled close, then cupped Gabi's chin in her hand.

"You doing okay, honey bun?"

To her shock, Gabi took one look at her and burst into tears.

"Everything's such a mess," she said with a moan. "I know you already know, because Samantha has a big mouth, so you can't deny that I've really screwed up this time."

Cora Jane gathered her close and let her cry herself out. She'd thought long and hard since hearing the news about the best way to handle it. Nothing, though, had quite prepared her for the self-derision she was hearing in Gabi's voice. When Gabi's tears had dried, she looked directly into her eyes.

"Now, then, young lady, you listen to me and listen good," she said in a tone intended to catch Gabi's attention. "You're having a baby, which from here on out we're all going to think of as the blessing it is. You broke up with a man who obviously didn't deserve you. You lost a demanding job that was draining the life out of you. And you're here with family who's ready to love you and support you in any way you need. I plan to see only the good in all that. I suggest you do the same."

A watery smile formed on Gabi's face. "I always

thought I got my ability to put a good face on things from Mom, but it was you."

Cora Jane smiled and squeezed her hand. "I have my moments," she said modestly. "Now let's back up a minute. Tell me how you're feeling, physically, not emotionally."

"Tired," Gabi admitted.

"Then you're in the right place. You can sleep as late as you want while you're here."

Gabi looked startled. "You aren't going to insist I come to Castle's at the crack of dawn for the bakery deliveries?"

Cora Jane chuckled, fully aware that her granddaughters all hated the early-morning demands of running a restaurant that served breakfast starting at 6:00 a.m. "Not this week, anyway," she responded. "Next week, we'll see how you're doing. I want you to concentrate on getting plenty of rest, fresh air and exercise right now."

"I love you," Gabi said, leaning against her.

"I love you, too, and this baby you're carrying. Now, Samantha just called from the house. She arrived a few minutes ago and has started dinner. Let's get Emily and head home, put our feet up and relax. Tonight we're going to focus on Emily and Boone's wedding. Tomorrow will be soon enough to tackle everything else."

Gabi smiled. "You sound as if we can fix my life up in an afternoon."

"Maybe not in an afternoon," Cora Jane conceded. "But it seems to me tomorrow evening might get things rolling."

Her granddaughter frowned at her. "Wade Johnson is not the answer," she said forcefully.

Cora Jane didn't argue. Instead, she simply smiled

at Gabi's emphatic declaration. "I suppose we'll have to wait and see, won't we?"

"Grandmother!"

"Come along," Cora Jane urged. "Emily's found the perfect wedding dress. I can't wait for you girls to see it."

"Emily has also found an excellent fabric for the booths in here," Gabi said slyly. "You don't seem nearly as enthusiastic about that."

"This old vinyl has served us well for a lot of years," Cora Jane said with a huff.

"Which explains why it has cigarette burns from the days when smoking was allowed and tears from rambunctious kids," Gabi countered.

"Your grandfather picked it out," Cora Jane argued, unexpected tears welling up in her eyes. "Every detail in here was the way Caleb wanted it."

Gabi stopped and stared at her. "It's because of Granddad you don't want to change? Not because you're being stubborn?"

Cora Jane chuckled. "Well, of course I'm being stubborn, but I'm nostalgic, too. It wouldn't feel right to come in here and see things changed too much. I know your grandfather's gone, but sometimes when I walk in here, I expect to see him coming out of the kitchen or catch a glimpse of him just outside on the deck."

"You need to tell Emily that," Gabi said. "She thinks you're just dismissing everything she suggests without a second's thought. It hurts her feelings."

Cora Jane sighed. "I know that. I guess I thought she'd figure it out when I kept balking."

"None of us are mind readers," Gabi said. "Not even you."

"I'll try to remember that."

Gabi studied her worriedly. "How does Jerry feel when you get all nostalgic about Granddad?" she asked, referring to the restaurant's longtime cook, who'd become a lot more to Cora Jane since Caleb's death.

"He understands, or says he does," Cora Jane said. "It may not make sense to someone your age, but in a way it's him knowing your grandfather that's made it easier for us to be together. He doesn't expect more than I'm ready to give. He knows I had one huge love in my life." She smiled. "And now I'm blessed to have a dear friend by my side."

"Just a friend?" Gabi asked.

Cora Jane chuckled. "That's all I'm admitting to, young lady, and all you need to know. Some things are meant to be kept private."

Gabi laughed. "I hope you'll remember that and stop pushing Wade and me together."

Cora Jane was so happy to see some color in her granddaughter's cheeks at the mention of Wade, she decided to leave well enough alone, at least for now.

"No meddling," she promised, then amended to herself, unless she saw a need for it.

Emily slanted a worried look in Gabi's direction. "Are you sure you're up for this? Maybe we should focus on you tonight," she said after they'd finished dinner and were settled in the living room. They were drinking herbal tea out of respect for Gabi's pregnancy, though normally by now Samantha would have made a pitcher of something a whole lot stronger. Cora Jane had pleaded an early morning and gone to bed, leaving them to spend the evening together. It was a sign of just how well she knew them and understood their need for sisterly bonding.

"Please, my situation is not going to change anytime soon," Gabi told her. "Tomorrow's soon enough. I want to see this wedding dress Grandmother's been raving about."

Emily's eyes lit up. "It's absolutely gorgeous. I found it on Rodeo Drive. I have a couple of fittings yet to do, but I have pictures." She whipped her cell phone out of her purse and clicked on a series of shots showing the dress from every angle.

"Oh, my God, it's gorgeous," Samantha breathed with genuine awe in her voice.

Gabi grinned. "You're going to look like an elegant princess, and here I was hoping you'd have all these ruffles and layers of lace so we could giggle behind your back."

"Ha, ha," Emily said. "As if I'd ever be caught dead in a dress like that. I'm understated all the way."

"Which means our bridesmaid dresses are, too?" Gabi inquired hopefully. "We're not going to look like something from *Gone with the Wind,* are we? Add in my pregnancy, and I'd look like a wayward balloon from the Macy's Thanksgiving parade."

"I wouldn't do that to you," Emily said. "Even if I can't have you two looking more beautiful than I do that day."

"What do you care what we look like?" Samantha asked. "Boone only has eyes for you."

Emily grinned. "Yeah, he does," she said with satisfaction.

"Where is he, by the way?" Gabi asked. "He did come with you, didn't he?"

"He took B.J. over to see Jodie and Frank tonight. To give the man credit, he's determined to see that his son has a relationship with his grandparents despite everything they did to make Boone's life miserable."

"And yours," Samantha said. "Have they accepted that the two of you are getting married?"

Emily's expression fell. "I think Frank's okay with it, but Jodie?" She shook her head. "She's going to blame me forever for ruining her daughter's life."

"Which you didn't do," Gabi said loyally. "You were completely out of the picture when Boone and Jenny were married."

"Jodie doesn't seem to give two hoots about reality," Emily said wearily. "It's sad, really. I almost feel sorry for her."

"Save your pity," Gabi said. "She seems to enjoy clinging to her misery over Jenny's death."

"Jenny was her daughter," Samantha said with sympathy. "Of course she's going to grieve for her."

"She just doesn't have to take it out on everyone around her, that's all I'm saying," Gabi countered.

"Okay, enough," Emily said. "Here are the dresses I have in mind for you. If you hate them, I have backups. And you can pick the colors, though I think Gabi would look beautiful in a pale sage-green and you'd look fantastic in soft yellow, Samantha."

She handed over her cell phone.

"Oooh," Gabi whispered. "They're gorgeous." She handed the phone to her sister.

Samantha's eyes widened. "Absolutely perfect."

Unbidden tears welled up in Gabi's eyes and spilled down her cheeks before she could stop them. "I wish I weren't going to look like a blimp," she whispered with a sniff. "By June 2, I'll be lucky if I don't go into labor in the middle of the ceremony."

Emily looked crestfallen. "When's your due date?"

"Mid-June," Gabi said.

"Then we'll move the wedding," Emily said without even an instant's hesitation. "A few more weeks won't be a big deal. Boone will understand."

"Not on my account," Gabi objected. "You wanted to be a June bride."

"June, July, August—it's all the same, really. And goodness knows, Grandmother will be relieved to have an extra few weeks to plan. As anxious as she is to seal this deal, she seems to think a proper wedding can't be planned in anything under a year. I'm testing her sense of decorum, as it is."

"But I know you," Gabi said. "You probably worked some sort of complicated miracle to get time off in June to do this right."

"And now I'll work another one for whatever the new date is," Emily said. "I don't want you to be miserable about the way you look, or worrying about swollen ankles or having your water break when you walk down the aisle. If I'd known about the pregnancy sooner, I'd have taken all that into consideration in the first place. It's all good, Gabi. I promise."

Gabi picked up the cell phone again and clicked on the image of the bridesmaid dress and a reed-thin model. "It would be nice to look like that for your wedding," she admitted.

Emily grinned. "Then it's settled. I'll check with Boone and we'll set a new date." She glanced at Samantha. "Any complications in your life I need to know about?"

"Not a one," Samantha responded.

"Don't let Grandmother hear you say that," Gabi advised. "Her meddling gene is just itching to take your life on, too. I'd lay money on that."

"Heaven forbid," Samantha said with heartfelt emotion. But even as she spoke, Gabi and Emily exchanged a knowing look. They might not know what Cora Jane had in mind, but they were certain of one thing—Samantha was not going to escape their grandmother's wiles.

Sitting on the narrow twin bed in the room she'd shared with Emily when they'd spent summers with Grandmother, Gabi felt a sense of peace steal over her. For the first time in weeks, her stomach wasn't in knots. It wasn't as if she'd reached any decisions overnight or written down the first word of a new plan. It was this place with the windows open, a salt-air breeze coming in and Cora Jane's old-fashioned glass wind chimes tinkling merrily on the porch down below. The sound was so familiar, so comforting, she could have been a child again, a child without a care in the world, with the whole summer stretched out ahead.

There was a tap on the door an instant before it was flung open.

"You up?" Samantha asked, though she was already in the room and settled on the other twin bed without waiting for an answer. "How'd you sleep?"

"Like a rock," Gabi admitted. "Best sleep I've had in ages."

"Even with that noise outside?" Samantha grumbled.

Gabi grinned. "You always hated Grandmother's wind chimes."

"Because they make an unholy racket. I'm looking for earplugs first thing today."

"Don't they remind you of summer at the beach?" Gabi enthused. "They say smell stirs memories—the salt air by the ocean, cookies baking, the scent of a Christmas tree—but for me it's those wind chimes. I feel just like a kid again."

"Yeah, they take me back, too," Samantha admitted. "I never slept a wink then, either."

"How can a woman who lives in Manhattan with garbage trucks, taxis and car alarms going off in the middle of the night be bothered by little pieces of glass making music in a breeze?"

Samantha shrugged. "All in what you're used to, I guess." A grin spread across her face. "So, tell me about this date you have with Wade tonight."

Gabi regarded her incredulously. "How on earth… Never mind. I know Grandmother overheard us. It's not a date. We're going out to grab dinner and see a movie. No big deal."

"Sounds like a date to me, and I speak from some experience. Unlike you, I have those kind of dates on a regular basis."

"Wade just took pity on me, that's all. He thought I needed a distraction."

"How thoughtful!" Samantha said, her expression amused. "You just keep telling yourself it's as innocent as all that. I'm so mad I wasn't there to see the two of you for myself. I would have known right off if sparks were flying. Grandmother said they were, but she's unreliable. She sees what she wants to see. Emily doesn't see anything except Boone these days. She didn't even know you spent close to a half hour huddled with Wade. Her powers of observation are pitiful."

Gabi sighed. "Is this why you wanted me to drive over here, so you could try to set me up with Wade? I thought you wanted to be supportive."

"Nudging you in Wade's direction is being supportive. He's a great guy."

"Who's probably not one bit interested in being saddled with a woman carrying another man's baby," Gabi said. "What sensible man would want to sign on for that?"

"If you ask me, sensible can be highly overrated. Wasn't Paul sensible?"

"Point taken," Gabi conceded. "But please, please, leave this alone. I can't take one more complication in my life right now."

"Which is why you need someone like Wade to help you shoulder the burden," Samantha insisted. "He'll make you laugh. Even when you were pretending to be oblivious to him this summer, he could still make you laugh."

"I doubt there are enough comedians in the country right now to make me laugh," Gabi said.

"I think Wade's up to the task," Samantha contradicted. "Grandmother says he had you smiling yesterday. And given that he asked you out *after* seeing that you're pregnant, obviously your situation hasn't scared him off. He gets points for that, too."

"Cora Jane needs to mind her own business," Gabi said with frustration, unwilling to admit that it had been surprising to find that Wade wasn't put off by her pregnancy. She wasn't entirely sure if that made him extraordinarily rare, or perhaps just a little bit odd.

Samantha laughed at the reference to Cora Jane's penchant for meddling. "Let me know if you find a way to make Grandmother stay out of our lives."

Yeah, Gabi was pretty sure it was mission impossible, too.

Three

The custom cabinetry Wade had built for a kitchen in an oceanside condo was giving him fits. Though his measurements had been checked and rechecked, once he started the installation, it was clear something was off. Tommy Cahill, the contractor who'd hired him for the renovation, was as bewildered as he was.

"I can't deal with this now," Wade said, glancing at his watch. "I have to be somewhere at six."

Tommy nodded. "I'll give it some thought. There has to be something obvious we missed. The top cabinets fit perfectly. These bottom cabinets…" He shook his head. "I don't know."

"I have an idea," one of Tommy's helpers chimed in, clearly eager to impress his boss.

"Oh?" Tommy said, his skepticism plain.

The young man, barely eighteen and wearing jeans that looked destined to fall to his ankles at any second, took a marble from his pocket and set it on the floor at one end of the room. As Wade and Tommy stared, it took off rolling toward the other end of the room. The two men exchanged an incredulous look.

"The blasted floor's not level," Tommy muttered. "Not even close. How the devil did I miss that?"

"We both did," Wade said, shaking his head. "Jimmy, you win the prize for figuring this out. What made you think of it?"

The kid shrugged, his cheeks pink. "No big deal. I helped my dad fix up our place. There wasn't a level floor in it. We had to compensate for that in every room."

"Well, it's going to make my life a whole lot easier tomorrow when I get back here." Wade met Tommy's gaze. "I assume you don't want to fix the floor."

"No way. Not in the budget."

"You need to double-check with the owner? Maybe they'd like to get it resolved now."

"They balk if I buy an extra box of screws," Tommy said with disgust. "Cheapest sons of a gun I've ever worked for. Let's just get this over with."

Wade nodded. "I'll do some fiddling with the base of the cabinets to level things out," he said, considering the problem and potential solutions. "I have more of the cherrywood in my shop. I'll bring it along in the morning. Thank goodness the guys measuring for the granite countertops aren't due for a couple of days. We should have this straightened out by then."

Tommy nodded. "That's what margins for error are all about. I never give a customer a schedule without building that in. Since the hurricane, with renovations and repairs going on all up and down the coast, I allow even more cushion. I work with great subcontractors, but they're all busier than ever right now."

Wade turned to the young man. "I owe you, Jimmy. Later this week we'll pick a day and your lunch will be on me. I'll take you to Castle's. Best burgers on the beach."

"Not that the food is the attraction for you," Tommy taunted, a grin spreading across his face. "I heard Gabriella's back in town."

"She is," Wade confirmed. "But I doubt she'll be at the restaurant that much."

Tommy looked surprised. "I thought Cora Jane put her granddaughters to work over there the minute they hit town."

Wade wasn't about to explain. He said only, "Not this time." He glanced at his watch. "Now I really do need to hit the road. See you tomorrow. I might be a little later than today. I have another project that could take some time first thing in the morning."

Since Tommy knew Wade would never blow a deadline for him, he merely nodded. "See you when you get here." He looked a little more closely at Wade and grinned. "You seem awfully eager to go. Hot date?"

Wade felt himself coloring. "Just dinner and a movie with a friend."

"A female friend?" Tommy pressed. "Gabi, maybe?"

"No comment," Wade replied emphatically, hoping to end the guesswork.

Tommy seemed to consider the remark telling enough. "Thought so," he said. "It's about time, if you want my opinion."

"Which I don't," Wade retorted. No more than he'd wanted his sister's or anyone else's.

His attraction to Gabriella might be the first step on the road to recovering from his grief, but he had a hunch given her pregnancy, this particular road he'd chosen was going to be a bumpy one. In the past twenty-four hours since he'd first laid eyes on Gabi's baby bump, he hadn't allowed himself even a second to consider just what a huge mistake getting involved with her might be. He'd been worried about her fragile emotional state, not his own. That, he suspected, would come later.

Gabi looked at the pitiful wardrobe of loose pants and T-shirts spread out on her bed and sighed. She couldn't go out with Wade looking like a refugee from a thrift shop. Maybe it wasn't a date, but she had more pride than that. Why hadn't she brought anything fancier with her from Raleigh?

Because she hadn't anticipated being seen in public any more than necessary, she reminded herself ruefully. Now not only was she going to be on display, tonight was going to be perceived as a date no matter how cleverly she or Wade tried to spin it.

She looked at the assorted pieces hoping to spot some combination that hadn't occurred to her before, but the sad truth was, even if she'd brought along everything in her closet back home, nothing would fit anymore. Who'd have thought a tiny little baby could have such an effect on her figure so quickly?

"Ah, just as I suspected," Samantha said, coming into the room again, this time without even bothering to knock.

"Whatever happened to the concept of privacy in this family?" Gabi grumbled.

Samantha merely grinned. "We're sisters. We have no boundaries. Besides, you're going to be very glad I'm here."

"Really?" Gabi said skeptically. "Why is that?"

"Because I'm about to save the day," Samantha told her, tossing a shopping bag onto the bed.

Gabi eyed the bag from a boutique with interest. "For me?"

"Of course. And maybe a little bit for Wade," Samantha added with a twinkle in her eyes. "Open it."

Despite the worrisome reference to Wade, Gabi seized the bag and peered inside, then drew out a simple A-line dress with a deep V-neckline. It was a shade of blue just slightly deeper than her eyes. She recognized at once that it had the potential to be stunning with her coloring.

"It's too soon for maternity clothes," Samantha said, explaining her choice. "And there's not a huge selection to choose from close by, but this is loose-fitting." She grinned. "And trust me, with that neckline, nobody's going to be paying attention to your baby bump."

She gestured toward the bag. "There's more. Keep looking."

Gabi retrieved a lacy bra and a matching pair of thong panties. She lifted a brow. "Seriously?"

Samantha laughed. "Hey, I told you I kept Wade in mind while I was shopping. The man's tongue will be hanging out."

"Wade Johnson will never lay eyes on these panties or this bra," Gabi said firmly, though her cheeks heated at the thought.

"Maybe not tonight," Samantha conceded. "But I predict the time will come when you'll be very happy to have on sexy underwear."

"Sure. Maybe in about seven months," Gabi said. "Or after this experience, possibly a whole lot longer. Men, in general, are not real high on my trustworthiness scale right now."

"Please, please allow room for an exception," Samantha advised. "You might be reeling right now, but keep your heart open."

"And my legs clamped permanently shut," Gaby countered. Still, she leaned down and hugged her sister. "Thank you so much for thinking of this. I was starting to panic."

"Hey, Emily and I will always have your back," Samantha said. "That's what sisters do."

And these days, Gabi had never been more grateful for that.

Given his late departure from the renovation site, Wade was running close to a half hour late by the time he got to Cora Jane's. Samantha opened the door and gave him a pitying look.

"Not a good way to start," she whispered under her breath as she let him in.

Wade's eyes, though, were on Gabi, who seemed to be regarding him with a malevolent look. She'd obviously put some effort into getting ready, but at the moment, she was seated at the kitchen table with a half-eaten sandwich in front of her. He winced at that.

"I am so sorry I'm late," he apologized. "A job got complicated and it took too long to figure out the problem. I needed to get home, take a shower and change. Given how beautiful you look, you wouldn't have wanted to be seen with me at the end of a long day at work."

He caught the faint softening in her eyes at his flattery, but she kept right on eating.

"You're going to spoil your dinner if you finish that sandwich," he said.

"I'm reconsidering," she said, speaking at last.

"Reconsidering what?" he asked, though there was little doubt what she meant.

"This whole dinner and a movie thing. I'm pretty sure it's a terrible idea."

He grinned. "And I'm equally certain it's a fabulous idea. Well, maybe not the dinner if you keep on eating now, but seeing a movie. It'll take your mind off things. And you did say you wanted your own bucket of popcorn."

She set the remainder of the sandwich back on the plate and regarded him with caution. "With extra butter?"

"However you want it."

"And a large soda, even if it means I have to visit the restroom every twenty minutes?"

"You can sit on the aisle," he said. "Take off whenever you need to."

"I might want candy, too."

He held back a laugh. With negotiating skills like those, no wonder she'd been a success. "Done," he said agreeably.

She stood at last. "Okay, then. Let's go."

"Are you satisfied that you've negotiated a deal you can live with?" he asked.

She appeared to give that some thought before nodding. "Yep. I think that's it."

"Okay, here are my demands," he said, drawing a startled look. "Don't look so shocked. The other side always has counterdemands. I'm sure you're aware of that."

"Fair enough, I suppose," she said, eyeing him suspiciously. "Tell me."

"We don't mention the baby or your job all evening."

"Done," she said without hesitation.

"Since I'm skipping dinner, we stop by Boone's Harbor for dessert after the movie," he added.

"Sounds reasonable," she agreed.

"And you forgive me for being late without calling," he added for good measure.

She met his gaze. "This time," she said solemnly.

"It won't happen again," he assured her. "At least, not without a call."

He heard a chuckle and realized Samantha had taken in the whole exchange. He frowned at her. "Anything you'd care to add?"

She shook her head. "Nope, I think you two have this under control, though the battle over the candy choices promises to get interesting. I can hardly wait to hear how the rest of the evening goes."

Gabi frowned at her. "Don't wait up."

Samantha's brows shot up. "My, my, are you thinking of moving things along that fast?"

Her sister gave her a look of dismay. "Stop that. You know that's not what I meant. I just meant I do not intend to come in here later and fill you in on my evening."

"Darn," Samantha said. "I was hoping to live vicariously."

"Well, forget it," Gabi told her emphatically, then nodded toward the door. "Let's get out of here before she starts with some kind of cross-examination. I'm pretty sure Grandmother designated her to be tonight's interrogator."

Wade laughed. "Where is Cora Jane?"

"Out with Jerry. Don't be one bit surprised if they're in the back row behind us at the movies," Gabi said, sounding resigned. "Are you beginning to see why I thought this was a bad idea?"

"So far, nothing you've said or anything that's happened has scared me off," Wade assured her. If anything, knowing how much her family cared about her made him that much more certain that she was a woman worth getting to know.

"Oh, come on," Gabi protested as she and Wade were seated at a table by the window at Boone's Harbor, the flagship restaurant of Boone's small chain of upscale seafood establishments. "Are you seriously telling me you believed anything about that movie was realistic? It was a glorified cartoon with live action."

"Okay, so maybe you needed to suspend disbelief just a little," Wade agreed. "But it was fast-moving and exciting."

"And that's all it takes for you to like a movie? Blow up a few things, drive at a breakneck pace through city streets, dangle from a ledge?"

Wade scowled at her. "You agreed to an action movie," he reminded her.

"I was being polite."

"Was that it, or were you looking for a choice that we'd wind up fighting about the way we are right now? You get to complain that I have no taste, that I'm insensitive, just a dumb guy, what?"

Gabi laughed. Those were all things she'd intended to throw in his face before she was done. "I may have to take it back. You might be just the teeniest bit sensitive if you picked up on all that."

"I'll have you know I was perfectly willing to go to a chick flick tonight," he said, his expression stoic.

"Oh, really?"

He pulled a wad of tissues from his pocket. "See. I was totally prepared for the tears."

Gabi regarded him with astonishment. "You're actually serious."

"Of course I am. I did not foist this movie on you, Gabriella. You picked it."

"Then I will take all the blame for selecting something mindless and unbelievable. You can hold it over my head, if you like."

"How about this? Next time, I'll choose the movie. I bet I can come closer to picking something you'll like than you did making a choice for me."

Just then the waitress came over to take their orders. "Hey, Wade," she said, giving him a friendly wink. "Are you having dinner or just drinks?"

He glanced at Gabi. "Feel like a meal or just coffee and dessert?"

"It's probably sacrilegious or something in a seafood restaurant, but I could actually eat a burger," she admitted. "I'm starved again."

"Two burgers, then," Wade told the waitress. "What to drink, Gabi?"

"Just water."

"And I'll have a beer," he said.

"Sure thing."

"Is Boone around?" Gabi asked.

"Actually, he left about a half hour ago with his fiancée."

Gabi grinned. "That would be my sister."

The woman's expression brightened at once. "You're one of the Castles." She frowned slightly. "Gabriella, I bet. I've seen Samantha on TV a couple times, and her coloring is different."

"Good eye," Gabi told her.

"This is Francesca Daniels, better known as Frankie," Wade said. "She was in the class ahead of me in school."

"Since we didn't go to school over here, I didn't know that many of the locals, even though I was around every summer," Gabi said. She glanced from the woman to Wade and back. "Were the two of you close?"

Frankie laughed. "No way. Wade only had eyes for one girl back then." Suddenly at a warning look from Wade, her expression turned solemn. "I'd better get your order in before the kitchen closes," she said hurriedly.

After she'd gone, Gabi studied Wade. "She certainly took off fast. What was it she almost said that obviously bothered you? Was it about whoever you were interested in back then?"

"It doesn't matter," he said.

She could tell from his expression, though, that it did. "Secrets already, Wade? Come on. You know mine. Fill me in on yours. Was the relationship back then serious?"

"Probably not so serious in high school," he admitted with obvious reluctance. "But we stayed together."

"For how long?"

"Until a couple of years ago," he said, then lifted his gaze to meet hers. "When she died."

Gabi felt her heart plummet. "Oh, my God, I had no idea. I'm so sorry."

"We'd been married, though briefly. Kayla was pregnant. Right before the baby was due, there was an accident. Neither of them made it."

He made the recitation in a calm, matter-of-fact tone, but she could see the turmoil in his eyes. "Oh, Wade," she whispered, and reached for his hand, twining her fingers through his. He pulled away.

"I don't talk about it," he said flatly.

She frowned at that. "That can't be good. Not that I think you should pour out your soul to everyone you meet on the street, but this was a huge deal, Wade. It had to be devastating."

"It was," he said simply.

When she would have said more, he held up a hand. "We put the baby and your job off-limits for tonight. Let's add this to that list."

"But it's obviously part of who you are. How are we supposed to get to know each other if all the important stuff is off the table?"

"For tonight," he said emphatically. "Tonight the goal is to distract you from your problems, not to saddle you with mine."

Gabi heard not only the warning note in his voice, but the plea behind it. Obviously his emotions were still raw. While she'd never been through anything as terrible as what he'd faced, she understood all about it being too soon to discuss some topics.

"Fine. I'll drop it for tonight," she agreed.

But something told her that until they *could* talk about it, there would be a huge part of Wade Johnson she couldn't possibly understand. The fact that she was suddenly a little more intrigued than she'd expected to be was definitely disconcerting.

Relieved to have killed the subject of his marriage for the moment, Wade hurried Gabi through their meal, claiming he needed to get her home so she could get some rest. In truth, he needed some time to settle down, remember this was about distracting Gabi from her problems, not letting her get inside his head. It most definitely wasn't supposed to be about seducing her, which seemed to be all he could think about at the moment.

Good grief, the woman was having another man's baby, and his mind was on sex. It had been on sex since he'd first laid eyes on her months ago. He needed to make a few adjustments for the current and very unexpected circumstances.

When they walked outside, she looked up at the sky full of stars, her expression enchanted. "The sky never looks like this in Raleigh," she said. "Too many city lights."

"I've never known anything else," Wade said. "Lived here all my life, and not much interest in trying anyplace else."

"You didn't go away to college?"

He shook his head. "I knew early on that I wanted to work with wood. My dad taught me custom cabinetry. He'd made a good living at it and claimed I had a knack for it, too. I just eased into the business, then took it over from him when he retired."

"Boone says you're the best around," Gabi told him.

"He seems to like the work I've done for him."

"So did Cora Jane." She grinned. "At least, I assume that's why she kept dreaming up jobs for you to do at Castle's."

He laughed. "Sweetheart, that was all about keeping me firmly planted in your path. She assumed if we brushed past each other enough, sooner or later we'd set off sparks."

She winced. "You knew that? How embarrassing!"

"I didn't object. You were just about the prettiest

woman I'd seen in a very long time. The work was easy enough. The eye candy was something special."

She frowned. "Thanks, I think."

"Trust me, it was a compliment." He noticed she was still staring up at the stars. "Want to walk along the docks before we head back to your place?"

"Yes," she said eagerly, heading for the closest one in the marina.

She stumbled slightly at the edge. Wade caught her hand, then kept it securely in his. "You warm enough?" he asked, almost hoping she'd say no so he could justify putting an arm around her.

"Perfect," she assured him.

"No doubt about that," he murmured before realizing he'd spoken aloud.

Gabi regarded him worriedly. "Wade, I'm far from perfect."

"Not from where I'm standing," he insisted.

She regarded him with frustration. "This can't go anywhere. You know that, right? Things in my life are just too complicated. I'll go back to Raleigh eventually, start over."

"Maybe," he agreed. "Nothing says we can't be friends, though, right?"

"I got the feeling just now that you might want more," she admitted.

"You're a beautiful, smart, funny, desirable woman," he said solemnly. "Any man who didn't think about having more with you would be a fool. That doesn't mean I expect it to happen." He grinned. "At least not overnight."

"I just don't want to lead you on," she said, stopping at the end of the dock and studying him with an earnest expression. "I've messed up a lot lately. You seem like a really nice guy. I don't want you to be one of my mistakes."

He took her by the shoulders and held her gaze. "You're making way too much of an innocent remark," he said quietly. "We've had a nice evening out. We've gotten to know each other a little better, shared a few laughs. Nobody's asking for more. Nobody's jumping ahead, least of all me. Believe me, I know all about not being ready for any complications."

She seemed to take in his words, then finally nodded. "As long as we're clear about what's going on."

"We're clear," he assured her. "No worries, okay?"

"Okay."

"We'll hang out when it feels right," he added.

"Hang out?"

"Get together," he explained. "Have a meal, maybe some conversation, whatever. No big deal."

Gabi might be the spin master in the Castle family, but Wade thought he was doing a pretty good job right now of putting together a line that would assure she'd let her guard down with him. One thing was definite—whatever he had to say or do to pull it off, he didn't intend to let tonight's date be their last.

Four

At loose ends for the first time in ages, Gabi wandered through her grandmother's house the day after her movie date with Wade. Though she had slept late, she felt restless and edgy. She knew perfectly well it was because her life had no structure right now, no purpose. For a woman who'd been driven to succeed, who'd worked eighteen out of every twenty-four hours more often than not, the empty hours she faced now were a cross to bear, not a relief.

When her cell phone rang, she seized it like a lifeline without bothering to check the caller ID. After she'd answered, she was stunned to hear Paul's voice.

"Gabriella? Is that you?" he repeated when she held the phone in shocked silence.

"What do you want?" she finally asked.

"I heard what happened at work," he admitted. "I'm sorry."

"Thanks," she said tightly. "If that's all, I need to be going."

"Wait!" he protested. "I thought we should talk, settle a few things."

"Paul, believe me, you made your position plain the last time we spoke. We have nothing left to discuss."

"Look, I'm really sorry about how I behaved. I was insensitive and selfish. You just caught me completely off guard with the whole baby thing."

"The whole *baby thing*," she echoed. "What a quaint way to put it! You and I conceived a child together. You acted as if I'd done that all by myself and solely to ruin your life. I can't tell you how cherished and special that made me feel."

"I said I was sorry," he repeated impatiently. "Look, I know I'm bungling this again. I just want to talk, figure out how to handle things from here on out."

"There's nothing for you to worry about," she responded. "I'm handling things just fine on my own. That's what I do, you know. I handle things. Isn't that what you suggested as you walked out the door? That this was just one more challenge for me to deal with?"

"That was before you lost your job," he said, as if she needed reminding. "You'll need some financial support for sure now. I want you to know I intend to step up, for you and the baby."

"Not necessary," she said. "From now on the less you have to do with me or the baby, the better. I'm not sure I could stomach the sight of you."

"Now you're just being shortsighted and stubborn," he said. "Having a child can be a huge expense. I'm the father. It's up to me to contribute to his or her support."

Gabi drew in a deep breath and reminded herself of what she'd read online about adoptions. "There's only one thing I want you to do for me, and it doesn't require one dime from you."

"What?"

"I want you to have papers drawn up relinquishing all parental rights."

The request seemed to stun him. "What?"

"That's it. I imagine any of those very expensive attorneys who play golf with you every week can handle that for you. You obviously didn't want this child. I just want to make sure that you legally relinquish all rights."

"But why?" he asked suspiciously. "I'm offering to pay child support."

"And I'm telling you, I don't want your money. This document is all I want. I want to be sure you don't wake up some day, decide you made a terrible mistake and try to disrupt this child's life."

"There's more to this," he said. "Normally you'd be battling tooth and nail to see that I paid dearly to ensure the child's financial future."

"Which just proves you don't know me at all. I don't want any part of you, and I can ensure the baby's future will be a good one."

"Now? With no job?"

"Not every company is as conservative as the one I just left," she said with more confidence than she felt. "I'll work again. Now, will you get the document or not?"

"I'll have to think it over," he said.

"Oh, for heaven's sake, Paul. I'm letting you off the hook, which is exactly what you said you wanted. Stop pretending this requires any deep consideration on your part. Grab the deal."

"Fine," he said, proving she was right about this so-called epiphany of his. There was nothing sincere about it.

"I'll have the papers drawn up and sent over by courier tomorrow," he added.

"You'll need to send them to Sand Castle Bay. I'm staying with my Grandmother at the moment."

"I suppose your sisters are there, too," he said with an unmistakable edge of sarcasm.

"They are. So what?"

"It explains a lot, that's all. The Castle troops have rallied, forming a united front against evil."

She almost laughed at the drama he was implying. "You're not evil, Paul. Just selfish and insensitive. I can assure you that my sisters have given you very little thought, much less hatched some nefarious scheme to get even with you." Not that Emily and Samantha wouldn't enjoy doing exactly that if she'd signaled she wanted it.

"I'm not sure I buy that," he said.

"It's the truth. You're just not that important. Now, I'll expect those documents by the end of the week."

"Maybe I should bring them in person, just in case you've had a change of heart once you're thinking more clearly. This could be the hormones talking."

"I'm hanging up now," she said, barely containing her fury over the sexist comment. "Otherwise, this will not end on a civil note."

Before he could respond, she disconnected the call, then threw the cell phone across the room. Samantha snatched it out of the air before it could hit the wall. Gabi winced when she saw her.

"How much did you hear?" she asked her sister.

"Enough to figure out it was Paul, and that you weren't any happier with the conversation this time than you had been when you gave him the news about the baby."

"He accused me of being hormonal," she reported indignantly, pacing to work off some steam.

Samantha chuckled. "Well, you probably are, but it's not exactly diplomatic on his part to point it out. Why'd he call? He did make the call, right? Not you?"

"Oh, no, this was all about him. He called to soothe his conscience. He wanted to throw some money my way."

"And you turned it down?"

"Of course I did," she said, continuing to pace. "I don't want his money. All I want is for him to relinquish all parental rights to this baby. That way, when I put him or her up for adoption, there won't be any complications."

Samantha frowned.

"Oh, don't look like that," Gabi grumbled. "I just wanted to cover that base. I saw my chance and took it."

"And if you keep the baby? Don't you think Paul owes it to you and your child to help pay expenses?"

"I don't need his money," Gabi insisted stubbornly.

"It might make a tidy nest egg for your son or daughter's education," Samantha said reasonably. "At the rate college expenses are rising, you'll probably have to mortgage not only your house but your soul to assure the kid can attend a major university."

"You think I'm being shortsighted," Gabi concluded with a sigh. "Maybe I am, but even if I keep this baby, I don't want Paul to have any say in his or her life."

"When the child gets a little older, he or she might feel differently," Samantha argued.

"Which is yet another recommendation for adoption, if you ask me," Gabi said irritably, putting a protective hand over her belly. "I'll be saving this child from all the bitterness and hard feelings."

"You don't mean that," Samantha said. "You're hurt and justifiably angry about the way Paul handled the news of the pregnancy, but surely you don't want to punish the baby by trying to keep the identity of the father locked away forever."

Gabi sighed. "Okay, no. You're right. Then I'd be behaving just as selfishly as Paul was when he said he wanted no part of the baby." She gave her sister an imploring look. "But you have to see how much simpler it could be for this child to be raised in a loving home with two parents who will dote on her and not have all this emotional baggage they're dragging around."

Samantha smiled. "I have boundless faith in your maturity, sweetie. You won't allow your emotional baggage to affect your child."

"I wish I were as sure of that as you are."

"Give it time," Samantha advised. "You have a few months to get your equilibrium back before you have to make a final decision. Just don't do anything hasty. Can you promise me that much, at least?"

As if to echo Samantha's plea, the baby fluttered in Gabi's womb, making his or her presence—and maybe even his or her opinion—felt. Gabi sighed, wondering once more if she'd really be able to let this child go when the time came, no matter how deep her belief that it was for the best.

All things considered, Wade thought, his evening with Gabriella had gone pretty well. He'd managed to keep himself from trying to steal a kiss when he'd taken her back to Cora Jane's. He wanted to believe the decision had been part of a greater strategy, but he had a hunch it had stemmed from a fear of humiliating rejection. No way was she ready for so much as a hint of his growing feelings for her. She'd made that plain enough with her little speech at the marina.

Fortunately, this morning he'd been too busy meeting with a new client and trying to solve the problem of leveling out the kitchen cabinets for Tommy to worry too much about Gabi's perception of their date.

As lunchtime neared, Jimmy sidled close, his expression hopeful. Wade chuckled.

"You interested in grabbing that burger today?" he asked the teen.

Jimmy's expression brightened. "Sure, if you have the time. I'm getting sick of the peanut butter and jelly sandwiches I've been bringing."

Wade frowned. "You're not going out with the other guys for lunch?"

An embarrassed flush crept up the boy's neck. "Nah, they're older than me. They don't want me hanging around. Besides, I need to put my paycheck aside to help out at home. Since my dad's accident, he hasn't been able to work as much. We can use whatever money I bring home."

"Your dad had an accident?"

"His right hand got cut real bad on a job a few months back. It makes it hard for him to do construction, you know? They say with rehab, it'll get better, but he hasn't been able to do the kind of rehab they recommended. He cut back on his insurance to save a little money. Mom told him it was a mistake, but he wanted to get her the new stove she wanted."

"So money's real tight," Wade guessed, resolving to see if there was anything he could do to help out. It was plain, though, that Jimmy had a lot of pride. He suspected he'd gotten that from his dad.

Jimmy shrugged. "We do okay," he insisted. He hesitated, then added, "If I could pick up some overtime, it would help."

"I'll see what I can do. You're a good worker, Jimmy. If Tommy can't find a few extra hours for you, maybe somebody else will be able to use you."

"I'll take anything," Jimmy said eagerly. "That'd be great, Mr. Johnson."

"It's Wade. Now, let's go grab those burgers."

He drove over to Castle's, which was already bustling with a lunch crowd.

"Any tables left?" he asked Cora Jane.

"I'll always be able to find room for you," she said.

"And this is Jimmy Templeton," Wade told her.

Cora Jane looked him over. "Any kin to Rory Templeton?"

Jimmy nodded. "Yes, ma'am. He's my dad."

"I thought so," Cora Jane said. "You look just like he did when he was your age. I was real sorry to hear about his injury. How's he doing?"

"Coming along," Jimmy told her. "I'll tell him you asked about him."

Cora Jane turned her attention back to Wade. "You were out mighty late last night," she commented.

"I wasn't aware Gabi had a curfew," he teased.

"I just meant that she got in too late for me to get any inkling of how things went," she said, her frustration plain. "And I thought for sure we'd see you at that chick flick at the multiplex, but there wasn't a sign of you."

"We saw the action movie," he reported, managing

to hide his amusement at having frustrated her spying mission. "Gabi's choice, by the way."

"Really? She hates that kind of movie."

Wade chuckled. "So I gathered. It gave her an excellent chance, though, to carry on about men having no sensitivity or taste when it comes to movies."

Cora Jane laughed. "Now that does sound more like her."

She seated them in the booth near the kitchen that Wade knew she normally reserved for family. "I'll send your waitress right over," she promised, then hurried off.

Not two minutes later, as he and Jimmy were just starting to study the menu, a familiar voice said, "You!"

He glanced up with a smile. "Gabriella, I had no idea you'd be working here today."

She shrugged. "I wasn't. I got bored at Grandmother's and drove over here. She snagged me in the kitchen just now and put an order book in my hands, then assigned me to this table."

Wade laughed. "She never gives up, does she?"

"Never. It would serve her right if I just sat down here with you and waited for some other server to take over this table."

"Do it," he suggested. "Of course, that would be playing right into her hands."

He noted that Jimmy was studying the two of them with obvious fascination.

"Jimmy, this is Gabriella Castle. She's Cora Jane's granddaughter."

"The one Tommy was talking about yesterday," Jimmy recalled, proving that he'd taken in the whole conversation about Wade's social life.

Gabi regarded him curiously. "That would be Tommy Cahill?" she guessed. "And my name came up?"

"Unfortunately, yes. Cora Jane is not the only meddler in Sand Castle Bay," Wade said. "Say another word, Jimmy, and our deal for that burger is off."

Jimmy looked chagrined. "Sorry."

Wade grinned at him. "Just teasing, but maybe we ought to talk about something else. Gabi, Jimmy here saved the day on the job I'm doing for Tommy."

"Not really," Jimmy protested. "I just had an idea."

"Which turned out to be on the money," Wade said, then filled Gabi in.

She smiled at the teen. "I'm impressed. Are you serious about working in construction?"

"It's okay for now," Jimmy said. "I sort of drifted into it by accident, you might say."

Gabi seized on the remark. "But you'd rather be doing something else?"

He nodded. "I kinda wanted to go to college, or at least to junior college, but it's not in the cards right now."

"What did you want to study?" she asked.

"Biomedical engineering," he said, his expression suddenly animated.

Gabi looked startled. "And you think you have what it takes? It's a tough field."

"I got pretty good grades in science," he responded.

"How good?" she asked at once.

"Straight A's," he told her proudly.

"Good for you," she told him, her expression turning thoughtful.

"What are you thinking?" Wade asked.

"Just pondering a couple of ideas," she said.

Wade let the subject drop because he got a feeling she didn't want to mention the ideas in front of Jimmy. The fact that she'd so obviously taken an interest in a boy she barely knew touched him on a whole new level, though. Not that she needed any additional recommendation in his book.

She stood. "It's obvious Grandmother is not sending anyone else to handle this table, so let me rustle up some food for you. I'm sure you need to get back to work."

"Two cheeseburgers with fries," Wade said at once. "Soda, Jimmy?"

The teenager nodded, his rapt gaze never leaving Gabriella. Clearly he was smitten. Wade knew all too well exactly how he felt.

Even after Wade and Jimmy had left Castle's, Gabi hadn't been able to shake off their conversation or the eager expression on Jimmy's face when he'd talked about biomedical engineering. She wasn't sure why that look had touched her, but it had.

Maybe it was because she understood what it was like to want something so badly and know it was just out of reach. That's the way it had always been in her relationship with her father. He hadn't withheld his love, just routine affection and approval. He'd given lip service to being a good dad. He just hadn't been around. While Emily had responded by dismissing him from her life and Samantha had feigned acceptance of Sam Castle's flaws, Gabi had spent years trying to earn his attention.

At the end of the day, still unable to shake the image of Jimmy's resigned expression of acceptance that he'd never achieve his dream, she pulled out her cell phone and called her father's private line.

"What is it?" he snapped impatiently when he answered.

"Always a pleasure to hear your voice, Dad," she said, not even attempting to keep the sarcasm from her voice.

"Gabriella?"

"Yep, it's me. I'm probably the only one of your daughters who dares to interrupt your work."

"Did you call for something specific or just to make a point about my sins as a parent?" he inquired.

"Actually, for once, I'm not calling to judge you. I need your help."

For an instant, stunned silence greeted the remark. "That's a first," he said eventually.

"I hope that means you'll take it seriously, then."

"Of course I will," he said impatiently.

"I'm staying over at Grandmother's," she announced. "Emily and Samantha are here, too."

"Why?" he asked, a worried note creeping into his voice. For once he sounded more concerned than exasperated that something inconvenient might be about to disrupt his life. "Is your grandmother sick?"

"No, we're making plans for Emily's wedding," she said, figuring that was the least controversial explanation she could offer. "Since President's Day weekend is this week, could you drive over? At least for a day?"

"I seriously doubt your sister wants my input on her wedding," he countered.

"She might like sharing her plans with you, though," Gabi said. "Be an interested dad for once. Couldn't you do that?"

After a lengthy pause, he finally said, "I'll drive over Saturday morning. Is that all?"

"I need you to bring an open mind with you," she added. "There's a young man I want you to meet."

"Someone you're seeing?"

"No, someone I just met today."

"I don't understand."

"You will," she promised. "I think he's going to remind you of someone."

"Who?"

"You," she replied softly. "See you on Saturday, Dad."

She hung up before he could have second thoughts and take back his promise to come.

"What are you up to?" Cora Jane asked, studying her intently.

Gabi glanced up at her. "You heard?"

"Enough to know that you've reached out to your father," Cora Jane confirmed.

"I'm hoping Dad will dig deep into that heart we all suspect him of having and maybe give a helping hand to a kid who needs it," she said.

Cora Jane regarded her worriedly. "Oh, honey bun, are you sure about this? Are you really ready to see your father right now?"

Gabi knew what she was really asking—was Gabi ready for her father to realize she was pregnant and start making judgments. "It's not about me," she said. "That kid deserves a break, and I think I know a way to make it happen. Dad's company gives some scholarships for qualified kids. They start taking applications around this time of the year. Usually the applicants are high school seniors, but I think under the circumstances

I can convince him to make an exception for Jimmy. Dad has the ability to make this happen for that boy."

Cora Jane shook her head. "You've always been an optimist where your dad's concerned. You've seen the good in him, even when he's done his best to hide it from all of you."

Gabi shrugged. "I'm not sure if I've even had a glimpse of it," she admitted. "But he is your son, Grandmother. Nobody raised by Cora Jane Castle could possibly be all bad."

Cara Jane chuckled at that. "You may be giving me too much credit."

"I guess we'll see on Saturday, won't we?"

And at the same time, she'd be able to face the risk that her father would turn his back on her for the mess she'd made of her life. At least by forcing the issue here and now, she'd be surrounded by people who loved her and didn't judge her.

If Sam Castle disowned her for making a mistake, well, it would only sever a tie that had never been very strong to begin with. Maybe it was time she knew once and for all if she could ever forge a real relationship with her father, or if she, like her sisters, was destined to have him on the fringe of her life forever.

Five

"Dad's coming over on Saturday?" Emily repeated skeptically. "You called him and he actually said he'd come?"

Gabi shrugged. "He said he would. I told him you were here and we were making wedding plans."

"And that was enough to drag him out of his office? I don't believe it," Emily said flatly. "So, what? Am I supposed to ask for his opinion on the flowers?"

Gabi exchanged a look with Samantha, then chuckled. "Maybe you should ask him to pay for the wedding," Gabi suggested. "After all, he is the father of the bride. That would be the traditional thing to do."

Emily's jaw dropped. "You think I should ask Dad to pay for the wedding? Seriously?"

"Why not?" Samantha said. "He's lucked out so far. Three daughters and this is the first wedding to come along. Gabi and I have saved him a fortune."

An expression of wicked delight passed across Emily's face. "It would serve him right, wouldn't it?" she said, a glint of amusement in her eyes. "Boone and I intended to pay for everything ourselves, but it would be worth it to see the look on Dad's face when I hand him the bills for the dresses and the flowers and the caterer. Do you suppose he even knows how to write a check? Mom always paid the bills."

"Stop it," Gabi scolded. "Somebody's been paying them since Mom died. Dad's not incompetent, just distracted."

"He's so distracted, it's a miracle he's not been living on the street, if you ask me," Emily retorted. "I guess that scary, efficient assistant of his stepped up after Mom died. What's her name? I always called her the guardian of the gate."

"Her name is Miriam and she's actually very nice," Gabi said, thinking how often it had been Miriam, not her father, who'd been there to take the sting out of some slight at school. "And she probably did step in to make sure Dad's life continued to run smoothly after Mom died."

"I always wondered if there was something more between them," Samantha said.

Gabi frowned at the suggestion. "While Mom was alive? No way. Dad could barely spare enough attention for his wife and kids. He didn't have time for another woman. Besides, Miriam must be close to seventy by now, so she's at least ten years older than Dad."

"But he did spend an awful lot of time at the office," Emily countered.

"Okay, enough," Gabi said impatiently. "Dad has his issues, but infidelity isn't one of them. I'm as sure of that as I am that the sun will come up tomorrow. You seem to forget that rigid moral code of his."

"Ah," Samantha said, her expression turning worried. "You mean the one that's going to find your situation intolerable?"

Gabi nodded. "That's the one."

Emily seemed to share Samantha's concern. "Gabi, why are you forcing this now? Samantha said you weren't willing to turn to Dad for help in finding a new job because you didn't want him to know about the pregnancy. What changed?"

She explained about Jimmy Templeton. "I saw a chance to help."

Emily's eyes brightened. "And a way to impress Wade," she concluded.

Gabi frowned at the suggestion. "This has absolutely nothing to do with Wade. He introduced me to the boy, that's all."

"And is he, by any chance, going to be bringing him by here to meet Dad?" Samantha inquired, her own smirk firmly in place.

Gabi uttered an expletive. "I need to call Wade, don't I? I was so busy worrying about getting Dad over here, I completely forgot about arranging for Jimmy to be here."

"Notice she's going to call Wade, rather than call Jimmy directly," Emily commented smugly.

"I notice," Sam agreed.

"You two are so annoying," Gabi muttered. "If you weren't my sisters, I doubt I'd have a thing to do with you."

"Sweetie, are you really sure you want to insult the two people who will be here to have your back when Dad shows up?" Emily inquired.

"Point taken," Gabi said at once. "Do you think I

should have Jimmy here when Dad walks in the door or later?"

"Definitely later," Samantha said.

"But he might not say anything about me being pregnant with Jimmy and Wade here," Gabi said hopefully.

"Or he'll explode, and the prospects for Jimmy will get buried in the fallout," Emily said. "I vote for later, too."

Gabi could see what her sisters were saying. "I'm guessing Dad will get an early start and be here by ten. I'll suggest Wade and Jimmy come for lunch around twelve-thirty," she decided.

Emily nodded. "After delivering your news and my wedding bills, we should have Dad revived by then, for sure."

Gabi frowned at her. "Not amusing."

Samantha laughed. "But sadly, probably accurate."

Wade listened with growing amazement as Gabi issued her invitation to lunch and explained the reasoning behind it.

"Are you serious? You think your dad could get Jimmy a scholarship?" he asked.

"The company offers a few every year. I'm familiar with the criteria. Granted, I don't know everything about Jimmy's situation, but he seems to me like the perfect candidate."

"Is the decision up to your father?"

"No, but his opinion carries a lot of weight."

"This is a huge risk," Wade said, unable to conceal his concern.

"What do you mean?"

"If I understand you correctly, you haven't really

talked this over with your dad. You have no idea how he's going to react. What if it goes badly, and we've gotten Jimmy's hopes up?"

To her credit, Gabi didn't automatically dismiss his concern. "Here's how I see it. Right now, Jimmy has zero chance of achieving his dream. This scholarship could change that. Isn't it worth it to at least try? In the end, if he isn't chosen, he'll be no worse off, but he stands to get everything he ever wanted, if he is."

"Well, it's definitely not up to me to decide," Wade said. "I'll run this by him, see what he wants to do. Like you said, it could be the opportunity of a lifetime. I knew you were coming up with some sort of scheme when you met him the other day. I could practically see the wheels turning in that brain of yours."

"I didn't want to say anything until I knew if I could at least get my father over here. He's not always available."

Wade heard the sad undercurrent in her voice and assumed she wasn't just talking about a busy timetable. "I've heard he doesn't have the best relationship with you and your sisters," he admitted. "Boone's mentioned it."

Gabi sighed. "Boone's exactly right. I've tried the hardest to change that, but even I have my limits. This is going to be an interesting visit for me, too."

"Why?"

"He doesn't know about the baby," she said.

"Holy cow!" Wade muttered, then asked, "Don't you think that's a lot to lay on him right before you ask him for a favor?"

Gabi was extraordinarily quiet for a very long time.

Finally she admitted, "To be honest, I think this is kind of a test, to see if he's ever going to step up as my dad."

"That's quite a test, especially for a man who hasn't been that involved in your life up till now."

"I'm thinking of it as indoctrination by fire. Emily's going to drop the bills for her wedding in his lap, too."

Wade was starting to view the whole lunch invitation as a disaster waiting to happen. He understood Gabi's desperate need to clarify whether she could count on her dad, but he didn't think Jimmy needed to be caught up in all the likely drama.

"Gabi, I get what you're trying to do here, for Jimmy and for yourself. I'm just not sure you've taken into account how bad things could get. Do you really want to put a teenager you barely know in the middle of that? It could be asking a lot of him."

She hesitated, then said, "I guess I never thought about what might happen if Dad reacts badly to all this stuff coming at him at once."

"Don't you think you'd better consider it?"

"I knew there was a reason I called you, rather than talking directly to Jimmy myself. You're so blasted calm and reasonable."

"I'm not sure, but somehow it doesn't sound like you mean that as a compliment," he responded. "How about this, though? I'll give Jimmy a heads-up, make sure he's available. Then I'll stop by around noon and we'll decide if it makes sense for him to join us. Would that be okay?" Left unsaid was that he would be there for backup, if things didn't go so well and Gabi needed a shoulder to cry on.

"A much better plan," she acknowledged, albeit with a grudging note in her voice.

Wade smiled. "Okay, then. I'll see you tomorrow. And, Gabi?"

"Yes."

"I truly hope your dad steps up the way you want him to, not just for Jimmy's sake, but for yours."

"Thanks."

As he hung up, Wade's only regret was that he wouldn't be there when Sam Castle first walked in the door and discovered his daughter was pregnant. How he handled that moment was going to set the tone for everything that followed.

Gabi walked into Samantha's room on Saturday morning wearing the dress her sister had bought for her date with Wade. She glanced in the mirror, then turned to Sam.

"How bad is it? Can you tell I'm pregnant?"

"Sweetie, you're what? Almost five months along? It definitely shows."

"But how closely does Dad ever look at us, really? He might not notice," she said hopefully.

"Trust me, even Dad will notice," Samantha insisted.

"Maybe I should change."

Samantha shook her head. "You can't hide it with a baggy shirt. Dad may be oblivious to just about everything, but he's going to notice you're carrying a child. Isn't that the point, anyway?"

"I guess I just wanted a chance to break the news to him, not throw it in his face the second he walks in the door."

"Then you should have called him when you found out, or when you were first fired," Samantha told her. She stepped closer and gave Gabi a hug. "No matter what, it's going to be okay. You have me, Emily and Grandmother firmly in your corner. And Wade will be here, too."

"Not at first," Gabi said, almost regretting that she hadn't asked him to come by earlier. He had an amazing knack for steadying her. She found it annoying sometimes, but mostly it was comforting.

Suddenly she was struck by a terrible thought. "Oh, no. What if Dad takes one look at Wade and thinks he's the father? What was I thinking? He's liable to punch him in the nose."

Samantha's barely controlled chuckle erupted into full-blown laughter. "I know it's not really funny, but can you imagine Dad punching anyone?"

Gabi chuckled, unable to envision it. "Well, this could send him over the edge. Who knows? We've never tested him quite like this before. I wonder if he has any idea how lucky he's been all these years. Not a one of us has ever gotten into serious trouble."

"Something tells me if Dad does lose it, Wade can handle the situation," Samantha reassured her. "He's so smitten with you, he'd slay dragons for you, if need be."

"Wade's not smitten," Gabi said. "We talked about it. We're just friends."

Samantha rolled her eyes. "If that lets you sleep at night, fine, but I know what I know. So does Emily. So does Grandmother."

Gabi's nerves took another jittery bounce. "Please do not make me any crazier than I am already, okay?"

The sound of a car turning into the gravel driveway had her going perfectly still. "Dad?" she whispered, swallowing hard.

Samantha peeked out the window. "Breathe," she

advised. "It's just Emily. Let's go downstairs so we're ready to present a united front when Dad does get here."

A half hour later when Sam Castle walked in through the kitchen door, Emily deliberately stepped in front of Gabi.

"Hey, Dad. Thanks for coming." She stepped closer and kissed his cheek, drawing a look of surprise.

"Well, sure," he said. "Gabi said you're making wedding plans."

"I am," Emily said, beaming at him.

"Want some coffee, Dad?" Samantha asked, also pressing a kiss to his cheek.

He regarded her with suspicion, but nodded. "Is your grandmother around?"

"She'll be here in a few minutes," Samantha said. "She had to deal with a crisis at the restaurant, but she called and said she was on her way home."

He accepted the cup of coffee that Samantha thrust into his hands and was about to sit at the kitchen table when he caught a glimpse of Gabi, who'd been standing with a chair in front of her.

"Gabriella?" he said, his voice thick with shock. He glanced from one sister to the other, then back at her. "Are you going to have a baby?"

Gabi stepped out from behind the chair. "I am," she said cheerfully, though there was no mistaking the nervousness behind her admission.

Sam blinked hard, then sat down. "You…are you… who's…?"

Gabi did her best to hold his gaze. "I'm about five months along. I'm not married. I'm not getting married. The father's no longer in the picture. In fact, I got the papers just yesterday legally relinquishing his parental rights."

"What the hell?" Sam blustered. "Is the man crazy? What kind of coward walks away from his child and the mother of his child?"

"I sent him away, Dad," Gabi said. "Anything else would have been a disaster. He didn't want this baby. He didn't want me."

Sam frowned at her announcement. "But, Gabriella, the man has responsibilities."

"I'll manage on my own," she assured him.

"What about work? How are you going to manage that demanding job and being a single mother?"

Gabi gave him a rueful look. "Not a problem. I no longer have a job."

He was starting to look a little pale, as if his head were reeling. "You quit your job, too! What were you thinking?"

"She didn't quit, Dad," Emily said. "They made it impossible for her to stay."

"When did this happen?"

"A couple of weeks ago," Gabi admitted.

At that, color returned to his face, though this time it was a worrisome shade of red. "Why didn't you call me?" he demanded, his tone indignant. "I could have made some calls, straightened out this mess."

"It wouldn't have helped," she told him.

"Are you looking for another job? Is that what this call of yours was really about? Did you want my help?" The questions poured out as he tried to make sense of what was going on.

Gabi shook her head. "No, Dad. I really did call to ask you to help someone else."

Sam sat back in his chair, his expression stunned. "I honestly don't know what to say. If your mother were here, she'd know."

Emily gave him a pitying look. "That's always the way it was, right, Dad? We were Mom's problem. You had better things to do."

"That's not fair, Em," Samantha said, quick to jump to his defense.

Gabi could see the scene deteriorating. "Okay, this isn't the time for that discussion." She met her father's gaze. "I'm sorry about this, Dad. I know it's an embarrassment."

"Stop that!" Emily said indignantly. "Don't you dare apologize to him. It's not about Dad. This baby is nobody's embarrassment. It's a blessing."

"Amen to that," Cora Jane said, letting the screen door slam shut behind her as she entered just in time to hear the exchange. "Sam Castle, this is your first grandchild we're talking about. Now, I expect you to get on board and give your daughter the support she's entitled to expect from her father."

Sam stared at Cora Jane with a shocked expression. "I'm not judging her, not for a single second. If I judge anyone, it's the son of a gun who put her in this situation." He drew in a deep breath, then turned to Gabi. "What can I do to help?"

Gabi blinked back tears at the sincerity behind the question. "You really mean that? You're not furious with me?"

Though he looked visibly uncomfortable, he opened his arms to her. "Never, baby. Never," he said as she launched herself into his embrace. "It must not have seemed that way all these years, but we are a family. I'll do my best by you, whatever you need."

Gabi found herself weeping in her father's arms as her sisters looked on with unmistakable shock.

"Well, now, that's much better," Cora Jane said eventually. "Honey bun, why don't you go and wash your face. I imagine Wade will be here shortly, along with that young man you wanted your father to meet."

Gabi felt her father tense.

"Wade? He's not..." Sam asked.

"No, absolutely not," she said hurriedly. "Wade's a friend who's been incredibly supportive since I got over here last week. He introduced me to the teenager I want you to think about helping, but Jimmy won't be here right away. We wanted things to calm down before we dragged him in the door."

"Okay, then," Sam said, visibly relaxing. He patted her damp cheek. "Why don't you run along the way your grandmother suggested? I need to ask Emily what I can do to help with the wedding. I brought my checkbook."

Emily's mouth gaped at that. She whirled on Samantha. "Did you warn him?"

"Not me," Samantha insisted.

"Or me," Gabi chimed in.

Cora Jane shrugged, her expression sheepish. "I might have reminded him that parents usually paid for their daughter's wedding."

"And thank goodness she did," Sam said. "Otherwise, I imagine it would have been one more thing to add to the list of mistakes I've made with you girls. I know there's a ledger somewhere with all your grievances listed in it. I also know it's likely I earned every one of them. Maybe I can finally start getting a few things right."

Emily came over to poke him in the arm, her expression filled with suspicion. "Who are you, and what have you done with our father?"

For the first time since he'd arrived, the tension in the room seemed to ease. The laughter that erupted wasn't forced. In fact, for that one shining moment, Gabi looked around and thought maybe, just maybe, they were going to pull off being a real family, complete with the involved, caring dad they'd always dreamed of having.

Cora Jane looked around her living room with satisfaction. Today had gone more smoothly than she'd first imagined possible when she'd realized Gabi had pressured her father into coming over for the day. Of course, she'd taken it upon herself to call Sam herself and warn him it was time to step up and do the right thing. She hadn't mentioned Gabi's pregnancy, just the little tidbit about wedding expenses, then advised him to arrive with an open mind and heart.

"You need to hear what they're saying for once and not start making judgments the instant you walk in the door," she'd said.

Naturally he'd reacted with his usual impatience. "Mother, what the devil are you trying so hard not to say?" he'd blustered. "I don't have time for word games and innuendo."

Cora Jane hadn't issued a lot of ultimatums with Sam, especially as an adult, but she issued one now. "You listen to me, son, you will make the time for your daughters. These young women lost their mother. I've stepped up and done the best I can by them, but that doesn't make up for you. They need their father in their lives, and you're going to be there. Understood?"

"I *am* in their lives," he'd protested.

"Oh, really? When was the last time you saw them? Christmas day, unless I'm mistaken. When was the last time you called? Never, I imagine."

Somehow she'd managed to get her point across, or at least that was how it seemed at the moment, with her son sitting in her living room, actually listening to Emily's excited talk about her wedding plans as they awaited Wade's return with Jimmy.

Cora Jane almost hated to interrupt her, but she thought Sam needed to hear a little about Jimmy before he arrived. "Gabi, why don't you explain to your father about Jimmy?"

Gabi jumped in eagerly and summarized her meeting with him, what she knew of his situation and her belief that he was the kind of young man who'd work hard to achieve great things if given a chance.

"You saw that in one meeting?" Sam asked skeptically.

Gabi nodded. "You'll see, too, Dad. This is a kid who works hard. I told you that he reminds me a lot of you. He doesn't make excuses. He just does what's expected of him and does it well."

Sam nodded. "I suppose you have his paperwork all filled out?"

Gabi shook her head. "But I did print out the application." She handed it to him. "See what you think after you've talked with him. If you agree he has a chance, then you can give him the application, maybe help to be sure it'll impress the people who make the final selections."

He turned to Cora Jane. "And you agree with her instincts about this boy?"

Cora Jane nodded at once. "I do. I've heard only good things about how hard he's working to help out his family."

"Okay, then. I'll look forward to meeting him." He gave Gabi a thoughtful look. "And this friend of yours, Wade? Should I be giving him a more thorough once-over when he gets back here, too?"

Gabi blushed. "Don't you dare. We're friends. That's all. I'm pregnant, remember?"

Sam winced. "Not likely to forget."

Cora Jane sighed with satisfaction at the color that rose in Gabi's cheeks at the mention of Wade. Yes, indeed, despite—or perhaps because of—Gabi's too-quick disclaimer, she thought the signs were excellent that the day was off to a very promising start.

Six

"So, why does Gabi want me to meet her father?" Jimmy asked Wade when they were on their way to Cora Jane's. "It's kinda weird. It's not like I really know her." He gave Wade an impish grin. "Unless she thought I was hotter than you and wants to date me. Maybe she needs his permission."

Wade frowned at the teen's impudence. "Not even a tiny bit amusing, kid."

Jimmy's grin merely spread. Eventually, though, he said, "But you do know what this is really about, don't you? How come you won't tell me?"

"Because this was Gabi's idea. She should fill you in," Wade explained patiently. "And you can stop speculating and pestering me now, because we're here."

He pulled into a driveway already crowded with cars, then was relieved to spot Boone getting out of the one just ahead of him.

"Hey, Wade," Boone said, walking over to shake his hand. "Jimmy, how are you?"

"Fine, Mr. Dorsett." He glanced at all the cars, then asked, "Is this a big party or something?"

Wade grinned. "Jimmy thinks he's the only one who's been left out of the loop on what this is all about."

Boone patted the teen's shoulder. "You're not alone, pal. Nobody's told me a thing, either. Emily called a half hour ago and asked me to show up. I came as soon as I'd dropped B.J. off at the soccer field."

At Boone's words, a sinking sensation settled in the pit of Wade's stomach. "Soccer? The same team my nephew Bryce is on?"

"I think so, yes," Boone replied. "Uh-oh, were you supposed to be there? B.J. gave me permission to skip this one. The kid will do anything for Emily. Plus, since we're mostly in Los Angeles, it wouldn't have been fair for him to get any playing time."

Wade was only half listening as he took his cell phone out of his pocket and hit speed dial for his sister. "This is bad," he told Boone as he waited for her to pick up. "I was expected there. You all better head on in. Tell Gabi I'll be there as soon as I deal with this. I have some ruffled feathers to smooth out."

"Where the devil are you?" Louise grumbled before he could say a word. "Chelsea, get down from there right this second. Peter, go grab your sister."

Wade winced. "Are you at Bryce's game?"

"Yes, and you're not. Didn't you promise me you'd be here to help me corral these kids? My husband conveniently had an emergency appendectomy to perform. Right now, I'd happily trade places with him."

"I'm sure the patient would be delighted about that," Wade said. "Then you could sue yourself for malpractice."

"Bite me," she said cheerfully. "How soon will you be here?"

"Sorry. I have to bail. And just as a reminder, I never promised to be there. You just take it for granted that I will be."

Dead silence greeted the remark. Well, it was silent except for the sound of Jason wailing.

"You did not just say you're bailing on me," Louise said at last.

"I'm afraid so. Something came up."

"Something more important than helping your sister and saving your nieces and nephews from certain catastrophe?"

Wade chuckled despite the hot water he knew he was in. "Now you're just being dramatic. Those children aren't in any danger with you. You just like having someone around who doesn't judge you when you talk about them as if they're little brats, which they're not, by the way."

Louise sighed heavily. "You'd better have a really, really good excuse."

"A date," he said, knowing he was opening up a can of worms, though it was the only excuse likely to satisfy his sister.

"Details," she commanded, clearly intrigued.

"Not likely," he responded. "Besides, you need to be keeping a close eye on those kids you claim are running amok. Talk to you later."

"Yes, you will," she said, a dire note in her voice. "Or I will hunt you down."

"Duly noted," he said. "Love you. See you soon."

"If you abandon me again, I'm going to take away your uncle privileges," she threatened. "My house tomorrow for Sunday dinner. We're eating at one."

"I'll be there," he promised, then sighed. He was

fairly certain the pot roast would come with a healthy serving of uncomfortable questions.

Gabi couldn't help herself. Since she'd left Jimmy answering her father's gently probing questions, and her grandmother, sisters and Boone were handling lunch, she kept drifting toward the door to check on Wade. She didn't want to eavesdrop on his conversation, but the somber expression on his face worried her.

"Problems?" she asked, stepping onto the porch when she saw that he'd disconnected his call and stuffed his phone into his pocket. He joined her, dropping a kiss on her cheek. The gesture was casual, brotherly even, but it sent a spark sizzling along her nerves. The reaction was so startling, she barely heard what he was saying.

"What?" she said, shaking off the disconcerting moment.

"My nephew has a soccer game," he explained patiently. "I'm usually there. I forgot all about it until Boone mentioned something about dropping B.J. at the field."

The butterflies already doing a dance in her stomach turned into rambunctious, fluttering birds. Big ones. "Oh, dear, do you need to go?"

He squeezed her hand. "Not a chance. Lou has already heaped a boatload of guilt on me. Tomorrow she'll throw a few more zingers my way. Same old thing. I'm used to it. Getting to yank my chain is one of her favorite things. Besides, she's starting to take my presence for granted. It's a bad habit, more than likely for both of us."

Gabi frowned. "Do you do this a lot? Bail on the kids, I mean?"

"Absolutely not," he said, his indignation plain. "In fact, that's my point. I'm over at that house almost every afternoon providing backup for her while she settles down after work and gets dinner on the table. Even the most dedicated uncle deserves an occasional break. My mistake today was not giving her a heads-up. Usually her husband's at the games, but he's a doctor and had an emergency call. Since she can't yell at him, I got the brunt of today's lecture."

Gabi relented. "It's nice, though, that she can count on you," she said, wondering who she'd be able to count on if she did decide to keep her baby.

It was all well and good for her grandmother and sisters to promise backup, but Emily was in Los Angeles, Samantha in New York and her grandmother here in Sand Castle Bay. Obviously they wouldn't be dropping by to babysit if she returned to her life in Raleigh and a new demanding job. A high-paying job, she reminded herself. She could afford a nanny or the best day care in town, if it came to that, she decided with a sigh of relief.

Wade regarded her curiously. "What was that for?"

"Just mentally solving a problem. Sorry."

"Care to share?"

"No need. Just thinking, though, that Louise is lucky to have you around."

"I'll always be here for her," Wade said. "I like her kids. I'll be honest, though. When Jason came along, about a year after my baby would have been born, I had a little trouble at first. Louise already had four fantastic children, and I'd lost my one and only chance for a baby. It didn't seem fair. It took me a while to accept that life isn't always fair and that none of it was that baby's fault, or Louise's. I still feel bad that I steered clear for a while."

Gabi liked that he had an actual flaw, one he could acknowledge. Up to now he'd seemed almost too good to be true; such a vast improvement over Paul, it made him a little too attractive.

"It sounds to me as if you were just being human," she told him. "We all feel resentful from time to time. At least you saw that you were being unreasonable and made peace with them."

Wade nodded toward the house. "Speaking of family dynamics, how's it going in there?"

"Surprisingly well," she admitted. "Dad didn't keel over when he found out I'm pregnant. He actually offered to pay for Emily's wedding, albeit the suggestion had come from Grandmother. And he was openminded about talking to Jimmy. I stayed with them for a few minutes, long enough to see that the second Jimmy realized what my dad does in the biomedical field, he had a million questions."

Wade shook his head. "Does that kid astonish you every time he opens his mouth? He's really something."

"Dad's clearly impressed. When I came to look for you, they were actually discussing some journal article Jimmy said he'd read online. There's not a doubt in my mind that Dad will do everything in his power to see Jimmy gets one of those scholarships. In fact, I wish he'd shown half as much interest in my career."

Wade frowned at that. "He didn't?"

Gabi shook her head. "Not to belabor the point, but I did everything I could think of to impress him, to follow in his footsteps, not as a biomedical guru, but working in the industry. He was oblivious. He wouldn't even help me get a job at his company after graduation, even though I was more than qualified."

"Why would he do that?" Wade asked.

"He said it would be awkward, that it would be perceived as nepotism."

"I'll bet that hurt."

"It did," she admitted. "Now, though, I get it. What if he'd been the one who had to fire me because I got pregnant? Can you imagine?"

"Do you think he would have?"

"Not a doubt in my mind," she said instantly, then hesitated. "Though he didn't react the way I'd expected him to when I told him I'd lost my job. He almost seemed to be on my side."

"Sounds as if the dad gene kicked in," Wade said.

Gabi smiled. "That was exactly it. It sure wasn't what I'd expected, given our history."

"So, what's next?" Wade asked.

"Lunch should be ready any minute," she told him.

He smiled. "I meant for you. How's that plan of yours coming along?"

Gabi sighed. "It's not. To be frank, I haven't got the first clue about my next step."

"I had a feeling that's what you were going to say," Wade said.

"Why?"

"Because all this focus on Jimmy was clearly a way to avoid dealing with your own situation."

Gabi was about to argue the point, but then realized she couldn't. Not really. "You're probably right. I did see a chance to help someone who really deserves it. It was a situation I actually thought I might be able to control, while my own?" She shrugged. "Not so much."

"And control really matters to you?"

"Of my life? Sure. What about you? Don't you like to know where you're headed, what you need to do to get there?"

"Not really. I tend to take things a day at a time, especially the past couple of years. I got hit upside the head with a lesson in what really matters. I also learned the hard way how little control we really have over those things."

Perplexed, she studied him, wondering how he could possibly live with the uncertainty. "But what drives you?"

Wade laughed. "I suppose I'm not driven, not the way you mean. I don't have huge ambitions. What I do have are things I love to do and a lifestyle that allows me to do them."

It was a laid-back concept that was totally alien to her. "I don't understand."

"Because you've always had a plan," he teased, then added quickly, "And that's not necessarily a bad thing."

"But you say it as if it is," she accused. "Structure's important to me. The past couple of weeks since I left my job, the lack of structure and focus has almost driven me crazy. I don't know what to do with myself, so I do nothing."

"Maybe that's what you need to be doing right now," he said.

"Nothing?"

"Exactly. Sometimes the best way to hear what's going on deep inside yourself is to be very quiet and still."

"You must not do nothing the way I do," she said in frustration. "I have about a million voices yelling at me to get busy, and not a one of them so far telling me what it is I should be doing. I need to sort through all that noise and make that plan. I should be updating my résumé, making lists of companies where I could inquire about jobs, start networking again."

"If you know all that, why aren't you doing it?"

"I don't know," she admitted. "I guess I'm not ready. Or I'm afraid they'll all have the same reaction to me being pregnant."

"Or maybe it's not what you really want anymore," Wade suggested quietly.

Gabi frowned, genuinely shocked by the suggestion. "What?"

He grinned. "A scary thought after all that careful planning for so many years, huh?"

"Of course it's what I want," she insisted, though there was no mistaking the defensive note that had crept into her voice. She recognized that as a clear sign she wasn't as sure of herself as she wanted to be.

"Then why haven't you printed out the résumés or made those calls?"

"I've been…"

"Busy? That's not what you said."

She scowled at him. "Who needs a shrink when you're around?"

He laughed. "Just throwing out a few things for you to consider. I don't know you that well. Maybe I've gotten it all wrong."

"You have," she said flatly. "In fact, first thing tomorrow, I'm going to come up with a new plan." She nodded in satisfaction. "There, you see. I have a manageable goal and a timetable."

"Good for you. I'll look forward to hearing all about

it. Now we probably need to go inside and see how things are going between Jimmy and your dad."

"Sure. Right," she said, her tone disgruntled.

Wade stopped her just before they went inside. "No reason to be upset, okay? You will figure this out."

"Of course I will," she said with a confidence she was far from feeling. She *would* figure it out, because this baby was coming and she had no other choice.

As people drifted into Cora Jane's kitchen to fill their plates for lunch, Wade pulled Jimmy aside.

"How's it going? Are you enjoying yourself?"

Jimmy's eyes lit up. "This is totally awesome, man. Do you know who Sam Castle is? He's, like, this icon in the biomedical field. Like the Bill Gates or Steve Jobs in that world. And you'll never guess what he told me."

"What?" Wade asked, though he had a pretty good idea.

"His company offers scholarships to outstanding science students. Even though I graduated last June, he says there are extenuating circumstances and he's sure I can qualify."

"That would be incredible," Wade said. "That's what you want? To go away to college and study to work in this field?"

"More than anything," Jimmy admitted. "I just never thought it could happen. Even before my dad's accident, I knew there wasn't enough money for me to go to a major university. Junior college, maybe, but that's not enough to land a really good job in this field."

Wade couldn't help wondering if money was so tight, how the Templetons would manage if Jimmy was no longer providing that little bit of extra income. As if the teen had read his mind, Jimmy's expression fell and he muttered a curse.

"I can't go, can I?" he said, disappointment etched on his face. "Not even if I win this scholarship? My family needs the money I bring home every week."

"If you get the scholarship, you will go to school," Wade said decisively.

"But Mom and Dad are counting on me," Jimmy protested, looking crestfallen. "I can't just bail on them."

"I'm sure there are ways to take a lighter load, maybe work part-time to help out," Wade said.

"Not if I'm going to get good grades so I can keep the scholarship," Jimmy protested.

Sam Castle obviously overheard him, because he stepped closer and put a hand on Jimmy's shoulder. "Don't worry about your folks," he reassured him. "We'll figure something out. The fact that they're your top priority makes me more certain than ever that you're the right person for one of these scholarships."

"That's right," Cora Jane said, joining them. "When a young person demonstrates such a sense of responsibility toward their family, that should be rewarded. Don't you even think of walking away from this opportunity if it comes your way. We'll all work together to find a way to make sure your family has whatever they need."

"They're not going to take charity," Jimmy warned, looking as if he hardly dared to hope there might be a solution. "Dad wouldn't allow it."

"And we'll see to it that they're not made to feel that's what they're accepting," Cora Jane told him. Her expression brightened. "The only thing keeping your dad from getting back to work full-time is his injury, right? And not being able to do all the rehab that's necessary?"

Jimmy nodded.

"I think I know just the person who can help with that," she said.

"Ethan?" Boone suggested, overhearing her.

Cora Jane nodded. "Exactly."

Jimmy's eyes lit up. "You think Dr. Cole might be able to help him find a way to do that rehab?"

"There's not a doubt in my mind," Cora Jane said. "I'll speak to him first thing Monday morning." She patted Jimmy's hand. "And don't you worry. He'll make it so your dad can pay what he can afford when he's able to pay it. The important thing is to get him well enough to work again."

Wade regarded her with astonishment. "Are you some kind of an angel, Cora Jane?"

She laughed at that. "Not likely."

"You sure about that? It seems to me you've come up with a couple of miracles today." He glanced toward Gabi and her sisters, who'd joined their father at the table and were all talking at once about wedding plans. Sam Castle looked surprisingly content despite the likely expense of their lavish ideas.

"Sometimes the best way to get the things you want in life is simply to ask," Cora Jane said, following the direction of his gaze. "Maybe it's time you started asking for a few things you'd like to have."

Wade shook his head. Gabi was nowhere near ready to hear what he wanted. First she needed to figure out who she was without her work to define her. He had no idea how long it would take for that to happen, but once it did, he'd be around if she had room for a man in her life.

In the meantime, he might have an idea or two about ways to prod the process along.

"Can you believe how well today went?" Gabi asked. Happily exhausted, she was stretched out across her bed with Samantha in a chair nearby. "It was like something out of a dream. Dad here and being all dadlike. Jimmy getting a real chance at the future he wants. Emily getting her fantasy wedding."

"And you with Wade looking at you as if he'd never seen anyone so beautiful," Samantha chimed in. "Quite the ego boost, if you ask me."

"Stop that. Wade's being a good friend. That's all."

Samantha laughed. "That line is getting very old, especially when all evidence points to something else going on. I saw the look on your face when he kissed you."

Gabi frowned. "Wade never kissed me, not that way."

"You mean he didn't plunder your lips like a man who's thoroughly besotted?" Samantha teased. "Is that what you want him to do?"

"No. And all he did was kiss me hello, on the cheek. It was hardly passionate."

"No, it wasn't," Samantha agreed. "But you looked as if your knees were about to give way, just the same."

"I did not," Gabi protested, though she could feel the heat climbing into her cheeks at the blatant lie.

"It happened again when he left," Samantha taunted. "I watched."

"Have you turned into some kind of sick voyeur?" Gabi snapped irritably.

"Nope, just an interested third party," Samantha responded, clearly not offended by the insult.

"You need a life," Gabi told her.

"So I hear, almost daily, from Grandmother, as a matter of fact."

Gabi sat up. "Seriously? Grandmother's starting to get pushy about your lack of a love life?"

"Unfortunately, yes. To be honest, I thought I was safe for a while or I wouldn't have shown my face here right now. I thought it would take a lot longer before she was satisfied that both your life and Emily's are under control." She grinned. "Apparently, though, she thinks she can take her foot off the gas where you're concerned and turn her attention to me."

Gabi was intrigued. "Any thoughts about who she intends to push in your direction?" She glanced at the football jersey her sister was wearing and chuckled. "Or do I even need to ask? She has ideas about you and Ethan Cole, doesn't she?"

"I doubt it's any coincidence his name came up today," Samantha conceded. "It's not the first time she's mentioned Ethan, then waited for me to react."

"And do you? React, I mean? I know you had a huge crush on him years ago, but it's been eons since you've crossed paths."

"He didn't even know I was alive back then," Samantha said. "I doubt it would be any different now. I'm sure he has women flocking all around him, now that he's a war hero and a hotshot doctor to boot."

Gabi wasn't so sure about that. "Is that what Emily says?" she asked skeptically. "Boone and Ethan are close. She probably knows the full scoop on his love life."

"I am not asking Emily about Ethan," Samantha said. "It's too pathetic."

"What's pathetic about trying to find out if the man is available?"

"It was a high school crush," Samantha reminded her. "Shouldn't I be long over it by now? Shouldn't I have some other serious relationship in my life, instead of a string of not terribly fulfilling affairs?"

"But you don't," Gabi reminded her. "And if you won't even see Ethan, how will you know if the crush died a natural death years ago, or if there's something to be rekindled?"

"You can't rekindle something that never was," Samantha said.

Gabi noted that she was arguing semantics, rather than facing the real issue of her feelings. That told Gabi quite a lot.

"He was older," Samantha continued, clearly determined to make her point. "He didn't know I existed. Could we drop this, please? It's not even worth discussing."

"I can drop it," Gabi agreed readily. "Grandmother? Not so likely. If she's got this particular bit in her mouth, you, my dear sister, are in serious trouble. Take it from me. She has good instincts and the persistence of a pit bull."

Samantha grinned at last. "Meaning you and Wade don't stand a chance, either."

Gabi winced. "I was afraid you might put that spin on what I said."

"It is the natural conclusion to be drawn from your comment," Samantha said a little too gleefully.

Yeah, Gabi was afraid of that, too. She hated the thought of Samantha, Emily and Grandmother being right about the two of them, almost as much as she wondered what it would be like to have a man as rock solid as Wade in her life.

"I don't know why all of you think he's right for me," she said with exasperation. "He's annoying. He thinks he knows me. He keeps pushing all this nonsense about me not really wanting to go back to the life I had."

Samantha regarded her with surprise. "He said that?"

"He did," Gabi said indignantly. "Can you believe it?"

"Interesting," Samantha said. "I think he might have a point."

Gabi scowled. "He does not have a point. The man barely knows me. I don't think we had one single conversation that lasted more than a minute when I was here last August."

"Which gave him lots of time to observe you," Samantha suggested. "And we all know he rarely took his eyes off you. Sometimes it's these quiet ones who have fantastic insights. You probably ought to listen to him, or at least think about what he's saying."

"And what?" Gabi asked incredulously. "Not go back to Raleigh? Not go back into public relations?"

"I don't know," Samantha responded. "After all, you did choose that particular path in order to prove something to Dad. Did you truly love the work?"

"Of course I did. I doubt I'd have been any good at it if I wasn't fiercely dedicated and excited about it."

"Or determined to show Dad he'd made a mistake," Samantha suggested slyly. At Gabi's indignant huff, she held up a hand. "Okay. I know that, in the end, the decision has to be yours. I'm just saying if you're ever going to change directions in your life, now could be the right time."

Gabi thought she was crazy. "Now? When I'm expecting a baby and have just told the father I don't want his support? Come on. If I decide to keep my child— and I'm not saying that's what I've decided to do—don't you think I should be looking for the best possible job in a field in which I have outstanding credentials?"

"And go back to working eighteen hours a day while a nanny raises your baby?" Samantha asked gently.

That question brought Gabi up short. She knew what it was like to be neglected by a workaholic parent. She and her sisters had had their mom to balance things, but who would her child have? A well-paid nanny? How could that be fair?

She sighed heavily. "I'm going to bed," she told Samantha.

"It's not even nine o'clock," Samantha said, looking surprised. "Are you okay?"

"I need to get up early."

"Why? You're not even thinking of going back to Raleigh tomorrow, are you?"

"No, but I need to start making some plans first thing in the morning and I want a clear head."

Samantha smiled. "Ah, yes. I was wondering when the yellow legal pads were going to come out."

"And now you know," Gabi told her.

She just wished she had even the tiniest clue what the first item on her list ought to be.

Seven

Spending Saturday with Gabi and her family had been a revelation to Wade. Though he'd intended to drop by again on Sunday, he recalled his promise to his sister. If he failed to show up for Sunday dinner with all the answers she wanted, he'd never hear the end of it.

He was also struck by another thought, a surefire way to silence the questions and maybe to make a point with Gabriella at the same time. Since he knew Louise would never object to him bringing a woman along for Sunday dinner, he started with the tougher sell. He called Gabi.

"What are your plans for today?" he asked when she answered her cell phone. He thought she sounded half-asleep, her husky voice incredibly sexy, even though it was after ten in the morning.

"Well, I came outside a couple of hours ago to make a few lists, but I think I fell asleep," she admitted.

He smiled at the exasperation in her voice. "Thwarted again, huh?"

"I'm beginning to think there's something wrong

with me. I just can't focus. Do you suppose pregnancy saps your brain cells?"

She sounded so serious, so bewildered, he couldn't help chuckling. "I wouldn't know about that, but you know my theory about your lack of focus," he reminded her.

"You think I don't want to make any decisions."

"Pretty much. But since you're not totally engrossed in making a list, how about joining me for a traditional Sunday pot roast dinner? I'm due at my sister's at one o'clock. You can see for yourself how she juggles things. You can ask her about that brain cell thing, too."

"You told me she counts on you," Gabi responded. "And she has a husband. I'd say the situations aren't even remotely the same."

"But you're smart. So is she. I'm sure you can pick up a few tips."

"What does your sister think is going on?" she inquired suspiciously. "With us, I mean."

"To be honest, I've only mentioned you to her in passing. You're not going to be walking into a roomful of people with high expectations. That would be *your* family."

That earned him a chuckle. "Point taken. Okay, I'm at the point when any distraction sounds idyllic. Shall I meet you there?"

"Nope. I'll come for you around twelve-thirty. No need to dress up, by the way. You'll just be getting all messed up. These kids show no mercy."

"Gee, you make this sound really special," she said dryly. "Maybe I should reconsider."

"It's not the kids who should have you reconsidering. Louise is an attorney, remember? She may not have expectations, but she will have questions, I'm afraid. Brace yourself. She didn't get a tough courtroom reputation for no good reason."

Gabi laughed. "Are you sure you want me to come? It sounds as if you're determined to scare me off."

"Not at all. I just don't want you accusing me later of not giving you a proper heads-up."

"No chance of that," she said. "I am duly warned and still desperate enough to take my chances."

Now Wade laughed. "I knew you were made of tough stuff. See you soon."

As soon as he'd disconnected that call, he made one to his sister. "I'm bringing a friend to dinner. Any problem with that?"

"A female friend?" she inquired hopefully.

"A female friend," he confirmed.

"Well, hallelujah! Did you warn her about the chaos?"

"I warned her about the chaos and about you."

"Me?" she asked innocently.

"Yes, you. Try not to pull a full-blown interrogation on her, okay?"

"Are we talking Gabriella Castle?" she asked.

"Yes."

Silence fell.

"Louise, is something wrong? You don't have some problem with Gabi that I don't know about, do you? Is me bringing her by a bad idea?"

"I heard she's pregnant, Wade," she said, her tone somber.

"I'm well aware of that."

"Under the circumstances—*your* circumstances—

are you really sure getting involved with her is smart?"
she asked, genuine worry in her voice.

Wade understood his sister's concern. "Believe me,
sis, it's the best idea I've had in a very long time."

"Okay, then," she said, though she sounded far from
satisfied. "I'll be on my best behavior."

"I'm counting on it," he said. That, and a whole lot
more. He hoped Gabi would see his sister's family, hear
about Louise's mostly successful juggling act and realize it was possible to have it all. And that he wasn't
a bad person to have around for that particular ride.

Louise Johnson Carter's home was in a gated golf
community. Designed in the Carolina architectural style
so popular in Sand Castle Bay, it was built up off the
ground to protect the living space from storm surges.
There were balconies on every level and sweeping views
of the golf course and water. Inside, the space was one
giant living area, with kitchen, dining area and comfortable seating for a large group of people. Bedrooms
were on a separate floor.

"Be careful where you step once we're inside," Wade
warned as he led Gabi up the first set of exterior steps.
"Even though the kids have a gigantic playroom, their
toys are underfoot everywhere. Periodically Louise or
Zack do a sweep of the house and stuff everything into
toy boxes, but that generally doesn't last more than a
couple of hours, and that's if the kids aren't home or
are sound asleep."

Gabi chuckled as she reached the landing and had to
sidestep to avoid a fire truck, a baseball bat and a tea set.
"A home is supposed to be lived in," she said. "This one
obviously is. I'd be more worried if it were too neat."

"What a refreshing attitude," the frazzled woman at the top of the steps said as she waited for them. "Some people seem to think this ought to be a showplace 24/7."

"She means Zack," Wade said as he reached his sister and kissed her cheek. "Lou, this is Gabriella. She prefers Gabi, though."

"Then Gabi, it is," Louise said at once. "I've heard a lot about you, but I don't think our paths crossed back in the day."

"I don't believe so, either," Gabi said. "And I love your home. The views are amazing."

"Thanks. I try to make it a point to sit on the deck with a glass of wine from time to time and enjoy them. Unfortunately, most of the time, I just fall straight into bed at the end of the day."

"Wade says you have a thriving law practice and five kids. I'm surprised you're not comatose by midafternoon."

"I would be if I slowed down long enough to realize how exhausted I am. Now what can I get you? Soda? Tea? Water?"

"Water would be great. And directions to the nearest restroom."

Louise laughed. "Oh, do I remember those days! It's right here on the left."

"It's awfully quiet around here," Wade commented. "What have you done with the kids?"

"Zack took them for a walk. Sometimes that wears them out enough that they'll be civilized through an entire meal."

Wade regarded her indignantly. "You never shared that tip with me."

"Because, my sweet brother, you can't handle all five

of them on a walk. You can barely keep up with them when they're contained right here in the living room."

"That is not true. They mind me."

Louise rolled her eyes. "They might if you ever corrected them." She grinned at Gabi. "Every night after he leaves here, I have to undo all the damage he's done. He is not a disciplinarian, which is why my kids adore him. You'll see. Just stay out of the way when they get back. They'll head directly for him."

Sure enough, just then a downstairs door crashed open and a child's voice shouted, "Unca Wade's here!"

Feet thundered up the steps. Gabi took a few steps back as four kids threw themselves at Wade with an exuberance that might have knocked him down had he not braced himself for them.

Louise shook her head at the sight, then turned to Gabi. "Why don't you come into the kitchen with me? He's going to be under siege for a while."

Gabi made a quick stop in the restroom, then followed Wade's sister into the huge open kitchen with endless expanses of granite countertops, tons of cabinets and a refrigerator that looked as if it could stock enough food for six families. For anyone who loved to cook, it was a dream kitchen. The aromas suggested Louise was one of those people.

"Something smells wonderful," Gabi said as she accepted a glass of water from Louise. "How on earth do you find time to cook a real meal and keep up with everything else?"

"To be honest, it doesn't happen every day. I manage some time on Sundays to put a few things together for the week ahead, but we rely on takeout more than I'd like."

"I've just about lived on takeout since college," Gabi admitted. "And I had no excuses."

"Except for a demanding career, I've heard."

"It took a lot of time, that's for sure."

"And now? How will you manage that and a baby?" Louise asked.

Gabi didn't want to discuss the adoption possibility or her job status with a woman she barely knew, so she merely shrugged. "I guess I'll figure it out," she said.

"Want the single piece of advice someone once gave me that keeps me sane?" Louise asked.

"Sure."

"Don't expect perfection. It's unlikely anyone will die if you don't get to the dusting one week. While a balanced, healthy meal is certainly desirable, if you have pizza one night, enjoy it. If your kid skins a knee while you're not around, don't blame yourself. It could just as easily have happened while you were standing right beside him. And if they leave the house wearing mismatched, inside-out clothes they chose themselves, just close your eyes and be glad they remembered to put on shoes."

Gabi smiled. "That sounds incredibly sensible. How long did it take you to buy into it? You must have been pretty driven to get through law school."

Louise chuckled. "You have no idea. I believe the message finally took root after Peter came along. He was my second. With Bryce, I kept thinking I should be able to manage it all. With Peter, I took a deep breath and started to accept that I couldn't. I still have my freak-out moments when I think I'm messing everything up. Ask Wade. But I'm getting better."

Gabi hesitated, considering if Louise might be the

perfect person, after all, to answer the question she hadn't been able to shake. "Do you think it would be insane for me to try to have this baby on my own? Look at all the backup you have, and you still freak out."

Louise looked startled by the question. "But you are having it on your own, or am I wrong about that? Is the dad in the picture?"

"No, he's not." She drew in a deep breath, then revealed, "But I've been thinking the best thing for the baby might be adoption."

Louise's eyes widened. "Oh, wow! I had no idea." A frown settled on her face. "Does Wade know about that?"

For a minute, Gabi was thrown by the concern she saw in Louise's eyes. "He knows."

"What does he think?"

"It's not something we really talked about. It's pretty much my decision to make."

"Gabi, I may be the wrong person to be asking about this," Louise said candidly. "I have absolutely nothing against adoption. I think it's a wonderful choice under many circumstances. I don't know enough about yours to know if that's the case."

There was something left unspoken. Gabi could sense it. She could feel it in a sudden coolness in Louise's attitude, but she didn't understand it.

And unfortunately, as the afternoon went on, nothing happened to change the chill in the atmosphere. As soon as she could politely do so, Gabi suggested to Wade that they should leave. She noticed that there was no argument from Louise.

Gabi sighed as she slid into Wade's car, leaned her head back and closed her eyes.

Wade slipped into the driver's seat, but rather than starting the car, he turned to her. "Mind telling me what happened between you and my sister? It was painfully obvious that something did. What on earth did she say to you? If she offended you, I'm sorry. She tends to get pretty protective where I'm concerned."

Gabi didn't try to pretend that she hadn't been aware of the tension. "It wasn't anything she said. It was me. I said something about adoption and it kind of freaked her out."

Wade heaved a sigh. "I can imagine," he said. "I'm sorry."

"What did I miss? Why would she react that way? And she asked if you knew I was thinking about it."

"Lou's very protective of me, especially since I lost Kayla and the baby. She's obviously aware that I have feelings for you." He met her gaze. "Can you see where this is going?"

It suddenly dawned on Gabi what he was saying. "She sees me giving up this baby as you potentially losing another child."

"Something like that."

"But, Wade, we're not involved," she protested.

"That doesn't seem to stop me from having feelings for you," he said ruefully. "She can see that. All her sisterly, protective instincts kicked in."

"I told you this was too complicated," Gabi said, feeling awful. "I'm so sorry. The adoption thing is on the table. I feel as if I have to consider it. Not to think about it would be irresponsible under my circumstances."

"Circumstances change," he said, his gaze direct. "I'm not saying yours have. It's way too soon to say that, but they do change, Gabi. Keep an open mind."

She shook her head. "Wade, you're great. I don't want to be careless with you."

"Hey, I'm a grown man. I can handle a few complications."

"But maybe—"

"No maybes," he said adamantly. "We're friends. I'm not walking away from that."

Gabi couldn't help wondering, though, if she ought to do what he so obviously couldn't or wouldn't do and walk away herself, especially if a decision she was likely to make about her child was destined to hurt him.

Wade thought the dinner at his sister's had gone well enough, at least until the adoption issue had come up. Despite that, Gabi had been great with the kids and had entertained them all with stories of spending her summers here working for Cora Jane. On the way home he'd suggested they stop for a cup of decaf at a small coffee shop, but she'd pleaded exhaustion. There'd been unmistakable relief in her eyes when he hadn't argued.

Back at her grandmother's he'd debated a kiss goodbye, one a bit steamier than those he'd bestowed up to now, but even though he'd longed to kiss the perpetual frown off her beautiful face, he'd figured she wasn't even close to ready for that. And it would definitely muddy those waters she was already fretting about.

Reining in his impulses had cost him, though. He'd been up most of the night, restless and edgy, and thinking way too much about her possible decision to give up her baby. When she'd first mentioned it in a casual way, he hadn't really taken in all the implications. Now he was forced to. Lou was right about one thing. It had the potential to rip his heart out.

A few months ago, he'd never have considered taking such a risk, but this was Gabi. Did he want to throw away what might be his one chance with her because of something she might never decide to do? Though the glib answer was no, he understood that he needed to give the question more thought and face the very real possibility that he'd once again wind up with a broken heart. Not today, though. Today he just wanted to get another glimpse of Gabi.

Since the lack of sleep had left him in desperate need of caffeine, he'd picked up two large containers of coffee this morning along with a box of homemade, still-warm doughnuts from a local doughnut shop, one of the most popular destinations in Sand Castle Bay.

He drove over to Cora Jane's, parked his truck on the street even though Cora Jane had long since left to open the restaurant, then walked around back. He knew instinctively he'd find Gabi out there, making yet another attempt to organize her life and get it back on track.

Sure enough, he found her with a yellow legal pad on her lap, sitting in a weathered Adirondack chair in a patch of sunlight. Her face was turned up to the sun, her eyes closed. She glanced up when he took the pad from her lap. She tried to snatch it back, but he moved out of reach, checking out the page.

"Nothing?" he said quizzically. "I thought you'd have a huge master plan for your life outlined by now. It is nearly eight in the morning, after all."

She scowled at him. "I thought so, too," she said with unmistakable frustration.

"Maybe it's too soon," he suggested yet again. "Maybe you need to let your mind settle down, instead of trying to force things. My best ideas always come to me when I'm not really thinking about work."

"I know you're right, but sitting around and waiting for some muse to strike isn't my way. And seeing everything your sister has accomplished, despite all the commotion in her life, just made me more determined to figure this out and get going."

"I understand that you're highly motivated, but your way obviously isn't working," he said, then waved the box of doughnuts under her nose to provide an immediate distraction.

Her eyes widened with delight. "They're still warm?"

"Of course."

"Any with chocolate icing and sprinkles?"

He grinned at her eagerness as she grabbed the box from him, then drew in a deep breath, taking in the scent of sugar and chocolate and warm, old-fashioned cake doughnuts.

"I can't remember the last time I had one of these," she murmured as she reverently lifted one from the box. Her expression turned ecstatic as she took the first bite.

Wade got a little turned on watching her. His mind drifted to all the other, far more intimate ways he might give her pleasure and earn that look. She finally caught him staring.

"Oh, did you want one?" she asked, her expression all innocence.

"Glazed, please," he said, because it was safer than mentioning what he really wanted.

Using a napkin to pick it up, she handed him one of the glazed doughnuts, then plucked a second one from the box.

"For the baby," she told him.

He grinned. "Of course it is."

She gestured toward the two containers he'd set on the table between them. "Is one of those decaf?"

He nodded, checked the marks the clerk had made and handed the decaf to her. "Here you go."

"You're turning out to be quite handy to have around," she noted as she blissfully sipped at the coffee.

"Glad to be of service. Now tell me what's on your agenda for the day."

"Getting my life together," she said at once, snatching the legal pad back.

"A little ambitious," he countered. "How about coming with me instead?"

"Don't you need to work today?"

"I can spare a little time for a worthy cause," he assured her.

"Where would we go?"

"I want to show you something."

She frowned at his deliberate evasions. "No clues?"

"Not a one. You'll have to trust me."

The fact that she didn't even hesitate before agreeing gave him hope.

"Okay, then, let's go," she said, though she cast a disappointed look at the remaining doughnuts.

"Bring them along," he said. "In case you get hungry. Lou was always starving. It comes with the territory."

She slid a glance at him. "You'll make a great husband someday, thanks to all these little tidbits of information you've picked up from your sister."

"She might have been an annoying pest, but she definitely had her uses," he agreed. "And give me a little credit. I was smart enough to pay attention and take mental notes." He sobered for a moment. "And I did have a trial run, albeit a brief one."

She looked startled by the oblique mention of his marriage, but gave the subject a wide berth. "I wonder why more guys don't do that?" Gabi murmured, her expression thoughtful. "Pay closer attention to what women need, I mean."

"I suspect they don't have any idea of the rewards that could come their way. For instance, having a beautiful woman look at them the way you looked at me when I handed over those doughnuts."

"How'd I look at you?"

"As if I had a lot more going for me than I did a couple of days ago," he said.

"Seriously? You think I can be won over by doughnuts?"

"Sweetheart, I'm hoping you can be won over by someone taking the time to treat you the way you should be treated. Doughnuts are just the beginning."

He worried that his candor might alarm her, but instead she looked amused, and maybe just a little bit intrigued. He kept his grin to himself. It was all going nicely according to plan. Who'd ever suspect that a laid-back guy like him even understood the importance of a well-defined plan? He had a hunch that was going to work in his favor with a woman like Gabi.

Gabi looked around in surprise when Wade pulled up to a garage beside a beautiful little cottage that had obviously been restored with a lot of loving attention to detail. Emily, the master interior designer, would have had a hundred questions about the work Wade had done. Gabi was merely charmed.

"Your house, I assume?"

"And my office," he said, gesturing toward the garage.

"I didn't know carpenters needed offices."

"That's because you've never seen my real work."

"I saw what you did at Castle's," she contradicted. "The cabinetry you built for Grandmother was lovely. Boone says you're the best in the region at that kind of custom work."

"It pays the bills," he said with a careless shrug.

Her gaze narrowed. "But it's not your passion?"

"It's definitely not my passion." He opened the garage door then.

Gabi halted beside him, her mouth agape. There were wood carvings everywhere, seabirds so exquisitely detailed they looked as if they might fly away. Decoys that had been hand-rubbed to a soft sheen, probably not intended to be put into the water, but displayed on mantels or in galleries.

The scent of wood shavings filled the air, a clean and earthy mix of cedar, pine and others she couldn't identify by their aroma.

"Wade, these are amazing," she said softly as she went from table to table, unable to resist running her fingers over the wood, certain at times she could feel each individual feather beneath her touch, the fluttery beat of a tiny heart.

"You're an incredible artist," she said, glancing away from the carving she was holding and into his eyes. "Why are you wasting your time doing cabinetry?"

He shrugged. "Like I said, it pays the bills, and I enjoy working with wood, no matter the form it takes. There's satisfaction in creating something beautiful."

She turned and looked at him. "Why did you bring me here? It's not just because you wanted to show off these beautiful things, is it?"

"Why do you say that? Maybe I wanted you to see another side of me or perhaps I felt in need of having my ego stroked this morning."

She frowned at the comment. "You're the least egotistical man I know. You're also sneaky. Given the context of our recent conversations, I know there's a message here for me."

"What do you think it is?" he countered, looking vaguely amused.

Gabi struggled to figure it out. She was sure it was staring her right in the face.

"That there's more than one way to find satisfaction in life," she said eventually, studying his face for some hint of approval. She felt ridiculously like a kid hoping the teacher would praise her for grasping an elusive concept.

"Very good," he said, his grin spreading. "And how does that apply to you?"

"I'm not sure. I already know there are other PR jobs out there and eventually I'll find one."

He looked oddly disappointed by her response. "If that's what will bring you satisfaction and fulfillment, I'm sure you will," he said.

Gabi frowned at his tone. "You've been talking to Cora Jane or Samantha, haven't you? They've been telling you that I was only doing this ridiculously demanding job because I wanted my father's approval, that my heart really isn't in it."

"They might have mentioned something like that," he admitted. "Are they right?"

"I'm very good at what I do."

"But that's not the same thing, is it? I'm very good at cabinetry. I have more work lined up than I can handle. I can take pride in that on a lot of levels."

Gabi glanced around the workshop again. "But this is what really makes you happy."

"Yes."

"Then do it. Commit to it."

"It's hard to walk away from a sure thing," he said, then looked her in the eye. "Isn't it?"

Gabi understood what he was doing. All this pushing and prodding to reevaluate her choices had probably been Grandmother's idea. Or maybe Samantha's. They'd known she wouldn't take the advice if it came from them, so they'd enlisted Wade. Unfortunately for her peace of mind, he'd made a very credible argument.

"I'll think about what you're saying," she said eventually. "You can report back that the mission was accomplished."

He chuckled. "Not the entire mission," he said, his gaze capturing hers. "I have one of my own. It's entirely separate from theirs."

Her heart stuttered at the look in his eyes. The conversation was suddenly taking a turn into uncharted territory. She could feel it.

"Oh?" she asked, unhappy because her voice shook.

He took a step closer, then another, then bent down. He waited, his lips so close she could feel the soft sigh of his breath against her skin. With one hand cupping her cheek, he closed the distance between them.

The tender kiss was the most sensual, erotic one she'd ever experienced. In its sweetness there was caring and carefully controlled passion, a combination with which she had no experience at all. The gentle demand of his mouth on hers stirred longings she'd never expected. Of all the bloody times for that to happen, she thought as she pulled away with regret.

"We can't," she whispered.

He smiled. "We just did."

"I mean *again*. We can't do that again."

Amusement twinkled in his eyes. "Is there some law I don't know about?"

She frowned at the ridiculous question. "Of course not."

"That man, the father of your baby, is he not as far out of your life as you've told me?"

"Oh, he's gone," she said without hesitation. That was one of the few real certainties in her life.

"Then I don't see the problem."

She took his hand, pressed it against her belly just as the baby gave a kick. "That's the reason," she said.

He smiled. "You think that kick means the baby doesn't like me?" he asked.

"No, I think the baby is a huge barrier to me even thinking about getting involved with anybody. My life's upside down, Wade. I already have more decisions to make than I can handle."

"I understand you have a lot on your plate, and I don't want to add to the pressure," he said. "I just want you to know where I'm coming from. I don't see the baby as an obstacle."

She frowned. "And it bothers you that I do," she guessed.

"A little bit, though I certainly can understand that the circumstances are complicated. Bottom line, though, if I don't have a problem with you being pregnant, why should you?"

"How can you not have a problem with it?" she asked with exasperation. No man could possibly be as accepting of another man's child—a child still in the womb—as he seemed to be. Could he?

"Because when I see you glowing like the expectant mother you are, when I feel that baby's kick, all I can think about is how amazing any child of yours is bound to be." He held her gaze. "That is *all* I think about, Gabi. It's the only thing that matters, not how the baby was conceived, how complicated it's made your life."

Though there were tears in her eyes at the sweet thoughtfulness of his words, she couldn't seem to stop herself from saying, "When it's real, when it's flesh and blood and screaming in the middle of the night, all of those things will most definitely matter."

Surprisingly, Wade looked oddly angered by her candid reply. "That's some other man talking, Gabi. Not me. Don't sell me short."

The intensity of his reaction, the fire burning in his eyes when he spoke, almost convinced her. Almost.

The irony, of course, was his claim that his mission to seduce and make her his was his own very personal one. Instead, she knew all too well that it was exactly the one Grandmother and her sisters had had in mind for months. How could she trust that they hadn't worked their very persuasive magic to tempt this sweet, gallant, vulnerable man into doing something he'd never do if his common sense had time to kick in?

And wasn't that exactly what Louise, who knew him best, had been worried about, that Wade was in way,

way over his head, perhaps for reasons even he didn't fully comprehend?

Seizing what he was offering would be so easy. She was desperately in need of unconditional backup and here it was, in the form of a man who had a whole lot going for him. But those complications she'd mentioned were real, and if she cared for him, even a little bit, she had to weigh his happiness as well as her own.

"Wade," she began.

He cut her off. "It's too soon. I'm pushing too hard. I know everything you're going to say."

"This habit you have of reading my mind is really exasperating," she complained.

He gave her a wry look. "You're into clueless men?"

She laughed at that. "Hardly. I believe I've had my fill of those."

He nodded. "That's something, then. We'll table this conversation for a later date. In the meantime, I'll see what I can do to convince you that I know exactly what I'm doing."

She studied him for the longest time, saw the total sincerity in his eyes, and wanted desperately to believe him. As she'd just thought, things would be so easy then.

But hadn't she learned all too recently that life was almost never easy and miracles were in short supply?

Eight

Not until Wade had dropped her off back at Cora Jane's did Gabi realize that she'd gone off with him without her cell phone. Since it hadn't been out of reach for more than a minute or two for years now, it was a shocking discovery.

"What is happening to me?" she muttered as she stared at the cell phone sitting in the middle of the kitchen table where she'd obviously left it after reducing a slice of toast to crumbs earlier this morning.

Emily walked into the kitchen in time to overhear her. She grinned. "It's a shock the first time you realize your phone is not the most important accessory you own, isn't it?" she commented.

"You're telling me," Gabi said.

"You might want to check for messages. It's been ringing ever since I got over here. I didn't want to answer for you."

Gabi picked up the phone and noticed there were indeed half a dozen messages, including one from her father. As if that weren't shock enough, there were two from the woman who'd fired her, Amanda Warren.

"Dad called," she murmured incredulously. "That has to be a first. I can't think of one single time in my entire life when he's initiated a conversation with any of us, can you?"

"Maybe Grandmother put some sort of magic potion in his food when he was over here Saturday," her sister suggested. "We certainly saw a different side of him then than I'd ever seen before."

"You mean warm and funny and human?" Gabi said.

"Yep, those were the surprises," Emily confirmed. "Are you going to call him back? Or at least listen to the message?"

"I'm almost afraid to," she admitted. "What if he's turned back into regular Dad?"

Emily grinned. "Well, better to find out now, don't you think? At least he hasn't stopped payment on those checks he wrote for the wedding. I deposited them this morning and made sure they all cleared."

Gabi stared at her in shock. "You actually asked the bank to make sure they cleared?"

Emily nodded. "I still couldn't quite get over the sudden generosity. I was afraid he might have second thoughts as soon as he left here."

Even though she thought Emily's lack of faith was appalling, Gabi couldn't entirely blame her. "You do realize Grandmother's going to hear about that next time she stops in to do her banking," Gabi said. "I doubt she'll be pleased."

"I told her I was going to do it," Emily said, then sighed. "But you're right. She wasn't happy. I got a ten-minute lecture on giving Dad a little credit. She was winding up for the thirty-minute version, but Jerry showed up to drive her to Castle's. He managed to calm her down. Amazingly he did it without taking anyone's side. I swear the man should have been a diplomat, instead of a chef."

Gabi laughed. "Jerry had years of dealing with Granddad while hiding his feelings for Grandmother. I imagine that was good training for keeping the peace."

Emily studied her sympathetically. "You do know you're only postponing the inevitable, right? You need to listen to that message or call Dad back."

"Much as I'd rather not, it could be better than listening to the two from Amanda Warren," Gabi admitted.

Emily's eyes widened. "Your old boss called you? Twice? That takes some nerve."

"Doesn't it? I can't imagine what she could possibly have to say that I'd want to hear."

"Maybe she's realized the company can't survive without you," Emily suggested.

"I was good, but I was hardly indispensable," Gabi responded, staring at the message screen on her phone as if just looking at it would help her to discern what had been said.

"Okay, then an apology," Emily said. "That would be nice. Or extra severance."

The likelihood of either of those things was too remote for Gabi to wrap her mind around it. She took another look at the message list and realized that Amanda's calls had come in surprisingly close to her father's.

"She called the first time just minutes after Dad did," she commented slowly. "Do you suppose that's more than a coincidence?"

Emily looked startled. "What are you thinking? That Dad spoke to her?"

"Dear God in heaven, I hope not," Gabi said with heartfelt emotion. "How humiliating would that be?"

Emily chuckled at her reaction. "I think it might be kind of sweet," she said. "I'm not sure I can imagine Dad getting all fatherly and protective, but it would definitely be nice to see."

Gabi was struck by an even more horrifying thought. "What if he called the CEO? He and Mr. Carlyle are colleagues, after all. Knowing Dad, if he was going to interfere, he'd go straight to the top."

"You do realize there's an easy way to find out," Emily said gently. "Play the messages."

Filled with trepidation, Gabi finally punched the speaker button for her father's message.

"Gabriella, I spoke to Ron Carlyle this morning about your situation," he began. "We agreed—"

Gabi groaned and cut off the message in midsentence. "I knew it. I just knew it."

"I think it's incredibly sweet that he wants to fix this," Emily said tentatively. "Don't you? I mean, really, Dad out on a limb for one of us? I'm telling you, the man has undergone some sort of miracle transformation."

Gabi didn't see that at all. All she saw was the embarrassment of having her father intervene in a professional matter. "He called the head of the company and what? Begged him to give me my job back? That's pathetic. Even if Mr. Carlyle got involved, I'd never be able to work with Amanda again. She'll hate my guts for going over her head."

"Or she'll recognize that you have strong allies and cut you some slack," Emily said. "Look at the big picture, Gabi. You loved that job. You gave it everything you had. You got a raw deal because of a pregnancy that shouldn't have impacted your job status one iota. Somebody is ready to right that wrong, thanks to Dad."

"We don't know that for sure," Gabi said. "Dad said he and Mr. Carlyle agreed on something, but we don't know what."

"Given the two calls from Amanda that followed, I'd say we have some idea," Emily said. "Keep listening." She studied Gabi with a suddenly somber expression. "Unless the real problem you're having is the realization that you don't want to go back. Is that it, Gabi?"

Was that it? Gabi wondered. Had some of the things Wade said to her earlier today gotten through to her on some level? Was she starting to want something different for the rest of her life? She'd lived with all-consuming work-related stress for a lot of years now. She'd always thought she was thriving on it, but had she been? Or had it been draining the life out of her as her grandmother and sisters believed?

"I don't know," she whispered, shocked by the words. "I don't know if I want to go back."

As the stunning revelation came out of her mouth, she watched her sister's face. Emily, after all, was the most driven one in the family next to her. She waited for her to say she'd be a fool not to seize the opportunity to go back if it was offered.

"Even after all this effort Dad went to, you don't have to accept whatever they're offering," Emily reassured her, startling her with the gentle, understanding reassurance. "You know what kind of people they are now. Nobody would blame you for not wanting to work with them again."

"Dad will," Gabi said. "Even though I didn't ask him to intercede, he'll be furious with me if I don't go back."

"That's on him, then," Emily said. "You can't run your life to please Dad."

But old habits were awfully hard to break, Gabi thought. At least for her. Emily or Samantha could make a decision like this without a second thought. Could *she?*

"I need to think," she said, shoving the cell phone in her pocket.

"Where are you going? You're too upset to be driving," Emily protested, trying to block her way.

"Then I'll go for a walk," Gabi said, not arguing the point about her state of mind. Emily was right about that.

An hour later she'd made her way to the bustling waterfront where she watched excited children with painted faces exiting a pirate-ship excursion, swords in hand. She smiled for the first time in what seemed like hours.

Would she be here someday with this child she was carrying? Would his or her face be split by a huge grin as they came ashore? Would their carefree laughter carry over the water? Did she even want that? Could she expect to have moments like that if she went back to the kind of career she'd so recently left behind? Or would work be so all-consuming once again that carefree moments with her child would be nothing more than an idyllic dream, just as they'd been for her and her sisters with a dad who worked nonstop?

It was ironic, really, that just this morning she'd been trying to sort through her jumbled thoughts to construct a new plan, fresh goals, only to have the old ones dangled in front of her. Of course, she didn't know for a fact that the opportunity to go back was real.

Sucking in a deep breath, she drew the phone from her pocket and listened to all three messages. Indeed, her father and Ron Carlyle had apparently agreed that the decision to let her go had been precipitous. And Amanda had been contrite in her messages, assuring Gabi that she could come back and resume her rightful role at the company. There'd even been the hint of a plea in her voice in the second message, as if she was getting pressured from above to make this happen.

So, now she knew, Gabi thought as she ended the final message. She knew she owed her father and Amanda a call back, but instead she found herself punching in Wade's number.

"Are you free?" she asked when he answered.

"Is everything okay, Gabi? Are you all right?" The immediate worry in his voice was unmistakable.

"I'm fine," she said. "I just need to talk to someone who isn't family. You seem to have a pretty clear perspective where I'm concerned. I'm not sure you know me as well as you think you do, but you're the first person I thought of who might help me sort this out."

"Where are you?"

She told him.

"Give me twenty minutes," he said. "Don't move."

She chuckled. "Well, I might have to hunt down a restroom, but I promise I will be in the vicinity."

"Did you have lunch?"

"Come to think of it, no. The last food I had were those doughnuts you brought by earlier."

"I'll bring lunch, too."

"Thanks, Wade."

"Anytime, sweetheart. You can always count on me."

As she hung up, she couldn't help wondering if it was worrisome that she was starting to believe that.

Wade called an order in to Boone on his way to meet Gabi. "Can you have your chef put together a couple of shrimp po'boys, some fries and coleslaw? I'll pick 'em up in ten minutes."

"Done," Boone said at once. "Do you have a date with Gabi? Emily's worried about her. She called a while back and said Gabi left the house a couple of hours ago, upset about something, and no one's heard from her since."

"She just called me. Let Emily know I'm on my way to meet her."

"She'll definitely be relieved," Boone said. "How about I throw in a couple of slices of key lime pie while I'm at it?"

"Now you're talking my language," Wade said. "That's the only pie I can't get at Castle's. Cora Jane says yours is the best, so why bother."

Boone chuckled. "My chef is going to be ecstatic to hear that."

Ten minutes later, Wade swung into the parking lot by Boone's Harbor and saw Boone waiting with two large take-out bags. Wade grinned at him.

"If word gets out you're doing curbside service, your business will probably triple," Wade teased.

"This courtesy is only for certain valued customers," Boone told him.

"How much do I owe you?"

"This one's on the house. Emily's convinced you're about to save the day and that we owe you, whatever that means. Do you have any idea?"

"Not yet, but I will get to the bottom of it," Wade promised, taking the bags. "Thanks, man."

"Anytime."

Once he reached downtown, it took Wade longer than he'd have liked to find a parking space in the busy waterfront area, but when he had, he found Gabi on a bench, staring at the crowds and the boats, though he had a feeling her head was a million miles away. The sun had dropped in the sky, and the air had turned brisk.

She glanced up when he sat down beside her.

"Want to go someplace quieter, where we can talk?" he asked, shrugging out of his jacket and handing it to her. "Put this on. The temperature's dropping. You don't want to catch a cold."

"I'm fine," she insisted, even as she pulled the jacket around her. "I like sitting here. I've been watching the kids."

"And wondering about yours?" he guessed.

She nodded.

"Have something to eat and tell me," he suggested, handing her the sandwich and opening the fries so she had access to those. He took the ice-cold bottled water out of another bag and gave her one of those, as well.

Rather than responding, she took an eager bite of the sandwich, then closed her eyes in ecstasy. "From Boone's," she said at once. "It's the only place in town that can make a po'boy this good."

"And it comes with his compliments," Wade said. "Your sister's worried about you. I gather you took off from the house a while ago and haven't checked in."

"I needed to think."

"About the baby?"

She shook her head. "I had some calls earlier, while

you and I were out. I'd left my phone behind, so there were messages."

"Bad news?" he asked, trying to figure out the weary tone in her voice.

Her unexpected laugh seemed forced. "A few days ago, I'd probably have thought just the opposite. My company suddenly seems willing to have me back in my old job." She met his gaze. "I can thank my dad for that. He made a call."

Wade's heart sank at the news, but he forced himself to hide his reaction and focus on her odd mood. She didn't seem nearly as ecstatic as he would have expected.

"You haven't called back, asked for details?"

She shook her head. "Not even my dad, much less my old boss." Her expression turned bewildered. "Why haven't I?"

He smiled at her. "You're not ready. You're not interested. You want them to stew." He shrugged. "It could be any of those things, or something else entirely."

"What do you think I should do?"

"Oh, no, you don't," he said at once. "This decision is beyond my pay grade. Your life. Your decision."

"But just this morning you were so clear about this being the perfect opportunity for me to change my life," she said.

"It is that," Wade agreed. "But you have to want the change. It's not about what I think. I was just trying to give you a different way of looking at things, to view this situation as an opportunity, rather than a catastrophe."

"You, Grandmother, Emily, Samantha—you all seem

to agree about that," she said. "I respect your opinions. I was starting to listen to you. Now this."

"And you're confused."

She nodded.

"Can you manage to tune out all the clutter, all the noise from the rest of us, and hear what your heart is telling you?"

This time there was no mistaking the frustration in her expression. "No," she said, clearly annoyed. "I don't like this new me. I used to be decisive. I used to know exactly what I wanted."

"Until someone took it away and gave you two minutes to question whether you've changed, whether it's still what you want."

He saw how completely this opportunity had turned her life upside down yet again. "Sweetheart, this is your chance. It seems you can have it all back. How often do chances like that come along?"

"No more often than chances to change your life," she said. She met his gaze. She drew in a deep breath, then said, "I can't believe I'm going to say this, but I think going back would be a mistake."

Wade resisted the desire to shout *hallelujah!* "Why?" he forced himself to ask.

"It doesn't feel right. I'm not sure what *is* right, but I don't think it's going back to an old job where they forced me out because I embarrassed them or violated some code they think their employees should be living by."

"Then that's your answer."

"You're not just saying that because it fits in with the message you were trying to get through to me this morning?"

"Not at all," he insisted. "I promise. I'm saying it because it seems as if you've come to this conclusion for reasons that make sense to you. You're listening to your gut instincts."

Slowly her expression started to brighten. "Maybe I am finally able to make decisions for myself again," she said happily.

"Any thoughts yet about the next step?" he asked.

"Hey, getting to this decision has taken me all afternoon. Don't get pushy."

Wade laughed. "Now you're catching on. One step at a time. One day at a time."

Her eyes widened. "Heaven help me, you're starting to rub off on me."

"Is that such a bad thing?"

A smile lit her face. "I guess we'll have to wait and see. If I wind up working as a waitress at Castle's and turn into a complete slug, it might not be so good."

Wade laughed. "I don't think you need to be worrying about that. Ambition may shift directions through a lifetime, but I don't think it disappears entirely."

"I hope you're right," she said, "because Grandmother likes to make me show up before dawn and I am so not that person!"

She peered at the bag they had yet to open. "What's in there?"

"Boone sent key lime pie."

"Oh, yeah," she said happily.

"You sure you want it?" he teased. "You're not full?"

"Give me my pie," she ordered. "I know all about your pie addiction. Grandmother's filled me in, but one of those slices of key lime pie is mine."

He handed it over. "I learned a long time ago never to argue with a pregnant woman over food."

"Just one more thing I'll have to thank your sister for," she said as she dug into the pie.

Wade wondered what she'd think if he admitted that particular lesson had come from his wife.

Nine

Cora Jane had heard all about Gabriella's dilemma from Emily, but at the moment she had another crisis to deal with. She wanted to do what she could to see to it that there were no obstacles standing in Jimmy Templeton's way should he win that scholarship. If that gave her a chance to size up Ethan Cole and make sure he was the right man for Samantha, so much the better.

What she truly wanted was to see the two of them together, but when she'd suggested to Samantha that she accompany her to the clinic, her granddaughter had begged off as if she'd rather eat dirt. She'd been so adamant in her response, Cora Jane knew she was definitely on to something, at least on Samantha's side. Rumors of that old crush hadn't been exaggerated.

"Well, she certainly shot you down," Jerry said, regarding Cora Jane with amusement as Samantha all but ran from Castle's.

Cora Jane chuckled happily. "She did, didn't she?"

"Which makes you more determined than ever, I'm sure," he said, then gestured toward the bowl of crab soup in front of her. "Finish that, or you're not going anywhere. You need sustenance if you're going to do all this meddling."

She ate a bit more of the soup to wipe the concerned frown off Jerry's face, then said, "I haven't been wrong so far, have I? Emily and Boone will be married by summertime. Gabi and Wade are getting closer."

"Both of those things might have happened even if you'd stayed out of it," Jerry suggested.

"You tell me how. With all that bad blood between them, Emily and Boone were almost never in the same city, much less the same room. Gabi and Wade had never once crossed paths till I brought them together," she said, then amended, "Well, I did have a little help from Boone with that, albeit unwitting help. He had no idea what I was really up to, at least not at first."

Jerry held up his hands. "I stand corrected. You're a master puppeteer. And now you have a new mission."

"Two, as a matter of fact. I need to get Ethan on board with helping out Jimmy's father with his rehab." She pushed aside the remainder of the soup, ignoring Jerry's disapproval. "I should get over to the clinic before he leaves. I want to catch him today."

Jerry heaved a resigned sigh. "Okay, then, let's go."

She regarded him with surprise. "You're coming, too?"

"How are you going to get there if I don't? I drove you in to work this morning, and Samantha just left with your car." He gave her a worried look. "You didn't forget all that, did you?"

"Oh, stop with your worrying. My memory's fine. I just have too much on my mind."

"Of course you do," he said wryly. "All these sneaky shenanigans of yours take up a lot of brain space."

She gave him a look that would have daunted a lesser man. He only smiled, even as she warned, "If you're not prepared to help, you can wait in the parking lot."

"Believe me, I can't wait to see how you manipulate this situation," he retorted. "I'll be right by your side."

She wasn't sure that was the attitude adjustment she'd hoped for, but it would have to do. "That's good, then. It'll be good to have your impressions of Ethan. I know he's a fine man and a fine doctor, but is he the right one for Samantha?"

"You're admitting to doubts?" he said, his expression incredulous.

"I'm admitting it won't hurt to have a man's perspective. A lot's happened to Ethan. The injury he suffered serving in Afghanistan could have left scars far beyond the physical ones."

"He lost a leg, Cora Jane. He's entitled to a few bitter moments."

"I know that. I also know he hasn't been seeing anyone since his fiancée left him. Could be there's a reason for that. Maybe he's *too* bitter for a relationship. That's not what I want for Samantha. I know she comes across as confident and sure of herself, but she's an actress, after all. That's what she wants people to see. She's taken a lot of hits, things haven't always gone the way she wanted them to. She needs a man who's strong and compassionate, not one who'll drag her down."

Jerry nodded. "I'll be sure to take along my checklist."

Cora Jane frowned at him. "You're not taking this seriously enough."

"How can I? Falling in love is not an exact science.

Lord knows if it were, I'd have picked someone a whole lot easier and less complicated than you."

Despite the very evident frustration in his voice, Cora Jane chuckled. "Maybe so, but you're stuck with me now."

He put his arm around her shoulders and pressed a warm kiss to her cheek. "I surely am."

To her shock and immense satisfaction, it didn't really sound as if he were complaining.

As soon as Cora Jane explained the situation with the Templetons and the opportunity that might be coming Jimmy's way, Ethan jumped on board without a single instant of hesitation.

"I'll see that Rory gets the rehab he needs," he promised. "And we'll work out payments he can live with. If this accident happened on the job, shouldn't workmen's comp have kicked in?"

Cora Jane shrugged. "I honestly don't know the details. I just know that he hasn't been able to do the rehab, so going back to work has been out of the question. Whatever income he has these days, it's not nearly enough. Jimmy's been doing his part to keep the family afloat financially, but his heart's in this biomedical research the way my Sam's is. You should have heard the two of them. I swear that boy was as up-to-date on the latest journal articles as Sam was."

Ethan grinned. "He sounds like an amazing kid. I'm happy to do whatever I can to help."

Cora Jane beamed. "I just knew I could count on you, Ethan. You were great when we brought B.J. in here after he'd cut himself, and Boone has always spoken so highly of you."

"Boone's a good friend," Ethan said, regarding her suspiciously as if he feared where she might be heading.

"I'm real pleased that he and Emily have finally worked things out," Cora Jane said.

Ethan merely nodded, clearly waiting to see what she really had on her mind.

"And you? I was real sorry to hear about you and your fiancée. She wasn't a local girl, was she?"

"No, we met in college. She was from Durham."

There was no mistaking the icy tone that accompanied the terse response.

"And you're not involved with anyone at the moment?"

A surprising smile tugged at Ethan's lips. "Cora Jane, where are you going with this? My social life isn't really any of your concern."

"I just hate to see a handsome professional man sitting on the sidelines," she said easily.

"I'm perfectly comfortable on the sidelines, thank you." He gave her a pointed look. "And I know all about your tendency to meddle. Boone has filled me in. If you're even thinking about getting involved in my life, don't."

Beside her, Jerry chuckled. "I think that's clear enough, Cora Jane. Let's go before he decides that helping Rory Templeton is going to come at too big a price."

"One thing has nothing to do with the other," she said indignantly, then studied Ethan worriedly. "You know that, right?"

"I know that. Don't worry. Rory will get his rehab."

Cora Jane gave a satisfied nod. "Okay, then. We'll be on our way. Stop by the house sometime, Ethan. We'd love to see you. Or come by Castle's, maybe for lunch one day. It'll be my treat."

"That's a generous offer, Cora Jane. Maybe I will."

As she and Jerry walked back to his truck, she allowed herself a smug smile. "That went well," she said.

Jerry didn't seem nearly as certain of that. "You really think so?"

"Well, of course it did. He's going to help Rory, and one of these days he'll drop into Castle's. I'll make sure Samantha waits on him, and we'll be off to the races."

Jerry shook his head. "Darlin', I love your optimism, but that man is not going to set foot in Castle's unless he comes with an armed guard. He knows what you're up to."

She faltered ever so slightly at his conviction. "You think so?"

"Oh, he may not know you have Samantha in mind, but he knows you have someone waiting in the wings. He wants no part of your scheme. He made that plain."

"But he'd be perfect for Samantha. Don't you think so? He's a fine man. Steady and honorable. Quick to lend a hand."

"And not looking for a serious relationship," Jerry reminded her.

Cora Jane waved off the comment. "No man thinks he wants a serious relationship until the right one comes along," she said confidently.

Jerry sighed heavily. "No matter what I say, you're not going to let this go, are you?"

"Of course not. I intend to see all my girls happily settled."

"And yourself?" he asked. "What do you want for you?"

She linked her arm through his. "I already have every-thing I need."

He gave her a tolerant look filled with unmistakable devotion. "Good answer, my darlin'. Good answer."

When Wade finally dropped Gabi off at Cora Jane's, the house was dark even though there was a car in the driveway.

"Samantha? Grandmother?" Gabi shouted as she started inside, flipping on the kitchen light.

"Out here," Samantha responded.

Gabi glanced across the porch and saw her sister settled into a rocker with what looked to be a margar-ita in hand.

"Uh-oh, bad day?" Gabi asked.

"Nothing that unusual," Samantha said, her voice filled with resignation. "I was up for a part in a series pilot being shot in New York. I didn't get it."

"Oh, Sam, I'm sorry," Gabi said, worried by her sister's dejected tone. "There will be other parts."

"Do you know how many times I've had to tell my-self that?" Samantha asked. "It's wearing pretty thin."

"But you can't give up," Gabi told her. "Acting was always your dream."

"But when do I accept that my career isn't really going to get off the ground? I've been a working ac-tress, sure, but I've spent more time waiting tables, bar-tending and being a hostess in a restaurant than I have actually acting. That's not what I signed on for. Maybe it's time to call it a day."

"And do what?" Gabi said, working to hide her shock.

Samantha laughed, but it was definitely forced. "Now that is the million-dollar question." She glanced at Gabi, then lifted her drink. "I hear your day was about as confusing as mine."

"You heard about Dad and my job?"

Samantha nodded. "I did. What are you going to do?"

"I'm going to turn it down," Gabi said.

Samantha sat up a little straighter. "Seriously? Won't Dad go ballistic?"

"More than likely."

"When do you plan to tell him? I'm guessing you haven't, because you don't have that shell-shocked look that comes from having him cut you into little pieces for not living up to expectations."

"I haven't quite worked up the courage," she admitted.

"Is that because you're not sure you're making the right decision?"

Gabi shook her head. "No, I'm sure about this. I just don't know if I'm ready for all the aggravation, especially when for a few shining hours the other day, Dad was on my side."

"That was definitely a long-awaited Hallmark moment," Samantha agreed.

Gabi glanced over at her. "We're quite a pair, aren't we?"

"Indeed," Samantha said. "At least Emily seems to have her future all mapped out. She's got the job of her dreams out in Los Angeles, and Boone found a way to drop everything here and be right there with her."

"Boone's a rare man," Gabi said.

"So's Wade," Samantha said slyly.

Gabi nodded. "Yes, he is."

Samantha's eyes widened. "Wow! No argument?"

"How could I argue with that? He was there for me

this afternoon. Amazingly, he never once pushed me to do what he wanted. He just poked and prodded till I figured out what *I* wanted."

"How do you see this playing out?" Samantha asked. "Between you and Wade?"

"It is way too soon to even think about that," Gabi said. "Maybe I know that going back to my old job is not the answer for me, but the rest of it?" She shrugged. "Not a clue. And until I have my life under control, I can't even think about dragging anyone else into it. The only other human being I have to consider right this second is my baby. Deciding what to do for my child has to be a top priority."

"So, you're still considering adoption?" Samantha asked, her tone surprisingly neutral given her past opposition to the idea.

"It just makes so much sense under the circumstances," Gabi said, but even she could tell there was no enthusiasm for it in her voice.

Samantha reached over and touched her arm, then waited until Gabi met her gaze. "But you want to keep the baby, don't you?"

Tears filled Gabi's eyes as her hand instinctively covered her belly. "Yeah, I do."

"Then do it," Samantha urged. "You can handle being a single mom, Gabi. You'll have the whole family's support, and something tells me you'll have Wade's if you want it."

Gabi held up a hand. "It's not fair for me to rely on him. It's just not. Maybe later, once I have my own life under control—"

Samantha interrupted. "Is Wade going to stand by patiently while you get to that point?"

Gabi admitted to herself that she'd wondered the same thing. To Samantha she said only, "I guess we'll see."

"How do you feel about the possibility of losing him if it takes too long for you to figure things out?"

"I haven't let myself think about that," Gabi declared. "I have more than enough pressure to deal with as it is."

But amazingly, for the first time, she could almost view that with excitement rather than dread. Perhaps it had taken closing the door firmly on the past to allow her to open the next one, which could lead to all the possibilities.

"Unca Wade, do you like that lady who was here with you?" Chelsea asked, her expression serious but not half as somber as Louise's as she awaited his reply.

"Gabriella is a very good friend," he confirmed, deliberately keeping his tone neutral.

Eight-year-old Bryce wandered into the living room with a can of soda. Not known for mincing words, he inquired, "How come Mommy doesn't like her?"

Louise flushed at the comment. "Bryce Carter, I never said I didn't like her," she corrected hurriedly. "What I said was, I have some reservations about the situation."

Wade had a hunch that his nephew had interpreted her remarks exactly right. "You do know that I'm a grown man who's perfectly aware of the pros and cons of getting involved with a woman under these circumstances?" he said, holding his sister's gaze.

"I'm not so sure of that," she replied, her big-sister I-know-best frown firmly in place.

"I am," he countered, lifting Chelsea into the air until she squealed. "You need to leave it alone."

"How can I?"

"Find a way," he said firmly, glancing from his niece to his sister. "And next time we're all together, you might also find a way to lose the attitude. You made everyone uncomfortable on Sunday."

Louise looked vaguely chagrined. "That's what Zack said. Since he's usually oblivious to the undercurrents in a room, I figured it must have been bad."

"It was," Wade confirmed. "Mother would have been appalled."

Louise laughed. "Who are you kidding? Mother would have done a cross-examination that would make me look like a novice. Did you not hear her when I brought Zack home the first time? It's a wonder the man ever asked me on another date." She grinned. "Of course, the fact that he did earned him a huge number of points for courage in my book."

Her expression sobered. "You do know I only want the best for you. I don't want to see you hurt again. What happened with Kayla and the baby twisted you in knots."

Wade sighed. He certainly couldn't argue with that. And Louise didn't even know all of it. If she did, she'd lock him in a closet until Gabi—and the danger she represented—left town.

Just then his cell phone rang. Caller ID showed it was Gabi. "I need to take this," he said, setting Chelsea down, then walking out onto the deck.

"Hey, there," he said quietly. "How are you doing? Any second thoughts?"

"None," she admitted. "I think I'm a little shocked by that."

He smiled. "And I think that just proves you made the right decision. Have you told anyone else yet?"

"Just Samantha."

"And?"

"She agrees with you that I'm doing the right thing."

"You do know it's not about her approval or mine, though, right?"

"No, it's about how it makes me feel, and I feel surprisingly good. Relieved, in fact. And excited. Maybe I needed this offer, maybe I needed the vindication that what happened was wrong, in order to move on."

"That makes sense."

"Are you in your workshop now?"

"No. I'm at Louise's, spending time with the kids."

"And your sister? Has she given you an earful about steering clear of me?"

"She's tried," he said. "I told her to butt out."

"Maybe you should listen to her. I'm not exactly a great bet right now."

"My decision, sweetheart. I'm not budging." If the occasional second thoughts popped up, he'd just go right on tamping them down.

"I probably shouldn't admit this, but I find that surprisingly reassuring."

Wade chuckled. "Whoa! That may be the most encouraging thing I've ever heard you say. I think I'm getting a swelled head."

Gabi chuckled, just as he'd intended.

"You probably shouldn't let it go to your head," she warned. "I seem to have a lot of very capricious mood swings. Who knows what tomorrow might bring?"

"I'll take my chances. What's on your agenda for the rest of the night? Are you going to call your father and break the news?"

"No, I thought I'd save that for morning. I'd like to get a good night's sleep without his criticism echoing in my head."

"Makes sense," Wade said.

"What about you?"

"I'll be here a little longer, then take off for home. I found this incredible piece of driftwood on the beach the other day. I want to figure out what's inside it."

"I assume you're talking about the form it might take when you carve it, not that you expect to find treasure."

"That is treasure," he corrected. "If you were an artist, you'd understand."

"I almost do," she said, her tone turning thoughtful. "Way, way back I remember sitting on Grandmother's porch with a set of paints she'd given me. I wonder if those paintings are still around here." She laughed. "They were so awful."

"You sure about that?" Wade asked. "How old were you?"

"Twelve, maybe thirteen, I think."

"Maybe they were just the work of an untrained eye," he suggested.

"And unskilled hands," she countered. "I'm telling you, nothing I painted was recognizable. It was the most frustrating experience of my life."

"So even then, you didn't want to do something if it wasn't perfect," he said. "No allowances for trial and error?"

"Pretty much," she agreed.

"Find the paintings," he encouraged. "I want to see them."

"No way. You're a real artist. These were the childish works of a total amateur."

"Every artist was an amateur the first time they drew something," he said.

"I know what you're trying to do," she said accusingly. "But we're not going to discover that I have some hidden talent as an artist, I can assure you of that."

"Then let me ask you this," he said. "How did you feel when you did those paintings?"

"Frustrated and annoyed," she said without hesitation.

Wade laughed and gave up. So maybe she wasn't going to discover that she could be another Grandma Moses. "I'd still like to see them."

"Why?"

"Because I didn't know you back then. It'll give me a clue about what you were like."

"You'd probably get more information from letting Cora Jane tell you stories about how I misbehaved."

"Trust me, she's already filled me in," he admitted. "Just about the only thing your grandmother hasn't done is show me a baby book with you lying there naked on a bearskin rug."

"That picture doesn't exist, thank God," Gabi said. "But if you really want some insight into that era of my life, maybe I will let you look through one of my yearbooks sometime. Not sophomore year, though. I was pretty pathetic."

"It's hard to imagine you ever looking pathetic."

"Imagine glasses, straight hair and acne. The epitome of a high school geek."

"No way."

"Oh, yes. I was a charmer. Samantha was the beautiful one. Emily was the bubbly one. I was the serious student dedicated to making my father proud, not that he noticed."

"What changed?" he asked. "You said that was your sophomore year."

"I met a boy, of course. He didn't know I was alive, but thanks to Samantha's efforts, I traded the glasses for contacts, got a decent haircut and with the help of a very skilled dermatologist my skin cleared up. I even went on a date or two, though never with the boy who'd caught my eye."

"Was he here?" Wade asked, prepared to find him and cut his heart out.

"No, in Raleigh." She fell silent. "You know, I think that was the best part of summer for me. When I was here, there was no pressure to be with a boy like there was in high school. I met plenty of them, of course, at the restaurant, but we hung out on the beach as a group. There was always a crowd. I never felt weird about not being paired off."

"I'll bet I would have fallen for you even back then," Wade said.

She chuckled. "Maybe I should let you see that sophomore yearbook, after all. I doubt you'd be so sure of that then."

"Try me," he said.

"Maybe I will. Good night, Wade."

"Talk to you tomorrow."

As he disconnected the call and turned to go inside, he saw his sister standing just inside the door, blatantly eavesdropping.

"Not a word," he warned quietly. "Not one single word."

"Not even if I'm scared to death for you?"

"Not even then," he said.

What he didn't dare admit was how scared he was for himself. Contrary to what his sister might think, he wasn't totally blind to the obstacles in his path. Nor was he oblivious to the comparisons to his past with Kayla. He was just choosing to ignore all that, because at heart he was an optimist. He couldn't let himself believe that happiness would be snatched away twice.

Ten

After she'd gone to bed the night before, Gabi hadn't been able to stop thinking about those paintings she'd mentioned to Wade. Something he'd asked had triggered a memory for her. He'd wanted to know not how they'd turned out, but how she'd felt when she'd painted them. It had suddenly struck her that though she'd been frustrated by her lack of skill, she'd loved the process.

While Samantha had been off on dates and Emily had been with Boone under Grandmother's watchful eye, she'd been on the pier out back or on the porch with her watercolors. She recalled being completely aware of her surroundings in a different way, the nuances of light and shadow, the richness of colors, the complexity of textures. Not that she'd been able to capture a single one of those things on paper, she thought ruefully.

Still, it might be interesting to take another look at them. She had a hunch her grandmother had never thrown them out. Cora Jane had saved too many other mementos of those years to have thrown the paintings away.

With her grandmother and Samantha gone, Gabi had

the house to herself and time on her hands. Her only chore for the day was to call her father and then Amanda Warren. Postponing those uncomfortable conversations seemed like an excellent idea.

While her grandmother's master suite was downstairs, there were three upstairs bedrooms in the house. Gabi and her sisters had used the largest almost like a dormitory when they'd visited. Another was reserved for other guests, including the occasional visit by both of her parents. The third was cluttered with things Cora Jane couldn't bear to part with. Gabi decided to start there.

She smiled as she came across old dolls, even a miniature baby carriage for one of Emily's prized babies, an expensive toy she'd begged for for months before Christmas. Now, the doll had been tossed haphazardly in the carriage, dressed in nothing more than a diaper and wearing a ragged pink bow in its skimpy remaining hair.

"Well, one thing's for sure, I would take better care of my child than Emily did of you," she told the poor doll, cradling it in her arms as she continued to poke through the clutter.

She found boxes of puzzles, kept for rainy days, along with board games faded from frequent use. She could still hear the squabbles that had accompanied those afternoon endeavors echoing in her head. How often had Cora Jane lost patience, bringing them into the kitchen with her so she could referee as she baked?

Finally, when Gabi was starting to think that perhaps her grandmother's sentiment hadn't extended to her paintings, she opened a dresser drawer and found them, lying flat, tissue paper layered protectively between each page. The beginner's box of watercolors, dried out now, was there, too.

Setting Emily's doll aside, she took out the drawings and studied them with a critical eye. Oh, they were awful, all right. Her memory definitely hadn't gotten that part wrong!

One featured several blobs of blue on a mostly green background. She could only assume it had been an attempt to capture the image of the hydrangeas at the end of the porch. It was memory, not execution, that suggested that. In another, gray boards with no shading stretched out over a flat blue surface. A stick figure— it couldn't be described as anything more—sat at the end of the pier with what surely must have been meant to be a fishing pole in hand.

"Not a lot of subtlety here," she commented, amused by her ineptitude. "It's little wonder I never picked up a paintbrush again."

And yet she could almost feel the sun on her shoulders as she'd painted, smell the tang of salt in the air, hear the slow, steady hum of the boats on the water. She could also remember how desperately she'd wanted to capture all of that on paper, to create an image her grandmother would treasure. As she touched these carefully preserved pages, she realized she'd done that, anyway, even if they weren't exactly worthy of being framed and hung on the walls.

Maybe watercolors simply weren't her medium, she thought. Or maybe she didn't have an artistic bone in her body, not the way Wade so obviously did.

"But it could be fun to try again," she whispered, considering it. She could take a class, maybe. Just for the sheer enjoyment of it. When was the last time she'd done that, spent time doing anything just because it appealed to her? She'd been too busy doing the things that she'd thought could help her get ahead.

"And look how that's turned out," she muttered, putting the paintings away. Maybe one day she'd show them to Wade. Maybe not.

Now she needed to deal with reality, make those dreaded calls.

Gently she returned Emily's doll to her carriage, covered her with a blanket and gave her a little pat. "Maybe my little girl, if that's what I have, will come back for you," she whispered, envisioning it. The image left her with a smile on her face and a tug of longing in her heart.

Suddenly starving, or perhaps only delaying the inevitable, Gabi piled some of Grandmother's freshly baked peanut butter cookies on a plate, poured herself a glass of milk and headed for the porch, cell phone tucked in her pocket.

Settled on the chaise longue, she ate one cookie, then another, sighing at each burst of flavor on her tongue. Just like looking at those paintings, peanut butter cookies reminded her of simpler times. Of course, so did chocolate chip cookies or oatmeal raisin. Hardly a day passed without Grandmother filling the big cookie jar on the kitchen counter with the cookies Gabi, Samantha, Emily and their friends loved. Cora Jane usually made dozens of each, taking the extras to the restaurant to be served with ice cream as one of the day's dessert specials. They were also sold in individual bags to beachgoers looking for something sweet to take across the street after lunch.

After her third cookie, Gabi could no longer even pretend that she wasn't trying to put off making those calls. She hit speed dial for her father's personal line, not one bit surprised to hear an even gruffer note than usual in his tone when he picked up.

"It's about time you got back to me," he grumbled impatiently. "I went out on a limb for you, Gabriella, and how do you repay that? By ignoring my call. By not bothering to call Amanda Warren. What is going on with you? Are you determined to self-destruct?"

"Hold on, Dad," she said, barely keeping a grip on her own patience. "While I appreciate what you tried to do, you need to keep in mind that I did not ask you to do it. You didn't even consult me to see if I wanted to go back to work there."

He fell silent, obviously considering what she'd said. "Are you telling me that I wasted my time?" he asked slowly. "Do you have no intention of going back?"

For just a moment, she thought he'd suffered a pang of regret, but that instant didn't last.

"How is that going to make me look?" he asked next, resorting to a more familiar refrain.

"Of course, it's all about you and your reputation," she said, unable to keep a bitter note from her voice. "You made this magnanimous gesture, and I'm just supposed to fall in line to keep you from being embarrassed. Is that it?"

"I thought you wanted that job," he protested. "You acted as if losing it was the end of the world. You sounded miserable. That's why I took it upon myself to make that call."

She tried to remember that he really had been trying to do a good thing. She softened her tone. "But you didn't ask me, did you?" she said more gently. "I know you thought you were doing a great thing. And I do appreciate what you did. It meant a lot to me that you wanted to help, more than you can probably imagine."

"But you're not going back there," he concluded, sounding resigned, if not especially happy.

"No, I'm not. They don't want me back, Dad. Not really. Ron Carlyle was doing you a favor. Amanda will never really forgive me for having you go over her head. It would be an intolerable situation."

After what seemed like an eternity, her father sighed. "I hadn't looked at it that way. I just thought what they'd done was wrong and I wanted to fix it."

"I know."

"Have you told them yet?"

"No. I wanted to talk to you first. I owed you that."

"Sweetheart, putting this little fiasco of mine aside, what will you do?"

"I have no idea. I'm still thinking that through."

"I can put out some other feelers, if you want," he offered.

"Thanks, Dad, but not just yet. I need to make sense of things. For so long I thought that job was exactly what I wanted, *all* I wanted."

"And you've discovered it's not?" he asked, sounding as stunned by that as she was.

"Maybe not," she said. "I'm beginning to think what I really want is a life, a messy, complicated, jam-packed life."

"And will that include your child?" he asked hesitantly. "I know you've been considering adoption."

"And yet you didn't weigh in on that?" she said, surprised that he'd known and kept silent.

"That's a huge decision in anybody's life, and one only you can make. After all, you'll live with the consequences, either way."

"But how do you feel about being a grandfather?" she dared to ask.

He chuckled. "You know, I'm not really sure. I made a lot of mistakes as a father. Maybe this could be a chance for me to get a few things right, even get one of those lives you were talking about."

"I think I'm going to faint," she told him.

"Seriously? Are you sitting down?" he asked, his immediate panic yet more evidence that a change was taking place, an astonishing one.

"I was just teasing, Dad," she reassured him. "I'm fine, just a little startled by the new you."

"I'm afraid I'm a work in progress, Gabriella. I imagine there will be a few setbacks when I'll revert to my familiar, self-absorbed ways."

"I hope not," she told him. "Emily, Samantha and I need you in our lives, exactly the way you've tried to be the past few days."

"Do you know, I don't think any of you has even so much as hinted at that before," he said. "Even your mother got used to doing things on her own."

"Sure, we're all independent, Dad, but that doesn't mean we don't need you. Remember that, okay?"

"I'll definitely keep it in mind."

"Thanks again for what you tried to do."

"No problem. If you change your mind and want me to make some more calls, just let me know."

"I will," she promised.

Relieved by how well that had gone, she placed the call to Amanda. When she reached Amanda's secretary and was told she was in a meeting, Gabi asked for her voice mail.

Knowing it was cowardly, she left what she hoped was a gracious and mostly sincere message. "Amanda, this is Gabi. Thanks so much for reconsidering, but I think it's better if we just leave things alone. I'm not interested in coming back. I want to move forward, not backward."

After she'd hung up, she shoved the phone back in her pocket and uttered a sigh of relief. It might be only temporary, this feeling of serenity that was stealing over her, but for now she knew she'd done exactly the right thing.

"My dad got a call from Dr. Cole last night," Jimmy told Wade excitedly. "Mrs. Castle must have talked to him, because he told my dad he'd arranged for him to get all the rehab he needs. At first Dad was, like, 'Oh, no, I can't afford that,' but whatever Dr. Cole said next convinced him."

"That's fantastic, Jimmy."

"You know the best part? My dad was actually smiling when he got off the phone. It's been a long time since he looked really happy. I owe all of you guys for that. He'd thank you himself if he knew."

"Hope will put a smile back on a man's face," Wade said, smiling himself. "How are you doing with all those papers Sam Castle gave you to fill out?"

"I've done everything but the essay part," he said, making a face. "I don't know what to say."

"Aren't you supposed to tell them why you're interested in college or in this particular field?"

Jimmy nodded. "But it sounds dorky when I put it on paper, like I'm just trying to suck up or something."

"Here's my experience," Wade told him. "If what you write is sincere, if you tell them what's really in your heart, it won't sound dorky at all. I heard your passion for this field when you were talking to Sam Castle. We all did. Just try to put some of that in writing. I'll read it for you when you're finished, if you want me to, or I'll bet Mr. Castle would."

Jimmy shook his head. "He's going to be giving this to the selection committee. I don't want him to feel like I'm trying to get an edge on the other kids or something."

Wade gave him an approving look. "And that shows the kind of integrity you have," he told the teenager. "You are such a shoo-in for this scholarship. You have all the traits of someone who's going to succeed."

"You're just biased," Jimmy said, though he looked pleased by Wade's assessment.

He hesitated a moment, and his expression faltered just a little. "Do you really think Dr. Cole and the rehab can help my dad so he can work again?"

Wade tried to be reassuring without making promises. "You know Dr. Cole lost a leg in Afghanistan, right?"

Jimmy nodded.

"And you've seen him getting around, running in a marathon even?"

Jimmy's eyes brightened. "And if he can do that, then my dad can get better, too," he concluded.

"I'd say he has a real good chance," Wade confirmed. "When's his first appointment?"

"He's getting an evaluation this afternoon. He'll start

rehab tomorrow." Jimmy regarded Wade hopefully. "I was thinking maybe I should go with him. Do you think Tommy would mind if I took off a couple of hours?"

"I don't think he'd mind at all," Wade said, proud of Jimmy for being so considerate of his father. "Go on and check with him."

Jimmy started off, then turned back. Shyly, he held out a hand. "Thanks, man, okay?"

"No thanks necessary. I didn't do any of this."

"You introduced me to Gabriella." A grin broke across his face. "Even though you knew she might fall for me."

Wade laughed at his impudence. "Go on, kid, before I change my mind and tell her she made a terrible mistake."

Jimmy didn't look even slightly worried about the threat. "I think it could be too late for that to matter."

"I think you're probably right. Now, go."

He shook his head, watching with amusement as Jimmy went to Tommy, his expression serious as he explained about needing time off. Tommy glanced over in Wade's direction, then nodded.

When Jimmy had left, Tommy came over to Wade. "Are you responsible for costing me one of the best young workers I've taken on in years?"

"Sorry about that," Wade said. "He has all this potential. How could I let it go to waste? Besides, if he told you about his dad, there's a good chance Rory will be ready to go back to work full-time long before Jimmy takes off for college. He'd be a good fit for you. He's both experienced and eager to get back to work."

Tommy's expression turned thoughtful. "No wonder you and Cora Jane get along so well. You share that meddling gene with her."

Wade laughed. "I suppose I never thought of it that way, but you could be right. In this case, I think it's for a good cause."

"I imagine that's what she always thinks, too," Tommy replied.

No doubt about it, Wade thought. And lately, with Gabriella in his life, he was in no position to argue with her reasoning.

"Retail therapy," Emily declared when she arrived at Cora Jane's right on the heels of Samantha, who came in dragging after a day of waiting tables at Castle's. "My treat. I just got paid an exorbitant amount of money for that consult I did on the ski lodge in Aspen."

"You should be setting it aside for your wedding," Gabi told her.

"And there will be plenty for that, especially now that Dad's picking up most of the tab," Emily replied. "But today I am taking my two favorite sisters impulse shopping. We are only buying things we love, not things we need. Just this once we're going to be totally impractical."

"Gabi will never be able to do that," Samantha teased. "She doesn't have an impulsive, impractical bone in her body."

"Hey, I'm carrying a baby, aren't I?" Gabi protested. "Surely that should get me a couple of points for doing the unexpected."

"True," Emily concurred. "So, are you two game? At the end of the day, the person who's bought the craziest, most impractical thing wins."

"What's the prize?" Gabi asked at once, getting into the spirit of Emily's challenge. There was a time when she'd liked nothing more than a good dare from her sisters. "And who decides who wins?"

"Grandmother decides," Samantha suggested at once. "She's impartial." She glanced at Emily. "Any thoughts about the prize?"

"Now that's a tough one. How about dinner for two at Boone's Harbor?"

Gabi lifted a brow. "How's Boone going to feel about you giving away a free meal at his restaurant?"

"He'll feel great if I win and he gets an entire evening with me with no interference," Emily said. "And we all know I'm the most impulsive one, so I'm bound to win."

Gabi looked at Samantha. "There's a challenge I can't resist. How about you?"

"Oh, yeah," Samantha agreed. "Any rules? You need to tell us now. You can't be making them up once we're out there."

"Fair enough," Emily agreed. "The impulse buy has to be something we really, really want, not just something we think will win."

"Oh, I like that," Gabi said. "I can hardly wait to get started."

They started close to their grandmother's, popping into shops with everything from sea-glass jewelry and art to fancy beachwear. Gabi stopped in front of a baby boutique, her gaze drawn to all the tiny outfits.

"Too practical," Emily declared. "Besides, we don't know yet if it's a boy or a girl. I think you could find out by now if you wanted to know."

"I know I could," Gabi agreed. "I don't want to."

"Because then you'd start wanting little pink things or little blue things for a baby you don't plan to keep?"

Samantha asked gently. "Doesn't that tell you something, sweetie? You want to keep this baby."

Gabi held up a hand, not prepared to discuss her evolving feelings. "Don't start on me again. What I might want and what's right are not necessarily the same thing."

She walked away and went into a shop with local art. Her gaze was instantly drawn to glass wind chimes sparkling in the sunlight, their sweet music stirred by the breeze of an air-conditioning vent. Something in her heart filled at the sound. She remembered sitting on Grandmother's porch, listening to a sound just like that, a merry tinkling that was all that was bright and cheerful about summer. The same music sang her to sleep at night now...and kept Samantha awake, she recalled with amusement.

Though she walked away, she kept being drawn back to the display of wind chimes.

"I want that," she whispered, stunned by the admission.

Samantha studied her curiously. "The wind chime? Which one? Is that your impulse buy?"

Gabi shook her head as an idea began to unfurl in her head. She wondered if it had been sparked by that serene sound or had her earlier examination of those inept paintings stirred some artistic trait she'd been unaware she possessed?

"I don't want to buy any of them," she told Samantha. "Although that one is lovely." She pointed to one with an iris painted on what looked like antique glass filled with tiny bubbles. The dangling shards of glass were multicolored in shades of green and purple.

She faced her sister and announced, "I want to make them."

Emily joined them just then and stared at her in confusion. "You want to make wind chimes? For kicks?"

"For a living," she corrected.

Both Emily and Samantha looked stunned.

"Do you have any idea how it's done?" Samantha asked.

"Not a clue," Gabi admitted. "But I can learn."

More excited than she'd been about much of anything recently, she headed for the cashier with the hand-painted glass wind chime in hand. "Was this made by a local artist?" she asked.

The girl shrugged. "No idea. I just work here."

"Could you find out? Or tell me how I could reach the owner."

"Leave a name and I'll have Meg call you," the girl said indifferently. "You gonna buy that?"

Gabi looked at the rippled shards of glass, the delicately painted iris on a larger glass diamond at the top. "Yes, please." It would always be a reminder of this epiphany of hers, even if it never led to a new career.

Emily appeared at her side with a credit card. "It's on me, remember?" She grinned. "I didn't think you had any grasp of the whole impulsive thing. You surprised me."

Gabi felt a slow smile spread across her face. "I surprised myself."

Emily turned to Samantha, who gave a slight nod. "Since neither Samantha or I have found a thing we couldn't live without, we declare you today's winner!" she told Gabi. "Let me know when you want that dinner and I'll make sure Boone makes the reservation."

"But we haven't been shopping that long," Gabi protested. "Either of you could still find something even better."

Emily shook her head. "Sweetie, it's not just about

the wind chime, though it is beautiful. It's about you wanting to learn to make them. That's amazing."

"And crazy?" Gabi asked, hearing just how insane it sounded after years of scaling the corporate ladder.

"Maybe just a little," Samantha said. "But you deserve to take a chance."

Though she happily clutched her package, Gabi wasn't so sure she agreed that now was the best time for her to be taking risks. "I'm going to have a baby," she reminded them. "I should be setting practical goals, don't you think?"

"Hey, maybe you'll turn out to be the best wind chime maker in Sand Castle Bay," Emily said. "In the world even."

Gabi gave her sister a fierce hug. "You know what I love most about you?"

"What?" Emily said, looking vaguely startled by the display of affection.

"You dream big, even for me."

"Well, of course I do. You're my sister. Sam, too. I want you both to have absolutely everything you want and then some."

Gabi grinned at them. "Can I have my prize tonight, please? And will the two of you be my guests for dinner? I know the prize was for two. I'll pay for the extra meal. I think all the soul-searching I've done today should be celebrated, to say nothing of dealing with Dad and Amanda without coming unglued."

"Amen to that," Emily replied. "And dinner for all of us is on the house." She gave them a wicked grin. "I'll make sure Boone gets suitably rewarded later for his generosity."

Eleven

Wade was about to head out to his workshop for the evening when his cell phone rang. He glanced at the caller ID as he walked.

"Hey, Boone," he said. "What's up?"

"You busy?"

"I'm not doing anything pressing. Why?"

"I just had a call from Emily. She, Gabi and Samantha are on their way over to the restaurant for some kind of celebration. She suggested you might want to join us."

"Emily suggested it?" he said, red flags flying. "Does Gabi know?"

Boone chuckled. "Hey, I'm only relaying the invitation. The behind-the-scenes machinations are way beyond me. You can't seriously want to miss this chance, though, can you?"

Of course he didn't want to miss it. "How soon?"

"They're on their way now," Boone said. "I gather they've finished a shopping spree and are coming straight here. I have no idea how the celebration thing fits in, unless they found an amazing bargain on shoes or something. That would be enough to make Emily's pulse race."

"I'll be there in twenty minutes," Wade promised. "I have to find my protective armor in case Gabi's not thrilled about my presence."

"You two aren't fighting, are you?" Boone asked worriedly. "Please tell me Emily's not trying to pull off some kind of public reconciliation that's bound to backfire."

"My guess is she's just meddling. I think the restaurant's china and glassware are safe enough."

"But you said…that bit about protective armor…"

"It was a joke, Boone," he explained patiently. "Gabi and I will behave in a thoroughly civilized manner. I can almost guarantee it."

"It's the *almost* that troubles me," Boone replied, then added in the resigned tone of a man growing used to being caught up in the Castle shenanigans, "See you shortly."

"Hey, Boone," Wade said, catching him before he'd had a chance to hang up. "You really don't have any idea what they're celebrating?"

"Not a clue. I just know I'm buying dinner."

Wade laughed. "And now *I'm* celebrating."

It promised to be an interesting evening, but then he hadn't spent a dull moment around Gabriella since they'd met.

When Wade arrived at Boone's Harbor, he found Boone and the three women at a round table by a window with an incredible view of the setting sun over the water. He knew perfectly well it wasn't coincidence that the only available chair at the table was next to Gabi.

Gabi's eyes lit with surprise when he pulled the chair out, but at least she didn't seem annoyed to see him.

"Where'd you come from?" she asked. "I thought Castle's was your hangout of choice."

"Definitely, but Boone called and alerted me that there was a celebration on tonight's menu here. He seemed to think I shouldn't miss it."

Rather than glancing at her soon-to-be brother-in-law for answers, she turned immediately to her younger sister as she said, "Is that so?"

Emily merely shrugged, feigning innocence and doing it badly. "I thought he might be interested in your news."

Wade studied Gabi's face. Her eyes did seem bright with excitement and her cheeks were tinted pink. "News?" he said, his curiosity stirred.

"I turned down the job at my old company," she reported. "Just the way we discussed yesterday." She gave Emily a defiant look. "See? No news there."

Wade pursued it, anyway. "And you're happy with that decision?"

"Very happy," she said. "Better yet, my father seemed to take it surprisingly well." She made a face. "At least after the initial shock of me rejecting his well-meant help wore off."

"Good for you."

"There's more," Emily prodded, clearly not satisfied with Gabi's piecemeal revelation. "Tell him the rest. Boone's dying to hear, too. I didn't fill him in when I called."

Wade watched as Gabi squirmed uncomfortably. "Is it something you're not ready to talk about?" he asked, wondering if they needed to let her off the hook.

"Sort of," she said, frowning at Emily. "It's one thing for Emily and Samantha to know, but you guys are bound to think I've gone off my rocker."

"I could never think that," Wade protested. "Your entire approach to life has been mature and methodical. I can't see that changing now."

"Well, I can, because I'm not sweet on you," Boone teased, then added, "but I'd never say it aloud."

"I do so appreciate that," Gabi replied, her tone tart.

Boone's expression sobered. "If you don't want to talk about it, Gabi, it's okay. Don't let Emily pressure you."

"Hey, it is *not* okay," Emily argued, poking Boone with her elbow. "Wade especially should hear this. I think he's responsible."

The comment worried Wade. Much as he might like Gabi, he didn't want to influence decisions she needed to be making for herself. He knew the sort of simmering resentment that could cause in the long-term. There were some mistakes he wasn't hell-bent on repeating, despite what Louise thought.

"Now I definitely want to know," he said. "How much trouble am I likely to be in?"

Gabi smiled and touched his hand. "No trouble. Not yet, anyway." She drew in a deep breath. "Okay, you know how you and I were talking about art last night?"

"Sure," he said, more bemused than ever.

"Well, I dug out those old paintings of mine this morning."

"And they were incredible?" he asked hopefully.

"Oh, no. They were every bit as awful as I'd remembered," she said, though she sounded surprisingly okay with that.

"I'm not following this," Boone said.

"Hush," Emily told him. "Just listen."

Gabi's flush deepened as Wade and Boone stared, awaiting the obviously big announcement.

"Just thinking about telling you all this is embarrassing," she said, her nervousness plain. "I've probably made a huge mistake. This whole idea is ridiculous. I can't imagine what I was thinking."

"Stop that this minute!" Emily commanded. "It most certainly is not ridiculous! Surprising, maybe, but not ridiculous." She jumped in to take over since Gabi obviously couldn't find the words to explain. "We were in this little art-and-gift shop, and suddenly Gabi took one look at these wind chimes and went all gaga over them. Right, Samantha?"

"Definitely gaga," Samantha confirmed, a grin on her face.

"It was like she had some sort of epiphany right there in the middle of the store," Emily continued. "She told Samantha and me she wants to make them."

Wade couldn't seem to keep his lips from curving into a smile. The ultimate businesswoman playing with bits of colored glass? He couldn't imagine it lasting, but for now it seemed like the perfect answer for the transition period she needed.

"Seriously?" he asked. "Wind chimes?"

Her expression sheepish, Gabi nodded. "I think so."

Boone looked totally perplexed. "Hold on a minute. For years you've been the single most driven member of the entire Castle sisterhood, leaving even Emily here in your dust, and now you want to give all that up to make wind chimes? That's some epiphany!"

"I was just thinking that if I'm going to change my

life, maybe it ought to be in a dramatic way," Gabi responded defensively. "And there's something special and beautiful about wind chimes. They've always made me happy."

Wade leaned closer and kissed her cheek. "Congratulations!"

Though Boone continued to look skeptical, he lifted a glass. "You know I wish you lots of success, Gabi."

"Thanks. Of course it remains to be seen if I have even the tiniest bit of artistic talent. For all I know, once I've had a few lessons all I'll have to show for it will be a lot of glass cuts and blood loss."

Samantha reached over and gave her hand a squeeze. "Whether you turn out to be the world's best wind-chime maker or not, I'm so impressed that you're going for this, Gabi. It's a daring move. I'm proud of you."

"Hear, hear," Emily said.

Wade could see the impact their enthusiasm had on Gabi. It was clear just how much she counted on her sisters' support. Her eyes were shining as they toasted her. And if there was even the tiniest shadow of doubt in her mind about her decision, for now at least, she hid it well.

Gabi accepted eagerly when Wade offered to drive her home after dinner. She'd been dying to hear his uncensored reaction to her decision.

Once they were in his car, she turned to him. "Okay, now tell me what you really think about all this. Am I insane to even consider something like this out of the blue?"

His somber expression as he faced her made her pulse beat unsteadily.

"Oh, no," she whispered. "You do think I'm crazy."

He shook his head at once. "It doesn't matter what I

think," he said. He was quiet for a long time before he faced her squarely and asked, "Just tell me one thing. Do you really, really want to give this a try? Or are you just desperate to seize on anything that doesn't require you to go back into the same old corporate grind?"

She frowned at the questions, mostly because he was asking things she'd been wondering herself, but avoiding answering. "Do you know how annoying it is that you always seem to cut right to the heart of things?"

"You asked," he reminded her. "How about an honest answer?"

She drew in a deep breath and thought about the question. "Maybe a little of both," she admitted. "I mean, I can see being passionate about something like this, about creating something so beautiful, something that will make people happy when they hear the sound on the breeze."

"But?" he prodded.

"I know I was also getting frustrated by not having made a decision. At least this is a step forward, even if it's not necessarily on the right path."

Wade nodded. "I had a feeling that might be part of it."

Her conviction wavered. "Should I just forget all about this?"

"Absolutely not," he said, surprising her.

"Why not?"

"Because changes aren't always black-and-white decisions. There's nothing wrong with experimenting, as long as you understand that the results might not be what you wanted or expected. It's never wrong to explore, to take risks, to shake things up as long as you understand why you're doing it."

"And I do know with absolute certainty that I want

something different," she said, confident on that point at least. "This certainly fits that criteria."

His eyes sparkled with amusement. "It certainly does. I think you successfully stunned both of your sisters when you made your announcement in that store and then Boone when you told us tonight."

"And you? You weren't even a tiny bit taken aback?"

"Nah," he said, then claimed, "I've known for months that there was an adventurous soul in there yearning to break free."

Gabi rolled her eyes. "You did not."

"Well, I have to admit I hoped there was."

"No dull, staid corporate type for you?"

He held her gaze then and leaned cross the console to cup a hand behind her neck, drawing her close. When their lips met, there was nothing dull or staid about the kiss that followed.

He leaned back, smiling. "No worries on that front. I suspect you'll always be able to keep my heart racing and me guessing."

Gabi studied him with wonder. "How can you see me that way, when nobody else does?"

"Maybe no one else has taken the time to look beneath the surface," he suggested, then added pointedly, "Not even you."

Gabi thought about that and realized it was entirely possible he was exactly right. She'd made up her mind at an early age that she had to impress her father to get his attention. When it hadn't worked, she'd tried even harder, never taking her eye off that single elusive goal. During the years when other teens changed course a half dozen times, she'd stayed on the straight and narrow. Whatever whims might have passed fleetingly through her heart had been determinedly ignored in favor of higher achievements.

"I feel as if I've picked the worst possible time to take off on some journey of self-discovery," she said.

"Because of the baby?"

"Of course because of the baby. Do you remember hearing about the flower children of the sixties? My impression was they were self-indulgent and irresponsible. Is that what I'm turning into?"

"I suppose it remains to be seen," he responded candidly, eyes twinkling. "But I seriously doubt all those old responsible habits of yours can be kicked that readily. You'll try this, and if it doesn't work out, you'll move on to something that does."

"You seem to have a lot of faith in me."

"Yes, I do," he said without hesitation.

His immediate belief in her was a revelation. How different her life might have been if she'd had even an iota of that from her father.

"I think you might be very good for me, Wade Johnson," she told him quietly.

The admission, coming as it did on top of so many other recent and unanticipated changes in her life, scared her to death. And, of course, there still remained the very big question of whether she could possibly be any good for him or whether he was trying desperately to recapture a time in his past when he'd had everything he wanted. Deep in her gut, she couldn't help remembering how tragically that had ended.

When Gabi finally got back to Cora Jane's, she was surprised to find her grandmother waiting up for her.

"Is everything okay?" Gabi asked at once. "You're never up this late."

"I thought we should talk," Cora Jane said. "Samantha told me a little about what went on today. Sounds as if you're looking to make some mighty big changes."

"And you disapprove?" Gabi asked worriedly. She'd been expecting her grandmother's blessing. Not having it would be an emotional setback.

"Of course not," Cora Jane said readily. "I'll always support you in whatever you want to do." She studied Gabi intently. "I have to admit to being surprised, though. Is this Wade's influence?"

"Maybe just a little," Gabi said, "but the decision was all mine. I don't want to go back to my old life, not any of it. In fact, I think tomorrow I'll speak to a Realtor about putting the town house on the market."

Astonishment lit her grandmother's eyes. "Really? What then?"

"I'd like to stay here with you, at least until the baby comes." She regarded Cora Jane hopefully. "Would that be okay?"

A smile spread across her grandmother's face. "You know it would be," Cora Jane said at once. "And to be honest, I wouldn't mind having a baby under my roof again, if you want to stay on for as long as it suits you."

Gabi smiled at the gentle nudge. "One step at a time, okay?" She studied her grandmother's pleased expression. "Grandmother, do you think there's a plan for us? You know, a bigger one?"

"From God?"

Gabi nodded, knowing that her grandmother's faith ran deep, even though she missed church more Sundays than not because of Castle's.

"Oh, I think He probably has a few ideas," Cora Jane told her. "But the way I understand it, He's left it to us to figure things out on our own. That would explain how so many folks manage to make a mess of things."

"I don't want to make a mess of this," Gabi said. "I don't mean the whole wind-chime thing. I'm talking about this baby. What if keeping it is all wrong? Would I be totally selfish if I decided to try to raise it on my own?"

"Honey bun, if you're asking if I think you'll be a good mother, the answer is yes. Just the fact that you're asking these kind of questions of yourself tells me that. I trust you completely to put the best interests of that baby first."

"I want to. I've thought all along it would be best if it were in a home with two loving parents. I certainly didn't want it to become a pawn in some never-ending battle between Paul and me."

"There's definitely a lot to be said for a child being with two parents who've been longing for a baby," Cora Jane agreed. "But it could be that you'll be able to give that sort of home to this child yourself."

It said a lot about what had been going on recently that she wasn't taken aback by the suggestion. "You're talking about Wade," Gabi said.

"The man is crazy about you," Cora Jane reminded her.

"But it's way too soon to even think about something serious like that developing between us," Gabi protested. "We're close, but it wouldn't be fair to make a decision for my child based on Wade being in my life to help."

"He'd be a wonderful father," Cora Jane said.

"I know that," Gabi said in frustration. "I've seen

him with his nieces and nephews. It's just that..." Her voice trailed off as she tried to put her concern into words.

Cora Jane remained surprisingly quiet, allowing Gabi time to think. When the silence dragged on, rather than filling it with advice, she stood, poured herself a cup of herbal tea, then sat back down, waiting expectantly for Gabi to pick up where she'd left off.

"Sometimes I worry that Wade's attracted to me *because* of the baby," she admitted at last.

To her regret, Cora Jane didn't immediately argue the point.

"I suppose it's natural to wonder about that since he lost his wife and baby not all that long ago," her grandmother said thoughtfully. "But have you considered the fact that he was hanging around here with his eyes glued to you back in August before you got pregnant?"

"He was here because you kept dreaming up jobs for him to do," Gabi reminded her. "I'm not sure we can base anything on that."

"Well, I happen to know for a fact that those jobs took days longer than they needed to, and that, missy, was because of you. Thank goodness I wasn't paying him by the hour." She shook her head. "I think you can put that worry out of your head. It's you Wade cares about. I believe the baby is just an unexpected blessing to him."

Her grandmother's insight reassured her to some degree, but Gabi wasn't quite ready to let go of the possibility that Wade saw her—and the baby—as a way to fill a huge emotional void in his life.

"Well, maybe there was a little chemistry on his part

back then," she conceded, not even trying to hide her skepticism.

"But not on yours?" Cora Jane asked, clearly amused. "Don't think I didn't notice how hard you worked to keep your eyes off him. You were not immune, Gabriella, and if you say you were, I'll call you on the fib."

Gabi blushed under her gaze, but didn't dare argue.

"And that standoffish behavior of yours was all out of some misguided sense of loyalty to Paul, I imagine," Cora Jane added. "If he hadn't been in the picture, well, I think things might have heated up pretty quickly."

Much as she wanted to save her pride, Gabi could hardly deny that Cora Jane was probably right about that. She'd honestly thought she was in a relationship back then, but it hadn't kept her from sneaking the occasional peek at the very sexy Wade, who was underfoot wherever she turned. With Emily and Samantha tormenting her about him, it had been all but impossible to ignore the man.

"Okay, so maybe there was a little chemistry back in August," she conceded. "It didn't go anywhere."

"Because you worked hard to make sure he knew you weren't available," Cora Jane said. "That didn't stop him from coming by here just about every afternoon after you'd gone, hoping I'd spill some little snippet of news about you."

She smiled. "And, of course, I got a good look at his face the day you reappeared here, very obviously pregnant. He looked as if Christmas, which was long past, had come around again especially early and just for him."

"You're exaggerating," Gabi said.

"Am I? How long did it take him to ask you out once

you'd told him you were no longer with Paul? Five minutes, maybe? Ten? No more than that. Does that sound like a man who's the least bit put off by you being pregnant? I'd say it's a man who's seen an opportunity and seized it. I respect a man like that."

Samantha scowled at her. "It is really exasperating to have an unrepentant spy in the family."

"Maybe so, but I take my role seriously," Cora Jane said, grinning. "Look, honey bun, I'm not saying you have to marry the man tomorrow. I'm just saying you should open your heart to the possibilities, just the way you've opened it to a new direction professionally."

"I'm barely out of a relationship with the baby's father," Gabi argued.

Cora Jane waved her hand dismissively. "You can call that whatever you want, but it wasn't a relationship in my book. I think Paul's behavior since you found out you were pregnant is proof that I'm right about that."

Gabi could hardly argue the point. "Okay, I'll think about what you said," she promised.

"Fair enough. Now what's your next step?"

"I'm hoping to speak to that gift store owner tomorrow. The cashier said she'd have her call me."

Cora Jane immediately looked flustered. "Oh, my goodness, I got sidetracked when you walked in the door and forgot to tell you. She did call. Her name's Meg Waverly. She says she'll be happy to give you the information you want. She needs to know if you preferred one style of wind chime over another, since she buys from several local artists. Just give her a call tomorrow on her cell phone or stop by the store around ten. She'll be there to open."

Gabi took the slip of paper from her grandmother

and glanced at it. There it was in black and white, the contact information for someone who might guide her into the next phase of her life.

How astonishing was that? And maybe just a little scary, since now she'd have to make good on all these pie-in-the-sky dreams she'd been expressing today.

Twelve

Wade had been avoiding his sister for a couple of days now. He knew that sooner or later he'd have questions to answer, but right now he simply wasn't up for the aggravation. Louise clearly didn't approve of his relationship with Gabi, and he was tired of defending himself.

What he didn't expect was to find his brother-in-law on his doorstep when he got home from dropping Gabi off at Cora Jane's after the dinner at Boone's Harbor. Zack's medical practice and hospital rounds usually kept him tied up until early evening, but then he hightailed it straight home. Wade frowned when he saw him. If Zack was here at this hour, he had to be on some sort of a mission.

"Kids okay?" he asked as he unlocked the door and waited for Zack to precede him inside.

"Wild, as usual," Zack said, then grinned. "But yes, they're great. Even when the house is a zoo, I stop and look around and ask myself how I got this lucky."

Wade heard the wonder in his voice and thought that maybe his sister was the lucky one. He hoped she knew and appreciated how devoted her husband was.

"How's Louise?" Wade asked, suspecting she was behind this unexpected visit.

"She's in a bad place," Zack said, his expression sobering at once. "She thinks you're mad at her."

Wade smiled. "She always was perceptive."

Zack looked startled by the response. "Then you *are* upset with her? I thought she was worrying about nothing. You two never fight. I wish I got along with my own siblings half as well as the two of you do. I figured you'd just been busy, maybe getting a life of your own."

"Well, that too," Wade conceded. "But I've gotten a little tired of her attitude about Gabi."

"She only said what she thought because she was worried about you," Zack said, jumping to her defense.

"I'm well aware of that." He looked his brother-in-law in the eye. "And I even appreciated the concern the first time, but she hasn't let up, Zack. It's time she gave me some credit. I lived through the emotional roller coaster that was my life with Kayla. I'm not likely to forget it. This is not the same situation."

"Can't argue with that," Zack agreed. "Gabi doesn't strike me as anything like Kayla."

"She's not, and the circumstances are entirely different, too."

"How? Maybe Louise would drop this if she understood," Zack said.

Unfortunately, the answer was just some gut-deep belief on Wade's part, not anything that his sister would find reassuring. "It just is," he said, knowing the reply was unsatisfactory.

"Come on, man. You know that's not going to cut it," his brother-in-law said.

"Just pass along the message, okay?"

"If I have to," Zack said, not looking very happy about the prospect.

"I'd appreciate it," Wade told him. "Now, then. You've said what you came to say. And I understand that Louise is worrying because I've been staying away. Is that it? Any other messages you're supposed to convey, or do you want a beer?"

Zack looked relieved to have the uncomfortable conversation behind him. "Absolutely. Being caught in the middle takes a toll. You and I, well, I like to think we're friends. Louise…" He shrugged. "What can I say? I want her happy."

Wade laughed. "I get that, trust me. I'm sure it's especially difficult to be between a stubborn rock like my sister and an equally stubborn hard place like me."

Zack lifted his beer. "Amen, brother."

"I'll stop by tomorrow," Wade promised. "On one condition."

"That she lose the attitude," Zack said.

"Exactly."

Zack sighed. "Good luck with that. When I suggested it, she told me I was reacting like a typical man who knows nothing about family dynamics."

Wade tried unsuccessfully to hide his amusement. "And you said?"

"That I'd never been an overprotective big sister, but I had some idea of the havoc that butting in where you're not wanted can do."

Wade winced. "She must have loved that."

Zack gave him a rueful look. "I'm here, aren't I? It's my punishment for not backing her a hundred percent. She sent me to do her dirty work."

"Ah, so there was more," Wade concluded. "Are you supposed to tell me to dump Gabi?"

"In so many words," Zack acknowledged. "She suggested I phrase it more delicately. When I reminded her that I was a typical man, that I didn't phrase things delicately, that even my bedside manner as a doctor has detractors, she threw a shoe at me. Thank heaven she has terrible aim, or that spike heel could have blinded me."

"Sounds like fun times at your place."

Zack nodded dolefully. "Which is why I'm going to have another beer after this one and hang out here. Want to watch some basketball? I think Carolina has a West Coast game tonight. Should be coming on about now."

Wade tapped his beer bottle to Zack's. "Sounds like a plan. Want pizza to go with it?"

"Absolutely, but weren't you at dinner earlier?"

"I'm a guy. There's always room for pizza," he said, placing the call for a delivery. After he'd finished, he held the phone out to Zack. "Should you call Louise to let her know you're staying?"

"Heck, no. Let her think we're bonding and that I'm getting through to you. That'll keep her happy enough."

Wade shook his head. "The dynamics of your marriage are a total mystery to me."

Zack laughed. "Me, too, my man. Me, too."

And yet Wade didn't have a doubt in his head that whatever those dynamics were, they worked for both Louise and Zack. He also knew that, as annoying as her tactics were, his sister wanted that same kind of strong, unbreakable bond for him. Sadly, she just didn't believe he could find it with Gabi.

* * *

After several frustrating tries, Gabi finally found a pair of slacks she could still fit into, even though the waistband had to be held closed with a safety pin. She found a loose-fitting blouse in Samantha's closet that had enough pizzazz to make the ill-fitting pants almost unnoticeable. She sighed as she studied the effect in her mirror. Clearly she needed to do some shopping soon, or else her only wardrobe was going to be comprised of elastic-waisted shorts and baggy T-shirts.

Excited about meeting Meg Waverly, she grabbed her purse and walked into the waterfront district, arriving at the shop right after it opened.

The woman who glanced up when she stepped inside looked to be in her late thirties or early forties. Her black hair was going unapologetically gray and had been pulled back in a tight knot that, despite its severity, flattered her face. Her eyes were a deep turquoise and alight with curiosity. She wore a pair of sea-glass earrings in that same shade of blue.

"Hi. I'm Meg. And I'll bet you're Gabriella Castle," she said.

"Good guess," Gabi replied.

"Not really. I seldom have customers wander in when the store first opens. Tourists seem to get a late start, and the locals are at work. Things don't pick up till closer to lunchtime. I can get a lot of my ordering and paperwork done in the morning. Today, though, I was expecting you to drop by. Now, tell me what I can do to help you."

"As long as you promise not to laugh hysterically," Gabi said. "This idea is a little new to me, so I'm fairly sensitive."

"But it has to do with wind chimes? Lily said you bought one yesterday and were asking who'd made it."

Gabi nodded.

"Just natural curiosity about the artist?"

"No." She took a deep breath, then explained. "I think I'd like to learn to make them, the old-fashioned glass kind like the one I bought. I was hoping there might be a class I could take or that the artist could recommend someone who could teach me or even work with me one-on-one—for a fee, of course." She regarded Meg worriedly. "Is that being too presumptuous? Would the artist consider me to be competition? Believe me, I'm not."

"I guess that remains to be seen," Meg said. "And some artists actually enjoy helping beginners. Others, not so much."

"And the one who made the wind chime I bought?"

"She's more openminded than most. You'll like her." Meg studied her openly. "Something tells me there's a story behind all this. No offense, but I don't meet a lot of people your age who suddenly decide to take up art, not in a serious way, anyway. Or did I misunderstand? Are you looking for a hobby?"

"I don't have much time to take up a hobby right now. I think I'd like to do this as a career."

"With no artistic experience?" Meg said, her expression incredulous. "Or do I have that wrong?"

"Nope. You're exactly right."

"Pardon me for being nosy, but what are you running away from? A man? Or a job? Experience has taught me it's usually one or the other. Personally, I moved to Sand Castle Bay and opened this shop when my marriage broke up," she confided. "I wanted a fresh start, and I thought this might be the perfect place to raise my rebellious teenage daughter." A fleeting smile crossed her expressive face. "The store, at least, is working out well."

"I want a fresh start, too," Gabi said, relieved that Meg understood.

"What did you do before?"

"Public relations over in Raleigh. Big company. High-stress job."

"And you left because?"

Surprisingly, Gabi wasn't offended by the personal questions. It was small-town curiosity at its finest. Most people around the area knew the details by now, anyway. She rested her hand on her stomach. "I got pregnant. Then I got dumped. Then I got fired."

Meg's eyes widened as she spoke. "Holy cow! I'm surprised you're still talking in complete sentences. I'd be curled up in bed in the fetal position with a drink nearby."

"I probably would be, too," Gabi said. "With the baby, though, that option's pretty much off-limits."

"So, instead, you want to make wind chimes?"

"Exactly."

Meg nodded as if it all made perfect sense. For that, Gabi was incredibly grateful.

"Let me make a call," Meg said. "As you said yourself, artists can be funny about this kind of thing, but Sally doesn't have a lot of the hang-ups some of the others do. In fact, I think the two of you probably have a lot in common. And she'll be honest with you. If you don't have a lick of talent, she'll tell you. She won't let you waste your money."

Gabi nodded. "And that's exactly what I want."

"Give me a sec," Meg said, then went into the back.

Gabi wandered through the shop again, captivated

once more by the selection of wind chimes. There were some she was certain hadn't been on display the day before, each one prettier and more distinctive than the next. She tried guessing which had been done by this particular artist, but she couldn't be sure.

"You're all set," Meg said when she returned. "She'd like me to bring you by her place, though, and I can't break free from here till around two after Lily comes in and things quiet down again. Would that work for you?"

"Absolutely," Gabi said eagerly.

"If you can wait until then to grab a bite to eat, I'll treat," Meg offered. "I want to hear more about this dramatic change you're trying to make."

"I may not be able to wait that late for lunch, but there's rarely an hour of the day when I'm not starving," Gabi said. "I'd love to join you."

"Then I'll tell Sally we'll be there around three-thirty or four. How's that?"

"Perfect. Thank you so much for doing this."

"My pleasure. I'll see you this afternoon. Meet me down the block at the Seaside Café. I'm parked close by and I'll drive from there after we've had a bite to eat."

"Looking forward to it," Gabi told her.

She left the shop with a sense of wonder. So, that's how it's done, she thought to herself. All these years when she'd been surrounded by colleagues, rather than friends, she'd been unable to imagine how real friendships were born. Something told her she was about to find out.

Since she was already in the shopping district, Gabi decided to poke around in a few shops to see if she could find the new clothes she desperately needed. She only found one boutique that had a selection of maternity clothes, but she did find two pairs of pants, a few blouses and even a couple of dresses that would suffice until she could drive back over to Raleigh or get to the one major department store in Sand Castle Bay.

Since it was still too early to meet Meg, she called Emily. "Where are you? Do you have time to grab a quick bite, or are you and Boone about to take off for the airport? I know you're flying back to Los Angeles tonight."

"I have some time," Emily said. "Where are you?"

Gabi told her the name of the sandwich shop on the waterfront.

"I won't have a ton of time," Emily said. "Order me a tuna salad on whole wheat and some iced tea. I'll be there in ten minutes."

"I should probably call Samantha and see if she wants to join us," Gabi said.

"She's at Castle's. It'll take forever for her to get away. Besides, she and I said our goodbyes last night. I'd like a few minutes alone with you."

"Then I'll see you soon," Gabi said, shaking her head as she disconnected the call. There was an old rivalry between her younger sister and her older sister that she'd never understood. Emily and Samantha were nothing alike, so the competitiveness made little sense. Still, it seemed that more often than not over the years, she'd found herself mediating between them.

She placed their order, then sighed, relieved to be off her feet. She glanced down and noticed that her ankles were slightly swollen. She'd read that was to be expected, but wasn't it too soon? She really did need to get back to Raleigh to see her ob/gyn. It probably made even more sense to find one over here if she intended to stay with Cora Jane and take these art classes until the baby was born.

"Why are you staring at your feet?" Emily inquired as she pulled out the chair opposite her.

"My ankles are swollen."

"Get used to it," Emily said. "I hear that's just one of the things you'll have to deal with for the next few months."

"Given your fondness for fancy shoes, how do you intend to cope with that?" she asked Emily. "You and Boone are planning to give B.J. some brothers or sisters, aren't you?"

Emily sipped her tea, her expression surprisingly wistful. "You know, if you'd asked me that a year ago—about having babies, I mean—I'm not sure what I'd have said. I never really thought about being a mom. Now, with Boone and B.J. in my life, it's just about all I think about." She studied Gabi. "Is it wonderful? Being pregnant, I mean? Knowing that you're carrying a tiny little human being inside you?"

Gabi considered the question. "Even though I'm not even remotely in love with the baby's father the way you are with Boone, it is amazing. Sometimes I just lie in bed at night with my hand on my tummy, waiting for the baby to move around. I can't help wondering if it's going to be a boy or a girl, what the baby will look like. I want to count the little fingers and toes."

Even as she spoke, she recognized the yearning note in her voice. "I'm so messed up about this, Em. I don't know what's right anymore."

Her sister smiled at her. "Yes, you do. Keeping this

baby is the right thing for you. It's in your voice. I can hear it. We all can."

"But I don't want to be selfish."

"You will give this baby a loving, supportive family. You'll be an incredible mom. There's not a doubt in my mind about that."

"How can you say that after all the years when I was totally absorbed by work, just like Dad?"

"Because you, of all people, know what it's like to have a workaholic parent," Emily said simply. "You won't be that person. I know that as well as I know anything."

Her sister's vote of confidence brought tears to her eyes. "Thanks for saying that."

"I said it because I believe it. Now, tell me what you've been up to today."

Gabi filled her in on her meeting with Meg Waverly and the planned visit to the wind-chime artist. "I'm really excited," she admitted. "Even though the sane, rational side of me says this whole thing is crazy, it feels amazingly right."

"Then go for it," Emily told her.

"How about you? Are you anxious to get back to Los Angeles?"

"Not so much to Los Angeles," she admitted. "But I love the work I'm doing for the foundation. We have two safe houses being remodeled right now, and we should be closing on three more properties in the next few weeks. Knowing that I'm helping to create places where these women and their kids can be safe and get back on their feet is incredibly rewarding."

"You look so happy," Gabi said. "I don't think I've ever seen you look happier, in fact. While some of that's obviously Boone's doing, the job is making a difference, too."

"I'm more than just happy," Emily replied. "I am so grateful that Boone understood how I felt about this and decided to open a restaurant on the West Coast, so we can be together."

"Any thoughts about making this your home base?" she asked.

Emily made a face. "How could I not consider it? This has been home for Boone his whole life. The headquarters for his restaurants is here. And, as he likes to remind me whenever he thinks I'm feeling particularly receptive, I have family here, and there are people around who might be in need of the kind of work I enjoy doing."

"Valid points," Gabi said.

"True," Emily agreed. "But I'm happy with things as they are. The West Coast suits me, and I think maybe Boone's coming around."

"Really?" Gabi asked doubtfully.

"Well, I hope he is," Emily amended. She gave Gabi a penetrating look. "Any particular reason you're asking this now?"

"To be honest, I'm thinking of sticking around here after the baby's born. It would be great to have you and Samantha both close by."

"Samantha? I don't see it," Emily said. "She's determined to stay in New York, even though it seems to me she's getting more and more frustrated by the lack of acting jobs coming her way."

"But you're not considering Grandmother's cleverness," Gabi said, grinning. "You know perfectly well she has something in mind for Samantha, or should I say *someone?*"

Emily laughed. "Not a doubt about that, now that you mention it. So, I suppose anything's possible. It would be awfully nice to have us all settled in one place, wouldn't it? Every time the three of us have been together, it reminds me of how close we once were. But thanks to flying, I'm not really that far away. Look how often I've been able to get back here. We'd have lots of time together, even if Boone and I stay in California."

"Not quite the same," Gabi said, though she tried to hide her disappointment. "Will you be away long this time?"

"A few weeks," Emily responded. "Now that the wedding date's been moved, I want to pick out some bridesmaid dresses for you and Samantha and bring them back here for you to try. Plus Grandmother gets anxious if I don't go over all the wedding details in person, even though we know she's perfectly capable of making all the right decisions."

"But it is *your* wedding," Gabi reminded her. "And you tend to be a bit of a control freak. I don't blame her a bit."

"Well, at least now she can drive Dad crazy over the budget. I think she's going to get a huge kick out of spending his money. A couple of weeks ago, she was grumbling about the cost of the flowers. Now she's considering doubling the order."

Gabi chuckled. "Go, Cora Jane!"

Emily laughed. "I know. I can hardly wait till Dad gets a look at that bill, and it's only the tip of the iceberg. One minute she was talking about baking the cake herself. Now she's wondering if we shouldn't hire some

Hollywood bakery she heard mentioned on *Entertainment Tonight*. She doesn't want any of the guests coming from L.A. to think we're a bunch of small-town hicks. Her words, not mine."

"How big is this guest list?" Gabi asked. "I thought you were just thinking family and a few friends."

"I was, but it started getting bigger and bigger. Grandmother doesn't want to hurt anyone's feelings. I think if she keeps this up, Boone's going to start pushing for an elopement, though I honestly don't think he'd ever deny Cora Jane anything she wants. I sometimes think the only reason he's marrying me is to be able to claim her as a relative."

"Everyone should have someone like Cora Jane in their lives," Gabi agreed.

"Which is exactly why you shouldn't even consider denying your baby that chance," Emily said, then held up a hand to prevent the not-fair protest on the tip of Gabi's tongue. "I'm just saying."

"Message received," Gabi assured her. "Now about those bridesmaid dresses."

"I promise you won't look ridiculous," Emily said. "This will be classy and elegant all the way."

"And Boone honestly didn't object to waiting till after I have the baby?"

"Actually, I think he was relieved. Things are heating up with the new restaurant. He wants to open by late spring. By delaying the wedding until later in the summer, he won't have to feel guilty if he can't get back here quite as much to help with the planning. This could be his last trip until after the opening."

"And you?"

"I'll be back with those dress samples before you

know it. I expect to see your wind chimes on display in Meg's shop by then."

"I think that might be an unrealistic stretch," Gabi said, then glanced at her watch. "And I'd better head over to the Seaside Café to meet her now. It's almost two."

"You're meeting at a café?" Emily said, her amusement plain.

Gabi merely grinned. "I'll be having dessert while she has lunch. These days I never miss an opportunity for more food."

"Which is definitely going to make the fittings for the bridesmaid dresses interesting," Emily noted.

"Yeah, you might not want to bother with fitting mine till after the baby comes. Anything else will be an exercise in futility."

"I'll keep that in mind. We'll focus on the style and color for now, and I'll have a seamstress on call right up until my wedding day."

Gabi nodded. "Definitely a wise plan. *My* plan is to lose every ounce of baby weight before I walk down the aisle, but the way I hear it, that is probably a little too optimistic."

"Samantha can probably help with that," Emily suggested. "The woman's a fanatic about exercise and diet. She's terrified if she picks up an ounce, the camera will add ten pounds."

"That is what they say," Gabi reminded her.

"But seriously, how often is she in front of a camera these days?" Emily asked, then winced. "Please don't tell her I said that. I know she's having a rough time of it. I don't want to make it worse."

Gabi gave her a penetrating look. "Are you sure you're not taking a tiny bit of satisfaction in her struggles?"

Emily looked taken aback by the question. "Do you really think I'm that shallow?"

"Not shallow, but you've always had this competitive thing going with her. I've never understood it."

"To be honest, neither have I," Emily admitted. "When I think back, I can't even pinpoint when it started."

"Maybe you ought to figure it out, because even this hint that you're taking pleasure in her current situation isn't very attractive. We're sisters, Emily. It shouldn't be this way, not between any of us."

"I know," Emily said contritely. "I'll work on it. I promise. I know it's ridiculous and petty."

"And mean," Gabi added.

"Okay, mean, too. Cora Jane would tan my hide if she'd ever heard me so much as hint that I was happy about Samantha's failures."

"Maybe even more important than stopping it would be figuring out why you feel that way in the first place," Gabi suggested.

"Any ideas?" Emily asked. "Because I'm at a loss. It seems as if it was always there between us."

"Not on Samantha's part," Gabi reminded her. "It's all on you, Em. And for the life of me, I can't figure out what she ever did to deserve it."

"Neither can I," Emily said miserably.

"But you'll work on fixing it?" Gabi pushed.

"Yes, Mother Hen."

Gabi gave a nod of satisfaction. "All I can ask. Now run along before Boone starts fretting about missing your flight. I'll get the check."

"Love you," Emily said, bending down to give her a hug. "Even if you did give my conscience a nasty poke."

"I live to make you a better person," Gabi told her. "Love you."

She watched as Emily left, her step a little slower, as if she suddenly had a lot on her mind. Gabi hoped she did, because it was way past time for this silliness between her and Samantha to stop. It was the sort of thing that could crop up at the most inopportune time, and she didn't want any sort of spat to spoil Emily's wedding.

Thirteen

Jimmy paced anxiously as Wade read his essay for the scholarship application. Every couple of minutes he'd pause in front of Wade, watch him intently, then take up pacing again.

"I'd be able to read faster if you'd sit down," Wade told him, amused. "Or at least stop jiggling the change in your pocket. You're messing with my concentration."

"If what I wrote was any good, wouldn't you be able to focus better?" Jimmy asked worriedly. "It's because it's awful that you're so easily distracted."

Wade studied the teenager and realized he really was panicked over this. "Sit," he ordered.

Jimmy dragged over a chair and straddled it.

"Now, I want you to listen to me very closely," Wade said. "I'm not finished yet, but this is not awful. Far from it."

Jimmy's eyes brightened. "Seriously?"

"Seriously," Wade assured him. "Now give me ten quiet minutes and I'll tell you exactly what I think. If you don't think you can sit still that long, get Tommy to put you to work. I'll find you as soon as I'm done."

Jimmy shook his head. "I'll wait."

"Quietly," Wade reiterated.

"As a mouse," Jimmy said, grinning. "That's what my mom used to say before church, that we had to be quiet as a mouse."

Wade laughed, remembering similar admonishments. "Okay, then. Let's give it a try."

He finished reading, though he was fully aware that Jimmy was still watching him intently, still looking half-afraid that Wade was about to rip his heart out with his criticism.

Before he could speak, Jimmy piped up. "English was never my best subject, so it probably needs some work on the grammar and stuff. Just tell me where I screwed up, okay?"

Wade held up a hand to silence him. "Jimmy, it's a wonderful essay. I promise you it's going to knock their socks off. You told them exactly why you want this, how hard you're willing to work, what you think will motivate you to be the best student ever."

"It's not dorky?" he asked worriedly.

"No," Wade assured him. "It's honest and sensitive, especially the part about how hard your dad has always worked and the lessons that's taught you about being responsible and being a good man."

"My dad's a great guy," he said simply.

"And that comes across loud and clear," Wade said. "And you know what else is loud and clear? What a fine young man you are."

Color rose in Jimmy's cheeks. "I just don't want it to sound dumb."

"There is nothing dumb about it. Want to go over to Castle's for lunch and let Gabi read it? She has a lot of experience with writing things to make a point. I'm pretty sure that's what press releases are all about, and the way I hear it, she writes exceptional press releases."

"Do you think she'd mind taking a look at it?" Jimmy asked hesitantly. "It's enough that she got me this chance. I don't want to be a pest."

"I think she would love to see the essay," Wade told him. "Let me make sure she's over there."

But when he called Castle's, Cora Jane told him that Gabi was meeting with the owner of the store where she'd found the wind chime and then going by to see the artist who'd created the wind chime she'd purchased.

"Tell you what," she said. "Why don't you bring Jimmy by the house for dinner this evening? I know Gabriella will want to see this essay of his, and she's bound to have news about this latest project of hers. I imagine you're anxious to hear all about that."

"Sounds great," Wade said eagerly. "What time?"

"Six-thirty? Jerry's coming by to put some fish on the grill. He stopped by the docks earlier. He told me today's catch was especially good, so he bought extra for tonight."

"Hold on a sec. Let me check with Jimmy." Wade told the teenager the plan, and Jimmy immediately agreed. "We'll be there, Cora Jane. Anything I can bring?"

"Just yourselves."

When he'd disconnected the call, he caught Jimmy grinning. "What?" Wade said.

"This worked out real good for you, didn't it? Thanks to me, you got yourself a date."

Wade frowned at him. "I don't think that's exactly true. Gabi doesn't even know about this, so if I have a date with anybody, it's with you and Cora Jane."

Jimmy immediately looked worried. "You think Gabi might not show up?"

Wade thought about Cora Jane's determination to play matchmaker. "Oh, I imagine she'll be there. Cora Jane will see to that," he conceded.

"Then in a way you owe me," Jimmy said.

"Do you really want to go there?" Wade asked, not even trying to hide his amusement. "Because without me, you wouldn't have met Gabi. Without her, you wouldn't have met her dad. And this whole scholarship thing…" He gave him a long look. "Well, I think you can see where I'm going with this."

Jimmy's impudent expression faltered only slightly at the reality check. "Still, I'm pretty sure I'm your ticket to getting tight with Gabi. She likes me. I don't scare her the way you do."

Wade frowned. "Scare her? You think I scare her?"

"That's the way it looks to me," Jimmy said with surprising confidence. "You get all intense and lovesick when she's around. That's got to be scary for a woman who's pregnant with some other guy's kid. I'm thinking you need to chill."

As much as he wanted to dismiss what Jimmy was saying, it struck Wade that the teen was displaying an astonishing degree of wisdom and insight. And unlike Louise's interference, he found Jimmy's meddling worth considering.

"Maybe you're going into the wrong field," he told him, his tone wry. "Maybe you should be writing an advice column."

"Nah. I think I'll stick to the whole biomedical thing," Jimmy replied, clearly taking Wade seriously. "Women and relationships are way too complicated."

"But you certainly seem to have Gabi pegged."

A grin split Jimmy's face. "Lucky guess. I was pretty much just trying to yank your chain."

Wade shook his head. "I'll pick you up at six-fifteen," he said. "Try to leave the smart-aleck attitude at home."

"What can I say? It's just who I am," Jimmy responded unrepentantly.

And that, Wade thought, might be annoying at times, but it was part of the charm that was going to make this exceptional young man a huge success someday.

Gabi left the Seaside Café convinced that her instincts about having met a new friend were correct. The ninety minutes she and Meg had spent getting acquainted had revealed that they had similar outlooks on life. They'd both come late to the concept of a more laid-back lifestyle.

While she didn't have a bad marriage in common with Meg, she did have the whole experience with Paul to color her view of relationships.

After listening to Meg talk about her ex-husband for several minutes, she regarded her with surprise. "You don't sound bitter."

Meg laughed. "That's because I have three years of recovery under my belt. If you'd met me right after I moved here, believe me, you would have heard a much different version. The vitriol poured out of me if anyone even mentioned my husband."

"What changed? Just time smoothing away the rough edges from the divorce?"

"That and the realization that my daughter needs her dad in her life. She doesn't need me bad-mouthing him at every turn. Not that the transition has been entirely about her. I've actually reached the point now where I'm glad about what happened. It made me reevaluate my life." She gave Gabi a penetrating look. "I think that's what you're doing, too. Maybe you'll thank your guy some day for turning your life around."

"Not quite there yet," Gabi said. "I'm still thinking he turned my world upside down. If I do find a new direction, maybe then that will change."

Meg nodded. "Then let's go and see Sally. She could be the key to unlocking this bright new future for you."

They drove to a small property hidden away in a thick grove of pine trees. The first thing Gabi noticed about the very ordinary house were the dozens of wind chimes hanging from the porch ceiling.

"Oh, my," she whispered as a breeze stirred and set off a musical symphony of sound.

Meg grinned. "It's something, isn't it? I feel good every time I step out of my car when I come out here. I've nicknamed it Wind Chime Point. We'll find Sally in her workshop, I imagine. Even though she knew we were coming, she probably lost track of time."

Reluctant to walk away from the sunlit rainbows of color and rippling sound on the porch, Gabi followed Meg around the side of the house. As at Wade's, the garage had been transformed into a studio. This one, though, was filled with light from huge, newly installed windows. Tables held panes of glass in every color imaginable. A very petite woman was standing at one of those tables with a cutting tool, creating rectangular strips from rose-colored glass. The music of a string quartet filled the room. Gabi immediately felt as if she'd walked into an atmosphere of buoyant optimism.

Meg walked around the table until she was in Sally's

line of vision. Even then, the artist gave a start. A grin spread across her face as she took off her goggles and gloves, then punched a button that quieted the music.

"Is it that late already?" she asked guiltily. "I promised myself I'd go inside and make sweet tea before you got here."

Meg laughed. "No need. We've just had a late lunch. Sally, this is Gabi Castle, the woman I told you about. Gabi, this is Sally Foster."

"I fell in love with your work the minute I saw it," Gabi told her. "I've always loved wind chimes, but yours are extraordinary. They're truly works of art."

A smile spread across Sally's face. "Did you tell her that flattery is a surefire way to win me over?" she asked Meg.

"I didn't need to say a word," Meg assured her. "She's sincere. She said the same thing to Lily when she came into the store, and then to me earlier this morning. The surprise is that she wants to give this a try herself."

Sally looked Gabi over as if trying to assess why anyone would suddenly make such a seemingly out-of-the-blue decision. "Any particular reason?"

"Lots of them," Gabi said.

Sally lifted a brow. "You do know nothing stays secret in this area for long. I imagine I could fill you in on your story. Pregnant. Dumped. Fired." She grinned. "How am I doing?"

Gabi laughed. "Right on every count."

"Don't feel bad. Everyone knew my story within days of my moving here, too. Took me a while to get used to that, but now I think it's part of the charm."

"To be honest, so do I," Gabi said, sensing another friend in the making.

"Why wind chimes?" Sally asked.

"Here's the very short version," Gabi said. "When I came over to stay with my grandmother a couple of weeks ago, the sound of the wind chimes on her porch took me back to childhood, when life was a whole lot simpler. They filled me with that sense of innocence and possibilities. When I saw yours, something just came together for me. I thought maybe if I could learn to create wind chimes, I could also create those same feelings."

Sally glanced at Meg, and a look of understanding and commiseration passed between them.

"That's a lot to expect from a wind chime," Sally said.

"Probably, but it is a dramatic change from my high-stress career, and I definitely need that," Gabi said.

"Been there," Sally said. "So has Meg, as I'm sure she told you since she can't resist talking about the transformation of her life since she moved to Sand Castle Bay."

"I don't spill my guts to total strangers," Meg replied with feigned indignation. "Just to kindred spirits."

"Well, it's evident to me that Gabi is a kindred spirit," Sally said.

"I think so, too," Meg agreed.

Sally turned back to Gabi. "So, you're here because you want me to give you lessons?"

"If you offer classes, that's fine, or I'll pay you for individual instruction. Whatever works for you. I'm happy to just help out and observe for a while, serve sort of an apprenticeship, if that's better."

Sally studied her thoughtfully. "I don't give classes," she began. "Don't have the patience for it."

Gabi's spirits sank.

"Oh, don't look so glum," Sally said. "If you're serious about helping out and observing, I imagine I can teach you a few things along the way. The goal, of course, will be to help you find your own style. It won't benefit either of us if you just try to mimic mine."

"Understood," Gabi said eagerly. "Believe me, I understand all about intellectual property. Where I worked before, people were very protective of their work. Obviously it was a very different world, but the principles are the same."

"And you don't mind doing some of the drudgery around here? You won't freak out if you're not producing great wind chimes by the end of the week? You strike me as the impatient type."

Gabi wasn't surprised that this virtual stranger had pegged her so well. "Yeah, well, that was the old me. I'm trying to become more mellow. I'll deal with your timetable. I just want to learn this the right way, not necessarily the fastest way."

Sally nodded. "Tomorrow," she said then. "Be here at ten."

"I could make it earlier," Gabi offered at once.

"I'm a night owl. Ten is good enough," Sally said. "Bring coffee. Mine is terrible, and you'll be saving me a trip into town."

"Done," Gabi agreed at once. "Thank you so much." She turned to Meg, who looked as pleased as Cora Jane when she saw a scheme coming together. "You, too. I can't tell you how much I appreciate this."

"We'll see how happy you are after Sally has worked you to death for a few days," Meg replied, but she was smiling when she said it. "Seriously, though, you couldn't be in better hands." She gave the artist a hug.

"Thanks. I'll speak to you soon. From the looks of the wind chimes on the porch, you'll have that next order ready for me any day now."

"Tomorrow or the next day," Sally promised. "I'll have my new helper here drop them off."

As she and Meg returned to the car, Gabi was filled with exhilaration. The happy tinkling of the wind chimes on the porch seemed to echo her mood.

"This is such a cheerful place," she murmured, though she felt a little silly uttering the words.

Meg merely smiled. "It is. If I were carrying a baby again, I'd want to be in a place just like this. I'm a big believer that, even in the womb, babies respond to their surroundings."

Gabi had never imagined herself buying into such a view, but now? She was pretty sure Meg had it exactly right. She couldn't have found a better place than Meg's so-called Wind Chime Point for her baby—or her—to spend the next few months.

It was after six by the time Gabi got back to Cora Jane's. All she wanted to do was put her feet up and sip on a tall glass of ice water, but there was a flurry of activity in the kitchen, with not only Cora Jane and Samantha there, but Jerry, too.

"Are we having a party?" she asked, fixing her water and dodging the fast-moving people in the room.

"Something like that," Cora Jane said. "Jimmy and Wade will be here shortly for dinner."

Excitement at the prospect of filling Wade in on her afternoon warred with sheer exhaustion. At her silence, Cora Jane took a closer look at her.

"You look plum worn out," she said. "Go take a catnap until they get here. Or at least splash a little water on your face and freshen up."

"Putting my feet up for a few minutes would feel wonderful," she admitted. "But don't let me sleep through dinner, okay?"

Samantha gave her a wry look. "As if Grandmother would ever miss a chance to throw you and Wade together." She waved her off. "Go. I'll come for you when he gets here."

Gabi headed toward her room but never made it past the living room. The sofa looked too inviting. She dropped down on the comfortable cushions, put her feet up and sighed. Heavenly!

The next thing she knew, she felt the light brush of lips across her forehead. Given the way her body instantly stirred at the touch, she doubted it was her grandmother or Samantha awakening her.

"Hey, Sleeping Beauty, you ready for dinner?" Wade asked softly.

She opened her eyes to see his gaze on her, a smile on his lips. "Hi," she murmured sleepily. "How long have I been asleep?"

"Long enough, according to Cora Jane. She says if you don't get up now, you'll never get to sleep tonight."

"When did you get here?"

"A half hour ago."

"You weren't in here watching me sleep, were you? That would be embarrassing. I think I might snore."

Wade laughed. "Even though I came in here just a minute ago, I heard no evidence of snoring. If that's really worrying you, maybe one of these nights you'll let me crawl into your bed and we can find out for sure."

Though she'd been half-asleep for most of their conversation up to now, she came fully awake at that. "Excuse me?"

"Well, that definitely got your blood pumping," he teased. "Rather than repeating it, though, I'll just let you ponder the idea for a while."

He held out a hand. "Dinner's on the table. The fish looks incredible. In fact, the whole meal does. I don't know how Cora Jane and Jerry did it after being at the restaurant from the crack of dawn until midafternoon."

"Grandmother loves being in the kitchen," Gabi said, taking his hand and letting him pull her up.

She thought maybe he pulled extra hard, because she stumbled straight into him. He caught her and held her close for just a second, long enough to add emphasis to his earlier taunt about spending the night with her one of these days.

She regarded him suspiciously. "What are you up to, Wade?"

"Same thing I've been up to for a while now," he said, not even trying to evade her direct look. "Trying to get your attention." He shook his head and lamented, "Jimmy says I'm going about it all wrong, though."

Gabi couldn't help laughing at the thought of the teenager giving Wade advice on handling a woman. "Isn't he a little young to be your romance coach?"

Wade gave her a rueful look. "You'd think so, wouldn't you, but he seems to have an amazing aptitude for that kind of thing."

"I can't imagine it. So, is he the one who taught you that maneuver you just pulled, the one that had me landing in your arms?"

"Absolutely not," Wade said, his expression innocent. "That was purely an accident."

"Not buying it," she told him. "I think you're sneaky. And if it wasn't Jimmy who planted that idea in your head, it was Cora Jane."

"I am definitely not taking advice from your grandmother," he said indignantly. "I may not be above courting her as an ally, but anything that happens between you and me will be all about us. She is not giving me dating tips. That would be just plain weird."

Gabi laughed as his masculine pride kicked in with a vengeance. "Okay, okay, these are your moves."

He glanced at her curiously. "Any of them working?"

"I didn't slug you just now, did I? And I haven't gone out of my way lately to avoid your company. In fact, when Grandmother told me you and Jimmy were stopping by for dinner, I was actually looking forward to filling you in on my day. I don't know what your standards are, but that could all be considered progress, I think."

"Absolutely," he agreed, clearly pleased.

Gabi noticed that several interested looks were directed their way as they joined the others at the kitchen table. Jimmy had a smirk on his face. Cora Jane's expression was smug. And even Samantha looked a little like the cat that swallowed the canary. Clearly the man had more than one ally in the room.

Jerry, however, regarded the two of them with sympathy, as if he understood the pressure they were under from too much unsolicited interference. He gave Gabi a reassuring wink.

Then, for a time after Grandmother said grace, the conversation quieted down as they passed bowls of corn pudding, salad and grilled vegetables to go with the perfectly blackened fish that Jerry had made with his personal blend of Cajun spices.

"Better than Boone's Harbor," Gabi declared when she'd tasted her first spicy bite. "Jerry, this is fantastic!"

"The man has a gift," Cora Jane declared.

"Unfortunately, she refuses to let me put this on the menu at Castle's," Jerry said with feigned dismay. "I've tried for years to talk her into it."

"And I've told him that grilled or fried fish is what our customers expect. Besides, now that Boone has a more Cajun menu at his restaurant, I see no reason to compete with that," Cora Jane said. "Seems to me restaurants should try to support one another, keep things different so we can grow our own loyal customer bases, rather than trying to drive one another out of business."

"I can't argue with that," Jerry admitted, regarding Cora Jane fondly. "And look how long that strategy has worked for Castle's. Who am I to try to force change on a set-in-her-ways woman with a mile-wide stubborn streak?"

"Stubborn? Set in my ways?" Cora Jane said indignantly. "This from the man who throws a fit if he can't find his favorite soup kettle?"

"I brought that cast-iron soup kettle from Louisiana," Jerry retorted. "It's been properly seasoned, the same as that skillet I brought with me. I'll bet you can't find me any chef worth his salt who doesn't have his favorite tools. Haven't you noticed on those TV chef competitions, they all show up with their own sets of fancy knives?"

"So you're calling yourself a chef now?" Cora Jane taunted as everyone at the table sat back to watch the sparks fly. "Weren't you just a plain old cook when you walked in the door to apply for a job all those years ago?"

"I was a chef then," Jerry said, "but you'd advertised for a cook. I didn't want to sound too fancy. Besides, I took one look at you and knew I'd do just about anything to get that job. I'd have called myself a busboy if that would have kept me around you."

The color rose in Cora Jane's cheeks at that. "I was a married woman!" she protested.

"And I didn't step one inch across a single line until after Caleb was gone and you'd had time to mourn," he reminded her. "I had too much respect for him and for you."

Gabi watched her grandmother's expression soften as she let Jerry take her hand.

"I'm grateful for that," Cora Jane said quietly.

Gabi noticed that Jimmy was studying the older couple with a thoroughly bemused expression.

"Are you two, like, dating or something?" he asked.

"It's the *or something* I want to know about," Samantha chimed in.

Jerry guffawed at the impudent questions, but Cora Jane frowned at both of them. To Samantha, she said, "Did I not have any influence at all over your manners?"

"Some," Samantha said, not looking the faintest bit guilty. "But you also taught me that if I wanted to know something, the best way to find out was to ask."

"I kinda figured the same thing," Jimmy said. He glanced warily at Wade. "Was I being rude?"

Before Wade could reply, Jerry jumped in. "I personally admire a man who's direct," he told Jimmy. "You never have to worry about what he's hiding. And, to answer your question, I am courting Cora Jane. One of these days I figure she'll give up and marry me."

Jimmy's eyes widened, but all he said was, "Cool!"

Gabi thought it was pretty cool, too. Cora Jane, however, looked fairly flustered by the very public declaration of a strategy that had been plain to her granddaughters for months now. It was about time Cora Jane had the tables turned on her. She wasn't the only one in the family, after all, capable of a little scheming.

Fourteen

After dinner, Jimmy volunteered to help clean up the kitchen, while Gabi took his essay into the living room to read. Wade hung out in the kitchen to lend a hand, as well.

Just as earlier, there was no mistaking Jimmy's nervousness as he awaited Gabi's verdict.

When she came back into the kitchen in just minutes with a smile on her face, not only Jimmy but Wade breathed a sigh of relief.

"It's okay?" Jimmy asked.

"It is so much better than okay," she said, giving him a hug. "You nailed it!"

"That's what Wade said, but he says you're some kind of expert when it comes to writing." He studied her face intently. "And you really didn't find any mistakes or anything?"

"Not a one," she assured him. "Do you have the application ready to go?"

Jimmy nodded. "This was the last thing. I can send it over to your dad tomorrow, if you think the essay's okay."

"Send it," Gabi told him, picking up a dish towel to help out with drying the last of the dishes.

Cora Jane might have professional-grade dishwashers installed at the restaurant, but here at home she insisted on doing the task the old-fashioned way. Over the years Gabi and her sisters had grumbled about it, but amazingly in retrospect she realized how wonderful the postdinner camaraderie had been. It felt that way tonight, too.

As soon as they'd finished, the teen looked at Wade. "I figure you're gonna be here awhile. Is it okay if I take off? I was gonna walk over to a friend's house."

"And you'll have a way to get home from there?" Wade asked him.

"He'll take me."

"Any curfew at home?"

"Come on, man. I'm almost nineteen," Jimmy retorted, looking at Wade as if he'd just arrived from some faraway planet.

"Hey, you're still living at home," Wade reminded him. "I imagine there are rules."

"Okay, sure, there are some," the teen admitted. "Clean up my room, help around the house, stuff like that, but I don't have a curfew." He turned to Gabi. "How about you? Does Cora Jane have you on a strict curfew? I wouldn't want old Wade here to get you in any trouble."

Wade chuckled. "Okay, point taken. Get out of here."

As Jimmy took off, whistling happily, Wade shook his head. "He's something."

"He is, indeed," Gabi agreed. "And you're good with him. He obviously looks up to you."

"Not just me," Wade said. "His parents have taught him to respect his elders, period. You saw him tonight. He doesn't hesitate to speak his mind, but he's quick to worry that he might have overstepped. He'll figure out how to make his way in the world."

"I think so, too," Gabi said. "Now, do you need to get home or do you have time for me to tell you about my day?"

"I always have time to listen to you," he told her. "Seems to me as if everyone else has taken off for bed, so we have the living room to ourselves. Or it might be nice enough to sit outside."

"Let me grab a sweater and let's walk down to the pier. Sitting on the porch would be nice, but I guarantee Samantha's window will be open and she'll listen to every word we say."

"Because that's what you would do?" he asked, his expression amused.

"That's what she *and* I did to Emily and Boone," she corrected. "I doubt Samantha has suddenly mended her ways."

Wade waited for her to get a sweater from upstairs, then walked with her across the lawn to the wooden pier. The grass was damp from an earlier shower, but now the full moon was out, casting a silvery steam of light across the water. Gabi could hear the chug of a boat's motor in the distance. Otherwise, it was incredibly peaceful with no nearby traffic to break the silence.

Though the air was pleasant, an occasional breeze stirred. Wade must have noticed her shivering, because he shifted to sit closer, then put his arm around her. She leaned into his side.

"If you're too chilly, we can go back in," he offered.

"I'm good," she said. "Your body's like a furnace."

"High metabolism," he claimed. "Tell me about your day."

Gabi described her meeting with Meg Waverly.

"Do you know her?" she asked.

"We've met. She carried a few of my carvings in her store. She's good people, as folks around here would say, no question about it."

"I think we're going to be friends," Gabi said, not even trying to keep a sense of wonder from her voice.

"Why do you sound so surprised about that?"

"Okay, I know this is going to sound pathetic, but I've never taken the time to have friends, not good ones, anyway. Emily, Samantha and I are close, and that seemed like enough. Friendships take time and effort. I never wanted that connection badly enough to take time away from work."

"But there must have been people you saw from time to time, had dinner with or lunch," he said.

"I had work colleagues," she said. "Sure, we went to lunch, even to dinner, but the talk was all about work. It's not as if we really knew one another. Not a one of them has called to check in since I left the company. I imagine there were even one or two who gloated about my downfall and my abrupt departure."

"What about neighbors? Had you lived in the same place for a long time?"

"Since college," she said. "It was a town house in a small development with a pool, tennis courts and a few other amenities. It's biggest attraction for me, though, was that it was close to my office."

Wade regarded her with disbelief. "You didn't make friends with people there?"

She merely shrugged. "They had gatherings from time to time. I never went. I barely knew my immediate neighbors by sight, much less the other people in the community." She studied his expression. "You're a people person, aren't you? You can't imagine living like that."

"You're right. I mean, I'm shut up in my workshop alone for hours on end, but I've always made time for friends."

"What do you do?" she asked, a note of envy in her voice.

"Go to ball games, have a few beers, play the occasional game of poker. I needed that social contact, especially after I lost Kayla. And there are always Louise and Zack and the kids to fill in the empty spaces in my life."

"That sounds wonderful," she said.

"If you kept people at arm's length, how did that guy fit in?" he asked.

She gave him a wry look. "He wasn't very demanding," she admitted. "And he was as caught up in work as I was. We understood each other."

"So it wasn't really a relationship," he said, sounding relieved. "It was a convenience."

Gabi frowned at the characterization. "That's not true."

He merely lifted a brow. "How so? Did you go out on double dates? Hang out with friends? Share the intimate details of your life the way you and I are doing right now?"

Tears stung Gabi's eyes at his probing questions. He was right. Whatever she and Paul had shared, it hadn't been a relationship. The bond had never been as intimate as the one she was forming with Wade, even after so little time.

"I'm sorry," he apologized before she could respond.

"I shouldn't be picking away at something that obviously worked for you."

"No, you're right," she said with a sniff. "What we had was sex now and then, when it suited us. It *was* a convenience, a way to feel as if we each had a connection to another person. God, that's even more pathetic than I realized. Maybe I'm incapable of having any more than that."

"I don't believe that for a minute," he told her. "You and I already have a lot more. We're talking right now, getting to know each other, becoming friends." A smile formed as he looked into her eyes. "And all without the benefit of sex, I'm sad to say."

She laughed. "And it has to stay that way, at least for now," she said, a chiding note in her voice.

"I was afraid you might say that."

She fell silent. A minute later, she dared to rest her head on his shoulder. It was the first time she'd made any sort of move in his direction on her own and it felt right. Surprisingly right.

"This is nice," she said quietly.

"This is definitely nice," he agreed.

For now, though, she knew it would have to be enough. She wondered if Wade would be able to live with that. Or if she would.

As she lay in bed in the morning, thinking about the night before, Gabi tried to recall a single day in her life when she'd spent so much time with a man just talking about anything and everything. Wade was right. They were becoming friends. Imagine that! She'd been in Sand Castle Bay just a couple of weeks, and she already had two budding friendships she thought she might come to count on. A third, if she put Sally in the mix.

Glancing at the clock, she realized she needed to get a move on, if she expected to pick up coffee and be on time for her first day with the artist.

An hour later, she was showered, dressed and had a box of doughnuts and two large coffees beside her as she drove to Sally's studio.

Once again, she paused in the yard to listen to the wind chimes and was charmed by them. She was actually laughing out loud at the sheer joy of that sound as she walked into the studio.

"There you are," Sally said, giving her a bright smile. She sniffed the air. "And if that box has doughnuts in it, you've just gone from part-time helper and wannabe artist to my new favorite person."

Gabi laughed. "These doughnuts do seem to have magical powers," she said, thinking of how Wade had bought just a sliver of her affections with them.

"Of course, if you make a habit of this, I'll have to run an extra five miles every day. Since I consider running to be torture, you might want to stick to coffee from now on."

"I've been telling myself that treats like this are for the baby, but since I know that's a lie, I promise this won't become a habit." Gabi looked around the workshop, eager to get started. "Now, tell me what I can do."

"You can sit down for a minute and enjoy a doughnut and talk to me. I know you said you were looking for some dramatic change in your life, but what exactly was this high-stress job you left?"

Gabi described the public relations work she'd been doing for more than a dozen years. "I was on a fast track for a vice presidency, or at least that's what everyone believed."

"Yet they forced you out? Why?" Before Gabi could answer, Sally's eyes widened. "Not because you got pregnant?"

"That was it," Gabi confirmed.

"Couldn't you have sued the pants off them?"

"Probably not. I mean, technically they planned to hide me away, rather than firing me outright. I'm the one who negotiated the buyout. Even so, my dad, who's fairly influential in those circles, went to bat for me, and they offered me my old job back, but I just wanted out. I mean, why would I want to go on working for people who think like that?"

"Still, I hope they compensated you well."

"It was a decent severance package," Gabi acknowledged. "Which is why I can take my time before going back to work. I can experiment with things like this, find out if I actually have any raw, previously unidentified talent. If it turns out that I don't..." She shrugged. "No real loss. I think I'll still have learned something that will bring me personal satisfaction."

She gave Sally a worried look. "Does that make you want to reconsider? I suppose I don't sound terribly confident or dedicated."

"No, you sound like a woman who's had a tough time and is trying to get her feet back under her. I can relate. This wasn't always what I did. Oh, I'd loved art and I'd taken a few classes working with glass, but it was just a hobby."

"Really? What was your career?"

"I worked for a major brokerage company until the bottom fell out. A lot of my clients lost their savings. It wasn't necessarily my fault. Most of them didn't even blame me for it. But I blamed myself. I decided I needed to get away, do something in which the only person impacted by my decisions is me."

She grinned and confided, "I've never been happier, but if you talk to my family, they're all convinced I've had some kind of breakdown. For the first couple of years I was down here, they showed up on a regular basis to see if I'd snapped completely."

"I think that may be what my father's worried about," Gabi told her, totally identifying with her situation. "He's left me half a dozen messages about other jobs he's heard about since I turned down the one at my old company."

"Not even tempted?" Sally asked.

Gabi shook her head. "Not even a tiny bit."

Sally took her last sip of coffee, tossed the cup into a trash can, then washed her hands. "Pull up that stool. You can watch what I'm doing. I usually try to cut a lot of these pieces of glass in various shapes and colors at one time, just to get that out of the way. I don't want to turn this into some sort of assembly-line manufacturing situation, but I can speed up this part of the process. That gives me more time to create the central art for each piece."

"I think that's what struck me when I saw them," Gabi told her. "The design of each piece is so amazing. I can recognize your style, but they're not duplicates."

Sally nodded as she put on goggles and gloves, then handed a set to Gabi. She talked as she began to cut. "I want them to be unique as much as possible, though I've had more than one request from a customer to do the same design that they bought as a gift last year. I do insist, though, that the stores that carry the wind chimes never display more than one of a design at a time. I think it's important the people feel as if they're buying a piece of art, rather than something mass-produced."

"Do you make your own glass? The colors are incredible, especially when they catch the sun."

"I do make some. I have a supplier for some. There's an artist here who is known for hand-blown glass pieces. You'll have to meet him. His work is incredible."

"I'd love to," Gabi said.

"He works with me sometimes, gives me pieces that didn't quite work out for him but that I can cut and use. Sometimes, if I have an idea for something a little more old-fashioned, I'll go to him with my design and he comes up with the most amazing glass for me. Of course, those pieces tend to cost an arm and a leg, so I try not to go too crazy with them. Not enough customers are willing to spend the money, especially if they're worried that it'll shatter in a windstorm."

"That is a risk, isn't it?" Gabi said. "I imagine it's why a lot of people prefer the metal wind chimes."

"Definitely safer," Sally agreed. "Though for me the sound isn't as sweet. We do temper the glass so it will hold up in a good stiff breeze, but a hurricane? Not so much."

She glanced up at Gabi. "You know where I get my favorite glass? Salvage yards. Every now and again I go scouting around and find old stained-glass windows that have been discarded because panes are broken and can't be replaced or whatever. There's not a salvage yard for a hundred miles in any direction where they don't know me. The second a window comes in, they call me." She gestured toward a window frame on another table. "Last week's find. Take a look at that glass. I'm guessing it has to be at least a hundred years old."

Gabi studied the window, much of the glass shattered but enough left to make several amazing, unique wind chimes. "This is beautiful. I love the tiny bubbles in the glass and the slightly rippled surface. I'd give anything to own something made from this."

Sally beamed at her. "Then you will. I might not get to it right away, but I'll remember to let you have first chance at anything that comes from that. I love knowing my pieces are with someone who can really appreciate the beauty of the glass."

Amazingly, even as Sally talked, she made quick work of cutting the more ordinary glass, mostly into rectangles, but a few bits were cut into triangles, circles and even an occasional S-shaped squiggle. After she'd worked awhile, she glanced at Gabi.

"Ready to give it a try?"

"I'm not sure my hand is steady enough," Gabi said doubtfully after watching the confidence and speed with which Sally worked.

"Hey, there's a bin right there at the end of the counter with my mistakes in it," Sally said.

Gabi glanced over and, sure enough, there were pieces of broken glass that hadn't passed inspection. "Okay, but I don't want to waste your good glass. Let me work on something you've already discarded."

"Fair enough," Sally said, extracting a couple of larger pieces from the trash.

Following the artist's patient directions, Gabi scored the glass, then tried to break it cleanly. She eyed the results with frustration. "It's just smaller pieces that aren't very good."

Sally laughed. "Did you expect to master it on your first try?"

"I'd hoped," Gabi admitted, then gave her a rueful look. "Unrealistic, huh?"

"I'd say so." She regarded Gabi with a meaningful look. "This is the real test, though. If you have what it takes, you won't give up. You'll keep trying till you get it right. After all, I imagine your very first press release didn't go out as written."

"Actually it did," Gabi told her, then winced as she recalled the versions she'd never shown anyone. "Of course, that was after the twenty or so tries that no one ever saw."

Sally tapped the broken bits of glass. "Consider these version one."

Gabi chuckled. "Meaning I have a long way to go."

"Oh, hon, don't we all?"

After years of thinking of her life as a succession of triumphs, it was a little humbling to realize she was back at step one and that this path could be littered with failed attempts. At the same time, she liked the whisper of anticipation and determination that came with the hope that tomorrow would be better and the day after that better yet.

Even though Wade was fairly certain that Gabi would be tied up with her new artist friend most of the day, he found himself stopping at Castle's after the lunch crowd had gone. He was hoping for a piece of Cora Jane's pie and a few of her insights. Instead, he found Gabi sitting in a back booth by the kitchen with her feet propped up on the opposite seat and her eyes closed.

"Well, this is an unexpected bonus," he said, lifting her feet so he could slide past them. "How'd your day go?"

"Sally's great. She even gave me a lesson on cutting glass today." She made a face at that. "I was terrible."

"Don't you think you're being a little hard on yourself for a first attempt?"

"That's what she said. She also said I looked as if I might faint from hunger, so she kicked me out."

"Good for her," Wade said. "Have you eaten yet?"

She shook her head. "Jerry's making me a grilled fish sandwich now." A grin spread across her face. "With french fries and cole slaw."

"I thought the kitchen closed an hour ago," Wade said, amused.

"Hey, it pays to have known the chef forever and to have an in with the owner," she said. "And since you're aware that the kitchen has closed, what are you doing here?"

"Cora Jane usually has pie left," he said simply.

"You mean she usually saves you a piece," Gabi retorted. "She must really like you."

"What can I say? I'm a charming guy."

Jerry came out of the kitchen just then with her lunch. He lifted a brow when he saw Wade. "Do I need to fix you a sandwich, too, or are you just here for the pie?"

"Pie's good," Wade told him. "What's left?"

"Apple and cherry."

"Cherry, with ice cream."

"Of course," Jerry said. "Something to drink?"

"Water will do. How come you're waiting tables?" Wade asked. "Where's Cora Jane?"

"When you turned up, she got it in her head she should stay out of the way," Jerry said, his expression filled with tolerant amusement. "However, I'm to let her know what's happening out here. I'm almost surprised she didn't ask me to snap a couple of pictures with my cell phone—discreetly, of course."

Gabi gave him a dismayed look. "Have you no shame, Jeremiah? Has Cora Jane reduced you to spying for her?"

Jerry grinned. "Hey, I thought I was doing the two of you a favor by keeping her out of your hair. If you'd prefer, I can send her right on out here to ask a few probing, uncomfortable questions."

Gabi immediately held up a hand. "Please, don't. I apologize."

"And well you should, young lady. Haven't I always had your back?"

"You have," she agreed at once. "Bless you."

"Okay, then," he said. "I'll be back with that pie."

After he'd gone, Gabi turned to Wade. "How's your work going?"

"I should be finished with this latest job for Tommy by the end of the week. He has another one starting next week."

She frowned at the response. "That's not the work I was asking about. Shouldn't you be working on your carvings?"

"I put in some time on them when I can," he said, suddenly on the defensive.

"But, Wade, they're so amazing. You need to focus on those."

"I seem to be spending a lot of my spare time on other interests these days," he said, regarding her pointedly. "I consider it a fair trade-off."

"Me, you mean? Wade, I don't want to keep you from the work you're meant to be doing."

"And I don't want to miss out on the chance to spend time with you," he countered with a touch of defiance. "Not when I have no idea how long you intend to stick around." He gave her a questioning look. "Any thoughts on that?"

"I'll be here at least until the baby's born," she responded. "After that, I guess I'll see how things are going with the whole wind-chime thing."

"Any chance I'd be able to influence your decision?" he asked, holding her gaze.

She looked taken aback by the direct question. At first he thought she might not even reply, but then she shook her head.

"I honestly don't know, Wade. This—" she gestured to him and then to herself "—I don't know how I feel about it. I like where we are right now, no question about it. But with so much else going on in my life, how can I even think about an actual relationship? You know perfectly well that my history of maintaining anything serious with men is all but nonexistent. We talked about that just last night."

"But you're not ruling it out?" he said, not entirely sure why he'd picked this particular moment to pressure her. Maybe it had something to do with an earlier call from Louise, who hadn't been able to resist making a few nagging comments about the disaster she saw looming on the horizon if he got too invested in something destined to fall apart.

Gabi looked into his eyes, and a faint smile touched her lips. "No, I'm not ruling it out." Her expression turned earnest. "But, Wade—"

"No *buts,*" he said. "As long as the possibility of more is on the table, I'm in."

"Why?" she asked, clearly bewildered.

"Because you're worth it," he told her, "and it amazes me that a woman as incredible as you needs to be reminded of that."

"You are so good for my bruised ego," she said, a smile blooming across her face.

"My pleasure," he said, wishing his skeptical sister could understand this draw Gabi held for him. He hadn't expected it, hadn't gone looking for it, but if he had his way, he'd spend a lifetime trying to put a sparkle back into those too-sad eyes of hers.

Fifteen

Even though he was reluctant to face another of his sister's disapproving looks, Wade forced himself to drop by Louise's after leaving Castle's. Despite his promise to Zack, he'd continued to put off the visit. It had finally dawned on him, though, that he was not only punishing Louise for wanting to protect him, but his actions were taking a toll on the kids he adored, as well. That had never been his intention, and yet, the proof of that hit him the instant he opened the door and four little bodies hurled themselves at him.

"Unca Wade, Unca Wade, we been missing you," Chelsea said, her little arms wrapped tightly around his neck.

"And I have lots of things to show you," Bryce said eagerly. "Mom took pictures at my soccer game and I got an A on my math test."

"Good for you!" Wade said, managing to give Bryce a high five, despite Chelsea's death grip on him. He looked at Peter. "How about you? What's up with you these days?"

"I hate my teacher," the seven-year-old announced

with stunning bitterness. Since he'd adored the young, enthusiastic first-year teacher just weeks ago, this was a shock.

"Why is that?" Wade asked him.

"She made him sit in the corner for misbehaving," Bryce revealed, a gloating note of triumph in his voice.

Wade's astonishment grew. Peter had always been so well-behaved it was kind of scary. Wade tried to catch his eye, but Peter had already turned his back on them and was trudging back up the stairs. Well, he thought, he'd get to the bottom of the uncharacteristic behavior soon enough.

Now he smiled at five-year-old Katrina, who'd been hanging back shyly. Less exuberant than the others, she was often left out of these initial greetings.

"Hey, short stuff, what do you have to say for yourself?" Wade asked.

She grinned at the affectionate name he'd adopted for her and sidled closer. "I missed you," she whispered.

He caressed her wild golden curls. "I missed you, too. I'll bet you haven't misbehaved at school, have you?"

She shook her head.

"But she peed her pants because she was too scared to ask to go to the bathroom," Bryce taunted.

Immediate tears filled Katrina's eyes. "I hate you," she told her brother. "I hate you, hate you, hate you."

As she, too, ran off, Wade regarded his oldest nephew with dismay. "Why would you do that?" he asked the boy. "You had to know you were embarrassing her and Peter."

For just an instant Bryce looked chagrined by the disapproval in Wade's voice. Before he could try to make excuses, Wade told him firmly, "These sisters and brother are your family. You're the oldest. You're supposed to have their back, not torment them, okay?"

He thought he detected an instant of real shame in Bryce's eyes, so he pressed the point. "Do we have a deal?"

Bryce now looked as if he, too, might cry, but he nodded. "Promise."

"Okay, then," Wade said, taking him at his word. He ruffled his hair affectionately, earning a faint smile.

Wade climbed the stairs to the living quarters and found Louise waiting at the top of the steps. He gave her a kiss on the cheek.

"Have you missed me, too?" he asked.

"You know I have. You stayed away too long," she said, a scolding note in her voice.

"I apologize for that."

She drew in a deep breath, then looked him in the eye. "I get why you did it, and from here on out I will try like crazy to keep my opinions to myself." She paused, then amended, "At least about Gabi."

"I'd appreciate it," he said, speaking just as solemnly as she had.

"But," she began, ruining the moment, "I just want to say that I heard what you said a minute ago about family having one another's backs. All I intended to do was have yours."

"I know that your intentions were good," he conceded. "All behind us, okay?"

A smile spread across her face. "Okay. You staying for dinner? I was planning on spaghetti, but since you've shown up, I can roast a chicken and make mashed potatoes."

Wade had considered making a hasty exit, but the

hope in his sister's eyes changed his mind. "Sure. I'll stick around."

He managed to disentangle himself from Chelsea and sent her off to join the other kids, then helped himself to a glass of sweet tea. "So, what's up with Bryce? It's not like him to be tattling on the other kids the way he did just now. And what about Peter getting punished in class?"

Louise shook her head, her expression bewildered. "I wish I understood it myself. Zack thinks it's just a phase with Bryce, but I'm not so sure. Not to dump a guilt trip on you, but it started when you missed that soccer game. And you haven't been coming around, either. I don't think you realize how much my kids count on you. They've asked about you every day and watched for you. It breaks my heart when dinnertime comes and I have to face the disappointment in their eyes."

Though he knew she was intentionally heaping on the guilt, Wade still flinched at the direct hit. He'd always taken his responsibilities as an uncle seriously. The last time he'd stayed away had been after Kayla's death, and he'd seen the toll it took. He should have remembered that.

"I'm so sorry. I honestly didn't give a thought to what my staying away would do to them. After the last time, I should have. It won't happen again. If I can't stop by, I'll at least call to speak to them."

As Louise took the chicken from the refrigerator and readied it for the oven, she seemed to be weighing something carefully before she spoke. Wade had a hunch he knew what was coming.

"Are you still seeing Gabi?" she asked, her tone carefully neutral.

"Yes."

"How's it going?"

"I like her," he said simply. "More and more all the time."

"How does she feel?"

He shrugged. "I think I'm making progress."

A frown crossed her face. "And that's enough for you? Some kind of maybe progress?"

"For *now,* yes," he said emphatically, hoping to dissuade her from pursuing the topic before their detente could be destroyed.

She drew in a deep breath, then gave a little nod. "Then I'll try again," she said. "If she's important to you, I need to make more of an effort."

Wade studied her. "What does that mean exactly? You'll invite us back to dinner?"

"No, I was thinking maybe she and I could get together for lunch sometime. Just the two of us."

"Oh, no," he said at once.

"Why not?"

"Because I don't entirely trust you not to warn her off," he replied candidly.

She gave him a gentle punch in the arm. "Give me some credit. I'm a little more trustworthy than that. And I have been duly chastised for my past behavior, so I'll observe the boundaries."

"You're not always quite so trustworthy when you're on a mission," he said. "And when you're convinced you're in the right."

"The mission's changed," she told him. "It's now about getting to know Gabi for myself, not about running her off. If you truly care about her, then she must have a lot going for her. I want to see that side and not just all the red flags."

"You promise?" he inquired doubtfully.

"Cross my heart," she said, sketching an exaggerated sign across her chest.

He deliberately caught and held her gaze. "Okay, then, but if I get wind of so much as a hint that you're trying to cause problems, you and I will have big-time issues."

"Understood," she agreed. Without looking away, she added, "If this woman really is the one for you, I just want it to work out. I love you. I want you to be happy. You deserve it."

He pulled her into a hug. "Thank you. Now let me spend a little time with the rug rats before dinner."

"Just don't give them that candy I know you have in your pocket," she said.

Wade regarded her with surprise. "How'd you know about that?"

"I know you. You always have a bribe handy. Why do you think those children love you so much?" She waved a finger under his nose. "After dinner and not one second before."

He laughed. "Yes, ma'am."

"I'll be watching," she warned.

"Never doubted it for a second."

But, he thought, as he joined the kids, how seriously could one little piece of chocolate hurt their appetites? He'd just have to make sure they all brushed their teeth before they came to the table.

When Gabi got back to Cora Jane's, she found Samantha packing, her expression grim.

"What's going on?" she asked her sister.

"I'm heading back to New York first thing in the morning," Samantha said, her tone surprisingly flat. "My agent called. I got a part in a commercial that's shooting in a couple of days."

Gabi studied Samantha's expression more closely. "Then why don't you look happier?" she asked with candor.

"Because it's a slight secondary role," Samantha responded. "If you blink, you'll miss me completely. I was up for the lead."

"Oh," Gabi said softly. "I'm sorry."

Samantha sank down on the side of her bed. "Don't be sorry. This is just the way it is. I probably have to learn to accept it."

"Meaning?"

"That once you hit a certain age, it's going to be harder and harder to get into commercials, unless I want to start auditioning for things meant for seniors like absorbent panties or denture adhesive. There's a big market for older actresses these days, but I'm caught somewhere in the middle."

Gabi wasn't sure which surprised her more, trying to imagine her thirty-five-year-old sister in a commercial aimed at seniors or the bitterness in Samantha's voice. Probably the latter, since in all these years she'd never before heard that kind of defeated attitude coming from her perpetually upbeat sister. She had no clue what to say to try to bolster her spirits. Acting was too far from her area of expertise. She had no idea if the bumps in the road were to be expected, something that was likely to pass, or if this was the pattern Samantha could expect from here on out.

She was struck, though, by a sudden idea. "Maybe I could help," she said, trying to work it out in her head before she said more.

Samantha stared at her. "Help how?"

"You have an agent," she said slowly.

"Obviously."

Gabi met her gaze. "But do you have a publicist?"

"Are you kidding me? I can't afford to hire a publicist."

"What about one you wouldn't have to pay, namely me? I'll bet I could plant your name in a few columns, get a little bit of a spotlight shining on you. That could help, couldn't it?"

"It couldn't hurt," Samantha said, her expression thoughtful. "Do you have time to do that?"

Gabi laughed. "Sweetie, I have nothing but time. I'll get my hands on the New York papers, start looking online to see what sort of opportunities there might be, then you and I can talk about a strategy. Maybe we should even have a conference call with your agent and decide the sort of angle that will get the attention you want in the right circles, with the commercial casting agents or Broadway casting directors, whatever. What do you think?"

"I think you're amazing for even offering to consider this. It could be my last chance."

"Stop talking about last chances," Gabi said firmly. "This is going to work. And from now on, all of our spin is going to be positive. Understood?"

Samantha still didn't look totally convinced, even though she seemed more optimistic than she had a few moments earlier. "I hope you're right," she said. "But I think it may be time for me to start being more realistic. If the parts simply aren't going to be there. I need to begin thinking about what comes next."

"In due time," Gabi told her, determined not to allow Samantha to sink into despair before they'd even given a good publicity campaign a try. Gabi sat beside her and nudged her with an elbow. "So, you're in? You'll work with me on this?"

Samantha glanced over at her, a smile on her lips. "I'm in," she said. "And if this works, I will pay you."

"Not even the tiniest chance I'll let you do that," Gabi said. "This is what sisters do, period."

She'd come to appreciate that kind of unconditional support lately. She'd had it from Emily and Samantha the moment they'd learned about the baby. Now it was her turn to return the favor.

Gabi, Cora Jane and Samantha had barely finished dinner when the phone rang. Samantha glanced at the caller ID and chuckled.

"Surprise, surprise, it's Wade," she announced, handing the phone to Gabi without answering. "For you, no doubt."

Gabi scowled at her sister, but took the phone. "Hey. I wasn't expecting to hear from you tonight. I thought you were going to spend the evening with your sister and the kids."

"I did," he told her. "And now I'm calling to warn you to be on the lookout for a wolf in sheep's clothing."

"I beg your pardon?"

"Louise wants to get together with you."

"Uh-oh," she said, immediately understanding his concern.

"My sentiments exactly, but she swears she will be

on good behavior, that she won't try warning you off, or make any trouble."

"And you believe that?"

"She did promise," he said. "But I'd still keep my guard up, if I were you."

"Maybe I should just avoid this little get-together," Gabi said, thinking that would definitely be the least stressful strategy.

"Have you met my sister?" he asked with a rueful laugh. "Evasion is not an option. She will hunt you down."

"Gee, what fun!"

"You can handle her. Just tune her out, if that's what you have to do."

"You don't want me to do my best to impress her?"

"Sweetheart, you don't need her approval. You have mine. Though it would be nice if the two of you could find a way to get along," he said wistfully.

Even though their relationship was far from certain, Gabi understood how important Louise's opinion was to Wade. "I'll be on my very best behavior, too," she promised, then teased, "First, though, she has to catch me."

"I'm sorry to put you in this position," he said.

"You're not putting me in any position," she said. "Louise is the one with the problem. Since you're my friend and I know how deeply you care about your sister, I'll try to smooth things over. I'm all about being surrounded by positive energy these days."

"You're an angel," he said.

"Some would say if I am, then I have a slightly tarnished halo," she replied. "I'll keep you posted if I hear from her."

"Oh, you'll hear," he said. "The only question is when."

"Good night, Wade."

"Night, angel."

Despite the troubling warning he'd just delivered, Gabi discovered she had a smile on her lips as she hung up.

"Trouble with the potential in-laws?" Samantha asked, obviously having eavesdropped.

"Pretty much," Gabi said. "If Louise has her way, Wade and I will never get past the holding-hands stage. Not that we're even there yet," she added hurriedly for her grandmother's benefit. Cora Jane could probably turn handholding into an engagement in the blink of an eye.

Even so, the remark about Louise's sour attitude caught Cora Jane's attention. Her gaze immediately narrowed. "What's her problem with you?"

"She's worried I'll break her brother's heart," Gabi said, then admitted, "I can't deny it's a real consideration. How can I fault her for that?"

"Worrying about loved ones comes with the territory," Cora Jane conceded. "Interference, though, that's something else."

Gabi exchanged a look with Samantha. "Isn't that the pot calling the kettle black?" she teased her grandmother.

"But I want the best for both of you," Cora Jane said, clearly convinced she was on the high road. "Trust me, it's entirely different."

"If you say so," Gabi said, smiling.

"I do say so," Cora Jane responded with a little huff. "And if you need me to have a word with Louise, just let me know."

Gabi managed to contain a chuckle until after Cora

Jane had left the kitchen. "Oh, she is priceless," she murmured when she and Samantha were alone.

"Absolutely priceless," Samantha agreed.

Gabi grinned at her and lifted her glass of tea in a mocking toast. "And just think, sister dearest, your turn is yet to come."

"Heaven help me," Samantha said with heartfelt emotion.

Gabi had come up with her first idea for an original wind-chime design, based on the graceful flow and colors of a weeping willow. She could see exactly how it should look in her imagination, had even roughed out a sketch on a piece of paper, but now she was completely stymied.

"What's the problem?" Sally asked, peering over her shoulder.

"I have this vision," she said, her voice filled with frustration. "But I don't have a clue how to execute it."

"You're going for the cascading branches and leaves of a weeping willow, right?"

Gabi regarded her with astonishment. "You can actually tell that from what I drew?"

Sally patted her arm. "Wild guess," she admitted. "The color clued me in more than the design."

"So, what do you think?"

"Great concept, but a little tricky to pull off on your first attempt at a solo project."

Up to now, Gabi had only worked for the past week on following Sally's step-by-step instructions and only on the simplest designs. Her results had been less than stellar, but even so, Sally had encouraged her to start trying to find her own style.

Gabi sighed heavily, her mood as dreary as the cold winter rain falling outside. "I'm beginning to have my doubts about all of this," she muttered.

Sally merely smiled. "Do you have any idea how much glass I blew through when I started? Come on, girl. Mistakes don't matter. It's not trying that's the kiss of death."

As a pep talk, it was about as effusive as Sally ever got. Still, Gabi had come to appreciate her gentle nudges and determinedly optimistic outlook. Even her harshest criticism was couched in language meant to encourage. If she was going to be an apprentice to someone, Sally had been the perfect choice.

Gabi drew in a deep breath. "Okay, then, let's talk about the basics. Does the design have any merit?"

Sally grinned. "It's terrific," she said, clearly not feigning her enthusiasm. "Wish I'd thought of it myself."

"Seriously?"

Sally's expression instantly sobered. "I will never lie to you, Gabi."

"So, I just need to work on the best approach for executing it," Gabi concluded. An idea came to her. "Is there any more of the green glass?"

Sally nodded, clearly pleased by her shift in attitude. "Over there. There are several shades of green, in fact," she mentioned casually.

"Ah, an honest-to-goodness hint," Gabi teased. "I thought you were determined to make me figure out every little thing on my own."

"What can I say? Sometimes I can't resist."

Sally went back to her own project, and Gabi gathered the material she needed to give hers another try. She was about to start cutting the glass, when there was a tap on the door, followed immediately by Meg stepping inside. Then, to Gabi's shock, she spotted Louise right on her heels.

"I brought company and lunch," Meg announced. "Louise stopped by the shop just as I was leaving to drive out here, and we decided to surprise you both with sandwiches."

"And cupcakes," Louise added cheerfully as she regarded Gabi with a hesitant smile.

"You're goddesses," Sally said, whipping off her goggles and clearing a space at a table. "Grab some stools. Since it's such a crummy day outside, there's no point in trying to traipse over to the house. We can eat right here."

This whole visit was definitely a turn of events Gabi hadn't expected.

"You three know one another?" she asked

"Louise helped us get all our business paperwork done," Meg said. "If you ever need an attorney, she's the best around. She tells me you've already met."

Gabi nodded. "We have."

"And got off to a very bad start," Louise said with a directness that stunned Gabi. "Actually, I begged Meg to bring me along today so I could apologize."

Her words clearly caught Sally's and Meg's interest.

"How so?" Sally asked.

"It's up to Gabi to fill you in on the details, if she wants to," Louise said discreetly.

"I think we should put it behind us," Gabi replied, determined to do just that, and not only for Wade's sake. If Louise was friends with these two women she'd come to admire, then Gabi wanted to give her another chance on her own merits.

Obviously picking up on Gabi's desire to put the subject behind them, Meg studied her, then said, "I swear your baby bump has doubled since the last time I saw you. How are you feeling these days?"

"I'm good," Gabi said. "But I do need to find an obstetrician here. I drove over to my old one in Raleigh the other day for my routine checkup and picked up my records."

"Mine is great," Louise told her. "Believe me, Zack compulsively checked out all of her credentials before he allowed me to walk into the office when I was first pregnant with Bryce. She's delivered all five of my kids."

"Now that's a recommendation!" Meg said.

"It sure is," Gabi agreed.

Louise pulled a piece of paper from her purse, glanced at her cell phone, then jotted a note. "Here's her name, number and the office address. Tell her I sent you." She hesitated, then asked, "Maybe I shouldn't ask this, but are you still considering adoption?"

Though it wasn't something she would have brought into the open in front of Meg and Sally herself, Gabi found she was actually relieved to have the subject out there. It helped, she supposed, that this time she didn't detect disapproval in Louise's voice. Nor was there any sign of it in Meg's eyes or Sally's. Instead, she saw curiosity, perhaps even a hint of sympathy.

"I'm still considering all my options," she told them. She met Louise's gaze directly. "It's getting harder and harder to think about giving up my baby."

Louise nodded in understanding. Now there was no mistaking the relief in her eyes. "I only asked because Dr. Hamilton can help with adoption if you do decide to go that route. So can I, if you make a final decision that it's the way you want to go. She and I have handled a couple of private adoptions that have worked out well."

Gabi couldn't hide her surprise. "Really?" she asked, but then it dawned on her that Louise's initial reaction hadn't been to the idea of adoption, but to a woman in her brother's life giving away her baby after he'd lost his own child.

Louise smiled as if she could read Gabi's mind. "Seriously," she replied solemnly. "Sometimes it is the best choice for everyone. Sometimes not. I only want people to be certain. Otherwise, it can lead to heartache."

Gabi nodded. "And that's exactly why I'm still thinking about this. I don't want to live the rest of my life with regrets. I want to do what's best for my child."

"And for you," Meg said, chiming in for the first time. "You matter, too, Gabi. And I, for one, think you'd make a terrific mother."

"You don't really know me that well," Gabi protested.

"Remember what we said when Meg first brought you here to see me?" Sally asked. "You're a kindred spirit. We're intuitive about these things."

"Besides, if I can actually meet the challenge of getting my teenage daughter out of high school, into college and settled in life, then raising a child should be a breeze for you. Look at the example you've had. Cora Jane Castle is a legend around here."

"An original, for sure," Louise agreed. "A strong, compassionate woman. And since she clearly adores my brother, she's obviously a woman of discriminating taste, as well."

"Ah-ha!" Sally said, her expression brightening. "That's the connection. Gabi and Wade!" She looked from Gabi to Louise and back again. "So what's the story there? Are you two an item?"

Gabi blushed furiously. "We're friends," she said very firmly, then said a little prayer of thanks when Louise didn't correct her.

A grin spread across Meg's face. "Not entirely buying that," she said. "How about you, Sally?"

"Not a word of it," Sally agreed. "Louise? You obviously know more than we do. What's the real scoop?"

"If Gabi says they're just friends, then I'm going with that," Louise said diplomatically.

"And on that note, I need to take off," Gabi said hurriedly. "Thanks for another great lesson, Sally. And thanks for the lunch. Great to see you both again," she said to Meg and Louise.

Though she doubted the speculation about her and Wade died with her exit, at least she didn't have to be in the room to keep up the pretense it was getting harder and harder to maintain. Because the truth was, lately her feelings for Wade were getting to be a little bit more than just friendly. And, though she'd never in a million years have admitted it to Louise, she shared some of her same doubts about the wisdom of that.

Sixteen

Gabi made an appointment with the obstetrician Louise had recommended, but when the time came to go, she was oddly reluctant. Cora Jane sensed it at once.

"Want me to come with you, honey bun? I know Dr. Hamilton. You're going to like her. She's no-nonsense, but she gives her patients her full attention and compassion."

"It's not that I'm afraid of seeing a new doctor," Gabi said, trying to put her finger on why she was having so much trouble getting herself to leave the house.

"Is it because Louise told you that Dr. Hamilton could help with an adoption if that's what you decided on?" Cora Jane asked with astonishing perceptiveness. "Are you suddenly feeling pressured to make that decision? Because you don't have to make it now. And you know how the rest of us feel. You don't have to give this baby up. Not ever. We'll welcome him or her with open arms."

"I know that," she replied. "And maybe that is the problem. As my due date starts getting closer, even though it's still a few months away, I *am* feeling pressured to decide one way or the other. And there will be an ultrasound today. Up until now I haven't wanted to know the sex of the baby, but for the past few days I've started thinking I'd like to know."

Cora Jane smiled. "But that will make this child even more real to you and make the decision to let go even harder," she guessed. "Is that what's worrying you?"

"Exactly." She looked to her grandmother for guidance. "What do you think I should do?"

"About learning the sex of the baby?"

"About any of it."

"Is knowing if the baby's a boy or a girl truly going to change your decision?" Cora Jane asked. "I mean, do you want a little girl, but maybe not a boy? Or vice versa?"

"No, no," Gabi said hurriedly. "That's not it."

"Then, if it were me, I'd want to know," Cora Jane said. "And I'll tell you why. You're going to be carrying this child for a while to come. It's natural to start talking to it. In fact, I've heard you doing it already. And I honestly believe babies come to know their mother's voice. I think this child, boy or girl, should know it's loved. Knowing the gender is a piece of that, don't you think? Maybe we shouldn't but we tend to talk to little boys differently than we do little girls."

Gabi found herself chuckling at that. "Grandmother, I think you just set the gender equality debate back about fifty years. If moms started talking to baby girls in the womb about being iron workers or truck drivers, what a different world we'd live in."

"I think maybe that's a conversation to have with them a little later," Cora Jane said wryly. "But you do get my point, don't you?"

"I do, actually," Gabi admitted. "And I think I want to know. It just scares me to think what that will do to my resolve to give the baby up."

"Honey bun, I think that resolve already has cracks in it a mile wide," Cora Jane told her.

Blinking back unexpected tears, Gabi whispered, "I think you could be right."

"Maybe we should back up a step or two," Cora Jane suggested. "Why did you consider adoption in the first place? Do you not want children?"

"When I was working nonstop, I don't think I ever really thought about it," Gabi admitted. "But lately I've realized that, yes, I do."

"Was it about losing your job and not being sure you could provide adequately for a child?"

Gabi shook her head. "Though that's certainly a consideration, I think I know myself well enough to believe that I'll get back on my feet. And I have savings and that severance package right now."

"Okay, then. Was it about Paul, about his very negative reaction?"

Asked directly like that, Gabi recognized that her grandmother was on to something. She nodded slowly. "I think so. I think two things were bothering me. That I'd come to resent the baby because of how angry I am at Paul, and that Paul would try to insinuate his way into the baby's life—and mine—at some point down the road. I don't want someone as selfish as he is to be an influence on this baby. Adoptive parents could assure that."

"I thought so," Cora Jane said. "Now that you've had some time, what do you think?"

"He's signed the papers giving up parental rights.

He's a nonissue," she said, her mood brightening. "This is *my* decision, isn't it?"

"I'd say so." Cora Jane regarded her approvingly. "So what are you thinking?"

"I'm scared to death, but I want to keep my child," Gabi said.

Now she simply had to figure out how on earth she was going to live with that decision. Knowing how compulsively she'd always approached the major decisions in her life, she should have started detailed planning for this baby the instant she found out she was pregnant, not now, months later. The old Gabi would have decorated a nursery by now and started looking for the best preschools. That she was this far behind on making those decisions was proof of just how rattled she'd been by all these changes in her life.

But, she thought, grinning at last, she'd just have to catch up. And there wasn't a doubt in her mind that she could do it.

Wade was stunned and delighted when he looked up and saw Gabi crossing his lawn in the direction of his workshop just as dusk was falling. It was the first time she'd deliberately sought him out at home, or anyplace for that matter.

He put down his knife and walked to the door to meet her. "Hey, you," he said softly. "What brings you by?"

She regarded him hesitantly. "Is it okay? Are you busy? I don't want to take you away from your work."

"I can always make time for you," he assured her. "Something on your mind? Let's go into the house and I'll make some tea for you. Even though the rain has finally stopped, there's still a nasty chill in the air."

"Tea would be great," she said, following him. "And I never have seen your house, just the workshop."

The reminder took him by surprise. "That's right. I was so focused on having you see my work the day I brought you here, I never thought to bring you inside."

In the kitchen, which he'd updated with all new appliances and cabinetry after buying the house, he made a pot of herbal tea and poured them each a cup as Gabi wandered around, commenting on the framed photos on just about every surface.

"The kids sure have grown," she said. "This one's Bryce, right? How old was he?"

"Four," Wade said, glancing at the picture she held, a smile on her lips.

She picked up the one next to it. "And this one? Is it Chelsea or Jason?"

"Look at the curls. That's Katrina."

"Ah, yes. She'll go through a period when she hates them, I'll bet. Then she'll discover that guys love to run their fingers through those masses of curls."

She came back to the kitchen table and sat down.

"Why the sudden interest in the baby pictures?" he asked.

"I had an appointment with Louise's gynecologist today," she said.

Wade was instantly on alert, wondering if bad news explained her odd mood. "Everything okay?"

"Perfect," she said, her lips curving slightly. "The baby's a girl, Wade." A full-blown smile broke across her face. "I'm having a girl."

"And you're happy about that," he guessed based on her expression, but unsure what this meant for the future. Had she made a decision to keep the baby? Was that what this was really about? Heart in his throat, he asked.

"I had a good talk with Cora Jane this morning," she replied. "She helped me to see things more clearly. I'd already pretty much decided to keep the baby, but this news clinched it." Eyes shining, she said, "I'm going to have a daughter, Wade. How could I ever give away my little girl?"

"Any second thoughts at all?"

She shook her head. "I knew this was going to happen. I just knew it. I think Grandmother did, too. I think that's why she encouraged me to find out the sex of the baby. She knows me too well. She knew that the second this baby became a real person to me, girl or boy, I'd never let go. Blast her for being so darned smart."

Wade chuckled at that. "You think Cora Jane somehow tricked you into getting her own way?"

"Well, of course, she did, the sneaky woman. And it's not just her way. She's insisted all along that keeping the baby was the right answer for me, too. I was just filled with all these doubts about whether I could do it, whether I should, whether I'd take my anger at Paul out on the baby."

"Nonissues," Wade said with conviction. He reached out and took her hands in his. "Admittedly, I haven't known you for very long, but if you ask me, there's not a doubt in the world that you can do anything you set your mind to. Come on, Gabriella. You blazed a trail through your company's PR department in record time. The way I've always heard it, you made a detailed plan, set your goals and never looked back. You can do the same thing when it comes to raising this baby."

She regarded him with surprise. "You really have that much faith in me?"

"Absolutely. Name one reason I shouldn't."

"A total lack of experience with kids," she said at once.

"Easy," he said. "We'll borrow Louise's. She always welcomes a break. And I hear the two of you have made peace."

"She told you that?"

"Yep, she told me all about her visit to Sally's studio, the lunch the four of you had out there and the public apology she made to you."

"I have to give her points for that," Gabi admitted. "I'm sure it wasn't easy for her to apologize at all, much less in front of her friends."

"I honestly believe she meant it," Wade said.

"I do, too. And it meant a lot to me. I don't think we'll be best friends overnight, but I think we'll get there."

He smiled. "That's what she said." He touched a strand of hair that the damp air had turned into a corkscrew curl. Just as she'd said earlier in reference to his niece's curly hair, he loved running Gabi's curls through his fingers. "Now, what are your plans for the rest of the evening?"

"I haven't made any. I just started out for a walk and impulse brought me here."

"Have you had dinner?"

"Of course, but I'm always starving."

"Any strong opinions about ice cream?"

"Absolutely," she said, her expression brightening. "Cover it with hot fudge sauce and I'm in." Just as the words left her mouth, her eyes widened in surprise and she put a hand on her belly. "If that kick is anything to go by, the baby agrees. She's going to be a girl after my own heart."

Which meant, for Wade, that she'd be irresistible, too.

As they walked to the closest ice cream shop, Wade noted that though Gabi seemed at peace with her decision, there was something still troubling her.

"You said something before about being uncertain how you'd manage as a single mom," he reminded her. "Is that really bothering you? I know I kind of dismissed it, but maybe it's something we should talk about."

She glanced over at him. "Do you really want to listen to me weighing all these pros and cons and tossing my insecurities out there for you to dissect?"

"If it's weighing on you, absolutely."

She nodded at the conviction in his voice. "Okay, I know I'm a competent human being," she began.

He merely smiled at the understatement.

"But just as you said a minute ago, I set goals. I go after what I want. I have long-range plans and strategies."

"Okay," he said, not entirely seeing the problem yet.

"I haven't even bought the first bootie for this baby," she lamented. "I have no idea where I'm going to live, so I can hardly set up a nursery. I'm playing at this whole wind-chime thing, which is not exactly a sure-fire career path."

"And none of that seemed as terrifying when you were convinced you were going to give your child up for adoption," he guessed.

"Bingo! Suddenly I'm feeling completely overwhelmed." She wrinkled her nose. "I have to say, I don't much like it."

Wade laughed, even though he knew it was the wrong reaction. At her immediate frown, he said, "Sorry. It's just that no one is ever entirely ready to have a baby, especially a first baby. You know Louise. She's probably every bit as compulsive as you've even dreamed of being, and she was absolutely freaked out before Bryce got here, even with Zack completely on board and me dancing attendance whenever he couldn't be around."

Gabi looked intrigued by his revelation. "Louise was freaked out?"

"You have no idea. She spent one entire week visiting private day-care centers and preschools. This in an area that doesn't have competitive waiting lists for these things. And, let me add, she was about as far along as you are now."

Gabi was smiling now. "I wonder if she still has the lists she made?" she murmured.

"I can just about guarantee it. Now, do you think you can let this go for the rest of the evening and enjoy your ice cream?"

"In a minute," she said. "Do you have your cell phone with you?"

He pulled it out of his pocket. "Here you go."

"Is Louise's number programmed in?"

Wade pulled it up and dialed, then handed her the phone. "I'll go inside and get the sundaes," he told her, but she was already hitting his sister with a barrage of questions.

Heaven help him! He'd wanted those two to get along. He hadn't realized that the bond they were likely to forge might exclude him, even for a half hour at a time, which seemed likely right now.

* * *

Gabi slept late on Saturday morning. When she finally wandered into the kitchen, she was startled to find both Emily and Samantha sitting there with big glasses of sweet tea.

"Where'd you two come from?" she asked. "And are you here to double-team me about something?"

"Not everything is about you," Emily said, then gestured toward two huge boxes sitting across the room. "Bridesmaid dresses. I found the perfect choices, so I had the store pack them up, ship them over and called Samantha to meet me here."

"Oooh, let's see," Gabi said, reversing directions to head toward the boxes.

"Not yet," Emily said. "I promised Grandmother she could be here when you try them on. I had my wedding dress sent over, too. I had the final fitting last week and unless something dramatic happens, like too many pieces of Grandmother's pie or bowls of Jerry's crab soup, I am ready to walk down the aisle." She frowned. "Well, except for the veil and the shoes and the bouquet, anyway."

"Are you sure we have to wait?" Gabi said, eyeing the boxes impatiently.

"Yes," Samantha said in her firmest big-sister voice. "You know how disappointed Cora Jane will be if we don't wait for her. She wants to make an occasion of this."

"Besides," Emily added, "I understand we have other news to discuss that could take some time."

"You heard that I've decided to keep the baby," Gabi said. "And that it's a girl."

"All of that," Emily agreed, giving her a fierce hug. "I'm so thrilled for you."

"And for us," Samantha said, giving Gabi a hug, as well. "We're going to be aunts!"

"Have you started thinking about names?" Emily asked.

"Can we go shopping for baby clothes now?" Samantha wanted to know. "I saw the cutest little outfits the other day. I was dying to buy them."

Gabi laughed. "Hey, slow down, you two. I just made this decision yesterday. I'm still getting used to it."

Her sisters exchanged a look.

"Meaning she wants to sit down and start making lists," Emily said.

"There is nothing wrong with planning and organization," Gabi said defensively. "Some people even think it's very wise to make sure all the bases are covered."

"Which people would those be?" Samantha inquired suspiciously. "It doesn't sound like Wade. He's pretty laid-back."

"But his sister isn't," Gabi said.

"You're taking advice from Louise now?" Samantha asked, her expression incredulous. "Just the other day weren't you two on opposite sides?"

"Long story," Gabi said. "We've found some common ground."

"Other than Wade?" Samantha asked.

"Yes, other than Wade," Gabi replied testily. "Maybe we ought to focus on something else." She looked pointedly at her older sister. "Why didn't you set up that conference call with your agent the way we discussed? I left you a couple of messages to remind you."

Emily looked puzzled. "What conference call is that?"

"Gabi offered to do some work as a publicist for me," Samantha explained. "I'm just not sure the timing's right, after all."

"But you said yourself that your career is slowing down. It seems like exactly the right time," Gabi protested, puzzled by Samantha's sudden lack of enthusiasm for the idea. "It needs the shot in the arm that a good publicity campaign can give it."

But even as she pressed, she saw Samantha's expression shutting down. "Samantha? What don't I know?"

"My agent dropped me," she said, her eyes filling with tears. "He said I don't seem as motivated as I once did and, combined with the whole age thing, he thought maybe he wasn't the best person to represent me anymore, especially if I intended to treat my career more like a hobby."

"A *hobby!*" Emily exclaimed incredulously. "Isn't it his job to find you regular work?"

"He claims parts have come up while I've been away and he couldn't send me on the auditions because there wasn't time for me to get back to New York. That's a crock, and we both know it," she said, heat returning to her voice. "He just wants to focus on younger, up-and-coming talent who will bring in more money."

"So much for loyalty," Gabi said, angry on her sister's behalf.

Samantha's smile was faint. "I'm not in a business known for its loyalty," she reminded them. "It's cut-throat from day one."

"Okay, so you'll get another agent, one who'll appreciate you and is tuned in to a different list of contacts," Gabi said.

"And how am I supposed to do that? My résumé

for the past year is pretty skimpy. Why would another agent want to bother? Success feeds on success and, let's face it, I haven't had much that can be described as successful lately."

"But I am going to make you sound like the best actress to hit New York in the past decade," Gabi said with determination. "That spin we talked about is going to turn the tide."

"I don't think there's enough spin in the world to sell an aging actress when everybody's looking for a youthful face," Samantha said, her discouragement plain.

"Then come out to Los Angeles," Emily suggested, her eagerness catching them all by surprise.

Gabi thought maybe Emily had taken her concerns to heart and was reaching out to her big sister for the first time ever.

"Get a fresh start there," Emily continued, her enthusiasm growing. "You know my friend Sophia has contacts all over the film industry, and Marilyn Jennings, who's chairman of the board of the foundation building these safe houses, is married to a studio president. I can almost guarantee you'd find a top agent and more roles than you can handle."

For an instant Samantha looked intrigued.

"It's not a bad idea," Gabi said, hoping to encourage the olive branch Emily was extending, if nothing else. "A fresh start could be just the thing to relaunch your career."

Once again Samantha's eyes filled with tears. "You two are amazing, but I need to think about this. I've never thought of myself doing movies."

"Hello," Emily said. "Where do you think most of those TV series are made? And there's a healthy theater scene out there, too. You can stay with Boone and me, so your housing will be taken care of until you land a few jobs."

Gabi could see that Samantha wasn't quite ready to make such a dramatic leap, and the pressure was starting to get to her. She could totally relate.

"Sweetie, all we're saying is that you do have options," she told her older sister. "Emily and I are behind you and ready to do whatever we can, no matter what you decide, okay?"

Samantha nodded, swiping at the tears streaming down her cheeks. "I need to go wash my face," she said.

After she'd gone, Gabi looked at Emily. "She's obviously feeling overwhelmed and off-kilter. I can relate."

"Me, too," Emily admitted. "That's how I felt when I had this fantastic job offer in Los Angeles and my relationship with Boone was just falling into place back here."

"Then we're agreed? We won't pressure her?"

"Agreed," Emily said at once. "Do you suppose Cora Jane knows about this?"

"I doubt it," Gabi said just as her grandmother walked into the kitchen.

"What is it you're wondering if I know?" Cora Jane asked, proving her hearing was as sharp as ever.

"That some high-falutin' developer wants to get his hands on some land around here for a big resort," Emily improvised.

Cora Jane looked as if she weren't buying that for a single second—not the response nor the supposed rumor.

"So, don't fill me in," she said. "I suppose you girls are allowed to keep a few secrets."

Emily bounced up and hugged her. "But we are very glad you're here. I wouldn't allow Gabi or Samantha so much as a peek at their dresses till you got home."

Cora Jane held up the bag in her hand. "And I brought nonalcoholic bubbly so we can celebrate while you do your little fashion show in the living room."

"Nonalcoholic?" Emily protested.

"Hey, I have a baby to think of," Gabi said.

"And we don't want your sister to feel left out," Cora Jane scolded. "This will do just fine. The real celebration is all of us being together for this big moment in your life, am I right?"

"Of course you're right," Emily told her. "Hey, Samantha, get your butt back down here. We're about to try on dresses."

With the true skill of an actress, there wasn't so much of a hint of Samantha's earlier dismay reflected in her eyes when she returned, and a deft use of makeup covered all traces of her tears. Her smile for Cora Jane's benefit was as bright as ever.

They carried the boxes into the living room. Samantha poked at one. "If the first thing out of here is orange, you can count me out."

Emily laughed. "Would I do that to you? I told you we'd be going with pastels, though since we've set the date now for late summer, I decided on slightly deeper shades."

She opened the box and pulled out a slim dress the color of a ripe peach and handed it to Samantha, then extracted a similar dress in turquoise for Gabi. She regarded them hopefully. "Well? What do you think?"

"Summer at the beach," Gabi said at once. "They're beautiful, Em."

"And that color was made for you, Samantha," Cora Jane said, her eyes shining with unshed tears. "You girls will be beautiful."

"And now for me," Emily said. "I'm changing in the bathroom, though. I want to make an entrance. Gabi, do you want to help? I can't reach all the buttons in the back."

Gabi went with her, then stood by as Emily extracted an exquisite fairy-tale dress with a beaded bodice and narrow skirt that swirled into a flowing train. It was the back that made her draw in her breath. It dipped low with dozens of small buttons drawing attention from the small of her back to well below her hips.

"Sexy, huh?" Emily said with a grin. "I figure if people are going to be looking at my backside during the service, then it ought to put on a show."

"It's stunning," Gabi told her. "And exactly right for you. It's elegant and classy, yet you'll look like a princess."

Emily beamed. "Exactly the look I was going for. Hurry with those buttons. I can't wait to see Grandmother's face."

"She's going to cry," Gabi predicted.

"Well, I know that. I just hope she'll get all the tears out of her system now, so she'll be all smiles on my wedding day."

"Not a chance," Gabi said. "She'll be as emotional then as the rest of us. I expect to bawl my eyes out."

Emily frowned at her. "Don't you dare. I don't want all my wedding pictures to look as if I made my entire family miserable by getting married."

"Fine. I promise we'll look as if we're relieved to be rid of you," Gabi teased.

"I thought older sisters were supposed to be more supportive," Emily lamented.

"You'd be thinking of Samantha. I'm here to be the thorn in your side."

Gabi opened the door, did a little flourish, then stepped aside to allow Emily her grand entrance.

As predicted, Cora Jane's eyes instantly filled with tears. So did Samantha's.

"Well, heck, if the two of you are going to cry, then who am I to be holding back," Gabi said. "Sorry, Em, but you're just so darn beautiful and we are so incredibly happy for you and Boone."

When she glanced at her sister's face, she noted that Emily, too, had tears in her eyes. Oblivious of her dress, she crossed the room and gathered them all close.

"You guys are the best," she whispered.

"And you, my sweet girl, will be the loveliest bride ever," Cora Jane said, then grinned. "At least until these two get with the program. I imagine they'll give you a run for your money."

All three of them laughed at the unmistakable challenge in Cora Jane's voice, but it was Emily who uttered a warning.

"Just as long as they don't steal my thunder, understood?"

"Yes, ma'am," Gabi said.

"Never dream of it," Samantha added. "This is your big day. The next few months are all about you, just the way you like it."

Emily frowned slightly at that. "Hey, wait a minute."

"It's okay," Samantha said. "We love you, anyway."

"And I'd like to point out that I'll be having a baby before this big wedding," Gabi commented. "I wouldn't mind at least a few minutes in the spotlight. In fact, after going through hours of labor, I may want a parade in my honor."

"Oops," Samantha said, grinning. "I almost forgot. You're not just getting a little pudgy around the middle. That's a baby you're carrying."

"So amusing," Gabi commented.

"Enough," Cora Jane scolded. She poured the nonalcoholic champagne into fluted glasses. "To the Castle women, each of you unique and amazing!"

"And to the woman who's been our example," Emily said, lifting her glass to Cora Jane.

After that, the tears flowed yet again, right along with the bubbly. Gabi hoped they'd always remember the moments of unity like this one and not the dissension and sibling rivalries that occasionally divided them. With luck and maturity, those were well and truly in the past.

Seventeen

Wade had been working with Tommy Cahill on a new oceanfront home for the past week. He'd also been keeping a close eye on Jimmy, whose usual exuberance and impudence were nowhere to be found. After several days of giving the kid his space and hoping Jimmy would come to him, Wade tired of waiting.

The kid had left the house, walked over the dunes and was standing by the ocean, his hands shoved in his pockets, his shoulders slumped. He could have been the poster boy for teenage angst and dejection.

Wade walked up beside him. He kept his gaze straight ahead, waiting some more.

"Hey," Jimmy said eventually.

"Hey, yourself." When Jimmy added nothing, Wade asked, "Everything okay?"

Jimmy shook his head. As Wade studied his expression, there was no mistaking the worry in Jimmy's eyes.

"Want to talk about it?"

After a long silence, which Wade patiently waited out, Jimmy revealed, "I haven't heard anything about the scholarship. Mr. Castle said I should be hearing soon."

"And did he tell you what he meant by *soon?*" Wade asked, knowing that what seemed like soon to an adult could seem like an eternity to a kid whose future was on the line.

"I thought last week, but I didn't get a letter or a call."

"Have you spoken to Mr. Castle? He could probably tell you if there's been a delay or if you're being a little too anxious."

"I don't want to bug him," Jimmy said, then hesitated before adding in a voice barely above a whisper, "And maybe I don't want to know."

"Ah," Wade said, seeing the real problem. "You're scared this means you're not getting the scholarship."

Jimmy gave him one of those disbelieving looks that all kids had mastered by their thirteenth birthday, if not before. "Well, duh! It's a real possibility, you know? But I've kinda started counting on it. I know that's a dumb thing to do, because the odds are against me. There are probably a hundred kids who deserve it way more than me."

"But we've all told you that you have a good chance, so you let yourself believe," Wade concluded, wondering if they'd done him a grave disservice to get his hopes up.

Jimmy nodded. "Crazy, huh? I mean a little while back I didn't think I had any chance at all of going to college, so this at least gave me some hope. I should be grateful, not acting like a big baby."

"You're not acting like a big baby," Wade said, fighting to hide a smile. "You're acting like a young man who wants this really badly."

"It's just that it's my big chance," Jimmy said earnestly.

"I know," Wade said, putting a hand on his shoulder. "And whatever happens, I believe with everything in me that things will work out for you."

"I suppose," Jimmy said, his tone still dejected.

"It's entirely possible," Wade suggested, "that they send out the rejections first. Not hearing could actually be a good thing."

"You think?" Jimmy asked, seizing at the faint hope Wade had tossed out.

"It's possible. What I do know is that worrying about it won't make things happen any faster." Wade decided a change of topic was in order. "How's your dad doing with rehab?" he asked, hoping he'd picked the right subject, one that would elicit a positive response.

Jimmy's eyes immediately brightened. "He's doing great. The doctor said he can go back to work pretty soon, and Tommy's talked to him and promised to put him on his crew as soon as he's ready."

"That's fantastic!" Wade said. "Why don't you focus on that for now? You'll have these other answers soon enough."

"I guess," Jimmy said. He glanced at Wade. "Thanks, man. Not just for the talk, but for all of it."

"Not a problem. I'll always have your back, okay?"

Jimmy grinned. "Hey, you need any help with Gabi?"

Wade laughed. "Thanks all the same. I think I have that covered for now."

"You sure about that?"

Wade wasn't a hundred percent sure of anything where Gabi was concerned, but he was a lot more optimistic than he'd once been.

"I'm sure," he said. "You'll be the first person I call, though, if I do need backup. Like you've said before, she's crazy about you."

"Awesome," Jimmy said, giving him a fist bump, his good mood obviously restored.

Wade watched him take off for the house, then smiled. Whatever happened down the road—for him or for Jimmy—they'd handle it. He believed that with everything in him.

Gabi was startled when Louise called on her cell phone at midmorning and invited her to meet for lunch.

"I can ask Meg and Sally to join us, if the prospect of spending time with me scares you," Louise said.

"I'd like to think we're past any problems or misunderstandings," Gabi told her. "Sure. I'd love to have lunch."

"Great. I'll bring along all those lists I told you about on the phone the other night. They're still up-to-date, thanks to the unexpected arrival of Jason. Mommy's little surprise, as I like to call him."

Her flip remark startled Gabi. "Wade had me thinking you'd wanted a big family."

"There's big and then there's five," Louise said, her tone wry. "I thought four was plenty, but sometimes we just don't know what life has in store for us." Then she suggested they meet at noon at the Seaside Café. "Will that work for you? I know you help Sally out most mornings."

"Actually today's the perfect day for it," Gabi responded. "Sally wants me to bring a couple of orders into town, so I'll just time those deliveries accordingly." She glanced over at Sally for confirmation. Sally nodded.

As soon as Gabi had disconnected the call, Sally asked, "Another step in the peace process between you and Louise?"

"I think so," Gabi said.

"You do know it wasn't really about you, right?" Sally asked. "Since her mom died and her father retired and moved away, Louise is even more protective of Wade. He took it real hard when his wife and the baby died."

"Of course he did," Gabi said. "That's totally understandable. From what I've heard, she was his childhood sweetheart."

Sally frowned at the characterization. "Something like that," she said, suddenly evasive.

"Hold on a second," Gabi said. "Are you saying they weren't a couple from way back?"

Sally regarded her guiltily. "Gabi, I am so sorry I got into this. I try my best not to gossip and it's not my place to be talking about this. It's just that I like you and it seems the story might be a bit more complicated than anyone's told you. I am not the right person to fill in the blanks, though. Ask Louise, if you want, or better yet, talk to Wade. It's his story to share."

Judging from Sally's tone, Gabi had the distinct impression that it was a story she very much needed to hear. Not from Louise, though. That would be too much like sneaking around behind Wade's back. She needed to hear it from him, because if it in any way affected the bond he seemed to have formed with her, it could change everything. She'd worried for a while that his real attachment was to the baby, not her. Cora Jane had tried to allay that fear, but was it possible Gabi had been right all along?

* * *

After his conversation with Jimmy, Wade had driven out to Sally's studio, where he'd just missed Gabi. When he'd heard she was meeting Louise in town, his blood had run cold. He wanted Gabi and his sister to be friends, but the accelerating pace of their friendship was just a little scary. He didn't entirely trust Louise to keep her promise about staying on good behavior.

It was twelve-fifteen when he walked into the Seaside Café and spotted the two of them huddled together over a table strewn with yellow legal pads and papers. They had iced tea at hand, but no food.

He grabbed an extra chair from a nearby table and put it between them, finally catching their attention. Gabi smiled, but his sister frowned suspiciously.

"What's up, Wade? Why are you here?" Louise asked.

"Am I intruding on a private business conference?" he inquired lightly, his gaze on Gabi.

"Absolutely not. Louise is just sharing some of her research with me. It's going to save me a ton of time," she said happily.

He nodded. "That's great."

"Don't you usually take your lunch to work?" Louise asked, clearly not pleased by his unexpected appearance.

"Usually. Today I didn't. I drove out to Sally's, intending to ask Gabi to go to lunch with me. Sally pointed me in this direction." He studied his sister with a narrowed gaze. "What's with the attitude? Did you have something on the agenda besides a friendly chat with Gabi?"

"Of course not," Louise said huffily. "I promised

you those days were behind us. I promised Gabi, too, for that matter."

"We're fine, Wade," Gabi assured him. "But I'd love it if you could stay. I'd like your input on some of these day-care centers. Louise said you've done renovations in a couple of them."

Pushing his concerns about his sister's intentions aside, he took the notebook Gabi was holding out and glanced over the list.

"Okay, aside from the fact that it strikes me as absurd to be looking for day care months before the baby even arrives, I'd say this one is the best-run facility I've been in." He pointed to the third one on the list, knowing full well it was where Louise had sent her own children.

Gabi nodded. "That's what Louise said, too."

"This does make me wonder if you've decided to stay here permanently," he said, trying to keep a hopeful note out of his voice.

"If it works out, yes," she said at once.

"Works out how?" Louise asked, her gaze narrowing. "You mean with my brother?"

"Louise!" Wade said sharply.

"Well, it's a fair question," his sister retorted.

"No, this is all about me," Gabi said. "And finding work that will fulfill me. As much fun as I'm taking lessons from Sally, I'm a long way from convinced that I have a future in the wind-chime business. And I absolutely do not want to take over Castle's and run it, even though I know it would thrill Cora Jane if I would."

"So if you don't find this satisfying work, you'll what? Go back to Raleigh?" Louise asked with another pointed look at Wade.

Gabi shrugged, clearly not ready to commit. "I'll just have to see."

"Stop nagging the woman, Lou," Wade ordered. "We're getting way ahead of ourselves. I know how you like to plan every last little detail of your life, but these decisions are months away from needing to be made."

Louise sighed and sat back. "Point taken," she said, though she didn't look particularly happy about it.

Wade managed to steer the conversation onto more general turf, and the rest of the meal passed without incident. Still, there was no mistaking Louise's eagerness to take off as soon as they'd finished eating. That alone suggested he'd been smart to intrude on this little get-together of hers. While she might not overtly try to sabotage the relationship, he imagined she could plant seemingly innocuous little seeds of doubt that would come back to haunt him.

As soon as she'd gone, Gabi looked at him curiously. "What was that about?"

"What?"

"You were borderline rude to your sister," she accused.

"I just don't think this was the innocent little get-acquainted lunch she might have led you to believe."

"What do you think it was?"

Trying to put his suspicions into words without sounding like an idiot was trickier than he'd imagined. "A reconnaissance mission?" he suggested.

"To learn my deep dark secrets?" Gabi asked, barely suppressing a smile.

"Learn yours? Tell you mine?" He shrugged. "Hard to say, but it struck me as a bad idea either way."

"Since there's not much about my life that you don't already know, I think we can dismiss that as a real concern," she said. She looked him directly in the eyes and asked, "How about yours? Are you hiding anything from me?"

The way she asked the question made him wonder if someone hadn't already planted a few seeds of distrust in her head.

"You know exactly the kind of guy I am," he said, though he couldn't seem to keep a defensive note out of his voice.

"I certainly thought so," she agreed.

He frowned at her phrasing. "Have you changed your mind?"

"Tell me more about you and Kayla," she suggested bluntly.

Wade was completely thrown that she would go there. He thought he'd given her as much information as she needed. Had somebody aroused her suspicions that he hadn't completely leveled with her? Who would do that? And what would they reveal?

"Any particular reason?" he asked, hoping he didn't sound totally paranoid.

"Curiosity," she claimed. "She was your wife, Wade. She was carrying your baby when she died. Isn't it natural for me to want to know more about her, about the kind of marriage the two of you had?"

Even though Wade didn't entirely buy it, he didn't want to create a problem where none existed by being evasive. "You know the basics. I was crazy about her. She got pregnant. We got married, but she died before the baby was born."

"And you were devastated?"

He frowned at any hint that he might not have been. "Of course. Has someone told you otherwise?"

"No. And believe it or not, I really don't listen much to idle gossip. You've never given me any reason to believe you haven't been completely honest with me."

"And yet, I get the feeling you don't entirely buy that I'm being honest now," he said, heat rising in his voice despite his best effort to keep his temper under control.

Her gaze clashed with his. "Sorry, but you're sounding an awful lot like a man who's holding something back. Since I've all too recently dealt with a man who turned out not to be very candid, I'll admit I don't like it."

Wade regarded her with shock. "You're comparing me to that guy? What's his name? Paul? Seriously?"

Even though he knew he *was* holding out on her, the idea that she would lump him in with that reprehensible jerk appalled him.

"I don't deserve that," he said bitterly. He was on his feet before she could respond. "I guess Louise was right about one thing. Coming here today was a really bad idea."

He tossed some bills on the table, then took off.

"Wade!"

Though her voice carried to him, he ignored it. That was a lot easier than ignoring the guilt that was suddenly eating at his insides.

Gabi was still fuming as she left the Seaside Café and drove over to Castle's. She stormed into the kitchen, poured herself a glass of tea, forced a smile for Jerry, then settled into the booth generally reserved for family. Two seconds later, Cora Jane appeared.

"How'd you even know I was here?" Gabi grumbled. Though she'd sought refuge right here under her grandmother's nose, she'd hoped for a little longer to sort out her thoughts before having any conversation with the very perceptive Cora Jane.

"Jerry called me from the kitchen and said you rolled through there looking like a storm cloud," Cora Jane said. "I have to say he got it about right. What's on your mind?"

"Men!" Gabi said emphatically.

Cora Jane's lips curved, but to her credit she managed to fight the smile and win. "Any particular man?"

Gabi drew in a deep breath and told her what had happened at lunch. "I was just trying to get things out in the open and he went crazy."

"Crazy? Or was he just offended because you made it seem you didn't trust him?"

"Well, I don't trust him now, after he got all weird on me. What on earth is he hiding?" She gave Cora Jane a plaintive look. "Do you have any idea?"

"Not a glimmer," Cora Jane said. "And I'm not the person to be asking."

"That seems to be the general consensus, but the person with answers isn't talking."

"Give him some time to settle down, honey bun. If there's something to tell, I have every faith that Wade will open up when he's ready."

"But I'm ready now," Gabi protested. "I'm starting to like him, to let him in. What if that's a huge mistake?"

"Does it feel like a mistake?"

"It didn't until about an hour ago," she said. "Now I have to wonder. All along I've thought his life was an open book, same as mine. Even when Sally hinted that might not be true, I didn't entirely believe her."

Cora Jane frowned. "This started with Sally?"

Gabi nodded. "She made an offhand comment, then immediately regretted it."

"You so sure about that?"

Now it was Gabi's turn to frown. "Meaning?"

"Was it a slip of the tongue or did she mean to stir the pot? How well do you know this woman?"

"Sally's not like that," Gabi protested, certain of that much at least.

"Do you know for a fact that there's never been anything between her and Wade? Could she be a tiny bit jealous?"

"No," Gabi said emphatically, then started to wonder. Did she really know that? Had Louise maybe tried to set them up at some point? It was something she might do. But would Sally deliberately try to sabotage the attraction between Gabi and Wade? Gabi honestly couldn't see that. Sally had been pretty direct about not being interested in a relationship these days. Still, maybe those remarks had been for Gabi's benefit, to keep her from guessing at an attraction that hadn't worked out.

"Well, I can settle that much," she told Cora Jane, taking out her cell phone and calling the artist. Confrontation might not have resolved much with Wade, but hopefully it would clear the air with Sally before Gabi started imagining nefarious schemes where none existed.

"Gabi, everything okay?" Sally asked at once.

"Can I ask you kind of an off-the-wall question?" Gabi said.

"Sure."

"Were you ever involved with Wade?"

"What?" Sally said, her tone incredulous. "Never.

Why on earth would you ask? Did he or Louise say something to suggest that we dated?"

"No."

"Well, as good-looking and sweet as he is, I have no intention of getting involved with anyone at this moment," she said, repeating her familiar refrain. "I'm just getting my own life on track." She hesitated, then asked, "Is this about what I said to you earlier? Are you worried that I had some kind of ulterior motive?"

"I'm ashamed to say it crossed my mind," Gabi told her. "Wade showed up and things got a little complicated over lunch, so now I'm second-guessing everything."

"Well, that's one worry you can put out of your mind. My only concern is for you. And I'm not even suggesting anything awful about Wade, just so you know. I'm just saying it sounds as if there are details you don't have, that's all. He's a good guy, Gabi, quite likely even better than you realize."

"Thanks, Sally. I hope I didn't offend you."

"No offense taken," she assured Gabi. "I actually appreciate that you asked me directly, rather than making assumptions that could have hurt our friendship."

"I'm glad I called, too," Gabi told her.

"See you tomorrow, then."

Gabi sighed as she disconnected the call. "Now I'm more confused than ever," she told her grandmother. "This big-deal secret is apparently something that turns Wade into a hero, not a jerk. If that's the case, why not just tell me?"

Cora Jane smiled. "Because it's obviously something Wade doesn't like to talk about but that Sally thinks you ought to know. Looks to me as if you'll have to practice a little patience until he's ready to talk."

"Have you ever once put patience on any list of my virtues?" Gabi inquired, exasperated.

"Nope, but now seems as good a time as any for you to get a little practice."

"Can't I just hunt Wade down and persuade him to talk to me?"

"Did he seem as if he was in a talking mood last time you saw him?"

"No."

"Well, then, that's your answer. This is one time when you need to listen to your grandmother."

"I always listen to you," Gabi claimed.

"And then do whatever you please," Cora Jane noted, then glanced up. "Besides, it doesn't look as if you're going to have to wait all that long for answers."

Sure enough, Wade was striding across the dining room, a determined glint in his eyes. His expression softened as he greeted Cora Jane with a kiss. Then he met Gabi's gaze.

"Can we talk?" he asked.

"You're in the mood now?" she asked, unable to keep the snarky note from her voice.

"Gabriella!" Cora Jane scolded.

Wade merely grinned. "It's okay. I gave her a rough time earlier. She probably didn't deserve it."

"Probably?" Gabi repeated with indignation.

"Okay, you *didn't* deserve it."

"Thank you," Gabi said. "And maybe I was a little bit at fault, and I am sorry for earlier and for my attitude just now. Being snippy is not the best way to mend fences." She frowned slightly. "You do want to mend fences, right?"

He nodded. "That's what I was thinking when I spotted your car outside."

"Then I'll leave you two alone," Cora Jane said. "I'll bring your pie and some iced tea, Wade. In the meantime, play nice."

Gabi smiled at the admonishment. She hadn't heard it in years. It had usually been directed at the more rebellious Emily. Gabi had always played nice. It was the trait that had gotten her ahead in the business world. She'd played nicely, but always to win.

Now she'd have to see if it could get the answers she wanted under these circumstances.

Eighteen

Wade found himself nervously dissecting the piece of apple pie that Cora Jane had brought to the table. He knew he owed Gabi not only an apology, but an explanation for what had happened earlier. Neither was going to come easy. Since the apology was the lesser of two difficult conversations, he started there.

"I'm sorry I got all bent out of shape at lunch," he said, looking her in the eyes. "The whole conversation stirred up a lot of bad memories for me, but you couldn't have known that."

"That wasn't at all what I'd intended to do," she told him. "I feel as if I'm groping around in the dark, Wade. Clearly there's some topic that's off-limits between us, but without knowing what it is, how am I supposed to avoid it?"

"That is a dilemma, isn't it?" he asked with a rueful note in his voice. He'd imagined dealing with this a million times, but it had never been as difficult as he was finding it in real life. Not only did it mean opening an old wound, it meant baring his soul.

Gabi waited, then began carefully, "Wade, I know we don't have any idea where this is going between us."

What he knew was that she was trying to fill the silence that fell while he sorted through what he wanted to say, what he *had* to say. "True," he said.

"But you've certainly hinted at wanting a relationship. Admittedly, my experience with relationships is pretty lousy, but I do think the cornerstone is probably built on honesty and communication. Since that was clearly lacking in my last so-called connection with a man, I'd like to get it right this time. Evasions aren't going to cut it with me."

"I couldn't agree with you more," he said. He gave her a wistful look. "Isn't it enough that you know I was married, that I lost my wife and baby in an accident?"

"If that's the whole story, then yes," she said at once. "Is it?"

Wade sighed heavily. "No."

As he let the silence drag on, her eyes widened. "Wade, you didn't cause the accident, did you? Is that what you don't want to talk about?"

"No! *God, no,*" he said emphatically, genuinely horrified that such a thought had even crossed her mind.

He understood, though, that nature abhorred a vacuum. Without answers from him, her imagination could spin completely out of control. Obviously she wasn't going to be satisfied with half-truths or evasions, either. Anything less than complete candor was going to leave room for the wildest speculation. He didn't know if he had Sally or Louise to thank for planting these seeds of distrust in her head, but it was up to him to set the record straight, to talk about something that only very few people knew. And no one—not one single person—

knew everything. He'd kept the secret for Kayla's sake, and maybe for his own.

"What have you heard about me and Kayla?" he asked, backing into the subject.

"That you were high school sweethearts. Even the waitress that night at Boone's Harbor talked about how you'd only had eyes for her." She frowned slightly. "Is that not true?"

"Oh, it's true," he said, unable to keep a hint of bitterness from his voice. "I was crazy about her almost from the day we met. We were in high school. She was new in town. I can remember like it was yesterday when she walked into my homeroom. Actually, she bounced in with this shiny brown hair practically down to her waist. Her hair seemed like it was shot through with gold."

A faraway smile crossed his face. "She had these incredible long, long legs, which she was showing off with a very short skirt. Add in a tight tanktop and, well, I'm sure you can imagine the scene. I think every boy in the room almost fell out of his seat. And every one of them did his stupid best to catch her attention."

"Except you," Gabi guessed.

He regarded her with surprise. "How did you know?"

"Not your style. When Cora Jane dragged you into Castle's last summer specifically for my benefit, you were completely low-key and laid-back."

"Maybe I'd just learned my lesson about overplaying my hand," he suggested.

"Nah," she said confidently. "So, what happened? Did she ignore you?"

He thought back to the way Kayla had gravitated right to him, as if she'd somehow sensed that she'd found a safety net. That's when they'd become friends.

Friends, he thought. How he'd hated that at the time. He'd wanted to be her boyfriend. Instead, she'd confided in him, trusted him with her secrets, tortured him with tales of her dates.

"She didn't ignore me," he said quietly.

Apparently something in his words or his tone sank in, because Gabi studied him even more intently. "But something went wrong, didn't it?"

"Not wrong exactly. She liked me well enough, but I wasn't really her type. She liked her boys wild—the wilder, the better, in fact. She thought of me as friend material."

"Oh, dear," Gabi whispered, her expression filled with compassion. "That whole wild thing is so not you. Or have you changed?"

He smiled at how quickly she'd caught on to the problem. "I haven't changed. Still the solid, responsible guy I've always been. Boring to a fault."

"You're anything but boring," she said heatedly.

He smiled. "Thanks."

"How'd you end up together, then? Did she finally mature and realize what a treasure she had in you?"

This was the hard part, the part he'd never wanted to admit to a living, breathing soul, not even his sister. He suspected Louise had guessed because he'd asked for some barely veiled legal advice, but for once in her life she hadn't pushed for more information. Even she seemed to understand that the topic was off-limits, that his pride demanded a shroud of secrecy over the rest.

"Kayla didn't go away to college, and the two of us stayed close. She hung out with a lot of college guys who came here to party during the summer. Then she got pregnant," he said simply. "And the guy didn't want any part of her or the baby."

Gabi looked stunned, obviously making the connection between that situation and her own. "But you stepped up?"

He nodded. "I wasn't going to let her face the pregnancy alone."

She studied his face. "But you did more than that, didn't you? You claimed the baby as your own? You let everyone think you were the one responsible for her being pregnant?"

He nodded. "Don't make me into some sort of saint, Gabi. It worked out for me. In fact, it was like a dream come true. I had the woman I'd loved and a child on the way. Maybe it wasn't the way I'd envisioned, but once we committed to marriage, we were making it work. We really were. It was harder for Kayla than me, but she tried. I think her feelings for me deepened." He shrugged. "Or maybe it was just gratitude, but we were doing okay."

"And then you lost them," Gabi said softly. "Oh, Wade, that must have torn you apart."

"You have no idea." He looked into her eyes, which had filled with tears. "Don't you dare cry for me," he said. "And don't start making comparisons."

"But here you are again, standing by me."

He could almost see her pulling away, twisting what had happened back then into a precursor of what was going on right now. "It's not the same," he insisted. "It's not. Kayla and me, we were a couple of young, foolish kids. I had this idealistic sense that I could save the day. You, Gabriella, don't need saving, not by me, not by anyone."

"But still—"

He cut her off. "No buts. Sure, there are similarities in the situations. Even if I wanted to deny that, there's Louise to remind me that I jumped into an ill-advised marriage because of an unplanned pregnancy. I assure you, though, that's where the similarities end."

"How can you say that? I am carrying another man's child, Wade. And here you are, ready to save the day."

He gave her an impatient look. "Did you not hear me just now? You don't need saving, and my attraction to you started long before I knew anything about the pregnancy, before you knew about it, as a matter of fact. This is not some weird pattern of behavior, Gabi. It's an unfortunate coincidence, that's all." He raked a hand through his hair, then corrected himself. "Not unfortunate. I didn't mean that the way it might have sounded. I'm glad you decided to keep the baby, but if you'd decided on adoption, that would have been okay, too. Despite what my sister thought, I would have accepted your decision."

She didn't look convinced.

"Gabi, what do you want me to say? I can't pretend that the past wasn't the way it was. And there is a blessing in the experience that you might not have considered."

"What's that?" she asked, a surprising tear rolling down her cheek.

"I can say with absolute, one hundred percent conviction that I don't have to be any baby's biological dad to love it with everything in me. The baby I lost was as much a part of me as if I'd provided the sperm, maybe even more so because I loved it without the tiniest reservation or doubt from the moment I felt it kick for the first time."

Gabi was openly weeping now, and he wasn't entirely sure why. Had he thrown her off with this revelation? Had he said too much? Gotten too intense?

"You may be the sweetest, kindest, most wonderful man I've ever known," she said as the tears continued to flow. "And that scares me to death."

The comment bemused him. "Scares you? Why?"

"Because now I understand why Louise was so afraid for you. Wade, I could break your heart."

"But you won't," he said simply. "I don't know how I know that, but I do."

"I wish I were half as sure." She stood. "Now I'm the one running off, but I need time, Wade. I need to think. I don't think I could bear it if you were hurt again, especially if I were the one responsible. This time you deserve your happy ending, and I'm not sure I can give that to you."

What she obviously didn't understand, he thought as she went, was that leaving, even now, made his heart ache as it never had before. As much as he'd loved Kayla, it had been with a naive, young man's passion. What he felt for Gabi went so much deeper. He believed they could build the kind of rock-solid foundation he wanted for the future, but not if his past and her doubts kept getting in the way.

As she had so many times as a teenager, Gabi called her big sister the minute she got back to Cora Jane's. Samantha had always been her go-to person for dating dilemmas. Now she had a doozy.

As she filled Samantha in, one thing seemed increasingly clear. She couldn't continue to see Wade. This was absolutely the wrong time to be involved with anyone, but especially someone with his particular baggage.

"Hold on a second," Samantha commanded when Gabi expressed that. "Do you think Wade is blind to the risk he's taking?"

"Not blind exactly. I just think he's minimizing the pain I could cause him if this doesn't work out between us."

"Sweetie, it could be he just thinks you're worth the risk," her sister said.

"I'm not," Gabi replied. "I mean, I know I'm a good person and worth loving."

"Do you really believe that?" Samantha asked. "Or have you been influenced by the way Paul treated you, as if you were nothing more than a convenience he could toss away?"

"Paul was an idiot!" Gabi said emphatically.

Samantha laughed. "Well, *I* know that. So does everyone else, but we weren't sure you did."

"Well, I do know it," Gabi said. "I might have had a pang or two when we first broke up, but I got over that the minute he agreed to give up his parental rights without a single hesitation or regret."

"Definitely a strong indicator of the kind of man he is," Samantha agreed. "So, what's really holding you back with Wade? Don't you have feelings for him? I mean if you're truly not attracted even a tiny bit, then pushing him away is definitely the right thing to do. Obviously he's a man who loves deeply. He deserves the same thing from the woman in his life."

Gabi thought of the few times when Wade had touched her, even kissed her. Sparks had flown, no question about it. More than that, though, she genuinely liked the man who was becoming her friend. He was solid and so, so different from the sort of workaholics who'd been in her life up to now. He had his priorities straight in ways she wanted to emulate. He actually had some idea of how to create a family, no matter the circumstances under which it had begun. She longed for the certainty that he had that anything between them was possible.

"He's been a good friend," she began. "That's how Kayla thought of him, too. I feel as if it's a pattern that's been established, as if I'm taking advantage of him the way she did."

"I don't think anyone takes advantage of Wade," Samantha said. "He chose Kayla, even knowing the situation. He's chosen you now."

"Maybe he's just one of those guys who can't resist rushing to the rescue," Gabi suggested.

"You didn't need rescuing when he met you," Samantha reminded her, echoing Wade's own words. "In fact, you claimed to have this hot relationship."

"So? I was unattainable, just like Kayla. Maybe it's not the rescuing he likes, but the challenge."

"Gabriella, listen to yourself. You're grabbing at any excuse that occurs to you. Stop it. Take a step back and think about the man you've been getting to know. Let's boil it down to the basics. Do you like him?"

"Yes," she replied unequivocally.

"Then, there you go," her sister said. "Start there. Nobody, not even Wade or Cora Jane, is suggesting you rush into anything."

"Well, I'm not so sure about Cora Jane," Gabi said wryly.

"Okay, I'll give you that one, but you see my point. You and Wade are at the beginning of something that could be very, very good. I'd give anything to have that with someone," Samantha said, an unmistakably wistful note in her voice.

"But you go out all the time," Gabi protested. "You've always dated more than Emily and me combined."

"Sure, I've dated," Samantha echoed. "That's very different. I've had one serious relationship in all these years, and it lasted a grand total of eight months, until I got a big part on Broadway and his career flatlined. Come to think of it, right now I actually understand how he felt."

Gabi heard the note of despair in her sister's voice and decided they'd spent enough time on her latest crisis. She owed Samantha some equal time.

"Have you given more thought to what you want to do? Are you going to take Emily up on her offer and go out to Los Angeles?" Gabi asked her.

"I really don't think I want to live in the land of sunshine, palm trees and plastic personalities."

"Wow! That's a little harsh, isn't it?"

"Yes," Samantha admitted. "I think I'm probably scared and, just like you, using any excuse to avoid making such a dramatic change."

"Or maybe you don't want this whole acting thing enough anymore. You've been willing to do whatever it took for a lot of years. Nobody could blame you if you were ready to call it quits. Or, if you do want to stay in New York and try to make something happen, I'm still more than willing to help you in any way I can."

"I did speak to a couple of agents this week," Samantha admitted. "And I called a couple of casting directors I'd gotten to know. I just wanted some realistic outside perspective on my chances."

"And? What did they tell you?"

"Both agents said they were familiar with my work and asked me to send over my résumé," she said, her tone brightening. "I'm including the reel of clips I've had put together from some of the TV shows and commercials I've done."

"How about the casting directors?"

"They said they had projects coming up and would consider me for a couple of things, if I get new representation. None of them seemed to think I should turn my back and walk away, though they were pretty candid about how my age could be an issue."

"Okay, then. Why don't we get a little proactive, create some buzz? How about it?" Gabi said eagerly. "Maybe your old agent just wasn't being aggressive enough and one of these new people will take you on and things will start to happen."

"God, you are so good for my ego," Samantha said. "You actually make it sound as if anything's still possible."

"I believe it is," Gabi told her. "The question is, do you?"

"After talking to these four professionals, I'll admit, I started feeling more optimistic."

"All right, then!" Gabi enthused.

"But," Samantha cautioned, "this is it. I'm giving it a few more months, not years. I don't want to be waiting tables when I'm fifty and talking about the days when I used to act."

"That seems reasonable," Gabi told her. "It never hurts to have a timetable in mind. But, Samantha, don't be afraid to change the timetable if it feels right, if you sense that the next big thing is just around the corner."

"Forget the next big thing. I'll be happy with just one tiny glimmer of hope."

"Okay, then. I'm getting paper and a pen. We're going to start making some notes."

For the next half hour, she interviewed her sister as she would any client whose story she wanted to sell.

"You know all this stuff," Samantha complained.

"But I can come up with better angles and livelier copy if I have the information in your own words. I'll draft a couple of things and run them by you in the next few days. I'll go back and look for the best places to plant some items in the media up there. In the meantime, can you try to find out what projects these casting directors are working on? Maybe we can hint that you're under consideration for something that's getting a lot of buzz."

"Isn't that dishonest?"

"Not if I handle it properly. Besides, PR is a game. You know that as well as I do. Once people start thinking you're a hot commodity, they'll all want to check you out."

Samantha laughed. "Does Dad have any idea how good you were at your job and what a jerk he was for not hiring you himself?"

"I doubt it," Gabi said. "But I've got an equally exciting client right now, and I'm going to make you a star."

"That may be overly ambitious, but I appreciate the thought."

"Love you," Gabi told her.

"Love you back."

"And we'll talk soon. Thanks for listening to me about Wade. You helped me sort through my thoughts."

"Anytime," Samantha said. "One last bit of advice— give the guy a break. Men like Wade aren't lurking around every corner."

Gabi smiled. "No, they certainly aren't."

And she probably needed to keep that in mind.

"So I filled her in about me and Kayla, and she walked away," Wade told Louise two days after his conversation with Gabi. "I haven't seen her since."

Louise stared at him in shock. "You told her *everything?*"

"Everything," he confirmed.

"Even the part you never acknowledged to me?" she asked pointedly.

He leveled a look into her eyes. "Even that."

"Have you called?"

"I left a couple of messages. She hasn't responded." He peered closely at his sister. "Are you gloating? Don't you dare gloat."

Louise frowned at him. "Do you honestly think I would ever be happy about anything that caused you pain? This is what I was trying to prevent. Gabi's life is obviously in turmoil. I doubt she can see anything clearly at the moment except that she's pregnant and has no career. It's not exactly the best time for her to form a new bond with a man, unless she's the clingy type that just needs a man to prop her up."

"That is definitely not who she is," Wade said, dismissing the possibility.

His sister nodded. "I agree, which means she's going

to want to get her feet back under her. Maybe then she'll be ready for a new man in her life."

Wade leveled a look at her. "I want to be that man," he said flatly.

Louise blinked at that. "You're that sure?"

"I'm that sure," he confirmed.

"What if she decides her best option is to go back to Raleigh? Would you seriously consider making a move?"

"I might," he said, though it was the last thing he wanted to do. He thought about the compromise Boone had reached with Emily, opening a restaurant in California to be with her while she worked on something that meant the world to her. How could he be willing to do any less, if that's what it took to make things work out?

"Boy, you do have it bad," Louise said. "I didn't think you'd ever leave Sand Castle Bay."

"I wouldn't want to," he conceded. "And I think the fact that Gabi put her town house in Raleigh up for sale is a pretty good indication that she's cutting those ties."

"Wade, you heard her say at lunch that she doesn't know what the future for her here holds. The whole wind-chime thing seems a little crazy to me. I think it's been some kind of creative outlet for her, but I seriously doubt her life's work is in cutting up bits of glass."

He frowned at her description. "You think Sally's an artist, right? You don't dismiss her work that way."

"Sally *is* an artist. Gabi's dabbling. And that is not meant as an insult. I think she's all but admitted that herself."

Even though Wade didn't much like his sister's tone, he couldn't really argue. For one thing, he hadn't seen a single finished wind chime. For another, Gabi's level of enthusiasm had waned as her days in the studio had passed without something to show for them.

And yet he believed that her love for the wind chimes, for Sand Castle Bay, for Cora Jane—maybe even for him—would all ultimately play a part in her finding happiness right here. He just needed to figure out how.

He stood. "I'm heading home," he announced.

"Before dinner?" Louise asked, startled.

"I'm working on a project," he said. "I need to get back to it."

"You're not mad at me for speaking my mind, are you?"

"No. I wouldn't have come to you if all I'd wanted was a sympathetic ear," he said with a grin. "For that I'd have called Zack and we'd have gone out for a beer. From you I know I'll get the unvarnished truth, at least as you see it."

Louise frowned. "Thanks, I think."

"It actually was a compliment," he said, dropping a kiss on her cheek. "Tell the kids I'm sorry I missed them. I forgot about the swimming lessons today. I'll see 'em soon."

He was on his way home when he was struck by an idea. He made a quick turn and headed into the countryside instead, winding up at Sally's. Since the lights were on in the studio, but not in the house, he wandered out and knocked on the door.

"Come on in," she called out.

He shook his head at her lack of safety precautions. "Shouldn't you know who's at the door before you invite them in?" he asked.

"Saw your car," she said succinctly, all her attention

directed at the piece of glass in front of her. "Have a seat. Give me a couple of minutes and I'll give you my full attention."

Rather than sitting, he moved closer to peek over her shoulder. She was working on the centerpiece of a wind chime, using bits of glass that would eventually be fused under high heat to create a colorful sailboat design. He recognized how delicate the process could be, so backed away and wandered around, looking at some of her completed work. He recognized her talent, both in design and in execution. He couldn't help wondering if anything Gabi had done had come close.

"There!" she finally said, a note of triumph and satisfaction in her voice. "Now, tell me what brings you by for the second time in the past couple of days. Is this visit about Gabi, too?"

"As a matter of fact, it is. I was wondering how the whole wind-chime thing is working out for her."

Sally regarded him with amusement. "Isn't that a question you should be asking her?"

"Oh, I definitely want her perspective, but you're the expert. I need your take before I go to her with an idea I've been toying around with since she came to town."

"Explain," Sally commanded.

"Well, if she's showing great potential and this is her future, then my idea isn't worth mentioning. I certainly don't want her to feel that I have no faith in her, if working with glass is her destiny or something."

Sally gave him a sharp look. "This is between us, right? You are never, not in a million years, going to repeat what I say to her?"

"Of course not."

She continued to look doubtful. "Because I like her, and I would never, ever want to hurt her feelings."

"Understood," he said, already beginning to get the picture.

"She doesn't have a lick of artistic talent," Sally said candidly. "Her ideas are spot on. In fact, she's had a couple of designs I wouldn't mind trying myself, but the execution?" She shook her head. "The pieces just aren't coming together."

"Couldn't that come with practice? She is just a beginner, after all."

"We were all beginners once," Sally agreed. "I remember that stage. Trust me, Gabi's at the stage *before* that, whatever that is. Don't get me wrong. She's made a few improvements. She tries so hard and gets so frustrated that I feel bad for her, but truthfully, I just don't see this happening."

Wade appreciated the candor. "So, should I encourage her, discourage her, offer an alternative?"

"If you have an alternative, I'd definitely toss it out there. I think she knows where this is going."

Wade nodded. "Mind if I try the idea out on you first? You might want to be involved."

It was evident he'd piqued her curiosity. "Tell me," she said eagerly.

"Actually, I've been thinking about something like this for a while. We—that is, the local artists—all have one or two favorite shops that sell our pieces, right? And we may go to a few shows during the season."

"Sure."

"What if we did something together, something bigger? What if we formed an art consortium of some kind with a gallery, but more important, some individual workshop spaces, so it could be a destination for tourists? They have these kinds of things in other cities, like the Torpedo Factory outside of Washington. I think there's something similar in Miami, as well. Lots of other places with a big artists' colony have them, too, I think."

Sally's eyes lit up. "I like it. I've been wanting to turn this space into a guesthouse. If I had a studio someplace like that, I could do it. But how does Gabi fit in?"

"She clearly has the right sensibility for what we do, even if she can't create wind chimes or whatever. And she has the sort of public relations experience that could put this place on the map. It could be a win-win for us and for her." He regarded Sally hopefully. "What do you think? Be honest. I don't want to even start down this road with her if the idea's off the wall and the other artists around won't embrace it."

"Oh, I'm sure there will be some holdouts," Sally said. "They don't call artists eccentric for no reason. But personally I think it's a fantastic idea, and I agree Gabi is the perfect person to pull it all together. She's organized. She can spread the word. I love it, Wade. I really do."

She gave him a knowing look. "Not that there's even a tiny bit of self-interest behind this for you, right?"

He could feel the heat climbing up his neck. "I want her to stick around," he said simply. "This could make that happen."

"If you need my help selling her on the idea, let me know," Sally said. "Frankly, I think she's going to jump all over this, and I think you're part of the reason. Her heart's here, Wade, because of family, sure, but also because she has feelings for you. I've seen it every time your name comes up. She may not be ready to admit that to herself yet, but she will if you give her time."

Wade gave her a hug. "Thanks. You won't say anything to her, will you?"

"Absolutely not," she promised. "This is your sales pitch to make."

Wade nodded, grateful for her insights. Sally had offered exactly the kind of encouragement he needed. Now he just had to figure out the right approach to take with Gabi to sell her. He had a feeling this was his best shot to grabbing everything he wanted. If she turned her back on this, it was entirely possible he'd have to face the prospect of losing her.

Nineteen

The box of shattered glass was beginning to get to Gabi. It had been weeks, and she had absolutely nothing to show for her efforts. Sally had been patient and encouraging, but Gabi was so frustrated, she was wondering if this whole idea hadn't been crazy. She'd even expressed that on occasion, but no one had suggested she quit.

Except her father, of course.

Just last night he'd sounded completely mystified by her ongoing insistence on exploring some artistic side of her nature she'd never once mentioned growing up. His exasperation with her refusal to return to Raleigh and her high-octane career was plain.

"You had a good job, Gabi, important work," he'd said. "You're giving it up to do what? Paint on glass?"

"To make something beautiful," she'd retorted. Would wind chimes save the world the way some of the research being done in Raleigh might? Of course not. But they brought beauty and innocent pleasure into people's lives in the same way other art forms did. She thought that shouldn't be dismissed so readily.

"If you insist on doing this, do it in your spare time," he'd argued. "Everybody needs a hobby."

"Do you?" she'd asked, amused that a man who worked 24/7 would even dare such a comment.

"Well, no, but most people have one. I'm sure that Wade fella could convert one of the bedrooms in your town house into a little workshop for you right here in Raleigh."

"Even if I hadn't already listed the town house with a Realtor, I'd need the spare bedroom for a nursery," she reminded him.

"You put the town house up for sale?" he asked incredulously. "Are you crazy? In this market? You'll lose a bundle. Gabriella, you're not thinking clearly. Call the Realtor and put a stop to this."

"Absolutely not. I may not be sure of much, but I am selling the town house."

"But where will you live?" he asked, as if housing options were limited to a precious few square miles in Raleigh.

"I'm planning to stay at Grandmother's, at least until the baby comes," she'd responded patiently. "Then I'll find my own place out here on the coast."

"You're going to regret this," her father predicted, his own patience obviously past its limits.

For the first time in her life, Gabi hadn't been crushed by his words or his judgmental tone, though today as she was tossing out yet another failed attempt—an unrecognizable hodgepodge of colored glass—she couldn't help wondering if it had been a mistake to reject her father's offer to help her find another job. Last night, though, her pride had kicked in and she'd told him emphatically that he was wrong.

She glanced once more at the box of shattered glass, proof positive that she wasn't the artist she wanted to be just yet, and shrugged. Even if her father wasn't wrong, that was okay, too. She'd have reached for something that had the potential to touch her soul.

"Sally, do you feel as if you're wasting your time working with me?" she asked.

"I like having you around," Sally responded.

"Not exactly what I asked," Gabi told her, wincing at the artist's carefully chosen words. "Can you see even a glimmer of talent?"

"Let me turn this around," Sally replied. "Are you ready to quit?"

"Not exactly, but I am frustrated. I'm not seeing much progress. I mean, in my mind's eye I can see exactly what I want to create, and I think the designs are pretty good. Then I start working with the glass and..." She shrugged. "Not so great."

Sally smiled. "Self-doubt is part of the process for any artist. Show me an artist who doesn't harbor any doubts, and I'll show you someone whose ego is wildly inflated and not necessarily based on talent."

Gabi grinned. She knew those types, too. She wondered what Wade would have to say about all this, but he'd been making himself scarce lately. He hadn't called after she'd ignored his first few messages. Nor had he been dropping by Castle's, according to Cora Jane, who was clearly miffed by that. Obviously he'd taken Gabi seriously when she said she needed time to sort through all he'd told her about his relationship with Kayla and that much-anticipated baby who hadn't been his biological child.

Over the past few days, she'd really started missing

him, and today with all these doubts swirling around in her head, she regretted that she couldn't simply call and bounce these worries off him. She respected his insights.

Well, she thought, there was really no reason she couldn't call. He wasn't the one who'd needed space, after all. She had. And right now, she didn't want it anymore. Maybe that was selfish, but she decided to go with her gut and make the call.

He answered on the first ring. "Hey, Gabi," he said, his tone cautious. "What's up?"

"I was wondering if you could come over to Cora Jane's for dinner tonight?"

"Is this her idea or yours?" he inquired suspiciously.

"Mine. She's actually going to a movie with Jerry tonight. I'm cooking, for better or for worse."

He chuckled at that. "Want me to bring takeout?"

She sighed. "It seems rude to invite you to dinner and then expect you to supply the food, but it might be smarter."

"Italian, Chinese, something from Boone's? What's your pleasure?"

"Pizza," she said at once. "And salad. I'll pick up some ice cream for dessert."

"What time?"

"I'm heading home now from Sally's. I'll probably try to sneak in a half-hour nap, but any time you're ready after five would be good. I'm not sure what your work schedule is like these days."

"I'm wrapping things up with Tommy in the next hour or so. I'll clean up, pick up the food and be there by five-thirty, most likely."

"Perfect. Thanks, Wade."

"No thanks necessary. I'm glad you called."

"Just like that?" she asked, amazed yet again by his accepting nature. Paul would have been in a snit for a week if she'd ignored even one of his messages. "After the way I treated you the last time I saw you?"

"Just like that," he said. "You needed time. I respect that. See you in a couple of hours."

Gabi disconnected the call and looked up to see a grin on Sally's face. "The man really is a saint," Gabi told her.

"A saint on a mission, I'd say," Sally replied.

"A mission?"

"He wants you, girl. You do know that, right? I mean, if you don't get that much, then you're not half as bright as I've been giving you credit for being."

Gabi sighed. "I just don't want to hurt him. Louise has been afraid of that all along and now I am, too."

"Wade's a big boy," Sally reminded her. "He's taken his share of knocks. Clearly he doesn't think you pose a threat to his serenity. Maybe you should trust him on that."

Gabi smiled. Maybe she should.

"How did you know you were good at carving wood?" Gabi asked Wade as they sat on the porch at Cora Jane's later that evening with the sound of wind chimes in the air.

Wade grinned at the plaintive note in her voice. Thanks to his recent conversation with Sally, he knew exactly where she was coming from.

"I'm still not a hundred percent sure," he admitted. "Each time I touch a new block of wood, I wonder if

I'll find the art inside." He glanced her way. "You're thinking too much about the mistakes."

"Well, of course I am," she responded irritably. "I do not have one single wind chime to show for all the hours I've been at this. There were one or two that were okay, but I don't want to settle for okay."

"Hours, huh?" Wade said, his tone dry. "Talk to me when you've been at it for months."

She frowned at his attitude. "At some point I do need to turn this into a living or give it up."

"No starving-artist lifestyle for you?" he teased.

"Hey, even you have a backup plan. You're doing all that custom cabinetry to pay the bills."

"And you have a severance package, plus you'll have some money from the sale of your house, and you can always work at Castle's. You and the baby will never starve."

She shook her head. "The severance package won't last forever and, as my father lovingly pointed out last night, the town house isn't likely to bring in big bucks. I'll be lucky to get the equity I have in it back. As for Castle's..." She shuddered. "Short-term, sure. As a career goal, not so much."

Wade gave her a considering look, wondering if she was ready to hear the idea he'd run past Sally. "I actually have some thoughts about something you could do, if you're interested in hearing them. I don't want to suggest that I don't have any faith in your artistic talents, though."

She smiled. "Believe me, after today I am more than ready for any ideas. I hate admitting I failed at anything, but I am very close to conceding defeat on that front. It's been fun and satisfying in some ways, especially getting to spend all this time with Sally, but mostly it's been frustrating."

"Maybe because you expected too much too soon. Should you give it more time?"

"I'm not going to walk out of Sally's studio tomorrow," she said. "But I wouldn't mind exploring some other options. What's your idea?"

"I've been thinking we need an artists' consortium, cooperative, whatever," he began, taking her at her word. He described the kind he had in mind, one where the artists would have their own workshop spaces. "I'd take a space for my carvings. I ran this by Sally recently, and she said she'd be interested, too. I think a gallery in which artists not only display their art but have room to work would be a real draw out here. I think people are as fascinated by the process as they are by the finished products. And the chance to meet the artist before buying his or her work could easily increase the value, too. With your organizational skills, you could pull this together, and with your PR skills, you could draw a lot of attention to it. Plus, I think you get the artistic spirit and could work with a lot of temperamental people."

She smiled. "Like you and Sally?"

"Hey, we're probably saints in comparison to some you'll run across."

Gabi's expression turned thoughtful. "It's actually a really interesting concept," she conceded. "It's definitely the kind of fresh new challenge that I could sink my teeth into."

The first faint hint of excitement in her voice told Wade she was already hooked. He waited as she mulled the idea over. "You really think a working gallery could draw artists and customers?" she asked. "Any proof of that?"

"Absolutely," he said at once. "I'll give you a couple of places you could check out online, get an idea of how they're run, what they offer. Some even offer classes, I think. I know how you love to do your research. I'll write them down for you before I leave. At least it'll give you a starting point."

"It would bring my interest in local art and my real professional training together, wouldn't it?" she said excitedly.

"And if I did my work there at least a couple of days a week, it would be something we could do together."

Gabi looked taken aback. "You mean a partnership?"

He grinned at her incredulous expression. "Just the first I have in mind for us," he teased. "We'll talk about the more important one another time. I'll give you some time to get used to this one first. I don't want you weighing too many different pros and cons lists all at once."

He laughed at her astonished expression. One of these days she'd finally catch on. Sometimes the very best things in life couldn't be planned the way Gabi wanted them to be. They simply happened when they were meant to. Thank heaven patience was one of his greatest virtues.

Captivated by Wade's idea, Gabi stayed home the next day and spent the morning on the internet. She did a bit of research for her planned crusade for Samantha, then turned to a search for artists' cooperatives. She found more than she'd anticipated. Some had an amazing internet presence in addition to a physical location. The more she read, the more excited she became.

One downside struck her, but it was personal. She liked Meg Waverly. She wondered if Meg and other local shop owners would view the launch of something like this as a betrayal, as unwanted competition both for stock and for customers. Only one way to find out, she decided, grabbing her purse and heading out the door.

Feeling more energized than she had in days, she walked briskly into town and arrived at Sea Delights just as Meg was giving last-minute instructions to Lily for the afternoon.

"I should have called," Gabi apologized, "but I took a chance that I could catch you. Are you in a hurry? Do you have someplace you need to be?"

"Out of here," Meg said wearily. "I feel as if ten busloads of tourists hit all at the same time this morning. That almost never happens, so I was here on my own. I am beyond ready for a break."

"Lunch?" Gabi suggested.

"Why don't I grab some bottled water and then we can ride over to the ocean and sit on the pier?" Meg suggested instead. "I love listening to the waves rolling in. That'll calm me down, and in no time I'll actually be able to have a civilized conversation with you."

"Works for me," Gabi said eagerly. "I haven't been there in ages."

Meg was silent driving over. Once she'd parked, they joined the crowds of fishermen and tourists on the recently built pier. They found a bench closer to shore where they were in less danger of being snagged by a fisherman's line and sat down, turning their faces up to the sun as waves crashed below them.

"This feels so good," Meg murmured. "I almost feel human again."

Gabi understood exactly how she felt. "I can't imagine why I haven't done this more often. I suppose it's because this pier hadn't been built when I was here for the summers I spent with Cora Jane, and after construction was completed, I was in and out of town too quickly to drive over and just plain relax like this."

"I honestly think I can feel my body unwinding," Meg said, then took a sip of water. She turned to Gabi, a grin on her face. "By the way, I've been wondering when I was going to see you."

"Oh?" Gabi said, perplexed by the knowing glint in Meg's eyes.

"Oops!" Meg said, her expression guilty. "Maybe I'm getting ahead of myself. Why don't you tell me why you wanted to see me?"

"Last night I was talking to Wade about an idea he had," Gabi began. As Meg's smiled broadened, she guessed, "You already know, don't you?"

"Wade mentioned it to Sally, but swore her to secrecy. She mentioned it to me, then swore me to secrecy. As you can see, I'm far better at secrets than she is, because I haven't said a word to a soul." At Gabi's lifted brow, she added, "Okay, maybe because it was only last night when Sally filled me in."

"So, what do you think?" she asked Meg.

"I love the concept," Meg said readily.

"You're not against the competition?" Gabi asked.

"Why would I be? I don't view it that way. People who come here to visit a place like that will fall in love with some of the shops already here, as well. I think it will be a win-win for all of us, especially if you're spending all the money and time on advertising and PR. It's one more way to sell the area as a destination."

Gabi grinned, finally allowing her excitement full rein. "I was really hoping you'd feel that way."

"Then you're intrigued by the concept?" Meg asked. "You might agree to do it?"

"I have a lot of thinking still to do, but I definitely think I'm more suited to doing something like this than I was to making wind chimes, much as I might love them."

"And how does Wade fit into this decision, if you don't mind me asking?"

Gabi thought carefully before answering. "I think working closely with him will be great."

Meg rolled her eyes. "Definitely not what I was asking."

Gabi laughed. "I know, and if I had an answer to your real question, I'd tell you. The good news, though, is that this project could give us time to figure things out. It takes off the pressure."

"Does he know you're giving this serious consideration?"

"Of course. I promised him I would."

"Have you considered how it would work? Would the artists own it? Would you? Who's going to find the right location? Rent the spaces?"

"All things on my list to discuss with Wade and figure out," Gabi said. "Any thoughts?"

"Well, as much as I like the idea of something owned by the artists, I have a hunch it would be impossible to get them to agree on which toilet paper to stock, much less the big decisions. My gut tells me, if you have the financial capability, you ought to start this as your own business and simply let them rent spaces to show their works or studios where they could do their painting, sculpting or whatever. If you also run the gallery, that would entitle you to a cut of sales, as well."

"Good points," Gabi said. "I can understand how operating this kind of business by committee could be tricky. Wade and Sally are both reasonable people with some business background, but I suspect there are artists who aren't especially business oriented."

"Oh, honey, you have no idea," Meg said. "They walk through the door of my shop all the time with the most outrageous ideas about pricing. If some of them had their way, I'd sell their pieces without taking any cut at all. If they won't listen to reason, I send them away, even if I'd kill to have something of theirs on display. If you can deal with them, more power to you."

Meg turned to study her. "Have I scared you to death with all these warnings about artistic egos?"

"Not at all," Gabi assured her. "I'm actually getting excited. All these ideas are starting to bounce around in my head. I'll sit down later and try to organize them into some sort of plan. In the meantime, what's going on with you? How's your daughter?"

Meg immediately frowned. "Now you've gone and spoiled my hard-won serenity," she said with a dramatic sigh. "I swear that girl could test the patience of a saint. When she's not dragging home the most inappropriate boys in her class just to torment me, she's not coming home at all and I get to spend my evening tracking her down. She must think I'm part bloodhound, because she makes it all but impossible. When I finally do corner her, she acts like my sole goal is to ruin her life."

"You're making me start to wish I were having a boy," Gabi admitted.

"I don't know that they're any less of a worry, just

different," Meg said. "I talk to other moms, and we all seem to be at the same stage, praying that we can get through the teen years with our kids in one piece and preferably not in jail."

Gabi thought of Jimmy and how different he was from the teens Meg was describing. "Do you know Jimmy Templeton? He graduated last year. He wasn't able to go to college because his family needed him here, but he's mature, responsible and smart, not at all like what you're describing. Of course, maybe he cleans up his act around Wade and me, but we both like him a lot. In fact, my dad's trying to help him get a scholarship."

"The name's not familiar, but I'm a comparative newcomer to the area and Analeigh's a couple of years younger. She's a junior this year."

"One of these days when the weather's warmer, maybe I'll throw a barbecue at Cora Jane's and invite Jimmy and you guys. I think he could be a good influence. I'm not suggesting a blind date, just that he's the sort of responsible kid that might offer her a different perspective."

"I'm ready to try anything," Meg said with evident frustration. "I'm certainly not getting through to her. I thought it would be easier here, but I guess kids are kids wherever they are, and if the opportunities for getting into trouble exist, any kid can find them." She gave Gabi a chagrined look. "Please don't get me wrong. She's not a terrible kid. She's just testing the limits and my last shred of patience."

Gabi regarded her with sympathy. "Something tells me one of these days you'll look back on this period and laugh about it, especially when she's all grown up and turns out to be just like her mom."

"I'm not entirely buying that, but I live to be proved wrong," Meg said, her tone heartfelt. "And now I'm starved. Do you still have time to grab a late lunch?"

"Absolutely. Breakfast was a very long time ago. Baby and I are more than ready for a big juicy burger, though I will probably settle for a nice healthy salad."

"Good thing," Meg said, "since I intend to take you to a cute little vegetarian place run by a friend of mine. You're not going to find any burgers on the menu, but the food is excellent and healthy."

"Lead me to it," Gabi said, following her back to the car.

A glance in the car's mirror showed her with bright patches of color in her cheeks and windblown hair, but she felt better than she had since arriving at Cora Jane's. She finally had a plan for the future that made real sense, one that she could envision turning into that fulfilling career she truly wanted. That it blended her professional talents and the artistic leanings of her heart made it even better.

As for Wade and what might be ahead for the two of them, well, that might be coming together, too. She just had to get past these nagging doubts that she was filling in for the woman he'd lost.

Twenty

After his conversation with Gabi, Wade practically held his breath for a couple of days waiting for her to make a decision. He had to force himself not to call and pester her. If he understood nothing else, he knew she was a woman who liked to look at things from every angle and make an informed decision. Hadn't that been exactly how she'd guided her career in PR straight to the top?

He knew that the process involved research, plus pages and pages of lists, plus conversations with people she relied on, such as Cora Jane. He imagined she'd go to Sally, perhaps Meg, maybe even her sisters. Eventually, though, she would come back to him with more questions, if not a final decision. Waiting for that moment, though, was getting to him. He'd wanted to pick up the phone and call her at least a dozen times, but he'd held back.

Hanging back, being patient—it was what he'd always done. In the end, he'd wound up with Kayla because of it. And though that had ended in terrible loss, for a time he'd had exactly the life he'd envisioned with her. He didn't doubt that the same strategy would work with Gabi.

But the stakes were bigger this time, his feelings even deeper. What if he waited too long, sat on the sidelines and, in the end, had to watch her walk away? With that fear at the back of his mind, it was getting harder and harder to be patient, even though he knew she was not a woman to be rushed.

When his cell phone rang and he finally saw her name in the caller ID, he dragged in a deep breath before answering.

"Hey," he said, proud of the casual tone he'd managed.

"Hey, yourself. Want to meet me at Castle's this afternoon? I'd like to talk some more about this idea of yours."

"I'll be there," he said at once. "What time?"

"Whenever you're free."

"I'm on my way now," he said at once, then laughed. "Not that I'm anxious or anything." It was downright pitiful how badly he wanted this, wanted her.

"You do realize we're going to talk about the artists' studio, not anything else," she cautioned.

"Yes, ma'am. I haven't asked any other questions yet," he reminded her. "One thing at a time, Gabi. One thing at a time."

And getting her to say yes to staying here on the coast was the first step to getting everything he wanted.

As Wade walked into Castle's by the Sea, Cora Jane stopped him.

"Thank you," she said, her expression solemn. "You've put the light back in my girl's eyes."

"She told you about the project I have in mind?"

"Every last detail, and believe you me, there are pages of them," she said, laughing. "Gabriella doesn't leave much to chance once she gets invested in something. She's a whirlwind, sweeping up information and sorting through it till it makes sense to her."

"What do you think of the idea?" he asked, curious to know her reaction. Cora Jane had her finger on the pulse of this community, probably more so than he did.

"I'd love it on its own merits," she said candidly, "but if it will keep Gabriella and my great-grandbaby close to me, then I'm a thousand percent behind it. Now get on over there before she wonders what sort of meddling I'm doing. I'll bring your pie in a minute. It's Mississippi mud pie today. Haven't tried that one in a while, but Jerry had a hankering for it, so I decided to indulge him."

"When do you intend to make an honest man of that old Cajun?" Wade teased. "Put the poor man out of his misery and marry him."

"We're doing just fine the way things are," Cora Jane said.

Wade couldn't seem to stop himself from asking, "Is that what Jerry thinks?"

"Well, no," she admitted. "But Jeremiah can't get his way about everything. It sets a bad precedent."

As anxious as Wade was to speak to Gabi, he hesitated. "If you don't mind me meddling…" he began.

She smiled at that. "Turnabout's fair, I suppose," she said with unmistakable reluctance.

"The man sat quietly on the sidelines for a lot of years out of respect for your marriage to Caleb. Maybe it's time to give a little thought to what he needs and not just what suits you." He held up his hands when

Cora Jane opened her mouth, clearly intending to protest. "I'm just telling you how I see it. You're perfectly free to ignore me."

"I suppose that's more latitude than I give you," Cora Jane grumbled. "I'll think about it."

"All I'm suggesting," Wade said.

He crossed the restaurant and found Gabi watching him curiously.

"What were you and Grandmother talking about? Were you forming a strategy about me?"

He laughed. "Nope. I was just putting in a good word for Jerry. Cora Jane seems inclined to stick with the status quo. I think her cook wants a lot more."

"We all think that, but she's stubborn as an old mule about changing things," Gabi said, her frustration plain. "I think it's less about loyalty to our grandfather than it is about wanting to experience a little independence after all those years of marriage. I suppose I can't really blame her for that."

"An interesting perspective," Wade admitted. "I hadn't really thought about that. I guess I was just identifying with Jerry hiding his feelings for so long, hoping for a relationship that might never happen."

A frown crossed Gabi's face. "Identifying with him? Are you talking about waiting for me?"

"You…and Kayla," he admitted. "I've done a lot of waiting in my life." He held her gaze. "I'm thinking I need to start being more proactive."

"Wade—"

He cut her off before she could utter whatever protest was about to form on her lips. "Just fair warning, sweetheart, not some kind of ultimatum you need to get all worked up about."

She stared at him for a long time. "You scare the daylights out of me sometimes."

"How so?"

"You're still reading my mind," she grumbled.

"The way I hear it, most women would be thrilled by that."

"Well, I find it annoying."

"Only because you're used to keeping your emotions under tight wraps."

A storm cloud rolled across her face. "I most certainly do not," she said, then sighed. "Oh, whatever. Of course I do. Emotions are messy."

"They are," he agreed. "But in the end, they're pretty much all that matters."

"I suppose I can't argue with that," she said with unmistakable reluctance. "Wade, I wish I could get past the idea that you've got Kayla and me all twisted up in your mind, that you're looking for a situation that mirrors that one."

"How many times do I have to tell you that the two of you are nothing alike? To Kayla, well, much as I wanted to believe she had real feelings for me, I was nothing more than a safety net. I'd be a fool not to have recognized that. It was enough at the time." He leveled an unrelenting gaze into her eyes. "I want more from you, a whole lot more. I knew it the first time I laid eyes on you. You left me speechless."

"Speechless?" she asked, looking intrigued.

He could recall the exact moment when Emily had been ogling him in a futile attempt to make Boone jealous and Gabi had walked into the dining room at Castle's, a bit of an ice-princess demeanor about her.

"You took my breath away," he confirmed, a smile

on his lips. "And if you recall, both Emily and Samantha were in the room and neither one of them fazed me. It was all about you from that first instant. If this thing happens between us, Gabi, it's going to be powerful and lasting. I won't accept anything less."

She looked shaken by his declaration. "I guess that's clear enough, then."

"Scared?"

"Terrified," she admitted.

He smiled. "You shouldn't be. Once you let down that well-honed guard of yours, I think you'll see what I see. Until then, maybe we need to focus on something else."

"The artists' workshop," she murmured, as if she'd just remembered why she'd called him.

Wade nodded. Because he couldn't resist, though, he leaned closer and captured her mouth with a kiss meant to chase away every last reservation. When he sat back, his pulse racing, Gabi looked dazed.

"There are just so many complications," she said with regret.

"There don't have to be." He kissed her again, taking his time, enjoying this long-delayed journey of discovery. "Still complicated?" he asked eventually.

She nodded, but she looked a lot less sure of herself. It was that expression that gave him more hope than he'd felt in a long time.

Gabi hadn't been anticipating the kisses. Even more, she hadn't been anticipating yet another bone-melting, breath-stealing response to it. The man had skills, she'd give him that. Add in his willingness to play a waiting game, and she was probably doomed.

Which wouldn't be such a bad thing, she realized as she studied him while he pored over the spreadsheets she'd organized in her attempt to answer every conceivable question about the artists' studio she was starting to envision.

"You've done a lot of work on this," Wade commented when he looked up.

She smiled. "You know me and my planning." She waved at the papers she'd brought. "That's the tip of the iceberg. Back at the house I have lists of my lists. Every time I think of some new angle, I jot it on a piece of paper."

"And then research the daylights out of it?" he asked, clearly amused and maybe even a little impressed.

"Well, of course. This won't be cheap to get started. And if we're going to do it, we want to do it right."

His brow rose. "We?"

"Well, it was your idea, and you suggested a partnership, so I'm running with that concept." She frowned. "Unless you weren't serious about that part."

"Hey, I'm all in," he told her readily. "I have some cash to invest, and I'll do the sweat equity and handle any renovations we need to do. Have you started looking around for a place that can accommodate what you're envisioning?"

"I found some space in a couple of the strip malls, but most of it's too small and I think the atmosphere's all wrong."

"I agree," he said at once. "How about an old house in an area that's been zoned for commercial use?"

"Much better, but I haven't had time to look around at those properties yet. Have you seen anything that could work?"

"Not really, but I'll definitely start keeping my eyes open now that I know you're interested in pursuing this. How do you see this working? Are you hoping to find other artists to invest?"

Gabi shook her head and explained Meg's theory about that. "Is she right?"

"She's right," Wade agreed. "I think it would be much smarter to make this your business—or ours, if that's your preference."

"I'm inclined to agree. I still think we should have a certain number of artists committed up front, though, say with reasonable two-year leases, so we know there's time to get this off the ground without a lot of turnover. Stability's going to be important, especially at the beginning. If we're successful, something tells me we'll have a waiting list of artists wanting spaces."

"How many were you thinking?"

"At least five to ten with workshop spaces and maybe double that selling their works in the gallery. I'd want at least one artist working in there at any given time, so we'd want a commitment of one day a week from each participating artist. The more days, of course, the better," she suggested. She frowned at the expression on his face. "What's wrong? Too ambitious?"

"No, I just love that you've put so much thought into this already. I knew you were the perfect person to pull this together."

"Hey, we're a long way from pulling anything off," she warned him. "I only have one artist so far, you."

"Sally's in," he reminded her.

"Okay, two. Do you know enough local artists to round out my list of contacts?"

"Between Sally and me we can come up with most

of the artists in eastern North Carolina. Meg has some contacts, too. Maybe you could consider having a guest studio space for an artist from out of the area to come in for a month at a time," he said.

Gabi beamed at him. "What a great idea! It's an on-going angle for promotion." She raised her hand for a high five. "What a team!"

Wade captured her hand and held it. "Keep thinking that way, darlin'. Keep thinking that way."

As it turned out, she was starting to think that way more and more often.

Wade was startled when he glanced around and re-alized it was dusk outside. He and Gabi had been talk-ing most of the afternoon, tossing around ideas, which she frantically scribbled down on one of her lists. He loved seeing this side of her, working at full stride, her mind engaged, right along with her enthusiasm. It made him even happier that he was at least in part responsible for having planted the idea that she was running with.

"Hey," he said, nudging her in the side. "Have you noticed that it's getting dark? I think Cora Jane and Jerry are long gone. We probably need to think about getting you and the little one some dinner."

Just then her tummy rumbled, emphasizing his point. She smiled. "I think you're right. Let's grab takeout and head back to Cora Jane's."

"You have your car?"

"Actually, no. Cora Jane picked me up so she could go with me to my doctor's appointment. If she's gone, I'm stuck."

"You're never stuck if I'm around," Wade said. "Let's go. Where would you like to stop for some food?"

"I'm dying for a hamburger," she admitted. "I got that into my head when I was with Meg a couple of days ago, but we ended up at a vegetarian place, and I still haven't had one."

"Want to stop and pick up the meat? I know a place that only sells the organic stuff with none of that pink slime filler. We can cook them ourselves. I make a half-way decent burger."

"Go for it," she said at once. "Just make sure you get all the fixings. I want tomatoes, cheese, onion, the works."

"A woman after my own heart," Wade said. "You can sit in the car and catch a quick catnap."

An hour later they were pulling into the driveway at Cora Jane's, where Wade spotted an unfamiliar car parked just behind Cora Jane's and the truck he thought to be Jerry's. "Looks like Cora Jane has company," he said. "Unless Jerry's gone out and bought himself a fancy BMW."

At his words, Gabi's eyes snapped open. She sat up straight, then muttered a curse.

"What?" he asked.

"Paul," she said succinctly.

Wade regarded her incredulously, a sinking sensation in the pit of his stomach. "The baby's father? That Paul?"

"That's the one," she said.

"What's he doing here? Did you have any idea he was coming?"

"Are you kidding me? He's the last person I want to see," she replied, though resignation was already settling on her face.

"It's not too late for me to pull right back out of the driveway," he offered, worried by the sudden pallor in her cheeks. "We can go to my place."

She sighed heavily. "Much as I would love to do exactly that, I can't stick Cora Jane with handling him."

"I'm sure she's probably delighted to give him an earful," Wade said. "Come to think of it, I have a few choice words for the man myself."

Gabi gave him a worried look. "But you won't say anything, right? I'm not up to a scene."

"No scene," Wade promised. Unless the jerk started it, he added mentally.

Inside, they found Paul seated at the kitchen table, his shoulders stiff, his expression uncomfortable. Wade studied him intently, trying to see what Gabi had once seen in him. He was handsome, he supposed, in the slick, polished way that some successful men worked hard to achieve. He was dressed impeccably in a suit that had probably cost a month's salary, French cuffs with eighteen-carat-gold cuff links and a Rolex on his wrist. A lot overdressed for a visit to the beach or to an ex-lover, in Wade's opinion.

Across from him, Cora Jane was eyeing him as if she'd found a particularly nasty poisonous snake in her garden. The silence was deafening.

When Wade opened the back door and Gabi stepped inside, Paul bounced up looking relieved, at least until he spotted Wade right on Gabi's heels.

"Well," he said with a little huff that spoke volumes about his reaction to finding Gabi with another man.

"Hello, Paul," Gabi said mildly, her head high. "This is a surprise."

"I thought we should talk," he said, his gaze riveted on her rounded belly. "About the baby."

"The baby's no concern of yours," she reminded him. "I have the paper you signed proving that."

"It's still my child," he insisted.

"No, *she's* mine," Gabi replied firmly.

Paul regarded her with a startled expression. "It's a girl?"

"Yes."

He glanced around at Cora Jane, and then at Wade. "Gabriella, could we speak privately?"

"I see no point in that," she told him, taking a step closer to Wade as if seeking his unspoken support. Wade put a reassuring hand on her shoulder.

Paul clearly got the message and just as evidently didn't like it. "So, that's the way it is? You've already hopped into another man's bed? Or was it his baby to begin with, one you just tried to pawn off on me?"

Wade's temper flared. "Hold on, pal," he said, taking a step forward.

Gabi interceded. "It's okay, Wade. Let him rant. He has no idea what he's talking about."

Cora Jane frowned at that. Though she'd remained quiet since Gabi and Wade had walked in, she spoke up now, her furious gaze directed at Paul. "Young man, if you dare to speak to or about my granddaughter that way again, I will have you thrown out of here."

Paul actually looked flustered by the threat, but he still put on a show of pure bravado. "By whom? Him?" he asked with a disdainful glance at Wade.

Jerry walked into the kitchen then, standing close enough to intimidate. "By the two of us, if need be," he said in his soft, Cajun-accented voice. "Though there's not a doubt in my mind that Wade could handle the job. He's very protective of Gabriella."

For the first time, Paul looked genuinely flustered by the united front he was facing.

"I'll speak to him privately," Gabi said, interceding. She stalked past him and headed for the living room. "Five minutes, Paul. Not a second longer."

Wade reluctantly watched her go. "I don't like this."

"I'm not exactly crazy about it, either," Cora Jane said. "But Gabi knows him better than we do. She obviously thinks she can handle him."

"And Wade and I are right here for backup if she needs it," Jerry added.

Cora Jane gave him a tender look. "It won't be the first time you've stood up for one of my girls," she said. "You were always quick to take on any customer who seemed to be bothering them."

"Of course," Jerry said. "Family looks out for family."

Wade gave Cora Jane a knowing look at Jerry's words and saw the tears in her eyes. She glanced his way.

"Oh, I know what you're thinking," she grumbled. "Just because the man is sweet doesn't mean I have to rush into anything."

Jerry obviously guessed exactly what she meant because his booming laugh filled the kitchen.

"But one of these days you'll give in," he said with conviction. "After all, I've been told I'm irresistible."

"If you're so irresistible, why didn't you marry years ago?" Cora Jane retorted.

"Because I've only had eyes for one woman and she was out of reach," Jerry said.

Wade had the distinct impression, though, that those days might be coming to an end.

When Gabi was alone with Paul, she noticed that his face was more haggard than she could ever recall seeing it.

"What's going on with you?" she asked, knowing that her concern was an old habit she hadn't quite broken.

"Second thoughts," he said tersely. "At least until I saw how easily you've moved on."

"I haven't moved on, not the way you mean. Wade and I are friends. He's been a real rock for me. I needed that after you bailed."

"Seriously?" he asked, obviously not believing it was possible for men and women to be friends. "You're not sleeping with him?"

"Paul, I'm carrying your child. It's not exactly the best time to think about being intimate with another man." Even if that man was so appealing it sometimes hurt to force herself to keep resisting him.

"Makes sense, I suppose. He's not really your type, is he? What's he do? Farm tobacco? Maybe knock back a couple of beers on Friday night?"

She regarded him with disgust. "You are such an incredible snob. How did I miss that?"

"Because I was exactly the kind of man you wanted, one with ambition and big bucks."

She shook her head. "Well, obviously that was a huge mistake. I must have missed the part about those things only mattering if the person has character. I think Grandmother and Jerry were right. You should go."

"Not until we've talked this through," he said stubbornly. "I want you to come back to Raleigh. Now that I've had time to get used to the idea of a baby, I think we could make it work."

She shook her head. "Sorry. Too late."

Her matter-of-fact dismissal clearly stunned him. "You don't mean that."

"Yes, I do," she said with conviction.

She realized that the past few weeks had changed her, made her stronger in ways she'd never imagined. She'd always known she excelled at her job, now she'd started to believe in herself as a person. She knew she could raise this child on her own, surrounded by a family who would fill her daughter's life with love.

And, irony of ironies, seeing Paul had accomplished something else. He was such a stark contrast to Wade, who'd never had a moment's uncertainty about being a part of her life or the baby's. It made her realize how lucky she truly was to have found him. Though she was a very long way from taking the blind leap of faith she knew Wade was hoping for, she knew that when she did, he was the man she wanted in her life.

She leveled a long look now at the man who'd turned her life upside down, but in a twist of fate, given her far more than she'd lost.

"Go, Paul. There is absolutely nothing I want or need from you."

He must have heard the certainty in her voice or perhaps she'd only said what he'd been hoping to hear, because he turned and left, without even looking back.

Good riddance, she thought, and went back to the man who understood the real meaning of character and commitment.

Twenty-One

"I don't like it," Cora Jane said when Gabi had filled her, Jerry and Wade in on the reason behind Paul's visit. "You may have gotten rid of him just now, Gabriella, but the fact that he came here in the first place strikes me as a red flag. Who knows when he'll have second thoughts again? Maybe decide he can't live without you?"

"Not a consideration," Gabi said flatly.

"Okay, then, can't live without claiming his daughter," Cora Jane said. "It's impossible to know what motivates a man who's used to getting whatever he wants. He could decide being a family man would be an excellent career move."

"I agree," Wade said as he set a platter of burgers on the kitchen table that Cora Jane had set. "You need legal advice, Gabi. Talk to Louise. If this is beyond her expertise, she can at least point you toward someone who can make sure you and the baby are protected."

Though Gabi wanted to believe they were both overreacting, she couldn't deny that it would be smart to make sure the law was on her side. "I'll talk to Louise," she promised. "But could we drop this for tonight?

I don't want to get indigestion. I've been looking forward to this cheeseburger for days."

Jerry put his big, comforting hand over hers. "Put this out of your mind. Something tells me that man came here just to swagger around with his big demands, so he could silence some last shred of conscience that's been bugging him."

Gabi smiled at Jerry's insight. "See, that's why I love you. You saw what I saw."

"The man might be an arrogant jerk, but he can still cause trouble," Wade cautioned them both.

"Which is why I *will* see Louise," Gabi stressed again. "Now, enough!"

"Okay, on to happier things," Cora Jane said with determined cheer. "Your sister called. Samantha was hoping to talk to you."

Gabi frowned. "Is everything okay?"

"I said happier things, didn't I? It seems those little items you managed to plant in a couple of gossip columns started some buzz in the right places. She has three auditions this week. One of them is for a recurring character on a prime-time show being shot in New York."

"That's fantastic," Gabi said, jumping up and getting her phone. "I need to call her back. I want to hear every detail."

Wade touched her arm. "After you've eaten," he said quietly. "You were starving when we headed over here and, thanks to Paul's impromptu visit, that was a couple of hours ago."

Her initial reaction was to chafe at being told what to do, but the real concern in his eyes kept her silent.

She sat back down and took another bite of the perfectly cooked cheeseburger before meeting his gaze.

"You do know that if this weren't so delicious, I'd have ignored you," she told him.

He laughed. "Absolutely, but I had to try. Sometimes you forget you're not the only one you need to think about."

Cora Jane smiled as she listened to him. "You're going to be a wonderful husband and father, Wade."

Gabi nearly choked on her food. After clearing her throat, she started to say something, but her grandmother silenced her with a look.

"I'm just saying what I think about Wade," Cora Jane said firmly. "I didn't say a thing about you."

Wade chuckled. "That's right. Who knows how many women might recognize these extraordinary skills of mine and vie for the chance to march me straight to the altar?"

Though he was joking, his words gave Gabi a pang. She didn't want some other woman being the beneficiary of his tenderness and caring. And yet that was exactly what she was risking by dragging her heels and not jumping into the relationship he so clearly wanted with her.

She dared to touch his cheek, even knowing it was an open declaration in front of Cora Jane and Jerry. "All those women," she said solemnly, "they'll have to fight me off first."

Cora Jane gave an immediate whoop at her comment, but it was the stunned expression in Wade's eyes that really got to her.

"You okay with that?" she asked, even as she wondered if she'd gone too far, too fast—not for his peace of mind, but for hers. Sure, she'd had an epiphany just now when she'd stacked Wade's attributes up against Paul's less than stellar character, but she hadn't envisioned leaping into a full-blown relationship just yet.

Wade's smile spread slowly. "More than okay, darlin'. More than okay."

Then, she thought as relief spread through her, she was more than okay, too.

Wade all but dragged Gabi out of the house after dinner and headed straight for the pier at the edge of the yard, either looking for privacy or with the intent of shoving her into the chilly water.

"If you suddenly intend to have your way with me, I have to tell you this is not the best place," Gabi told him, amused by his eagerness to get her alone. "This old, weathered wood has splinters and the bench isn't much better."

He gestured for her to sit, then began to pace. When he continued to say nothing, she grew concerned. Had she gone too far earlier? Had she inadvertently turned a game into something too serious?

"Something on your mind, Wade?"

He slowed then and looked directly into her eyes. "What was going on in there earlier?"

"Going on?" she asked, though she knew perfectly well what he meant. She needed to buy time, scrambling to protect these fragile new emotions she'd only tonight recognized for what they were—a prelude to solid, enduring love, the kind she'd never allowed herself to imagine finding.

"Have you suddenly decided you're ready for a relationship?" he asked, as if he couldn't quite believe it was a real possibility.

"Yes," she said at once, then tempered her response in the interest of complete candor. "More or less."

"Now that's reassuring," he said dryly. "Exactly what every man dreams of hearing. So, was this sudden decision because of Paul's unexpected visit? Are you starting to think if you and I get serious, we can present a united front to a judge or something?"

Gabi stared at him in dismay. "Are you crazy? That never crossed my mind. Paul has nothing to do with this. Well, other than the fact that he made me see what an incredible man you are. I believe Jerry's right. He came over here, postured for a bit, and will never be seen or heard from again."

"Then that leaves what? You can't tell me you had a sudden epiphany over burgers and decided you were madly in love with me."

Gabi knew she shouldn't, because he was so obviously worked up over this, but she smiled. "Maybe I did," she said softly. "Not because you made a great burger, though."

His gaze narrowed. "Why, then?"

Since it was her fault they'd ventured into previously forbidden emotional territory, she owed him honesty. It was hard to admit, though, that she'd been half-crazy with jealousy there for a minute.

"Was it because I mentioned all those other women?" he asked, looking bemused by the possibility that an innocent remark had accomplished what all his other efforts had failed to do. "Did I make you jealous, Gabriella?"

Gabi sighed. There it was. "A little, yes," she said,

then added hurriedly, "but it was Paul who clinched it. You probably owe him."

Wade didn't look especially pleased by that. "How so?" he asked, his expression dark.

"I finally saw him for who he really is tonight. It made me realize what a close call I'd had and how incredibly lucky I am to have found you. And then you went and mentioned all those other women recognizing what a catch you are." Blushing, she admitted, "It kind of freaked me out."

He stared at her, his expression incredulous. "You really were jealous? Of women who don't exist?"

"Maybe just a little," she said. "I just knew I didn't want you to be with *those* women."

His lips quirked at that. "Really? You think I should be with you?"

"Yes, at least compared to them, if that makes any sense."

His laugh carried over the water. "It does make a crazy kind of sense if a woman is crazy in love and just starting to figure it out. Any possibility that could be the case?"

Though she hated confessing the unexpected turn her emotions had apparently taken, she nodded. "Could be."

Now his whoop mirrored Cora Jane's earlier.

"You don't have to get arrogant and smug about it," she grumbled. "It's still not a sure thing. I think pregnancy has used up a lot of my brain cells. I might not be thinking clearly."

"Oh, but you are," he said confidently. "There is no turning back now, Gabriella."

He pulled her up and into his arms, seemingly oblivious to the very evident reminder that she had belonged to another man not that long ago. This time when he kissed her, she held back nothing. And despite the dizzying sensation that caused, she knew one thing with absolute certainty. She'd never been in safer, more loving arms.

"I'm telling you this situation has the potential to get really ugly," Louise told Wade when he stopped by her house the day after he and Gabi had finally, inevitably declared themselves to be a couple.

"Obviously Gabi filled you in on what the baby's father had to say when he turned up here yesterday," Wade said, taking a sip of sweet tea.

"Yes, and it scares me to death. He's unpredictable, Wade."

"Don't you think you can fight him and win?" Wade asked her, worried on Gabi's behalf. "Can he rescind that piece of paper he signed?"

"He could certainly try and, in the right circumstances, he just might win. I'm not saying he could take custody from her, but he could definitely win visitation with his child unless there's some overwhelming reason to declare him unfit."

"And that's what you told Gabi?" he said, regretting he hadn't gone to Cora Jane's looking for her, rather than stopping off here first. She must be freaking out.

Louise nodded. "I also told her she might be wise to grant him limited visitation, rather than trying to cut him out of the baby's life. It would be one thing if she wanted to put the baby up for adoption and give her a clean start, free from ties to her birth parents, but now that she intends to keep the baby, it's a whole new ball game."

"Lou, you didn't see this guy. He wasn't over here throwing his weight around because he gives two hoots for that baby. Whatever his motivation, it wasn't about love for his child. If someone told him he had to care for a child, I can almost guarantee he'd pass out cold... or hire a nanny so he never had to set eyes on the kid."

"That doesn't necessarily make him a bad father figure. After all, single fathers do work. So do single moms. Or even married couples who both work. They all have to make responsible arrangements for their children."

He frowned at her. "Whose side are you on?"

"Yours, at the moment. If Gabi actually hires me, I'll be on hers, of course."

"I'm not the one who needs a lawyer," he reminded her.

"No, but you do need someone looking out for your interests. You're getting more invested in this woman and this baby by the minute."

"No news there," he said, seeing no reason to debate the point. "In fact, when the timing is right, I have every intention of marrying her and treating this child as if it's my own."

Louise's expression turned sad. "That's what I'm worried about. The baby isn't yours, Wade. This little girl belongs to another man, who could claim at any moment that he wants a role in the baby's life. It's not like it was with Kayla where the dad was completely out of the picture."

He scowled at her. "Do you think I'm too stupid to figure out the difference?"

"Of course not. I just know what a soft heart you have. I don't want it broken again."

Despite his frustration, Wade smiled at the fiercely protective note in her voice. "Aren't you the one who once made a speech to our folks about being allowed to make your own mistakes, that it's part of being an adult?"

She smiled ruefully. "Well, yes, but that was me. This is you. I want so badly for you to be happy and to have everything you deserve."

"And Gabi's the woman who can accomplish both of those things," he assured her. "I know it, Lou. That's not to say there won't be bumps in the road. They're part of life. And maybe Paul will turn out to be the biggest, pain-in-the-ass pothole of all, but it doesn't scare me. The *only* thing that scares me is the thought of losing Gabi."

Louise regarded him with surprise. Obviously she hadn't been prepared for such an ardent declaration. "You really are in love with her, aren't you?"

"Head over heels," he confirmed.

She nodded slowly. Though there was still worry in her eyes, she said, "Then we'll do whatever it takes to minimize the damage this man can do to her, the baby and to you."

"Thank you."

And if worse came to worst and Gabi had to share custody with Paul, he'd find some way to make that work out for all of them, too. After all, if Gabi had once had feelings for him, misguided though they might have been, surely Paul couldn't be all bad.

It was a surprisingly warm day, even for mid-March, so Wade had left the garage door rolled up while he worked on his latest carving, a blue heron made from the last piece of driftwood he'd found washed up on shore. He heard a car slow, then stop outside. When he glanced up and saw Sam Castle standing in the doorway, his jaw dropped.

"Hello, sir," he said, unable to keep a note of caution from his voice. "What brings you by? Gabi didn't mention you were coming for a visit."

"She doesn't know I'm here," Sam said, walking in without an invitation and wandering through Wade's studio. After pausing to study several carvings, he stopped beside Wade. "I thought we should talk."

Wade frowned at his somber tone. "About?"

"Gabriella and this insane notion she's gotten in her head about making wind chimes. I've tried talking sense into her, but she's not listening. I have a feeling you're behind that."

"I think you're wrong about that," Wade said. "I haven't tried to influence her. And you're not entirely up-to-date. She actually has new plans."

Sam's expression brightened. "She's coming back to Raleigh?"

"No, sir, but you'll need to ask her to fill you in."

"But the bottom line is you want her to keep hanging around over here so she'll be close by, don't you? I've seen the way you look at her."

"If you're suggesting I'm attracted to her, then yes. If you're saying you think I'd try to keep her away from doing anything she wants to do wherever she wants to do it because of that, you're flat-out wrong. I just want her to be happy. She wasn't happy when she got here. I don't think she'd been happy for a long time."

Sam looked surprised by that. "She loved that job. She excelled at it."

"And it was killing her," Wade countered. "You know why? Because she'd worked so hard for so long, all to impress you, and it never worked."

"But I was proud of her," Sam said, clearly shaken by Wade's direct, uncensored words.

"And you told her that frequently? Ever?"

The older man looked chagrined. "No."

Wade nodded. "That's what I thought."

"All of that's beside the point," Sam argued. "She's too good at what she does to be wasting her talent trying to be some kind of artist. Who does that?"

Wade made a pointed survey of his workshop. "Well, I do, for one."

Sam looked vaguely taken aback. "You make your livelihood from this?"

"This and custom cabinetry," Wade told him. "Last year I earned more as an artist than I did from the cabinet work."

"But you haven't walked away from your nuts-and-bolts job, have you?" Sam asked, his expression triumphant. "That's all I'm saying. If Gabi wants to do this as a hobby, more power to her. But she shouldn't walk away from a lucrative career to dabble, especially not now with a baby on the way."

"Sir, no disrespect, but Gabi has a very good head on her shoulders. You should know that. It's why she's made some changes in her plans. I'm sure she's considered this new goal from every angle. Give her some credit."

Her father regarded him with frustration. "You're not going to help me make her see sense?"

"Not if your idea of sense is to go back to the life

she was leading before, which was sapping all the energy out of her."

"I should have known," Sam said, shaking his head. "You're living in a dreamworld, the same as she is. My mother's no better. I'm sure she's had a hand in persuading Gabriella to stay in Sand Castle Bay. Nothing would please her more than to hand off that albatross of a restaurant to one of the girls."

"You're wrong again," Wade said. "Cora Jane has made it plain that she would love having Gabi and the baby close by, but she hasn't once tried to influence her. Rather, she's been supportive of Gabi finding her own way. That's what I've tried to do, as well."

Sam ran his fingers through his hair. "Gabi was the most ambitious of all my girls, the most like me. I just can't see how she could make such a radical change without being pressured."

"Well, I can assure you that she hasn't been," Wade told him. "And since you came to me, I feel there's one thing I'm entitled to say. It seems a little late for you to decide to play the all-knowing daddy. There were a lot of years when she needed that from you and didn't get it."

Sam flushed at the harsh words, but rather than lashing back, he merely nodded. "I'm trying to make up for that now," he said simply.

"Then a word of advice," Wade said. "Focus on what Gabi wants and needs, not what you think is best for her. That's all I've tried to do. I've just encouraged her to explore her options. I haven't once told her what she ought to do." He held the older man's gaze. "Just a thought."

He wondered, though, if a man with Sam Castle's

success and arrogance was capable of leaving Gabi free to make her own choices and her own mistakes.

"There's something else we need to talk about," Sam said.

Something in his tone alerted Wade that this could be an even touchier topic. Only one subject he could think of fell into that category.

"Is this about Jimmy?"

Sam nodded, his expression filled with regret. "He's not getting the scholarship. He was on the short list and I lobbied for him, but there were just too many candidates with sterling credentials. The committee had to make a tough decision, and Jimmy didn't make the cut."

Wade heaved a sigh. Though the news wasn't entirely unexpected, it was disappointing. "He's going to be devastated."

"I know," Sam said. "I've had a couple of conversations with him recently, so I know how much he was counting on this. I tried to keep him from getting his hopes too high, but at that age, it's hard to accept that rejection is a possibility."

"He knew," Wade said. "He discussed it with me. He was afraid that not hearing anything meant he wasn't going to get it. He's prepared for bad news."

Sam looked skeptical. "You ever known a nineteen-year-old kid who's really prepared for bad news, especially news that's going to ruin his chances at the bright future he deserves?"

"Jimmy's taken a lot of hits in his young life. He may be more prepared than most," Wade said.

"In a way, that's what makes this even harder. The kid could use a break," Sam said, sounding genuinely dismayed. "It's killing me that the news isn't what we'd hoped for. Though I wanted to talk to you about Gabriella, I also wanted to drive over here today so I could talk to Jimmy in person. I didn't want this news coming from somebody he's never even spoken to before."

Wade regarded him with surprise. "That's very kind of you."

Sam shrugged. "I'll admit it, the boy got to me. He reminds me of someone else—me when I was his age. Gabi mentioned it herself when she first told me about him." He met Wade's gaze. "Which is why I want to fund his education myself."

The statement left Wade openmouthed with shock. "You'd pay for him to go to college? Why?"

"Because he deserves this chance, and I have the means to give it to him. I know I wasn't always the best father to my girls, but I have an opportunity to help this boy. Maybe that'll make up for some of the things I didn't do in the past. A little karmic balance or whatever they call it."

Wade smiled hearing Sam Castle, a man dedicated to scientific pursuits, talking about karma.

"Now, here's the big question," Sam said. "Do I tell him I'm behind this or let him think he won the scholarship or even just tell him I've found a different scholarship for his education."

"You tell him the truth," Wade replied without hesitation. "Not so you can take the credit for saving the day, but because the truth will eventually come out, and he needs to know it now, from you. What you're doing is incredibly generous. He should know that."

"Okay, that's the quick, easy answer and I agree on almost every level," Sam said, "but you know this fam-

ily. You know Jimmy. Are they going to think it's charity and dismiss it out of hand?"

Well, hell, Wade thought, surprised by Sam's perceptiveness. That *was* a real concern. He gave it the
consideration it deserved.

"I think it depends on how you handle it," he said
eventually. "Give Jimmy the option of paying you back."

"I don't want his money," Sam protested. "I don't
want him to leave school saddled with debt."

"Not even if that's the only way he'll accept the
offer?" Wade asked. "Run this by Gabi, but I think
I'm right. I think this is the only way Jimmy will accept your help." He smiled. "Of course, when the time
comes and he's some rising superstar in the biomedical
field, you can always turn down the payments he sends
you or put them into a scholarship for another young
student who shows promise."

Sam grinned. "I like the way you think. That's what
I'll do. I think I'll call my mother and see if we can pull
together a little gathering at the house for tonight. We'll
turn this into a celebration. You'll be there, of course."

"I wouldn't miss it," Wade told him. Not only did
he want to see Jimmy's face when he got the news,
but he wanted to be there in case Sam decided to start
something with Gabi over her decision to stay here on
the coast.

"By the way, sir, before you go, there's something I
need to discuss with you," Wade said impulsively, hoping this would be the most persuasive argument yet
against Sam trying to get Gabi back to Raleigh. "From
what you said earlier, it's clear you already have some
idea that I'm in love with your daughter."

To his surprise, Sam actually looked taken aback. "I knew you were close, but this hardly seems the time…"

"Which is why I haven't pushed her too hard," Wade agreed. "But I do plan to ask her to marry me when the time is right. I'd like your blessing for that. I also thought you might find it reassuring to know she wouldn't be giving up everything to stay here. She might be gaining more than she loses."

For an instant, Wade thought Sam might argue, but then a smile spread across his face. "I have the feeling you're absolutely right about that," he said. "I may not know you well, young man, but I like what I've seen. I like how you're looking out for my daughter and for Jimmy and even my mother. I doubt I'll have any say over whatever decision Gabi makes, but I think she'd be doing just fine if she does choose you."

For a visit that had begun on a contentious note, Wade thought it had turned out pretty well. Of course, he might be busy lining up all his ducks, but he had a hunch Gabi was still a long way from being ready to align hers in the same row.

Twenty-Two

The hastily pulled together gathering at Cora Jane's seemed to Gabi less like a celebration than a wake. She didn't know what was going on, but the somber expression in her father's eyes when he'd arrived earlier didn't bode well for a fun evening.

The fact that he'd alerted her that he wanted to have a private conversation at some point didn't sound promising, either. She joined Cora Jane at the sink, where her grandmother was rinsing off vegetables for the salad.

"Any idea why Dad turned up here today?" Gabi asked her.

"Not a clue. He called me earlier and said he was on his way and would I mind having a few people over. Of course I said it was fine. He didn't fill me in on the guest list. I invited Jerry, but the rest of this is your father's show."

"It sure doesn't feel like a happy occasion," Gabi said.

"Or maybe your father simply isn't used to throwing a party. Go offer him a glass of wine. Maybe he'll loosen up, instead of looking as if he's about to make some doomsday announcement."

Gabi poured a glass of her dad's preferred cabernet sauvignon and took it to him.

He frowned when he saw the glass in her hand. "Should you be drinking?"

"I'm not. This is for you. Grandmother thought you looked as if you could use it."

He smiled. "Funny. All I remember right now are the years she watched me like a hawk to make sure I *wasn't* drinking. As a teenager, I could have sworn that woman had eyes in the back of her head."

Gabi could imagine it. She and her sisters had also discovered there was very little they could get by Cora Jane. "And you were how old?"

"Sixteen, seventeen," he admitted with a grin that made him look younger than the late fifties he was now. "She was very wise to keep a close eye on me."

"I think you're safely past the age when she's worried about you on that front," Gabi told him. "So, what's the big announcement, Dad? Why did you want Grandmother to have people over tonight?"

He smiled at her impatience. "You always did want to be the first to know everything."

"It's a trait that's come in handy doing PR," she told him. "The more you know ahead of time, the better you can spin the story."

"But I gather you have no intention of doing that any longer," he said, then gave her a sly survey. "Or do you?"

She regarded him curiously. "Did someone mention my plans to you?"

"Wade alluded to something, but he said the details needed to come from you."

His response unnerved her. "When did you speak to Wade?"

"Earlier today. I had a couple of things I wanted to discuss with him. Your young man has a good head on his shoulders."

Though Gabi considered that high praise from her father, who'd never had an approving word to say about any of the men in his daughters' lives, she felt compelled to say, "Wade is not my young man."

Her father smiled. "I suspect he'd disagree."

Gabi didn't know what to make of her father and Wade suddenly becoming chums. He'd never taken the time to get to know any of the boys she, Samantha or Emily had dated. It had been up to their mother or grandmother to vet them. The thought of him and Wade sharing confidences sent a chill through her.

"Was I one of those topics the two of you discussed?" she asked.

"Yes, but you'll probably be very happy to know he put me firmly in my place and then referred me to you for additional information on your future plans."

Gabi couldn't help smiling. "Good for Wade," she said, thinking his attitude must have come as quite a shock to her father, who was used to being in command of all situations.

"So, what's ahead for you, Gabriella?" he asked. "I gather the obsession with wind chimes has worn off."

"Not worn off exactly," she told him, then acknowledged ruefully, "It seems I have virtually no talent."

She braced herself for an I-told-you-so, but he merely asked, "Then what are your plans? I know you must have something all mapped out. You've never left your future up for grabs."

To her surprise, he sounded genuinely interested. She described the business she intended to start. "It will combine my appreciation for local art with my professional skills," she concluded excitedly. "Wade and I are both looking for exactly the right space, and I already have firm commitments from a few artists for the first two years. I need more, but it's a good start."

His surprise—and maybe even a hint of approval—shone in his eyes. "You sound happy," he said.

Though he smiled, Gabi could see a lingering trace of sorrow in his eyes, as well, as if he regretted the dramatic shift in direction her life was taking…away from his world.

"I'm really excited," she confirmed. "I know you'd hoped I'd change my mind and come back to Raleigh, but this feels right, Dad. It really does."

"And where does Wade fit in?"

"We're still working that out," she said.

"But you care for him?"

She nodded. "I do."

"Then you're making the right choice, sweetie. I wish you'd made a different one, but your happiness is what matters. And this is not a bad place to raise a child."

"Summers here were certainly some of the happiest times of my life," Gabi told him. "I want that for my daughter."

Just then the back door opened, interrupting the rare moment of accord between them, and Wade came in with Jimmy. Seeing the teenager, Gabi suddenly gathered what this evening was all about. She looked up at her father.

"He got the scholarship?" she whispered.

The slight shake of her father's head dismayed her, but something in his expression told her that wasn't the end of the story. For once she was going to have to exercise some of that patience that had always been in short supply.

Jimmy crossed the kitchen, his expression eager, but his steps halting, as if he couldn't quite decide between anticipation and dejection. Apparently Sam's carefully neutral expression was giving him no clues.

Gabi glanced at Wade and knew at once that he knew, but he, too, was giving nothing away.

"Oh, for heaven's sake," Cora Jane said impatiently. "Don't keep us in suspense, Sam. Is this about the scholarship?"

"Is it?" Jimmy asked, real fear in his eyes now.

"I'm afraid so," Sam said, putting his hand on the boy's shoulder. "You were a finalist, but you didn't make the cut, son."

Jimmy's shoulders slumped and he fought to blink back tears. "I figured," he said, his voice trembling. He turned away from Sam, from all of them, then took a step back. "I gotta take a walk or something, okay?" He sounded desperate to leave before those tears fell.

"In a minute," Sam said, keeping him in place. "The scholarships being offered by my company aren't the only ones out there."

"Sure, but it's too late to try for anything else," Jimmy said despondently.

"You don't have to apply for this one," Sam told him. "It's already yours."

Jimmy lifted his head, looking as if he hardly dared

to hope. "Seriously? How come? Did you show my application to somebody else?"

"I didn't have to," Sam told him. "I'd already seen it."

"You!" Jimmy said, clearly shocked.

Gabi was equally stunned, but the smile spreading across Cora Jane's face told her she hadn't imagined what her father had just said.

"Good for you, Sam," her grandmother said approvingly.

"But I can't take your money," Jimmy protested, though he looked as if it was killing him to say no. "It would be wrong."

"There is nothing wrong with accepting help when it's freely offered," Cora Jane told the teen adamantly.

"And if you feel strongly about it," Sam told him, "we can always think of it as a loan, though I'd prefer to consider it a scholarship for a very deserving and promising young man."

"Maybe I could pay you back," Jimmy said, finally allowing himself to consider the possibilities. "It might take a long time, though. I know it's a lot of money."

"Money well-spent," Sam said. "And here's another possibility. We could even structure it so you'd come to work for me as a paid intern for a year or two in return for the scholarship. Whatever it takes to make you comfortable. I want this opportunity for you, Jimmy."

Sam looked deep into Jimmy's still-troubled eyes and sought to further reassure him. "Son, you've earned this chance. And the fact that you want to pay it back in some way is just one more example of the kind of young man you are, one who's worthy of getting a decent break. Please let me do this for you."

"I don't know," Jimmy whispered, then glanced over at Wade. "What do you think?"

"I think it's the opportunity of a lifetime," Wade told him.

"But my dad—"

"Your dad wants the very best for you," Wade told him. "Talk it over with him. You'll see."

"And I'll sit down with him, too," Sam said, then stressed, "This is not charity, Jimmy. This is an investment in the future of my field. I expect great things from you."

A slow grin spread across Jimmy's face as he finally allowed himself to seize on the hope right in front of him. "You won't regret this, Mr. Castle. I swear you won't."

"I'm as sure of that as I've ever been of anything," Sam replied.

Gabi crossed the room and impulsively hugged her father. "I've never been more proud to be your daughter," she whispered. "You did a good thing here tonight."

"I couldn't let that boy down," her father said simply. "I just couldn't." He held her gaze. "And I hope I don't let you or your sisters down ever again, either."

It was the first time he'd ever made such a promise. Gabi knew if he'd made it before, she'd have had difficulty believing in it, but tonight, after what he'd done for a boy who needed his help, she did.

Emily took one look at Gabi's expanding waistline, put her hands on her hips and griped, "Well, there's no way to do a dress fitting with you this weekend."

"Thank you so much for reassuring me about my blimplike proportions," Gabi retorted as she fingered the gorgeous material of her bridesmaid dress. "You know exactly how pregnant I am. The baby's due in less than two months, which as you may recall was exactly the reason you postponed your wedding date till later in the summer. Don't start hassling me now."

Emily grinned, turning to Samantha. "Are these pregnancy hormones talking? She's awfully cranky."

"And still in the room," Gabi replied irritably. "And getting less and less inclined to throw you a bridal shower by the minute."

Samantha laughed openly. "It's so much fun having sisters," she said. "We're always so compatible."

"Speak for yourself," Gabi grumbled. She'd been like this for a couple of weeks now, ready to take offense at anything and everything, exhausted most of the time and eating ravenously. The secret longing she'd had to be one of those pregnant women who glowed with good health and carried their babies like little basketballs in their tummies didn't seem to be panning out. She waddled and she hadn't seen her feet in days. She'd finally given in and gone to a salon for a pedicure.

Amazingly, Wade seemed as attracted to her as if she'd fit the magazine cover stereotype of maternal bliss. He still claimed she was beautiful and never seemed to tire of rubbing her shoulders or even her swollen ankles. In fact, she wished he were here right now to massage away the tension this entire conversation was causing in her shoulders.

"She's thinking about Wade, isn't she?" Emily asked, again as if she weren't in the room.

"How can you tell?" Samantha asked, studying her.

"Sappy expression," Emily said. "When did that happen, by the way? Last time I was here she was still holding him at arm's length."

Gabi scowled at the pair of them. "Since you seem content to talk around me, I think I'll go downstairs and get something to eat."

"No!" Emily said, even as Samantha stepped in front of the door to block her way.

Gabi scowled at them. "What is going on with the two of you? You're acting weird. I don't buy for a second that you came back this weekend for more dress fittings."

"Not just fittings," Emily insisted. "Grandmother has an endless list of wedding details she wanted to run past me."

"And I came just to thank you in person for giving my career a much-needed boost," Samantha said. "I've had two parts recently. Neither was exactly star-status, but at least I was working again. Both of the casting directors mentioned the blurbs they'd seen in the paper, said it had reminded them of how much they'd liked me in other roles."

Gabi saw the sparkle in her big sister's eyes and smiled. "I'm glad. I told you all you needed was a little buzz."

"Well, it remains to be seen how long it lasts, but I do have a callback for another part next week."

"What about the prime-time series?"

"The recurring role went to someone else, but they did give me a couple of small parts in upcoming episodes. The writers said they'd keep me in mind when they're developing scripts for next season."

"That's fantastic," Emily enthused. "Sounds like this was just the shot in the arm your career needed."

"We'll see," Samantha said. "I've had runs like this before that went nowhere."

"This is a discouragement-free zone," Gabi declared. "Only good thoughts allowed here. You have work. Emily's getting married. I'm having a baby, and this art studio project is catching fire."

"And you have Wade dancing attendance," Emily teased.

Gabi smiled. "That, too." Suddenly she frowned and glanced around the room. "Why are the windows closed in here? It's getting stuffy. It's gorgeous outside. Let's let in some fresh air."

"You're probably just having a heat flash or something," Samantha said hurriedly. "I'm actually a little chilly."

"Yeah, me, too," Emily said.

Gabi regarded them oddly. "A pregnancy hot flash? Are you kidding me?"

"I'm telling you, it's chilly in here," Samantha repeated, pulling her sweater more tightly around her to emphasize the claim.

"Okay, that's it," Gabi said. "If you don't want the windows open, then I'm going downstairs for something cold to drink."

She left the room before they could stop her.

Before she was halfway down the stairs, she heard Emily holler, "Gabi, bring me up some bottled water, too, okay?"

Since she'd shouted it as if she wanted to be heard in the next county, Gabi could hardly pretend not to have heard the request. "Sure. Samantha, do you want anything?"

"No, I'm good," she said, though she sounded as if she weren't that far behind Gabi when she spoke.

Gabi stepped off the bottom step, turned into the living room and was overwhelmed by shouts of "Surprise!"

She halted in shock and was almost trampled by her sisters, who were, in fact, right on her heels.

"Is this for Emily?" she asked in confusion, then spotted the pink decor and all the baby shower paraphernalia.

"Are you surprised?" Samantha asked, putting an arm around her. "We really, really wanted it to be a surprise."

"Surprised?" Gabi repeated. "I'm in shock."

Cora Jane stood by the table of gifts, beaming. Meg, Sally and even Louise were grinning at her. Since her circle of friends was still small, Jerry and Wade were here, too, though Jerry looked decidedly uncomfortable, as if he'd much prefer being in the kitchen cooking up the feast for the occasion.

"I can't believe you all did this," she whispered tearfully.

"I've been planning it since the second I found out you were pregnant," Samantha said. "If all else failed, this was going to be my last-ditch attempt to convince you that you have to keep this baby. Thank goodness it's just a full-fledged celebration now."

"Isn't it early to be having a baby shower?" Gabi said, even as she gravitated toward the gifts, eager to see what the beautiful packages held.

"Actually, we're all agreed that your due date was miscalculated," Louise said. "I have some experience in this area."

"Some?" Meg said wryly. "I'd say five babies qualifies as more than *some*."

"Bottom line, we didn't want to wait, especially since Emily said she could get back here this weekend," Samantha said. "Now, since I know you're always starving, food first, then presents. Jerry's been slaving in the kitchen since dawn."

Gabi's eyes widened. "Since dawn? What about Castle's?"

"I closed it down for the day," Cora Jane said.

"But you *never* close down the restaurant," Gabi protested. "And it's spring. There are tourists."

"Not a one of them's as important to me as you and this baby are," she replied emphatically. "And I'll close it down again for Emily's wedding."

"But the employees," Gabi protested, feeling guilty about causing them the loss of a day's pay.

"They got paid. So, now they owe you for an unexpected day of paid vacation," Cora Jane said. "I'm sure the next time you stop by, they'll be circling you like anxious little hummingbirds to make sure there's nothing you need. I would have invited them today, but they've already been making their own plans to throw a shower."

"Grandmother!" Samantha protested.

"They never intended it to be a surprise. Not a one of them can keep a secret."

"And apparently neither can you," Emily teased her.

Cora Jane gave her a miffed look. "I kept this one, didn't I? Don't be disrespectful."

"Okay, enough," Jerry said. "Let's eat!"

After a meal that was too much even for her, Gabi was settled regally in a chair while her sisters brought presents to her. The tiny outfits earned plenty of *oohs* and *aahs,* but it was Wade's gift that brought stunned silence.

"I'm lousy at wrapping, and this was a little too cumbersome, anyway," he said, then left the room. When he returned, he was carrying an exquisite, handcrafted cradle with frolicking bunnies carved into the headboard.

"Oh, Wade," Louise whispered when Gabi couldn't even gather her composure to speak.

"It's the most beautiful cradle I've ever seen," Gabi finally managed to whisper, her voice thick with tears. There was no mistaking the love he had put into every detail. "Thank you so much. What made you think of the bunnies?"

"Other than the dozen times you mentioned how much you'd loved the Beatrix Potter books?" he said wryly.

She touched the beautifully soft pink liner that had been chosen with such care to complement the cradle's design. Tiny bunnies danced across that fabric, as well. "Where did you find this? It's perfect."

He grinned sheepishly. "I had a little help with that. I asked Meg where to look."

"I was flying blind, though," Meg said. "He refused to tell me anything other than that he wanted something with bunnies and he wanted it to be pink." She glanced approvingly at Wade. "You did good, pal."

"You did really good," Louise confirmed.

Despite the accolades coming his way, Wade's gaze never left Gabi's face. "You really like it?"

"I would love anything you made for the baby, but, Wade, this is incredible," she told him, reaching for his hand.

Though he'd told her in words so many times how he already cared for this baby she was carrying, right here in front of her was the proof. He'd poured his whole heart into making this gift.

When he leaned down to touch his lips to hers, she looped an arm around his neck and held him in place. "I love you," she whispered against his lips.

She could feel his smile against her face. As he stepped away, that smile had become a full-fledged grin.

"You don't get to take that back, you know," he told her, holding her gaze.

"The cradle? Never."

"Not the cradle. What you said."

"What did she say?" Louise asked.

"Between us," Wade told his sister.

Gabi's own smile grew. "Wouldn't even try to take it back," she told him.

Though she hadn't imagined any of this—not the baby, not the new direction for her career and definitely not falling in love—it seemed she was all in for every single, exciting moment of it.

Twenty-Three

The Art Colony Studios and Gallery opening was scheduled for the weekend before Memorial Day. Gabi was still astounded that everything had come together so quickly. The fact that she'd had the stamina for all the hours of work it had entailed was something of a miracle, too. She had Wade to thank for sticking close every minute to do any task she assigned to him. Even Emily and Samantha had come home this week to pitch in.

Beside her now, Emily gave her a hug. "This place is amazing," she assured Gabi. "I still can't believe that you were able to turn this house into a gallery for working artists in such a short amount of time."

"I had help," Gabi reminded her. "Wade did the renovations with help from Tommy Cahill, Jimmy and Jimmy's dad. And I seem to recall that you contributed your share of ideas for some of the design details. Tommy said he was in awe that you could handle so much from clear across the country. I think he was terrified you'd sweep in here this week and tell him he'd gotten it all wrong."

"Not a chance," Emily said. "Believe me, I know when somebody understands the effect I'm trying to achieve, and Wade was completely on board when I went over the sketches with him." She gave Gabi another hug. "Thank you for giving us the leeway to handle that side of things."

"I trust your taste and I trust Wade," Gabi said simply, then grinned. "Besides, Wade showed me everything and got my stamp of approval."

"Smart man, who obviously knows your control-freak tendencies very well," Emily said. "Are you happy, Gabi? Really happy? Is this what you want? Staying here with your baby?"

"It is," she said without hesitation.

"And Wade? Where does he fit in? He's pretty invested in the relationship. Are you?"

Gabi leaned in to her sister and confided, "I'm in love with him. I finally told him that the day of the baby shower. I have no idea how it happened or why. He's so different from the men I always thought I wanted, but he's perfect for me. It kind of annoyed me at first that he seemed able to read my mind, but the truth is, he really gets me."

"I imagine it helps that he's gorgeous and devoted to you and the baby."

Gabi's smile spread. "Oh, yeah. It definitely helps."

"Any plans?"

"Too soon. Things need to settle down, and then we'll see. Right now we're both caught up in everything that's happening. Once this place is open and the baby's here, some of the glow could wear off."

Emily frowned. "You don't really believe that, do you?"

"It could happen," Gabi insisted. "Wade's had this idealized dream of the perfect family for a long time.

A part of me still worries that I'm only filling in for what he lost when Kayla and the unborn baby died in that accident."

"Honey, he doesn't look nostalgic when he looks at you. Seems to me he's very much in the moment. I know because it's the way Boone looks at me. I so want that for you and for Samantha. I'm pretty sure all it's going to take for you to have it is for you to say yes when the time comes."

Gabi wanted to believe that, too, but caution had her holding back on a full-fledged commitment. Maybe if she'd never known the whole story, maybe if Louise hadn't so openly expressed her skepticism—and who knew Wade better?—maybe if the situations hadn't been so similar, perhaps then she could have trusted her heart... and Wade's. As it was, well, she figured time would tell.

Wade stood off to the side as Gabi worked the crowd who turned out for the opening of the Art Colony Studios and Gallery. She was clearly in her element. Though she'd been complaining for days that she couldn't find a decent maternity outfit suitable for the occasion, Emily had apparently shown up and saved the day with a simple dress she'd found on Rodeo Drive. When she'd mentioned the name of the designer, Gabi had squealed in excitement, though Wade didn't have a clue who it was.

What he did know was that the midnight-blue material shimmered beneath the lights that had been carefully directed to showcase the art in each of the individual studios and in the main gallery. Those same lights seemed caught up in Gabi's eyes, sparkling like the small diamonds at her ears. She'd swept her hair up in a way he'd never seen before, exposing her neck and causing him to fight the urge to sneak a kiss behind her ear where a stray curl brushed against delectable skin.

She was so incredibly beautiful, it blew his mind to think that one of these days she was going to agree to be his. One of these days, when he had the nerve to ask. One of these days, when life had settled down just a little.

Across the room, he caught her eye and winked. She gave him a quick little thumbs-up, a grin spreading across her face as she continued to chat with someone who'd shown up from the newspaper in Raleigh, an old contact she'd told him was coming as a favor to her. He figured there must be a lot of old contacts who owed her favors because there were TV cameras all over the place and reporters were interviewing the artists in a sort of controlled chaos that she'd orchestrated.

Wade had told her to concentrate on giving the other artists all the attention tonight, but he realized she was heading his way now with a photographer in tow.

"Glenn, I want you to meet Wade Johnson. Not only is he the founder of this gallery along with me, but these amazing carvings are his works. Glenn's here from Asheville, Wade."

"Stunning," Glenn said, his attention immediately drawn to the carvings of coastal birds in Wade's studio. "This one looks as if it's about to take off in flight. I know of some shops back home that would love to carry your work."

"Not just yet," Gabi said, a possessive tone in her voice. "For now, he and his work are all mine."

Glenn laughed and immediately backed off. "Okay,

then." He turned to Wade. "Trust her. She knows what she's doing. She'll make you a force in the art world."

He took a few photographs of Wade at work, then wandered off. Wade tucked an arm around Gabi's shoulders. "What if I don't want to be a force in the art world?"

"I don't think you're going to have much choice. Your works are going to make you a star."

"I could be some private recluse," he said. "Just imagine the PR mystique."

"It's going to be hard to maintain that and have a studio right here in plain sight," she reminded him. "Besides, you're way too cute to be a recluse."

"And you don't mind sharing me?" he asked, a little disappointed by her willingness to do just that.

"It's your talent I'll be sharing," she told him firmly. "Never you. I thought I'd made that clear."

"That's better, then." He rubbed a thumb across her cheek. "Are you happy, Gabriella? You look happy."

"I am," she said. "Pulling this together, working with you—it's been amazing."

"But the hard work is behind you," he said. "Are you going to be bored from here on out?"

"Are you kidding me? The hard work is just getting started. Sure, we've created early buzz and all this attention tonight is incredible, but the key is to keep finding new angles to promote, to keep this place out there with fresh new artists and innovative ideas. A great opening is just the beginning."

He smiled at her enthusiasm. "And you already have some of these innovative ideas, I'll bet."

"Absolutely. Why do you think I didn't mention the guest artist program in the early press releases? That's another stage. And then we'll have classes. That's another campaign. And maybe an annual Christmas in July event. Or a red-white-and-blue event for the Fourth of July. I was in a store once that did that. It got people looking closely at everything."

He regarded her blankly. "Why?"

"Okay, let's talk about a painting. If the customer can find a hint of red in it—or of just white or blue—they'd get a ten percent discount. If they find two of those colors, it's twenty percent off, and thirty percent if they find all three colors in that same painting. Believe me, people study the details. And when people look that closely and are assured of the best discount, they buy."

"I'm not sure that's going to do much for my wood carvings," Wade said, though he was impressed by the clever concept.

"Which is why you put colorful tags on them," she said. "Maybe you create an all-blue logo for some or a red-white-and-blue tag for something you really want to move that weekend. You can be as stingy or as generous as you want to be. You'll see. It's going to be fun."

"I trust you," he said. "Now, how are you feeling?"

"I feel incredible," she said, though there was an unmistakable weariness in her eyes.

"How about ten minutes off your feet and a plate of the excellent hors d'oeuvres that Jerry made?"

"I should be circulating," she protested. "I want to be sure all these media people get the interviews they need."

"I've never seen a more contented roomful of media types," Wade told her. "Look around. They can spare you for a few minutes."

She glanced around, then nodded. "Sitting down would feel good."

Wade settled her on a chair in her office, then went for the food and a glass of the nonalcoholic champagne he'd made sure they had on hand for her and anyone else who preferred it. He ran into Cora Jane, who was overseeing the buffet table.

"How's our girl doing?" she asked. "She's been moving so fast, she reminds me of those hummingbirds that hover for an instant, then move on to hover over something else."

"Dead on her feet, but exhilarated," he told her. "I've persuaded her to sit down in her office for a few minutes. Can you put together a plate for her, while I pour her some of the fake bubbly?"

"Of course I will," Cora Jane said.

When Wade returned from the small kitchen they'd put in for a communal lunch area, Cora Jane had piled tiny sandwiches on a plate along with small key lime and cherry tarts.

"This is a hungry crowd," she told him. "It's a good thing we're winding down. The food's almost gone. If the show's been half as big a hit as Jerry's appetizers, I'd say this place is going to be a huge success."

"Once your granddaughter seizes on an idea and runs with it, there's nothing she can't accomplish," Wade said. "I'm in awe of her. I knew this was a good idea, but she took it to a whole other level."

"Seems to me the two of you make a good team," Cora Jane told him slyly.

Wade laughed. "You can stop nudging, Cora Jane. I'm on board."

He returned to the office to find Meg and Sally sitting with Gabi.

"Here's the man of the hour," Sally said. "Wade, what you and Gabi have accomplished here is nothing short of miraculous. I was interviewed by two different TV news crews. I doubt I said anything scintillating enough to get on the air, but it was fun. I felt like a celebrity."

"You can thank Gabi for that. She must have called every contact she ever had in the North Carolina media and beyond."

Gabi grinned, beckoning for the plate of food. "Most of them," she agreed. "But I held out a few for the next time I need some big favors."

She popped a small chicken salad biscuit in her mouth and closed her eyes. "This is heavenly. I think I could eat a dozen of them."

"Well, according to Cora Jane, you're out of luck. She says the food's almost gone, so I imagine the crowd will start dispersing soon."

"Just in time," Meg said, regarding Gabi worriedly. "You look beat. I hope you're taking tomorrow off to get some rest."

"How can I? It's our official opening day. I'll be needed here in case there are any glitches."

"Well, you can at least sleep late," Sally said. "Wade, see to it. Make sure she doesn't set foot in here before eleven. I can make sure the place opens on time and hold down the fort till she arrives."

"And I'll come over and pitch in, too," Meg offered. "I have Lily on at the shop tomorrow, and I even persuaded my daughter to help her out, so that's covered."

"That's so sweet," Gabi said. "But really, I should

be here by nine at least to make sure we're set for the opening at ten."

"Eleven and not a minute earlier," Sally repeated.

Wade grinned at Gabi. "See, you're not the boss of everything," he told her. "There are people here who have your back. Stay home and rest and I'll bring fresh doughnuts when I come to get you."

Gabi's eyes lit up. "Chocolate-iced with sprinkles?"

"An entire dozen of them," he promised.

"Then I suppose if I'm here by eleven, that'll be soon enough," she said docilely.

"Who knew she could be bought with doughnuts?" Meg said, clearly amused.

Wade chuckled. "How do you think I got her to notice me in the first place? It wasn't my good looks or sexy banter. Nope. It was those doughnuts that worked like a charm."

Gabi patted his hand. "Don't be smug. I'm capable of buying those doughnuts for myself, you know."

She started to get up, struggled a bit, then held out her hand. Wade pulled her to her feet. "Ready to go home?"

"Not just yet. I need to make the rounds and say good-night, make sure there are no last-minute requests for interviews."

"Fifteen minutes," he told her firmly. "Then we're out the door."

"Ooh," Sally mocked. "I do so love a man who takes charge."

"More like a man who *thinks* he's in charge," Gabi retorted, but she did leave the room with Wade. That gave him at least a faint hope that she'd wrap things up in the allotted fifteen minutes.

And then they could be alone so he could tell her how absolutely incredible and amazing he thought she was to have pulled off tonight's coup.

Gabi rubbed her back. It had been aching all day. She attributed that to going up and down the steps at the gallery all day long.

The opening night success had continued for the past two weeks of full operation. So far, the freshness of the idea and the excitement it had been generating around the community and the state hadn't worn off. She'd discovered that showcasing a variety of works that might bring joy, beauty or serenity into someone's life was astonishingly fulfilling. Wade had been right that there were many ways to find satisfaction.

Wade had been right about many things. She hadn't quite decided if that trait was annoying or endearing. At the moment, with him hovering over her with a worried frown, she was finding it annoying.

"You're in labor," he repeated for the tenth time in an hour.

"Don't be ridiculous. I'm not due for another two weeks."

"Perhaps the baby hasn't seen the schedule you posted on the fridge," Wade retorted. He pulled his cell phone from his pocket, muttered a few words, then handed the phone to her.

"Hi, Lou," Gabi said to his sister, giving him a wry look.

"If Wade says you're in labor, you need to go to the hospital," Louise told her firmly. "Ignore him at your own peril. I did with my first and almost had Bryce in the backseat of the car. My brother has some sort of uncanny ability to predict these things. With Chelsea, I didn't even have a twinge. Wade took one look at my face and drove me to the hospital."

"Please," Gabi protested, unconvinced.

"I'm telling you, he's in touch with some kind of feminine higher power or something. Trust his instincts."

"Okay, thanks," Gabi said, still scowling as she hung up the phone. "You want to go to the hospital, we'll go, but do not call my grandmother or Emily yet. This baby might not be here for days."

He grinned. "Yes, dear."

Several hours later, a squalling, rosy-cheeked baby girl was placed in Gabi's arms. Tears filled her eyes as she stared into that sweet face, but it was the awed expression in Wade's eyes that stole her breath.

"Whatever made me think I could do it?" she murmured.

Wade studied her as if not quite sure he dared to believe her. "Do what?"

"Let her go," she whispered. "I know I'd already made the decision to keep her, but looking into her sweet little face, I can't even conceive how I ever considered anything else."

"Not a single doubt?"

"Not a one," she told him. "And it's not even the way she makes me feel, though right this second I'm awash in all these incredible maternal instincts."

"If it's not that, then why are you so sure you've made the right decision?"

She smiled at him. "I saw the way you looked when you saw her for the first time. This little girl belongs with you, with us. I've never been more certain of anything than I am of that."

"I fell in love with her months ago," he admitted. "And with her mother long before that."

"Even though I'm still a work in progress?"

"I'm an artist. Works in progress are filled with possibilities and surprises." He sat on the edge of the bed and touched her cheek. "I can't imagine there will ever be a day when you don't surprise me."

"I like things all planned out," she reminded him. "How will that work?"

"We'll balance each other."

"Or drive each other crazy," she argued.

A smile spread across his face. "I can live with that, too. Can you?"

Gabi glanced from the precious bundle in her arms—this child she'd never expected to hold, much less keep—then into the eyes of the equally unexpected man who made all things seem exciting and possible. "I can, yes."

"Then I guess we should talk about a few things."

She held her breath. "Such as?"

"A name for our daughter for starters." He held her gaze. "Because she will be ours in every way that matters."

"Daniella Jane," she said at once.

He smiled. "That was awfully quick."

Gabi sighed. "As soon as I realized I wasn't going to be able to let her go, I started a list. I pretended I was just doodling some ideas, but it was more than that. Daniella seemed to stick and I wanted the Jane for Grandmother."

He touched a gentle finger to the baby's cheek. "What do you think of that, Daniella Jane?"

The baby actually seemed to coo her approval,

her blue eyes wide, if not yet focusing. Gabi honestly thought she was responding to the sound of this man's familiar voice.

"She already knows you," she said.

"Well, of course she does. She and I have had several conversations lately about how stubborn her mom is."

Gabi stared at him indignantly. "Is that so?"

"Well, you can't deny that you have yet to say exactly how I'm going to fit into this future you're starting to envision."

"Don't you know by now?" she whispered. "I can't let you go, either."

A smile broke across Wade's face. "Then I suppose we should talk about making it official," he said, his gaze locked on hers. "I love you, Gabi. And I love Daniella. I want us to be a family. In fact, I think I've been waiting for a very long time for this exact family to come along. Will you marry me? Soon? And before you ask, I already have your father's blessing. He gave me that weeks ago."

"You asked my father?"

He nodded. "You might not see yourself as a traditional kind of woman, but I am a very traditional guy. I wanted to cover all my bases. And we *know* Cora Jane is on board."

Gabi laughed, relieved by his eagerness. How many times had she tried to shoo him away? More than she could count, but he'd stuck like glue. "I will, but it may not be soon. I want to fit into a decent wedding gown. And Emily's wedding is coming up. I can't steal her thunder."

"You'll be beautiful no matter what you wear."

She laughed at that. "Keep on saying things like that

and people will wonder about your eyesight. That's not a good thing for an artist."

"Sweetheart, one look at the two of you, and they'll know I have an eye for beauty. Now we'd better get your grandmother and sister over here or we'll never hear the end of it. I think Cora Jane wanted to be in the delivery room to be sure the doctor knew what she was doing."

"Not to worry. I'll tell her you took very good care of me. Thanks for subbing as my birthing coach, by the way. You were like an old pro. It must be all those times you pinch hit when Lou's husband couldn't get to the hospital in time."

He shook his head. "It was nothing like those times," he argued. "This was you. And Daniella. I've never been more terrified in my life."

She laughed. "*Now* you tell me." She squeezed his hand. "It's okay. I never would have guessed."

He winked at her. "Another three or four times and I'll probably have it down pat."

"Once more, and we'll talk," she said sternly.

But even as she said the words, she knew that after all he'd given her in terms of confidence and a new direction for her life, she'd give this man whatever it took to make him happy. And she'd do it without ever looking back at the life she'd left behind, because the future promised to be everything she'd ever dreamed of.

* * * * *

Keep reading for a sneak peek at the thrilling conclusion to the Ocean Breeze trilogy, Sea Glass Island, from #1 New York Times *bestselling author Sherryl Woods. Coming in July 2023!*

One

Samantha plunged a spoon into a pint of Ben & Jerry's Cherry Garcia, then sighed as the decadent ice cream melted in her mouth. Guilty pleasures like this were about all that kept her going these days. With enough Ben & Jerry's came hope that her acting career would pick up. A positive attitude had helped her to weather tough times in the past, after all.

It was getting harder and harder to believe, though. The silence of her phone lately had been deafening. In late spring, she'd had a minor role in a prime-time TV show that filmed in New York, but it hadn't led to other opportunities despite the enthusiasm of the director and the producers. Fall season shows were back in production, but she'd received none of the promised job offers, not even for bit parts.

She hadn't had a single callback for a commercial in weeks. If it weren't for her job as a hostess at a high-priced Upper East Side restaurant, she'd be in the most serious financial trouble she'd faced since coming to New York over fifteen years ago. Even with that, she'd had to dip into her savings already.

Though her sister Gabriella had mounted a terrific PR buzz campaign for her back in the spring, its effects had worn off in weeks, rather than months, and now, once again, she was struggling. She'd worn out her list of contacts. But with everything going on in Gabi's life these days, Samantha hadn't felt she could ask for more free publicity assistance. Gabi was adjusting to being a single mom and trying to work things out with the very patient man in her life, who'd agreed to postpone their own wedding until after their sister Emily's in a few weeks.

Ever the optimist, Samantha had survived discouraging times more than once since arriving in New York just out of high school as a fresh-faced girl with stars in her eyes. This dry spell, however, was the worst she could recall. More disturbing was that now it came with pitying looks from other actresses up for the same roles. Her once exuberant, supportive agent had started dodging her calls, then parted ways with her. His replacement, though enthusiastic, hadn't gotten promising results.

Samantha had been in New York long enough to read the handwriting on the wall. She was thirty-five, and while still beautiful, she was past her prime. Parts that once would have been hers for the asking were now going to women in their early twenties. It didn't seem to matter that the casting call was for someone her age, or even older. At the same time, she wasn't quite old enough for the burgeoning niche for older actresses. There wasn't enough optimism in the universe to counter that harsh reality.

When her phone rang, she lunged for it, which told

her just how desperate she'd become. She didn't like the feeling.

"Samantha, hey. I'm so glad I caught you," her youngest sister, Emily, said, as if finding her at home was a rarity, rather than commonplace these days. "We need to talk. Now that Gabi's had her baby, it's time to get serious about my wedding. It's just around the corner."

Despite her generally sour mood, Samantha smiled. "Does Boone have any idea you weren't *always* serious about the wedding?" she quipped. "Remind me, when is it again? Sometime next year?"

"Very funny. It's less than a month away."

"That soon?" Samantha teased.

"Soon? This has been forever in the making. How long were Boone and I apart? Years and years. We need to make up for lost time."

The excitement in Emily's voice was wonderful to hear, Samantha thought, trying not to envy her. She and Boone did deserve this long-delayed happiness.

"When are you coming to North Carolina?" Emily prodded. "You have to have another dress fitting, not that you ever gain an ounce. It's more of a show of solidarity with Gabi, who's still fighting baby weight. And there's the bridal shower Grandmother and Gabi are throwing, then the rehearsal dinner. I'm thinking we need a bachelorette night, just us girls. I want you here for every minute. This is going to be the absolute best summer the Castle sisters have ever had in Sand Castle Bay."

"I wouldn't miss any of it," Samantha assured her. "After all, wasn't I the one who predicted last August that you and Boone were going to get back together?"

"Yes, you demonstrated amazing insight, but it

wouldn't be the first time that some irresistible part came through at the last second and you bailed on me. My college graduation comes to mind."

"Well, there's no way I'd bail on your wedding," Samantha reassured her. The likelihood of a plum role being offered was abysmally small. Besides, she'd never let Emily down after promising to be her maid of honor. The fact that Emily had even asked had come as a surprise. Their relationship had been tainted by some kind of sibling rivalry she'd never understood, but her sister seemed to be sincerely trying to leave that in the past.

"I'm driving south the day after tomorrow," she told Emily, not mentioning that the wedding was providing the perfect excuse to leave New York behind during these depressing dog days of summer. "I'll be there to do whatever you need."

"Are you bringing What's-his-face with you? The guy from the network or the producer? I lose track."

"Truthfully, so do I," Samantha admitted. "There's no one I'd want around for an occasion as important as my little sister's wedding."

There was a faint hesitation on the other end of the line and then Emily asked slyly, "Not even Ethan Cole?"

Samantha's heart did a predictable little stutter step. "Why on earth would you bring up Ethan? He's ancient history. Not even history, come to think of it. He never even knew I existed back in the day."

"Aha!" Emily said triumphantly. "You do still have feelings for him. I told Gabi you did. She thinks so, too. Our powers of observation are every bit as good as yours when it comes to romance."

"And you got that from my asking why you mentioned him?" Samantha inquired irritably, hating any possibility that at her age she could be wearing her heart on her sleeve for anyone to detect. Especially when the man in question probably wouldn't even recognize her if their paths crossed.

"I got that from your wearing his old football jersey around the house the whole time you were home after the hurricane last summer," Emily responded. "And, amazingly, it disappeared after you went back to New York. I'll bet it's in your closet up there right this minute."

"It is not," Samantha retorted, glancing down at the gold-and-green jersey she was currently wearing. So what if she still harbored a not-so-secret crush on the star quarterback from the high school? Three years older and surrounded by throngs of local girls, Ethan had never once noticed her back then. She was a summer kid, not even a blip on his radar. She seriously doubted he'd discovered deep feelings in the intervening years just from spotting her in some detergent commercial, and that was even assuming he knew it was her.

"You know he never married," Emily said casually. "And he and Boone play golf together. Boone's asked him to be in the wedding."

Samantha's stupid heart did another of those annoying little telltale hop, skip and jumps. "Not on my account, I hope."

"Of course not," Emily said. "But he is Boone's best man, which means you'll be seeing a lot of him."

Samantha groaned. She'd expected this sort of matchmaking from her grandmother, who'd actively campaigned to see that Emily and Boone were reunited and had done her share of manipulating to see that Gabi wound up with Wade Johnson. Samantha had been cer-

tain, though, that Cora Jane would show a little more respect for Samantha's ability to find her own man. Then,
again, there wasn't much evidence that Samantha had
made any particularly good choices up to now. The men
she'd dated had been seriously lacking in staying power.

"Did Grandmother put you up to this?" she asked
testily.

"Up to what?" Emily replied innocently. "I told you,
Boone and Ethan have been friends forever. Their fami-
lies go way back. It makes perfect sense that he'd want
Ethan in the wedding."

"I suppose," Samantha conceded.

"Gotta run. I love you," Emily said. "See you soon."

"See you soon," Samantha echoed.

Suddenly going back to Sand Castle Bay for her sister's wedding had gotten a lot more interesting…and
maybe just a little dangerous.

Gabi held Daniella Jane in her arms, rocking her
gently as she studied the color in Emily's cheeks.

"Well, did you find out whatever it was you wanted
to know when you spoke to Samantha?" she asked.

"Oh, Samantha still has it bad for Ethan, all right,"
Emily replied with a smirk.

"Which means you intend to meddle," Gabi guessed.

"Well, why not?" Emily inquired, reaching to take
the baby from Gabi's arms and cooing to her. "Grandmother does it all the time."

"And gets away with it because she's Cora Jane and
we love and respect her," Gabi reminded her. "You and
Samantha haven't always seen eye-to-eye on things, not
that I've ever understood why that is."

Emily made a face that had the baby gurgling with

what could have been delight…or a dire portent of something else entirely.

"I know that's all on me," Emily admitted. "And the worst part is that I honestly don't remember when it started. If I was going to feel this competitive nonsense, it should have been with you. We're the driven, ambitious ones. Or at least you were until you turned all mellow and had this beautiful baby. She's the one and only thing good to come out of your relationship with Paul the slimebag. Now you've fallen madly in love with Wade, and as much as it pains me to see, now you're just plain sappy."

"Hey, I have a thriving art gallery with a dozen temperamental artists working on-site. I'm trying to turn that into a tourist destination," Gabi protested. "I haven't exactly slacked off. I just redirected my goals."

"Yeah, yeah," Emily said. "You're missing my point. I can't figure out why I've always had this thing with Samantha, but I honestly do want to put it behind us. It's past time. I don't want any of those old lingering feelings to spoil what should be the happiest time of my life."

"Amen to that, and asking her to be your maid of honor was a really sweet gesture," Gabi said. "I know how much she appreciated it."

"It doesn't exactly make up for the way I've treated her over the years, as if her sole role in life was to annoy me." She tickled Daniella, then grinned as the baby squirmed. "Lordy, but she's cute. I think I want one."

Gabi laughed. "I have a hunch Boone will be more than willing to cooperate, but you might want to get this wedding behind you first."

"First, Boone and I have to be in the same place at

the same time if we're going to make a baby," Emily grumbled. "He's checking in on all his restaurants on his way here from Los Angeles."

"So you'll be apart how long? A whole twenty-four hours?" Gabi teased.

"Two days actually," Emily replied with a dramatic sigh.

Gabi laughed. "You are pathetic. You were apart for years before you reconciled. Even after you got back together, your work kept you in different cities for quite a while."

"And now I'm spoiled," Emily conceded. "With Boone in Los Angeles with me while I work on those safe houses for abused women and families, I've discovered just how amazing living together can be. I had no idea I'd adapt so quickly to having someone in my life 24/7. Add in B.J. and instant motherhood, and it's been the most incredible few months ever."

"It really is wonderful to see you so ecstatically happy," Gabi told her. "It's great that you and B.J. formed this immediate bond. Not every stepmother is so lucky."

"Believe me, I've heard the stories," Emily said. "How about you? I can see what a contented mom you are, but what's the scoop with you and Wade? Why hasn't he moved in here?"

"As broad-minded as Cora Jane may be, I don't think I want to test her limits by suggesting that my boyfriend and I live together under her roof. Wade and I are committed to working things out. That's enough for now."

"You're really happy?" Emily asked, studying her worriedly. "Staying here in Sand Castle Bay is what you want? And the gallery's enough for you?"

"I have more than a job here, Em. I have family and a wonderful man and that little munchkin you're holding. My life is full. I don't need a ring on my finger just yet. I certainly don't need to go back to the stressful, demanding life I was leading in Raleigh. Besides, I think Dad would stroke out if I hit him with another wedding bill right now. You haven't been here when Grandmother's handed over the invoices for yours. Poor Dad's just grasping the reality that weddings don't come cheap, especially with a daughter who has very expensive taste."

"Hey, I'm not the one who insisted on inviting half the state of North Carolina. You can thank Dad and Grandmother for that. Boone and I would have been content with family and a few friends."

"So you say now," Gabi said, "but I never heard you putting up much of a fuss as the guest list grew and grew and started to include half of Los Angeles."

"Well, it is what it is now," Emily said blithely. "Let's get back to Samantha. Any idea what's going on with her? She didn't sound all that happy when we spoke just now. Is her career faltering again?"

Gabi winced. "I'm ashamed to say I haven't given it much thought. I've been a little distracted lately."

"Understandable," Emily said. "She hasn't asked for your PR help, has she?"

"No, but she wouldn't. I had to badger her into letting me help a few months ago. It seemed to be effective, so I guess I just assumed that things kept on snowballing. In a good way, that is. That's how it is sometimes, one job leads to another, but I shouldn't have taken that for granted. I should have asked," she said, feeling guilty.

"Why? Not everything is up to you to fix," Emily said, an oddly defensive note in her voice. "If Samantha wanted help, she could have said something. That's her way, though. She just suffers in silence, then resents it when nobody jumps in to save the day."

Gabi regarded her younger sister with dismay. "That's not true, Emily. Samantha's not like that. Why would you even say something so cruel?"

Emily looked taken aback by Gabi's vehemence, then buried her face in her hands. "Because I'm mean and spiteful," she said in a small voice, then lifted her gaze to meet Gabi's. "What is the matter with me? I always see the worst in her, even when she's done nothing wrong."

"It's times like this when I really wish Mom were still around," Gabi said softly.

Emily blinked back instant tears at the unexpected reference to their mother, who'd died several years ago. "What does Mom have to do with this?"

"Maybe she would understand why you have this attitude toward our big sister. Dad certainly wouldn't have any idea. He was oblivious to everything going on at home when we were growing up. I doubt Grandmother was with us enough in the early years before Mom died to know the root of the problems between the two of you."

Emily sighed. "And it's increasingly obvious that it isn't something I can just wish away. These careless, hurtful words just pop out of my mouth sometimes, and I have no idea why."

"Then dig deeper and figure it out," Gabi advised. "You and Samantha both mean the world to me, and I don't want to be caught in the middle. I want us to be sisters, in every positive, loving sense of the word, okay? In fact, in my dream scenario, you and Boone eventually settle back here and Samantha marries a local, too, and we all live blocks apart so our kids can grow up together."

Emily nodded, her eyes still misty. "I want that, too," she insisted. "Well, maybe not moving back here full-time, but the rest. I will work this out, Gabi. I promise. Maybe once she's here, Samantha and I can sit down and hash this out. Who knows? Maybe she stole my favorite doll when I was two and I've blocked it from my memory."

Gabi smiled at the idea of something so innocuous causing a rivalry that had lasted for years. And Emily's earlier accusations about her sister harboring simmering resentments seemed to speak of something much more complicated.

"Just work it out, sweetie. Whatever it takes."

Emily settled Daniella back in Gabi's arms and gave her niece a last pat, then pressed a kiss to Gabi's cheek. "Done," she promised.

Gabi watched her sister leave and wondered if it could be that simple.

Ethan Cole had just seen his final patient of the day, a tourist who'd managed to slice open her foot on a rusty nail on one of the stray boards still around after a recent storm had ripped through the coastal areas of North Carolina. Though most of the shoreline had been cleaned up immediately, debris still washed ashore from time to time, especially along a few more deserted areas of the beach. He'd given her a tetanus shot and four stitches and told her to come back if there was even a hint of any infection at the site of the injury.

He was just finishing up his notes when the door

pushed open again and Boone Dorsett wandered into the small emergency clinic that Ethan had established with another doctor who'd also served in Iraq and Afghanistan. They'd agreed that the emergencies here in a small coastal community were unlikely to rise to the level of anything they'd coped with on their tours of duty in the military. Bumps, bruises and a few stitches were a day at the park compared to anything they'd seen, or in Ethan's case, experienced firsthand.

He'd lost his lower left leg to an IED explosion in Afghanistan. While that might not have kept him out of an operating room once he was back stateside, it had gone a long way toward changing his need for the adrenaline rush of spending hours in a trauma unit or performing complicated, high-risk surgical procedures.

"You busy?" Boone asked, his tone nonchalant but his expression harried.

Ethan studied his friend's face. "You look like you need to talk. Wedding jitters?"

Boone sat down, one leg bouncing up and down nervously, even though he uttered a denial.

"If it's not about the wedding, what's going on?" Ethan asked. He'd heard it was the best man's duty to keep the groom calm and focused and make sure he turned up at the church on time. Emily Castle had made that very clear to him. So had her grandmother. It was Cora Jane's admonition that had resonated. She'd threatened him with bodily harm if he failed to deliver Boone precisely at ten-thirty two weeks from Saturday.

"There's something you maybe need to know," Boone admitted.

"Okay," Ethan replied slowly. "What?"

"You're the best man, right?"

"So you keep telling me."

"That means you have this sort of obligation to spend time with the maid of honor."

Ethan stilled. "What does that mean, 'spend time with'? We walk down the aisle together at the end of the service, right? Maybe sit next to each other at the head table and deliver our heartfelt toasts about how inevitable it all was that the two of you wound up together?"

"I think maybe Emily is expecting a little more than that," Boone acknowledged, squirming uncomfortably.

Ethan's gaze narrowed. "And why would Emily be expecting anything more? And why are you warning me?"

"Because I don't want you to be blindsided. I know how you are about dating. Ever since you got back from overseas, you've been this social recluse."

"I was still engaged when I came back," Ethan reminded him. At least he had been for about twenty minutes, until all the hero worship died down and Lisa had admitted she didn't think she could stay with someone "who's not whole." It was the first time Ethan had really seen himself as others probably saw him, as someone who was no longer quite the same man he used to be.

The only good thing to come out of that ugly breakup was his increased determination not only to ensure that his injury put no limitations on his life, but to see that kids with physical disabilities learned to view themselves in a positive way. That mission to salvage his own dignity and help others had given his life a much-needed purpose. Project Pride filled hours that otherwise might have been spent on this so-called social life Boone—or more likely, Emily—thought he needed.

"It's been three years since you split with Lisa," Boone pointed out.

"Since she dumped me," Ethan corrected to keep the record straight.

"She was a self-absorbed twit," Boone said with feeling, "but let's not go there. My very low opinion of your ex is not the point."

"Then what is the point?" Ethan asked, frowning.

There was no mistaking his friend's discomfort as Boone finally muttered, "Heaven only knows why, but Emily seems to have gotten this idea that you and her sister Samantha are perfect for each other."

"Excuse me?" Ethan said, hoping he'd heard incorrectly.

"Come on, Ethan," Boone said impatiently, "you know exactly what I said. I didn't leave a lot of room for misinterpretation."

"Samantha, the maid of honor," Ethan said, finally getting all the implications of this little scheme of the bride-to-be. He shook his head and directed a warning look at his friend that he hoped would put the fear of God into him. "No way, Boone! You need to tell Emily to forget it. Being subjected to matchmaking, meddling or whatever you want to call it, that's definitely not part of what I signed on for."

Boone gave him an incredulous look. "Have you met Emily? She's got me in here spouting off like a blasted girl about stuff that is absolutely none of my business!"

"Okay, she's tough and determined. I'll give you that, but you're tougher," Ethan said.

Boone shrugged. "Not so much."

"I'll bail on you," Ethan threatened. "I swear I will."

Boone merely rolled his eyes in disbelief. "No, you

won't. Besides, I can kind of see it. You and Samantha. She's beautiful. You're handsome. You'd make gorgeous babies, and that is a direct quote from Emily, by the way."

Ethan stared at him. "What has happened to you? Since when do you get involved in matchmaking, much less on the basis of how pretty any resulting babies would be?"

"Emily was very convincing," Boone said, then grinned. "Besides, she says Samantha had a crush on you back in the day. She seems to think this is destiny or something."

Ethan searched his memory, but no image came to mind, just bits and pieces of more recent gossip. "Isn't Samantha an actress? Younger than me by a couple of years at least? She went off to New York to be a star or something? Does that really sound like someone who'd be suited for life with a small-town doctor? The whole Lisa experience pretty much cured me of having unrealistic expectations when it comes to women."

"Emily believes Samantha is ready for a change of direction. She keeps talking about Samantha's summer of transformation or some such. Believe me, she has a plan."

Now Ethan couldn't hide his amusement. "And how does Samantha feel about that?"

"She might not have figured it out just yet," Boone admitted. "But she will, once Emily spends a little time with her. I have complete confidence in Emily's powers of persuasion. She's also highly motivated. She and Samantha haven't always been on the best terms. I think she sees this as a chance to turn that around and truly bond with her older sister."

"By delivering a man into her life?" Ethan asked incredulously. "One she may not even want?"

"Emily's convinced she has this right," Boone countered. "And just so you know, I think Cora Jane's on her side in this, too. She has an uncanny knack for these things. If you ask me, you're pretty much doomed. I'm just giving you fair warning."

"Just because Emily—or Cora Jane, for that matter—can obviously twist you around her little finger and get you to buy into all this sisterly bonding and destiny nonsense doesn't mean she'll have the same effect on the rest of us," Ethan said.

In fact, he could pretty much guarantee he wouldn't get with the program. He'd had his fill of silly, shallow women who thought looks were everything. His ex-fiancée had seen to that.

He realized exactly how bitter that made him sound. Well, he *was* bitter. In fact, he'd been counting on that for quite some time now to keep his heart safe, no matter who was scheming against him. Up to now it had worked like a charm.

Then, again, he hadn't tested it against the likes of Emily and Cora Jane Castle just yet. That, he was very sorry to admit, was just a little worrisome.

HARLEQUIN
PLUS

Try the best multimedia subscription service for romance readers like you!

Read, Watch and Play.

Experience the easiest way to get the romance content you crave.

Start your **FREE TRIAL** at
www.harlequinplus.com/freetrial.